Epitaph for Mister Wynn

Keith Wheeler

Also by Keith Wheeler

THE LAST MAYDAY

PEACEABLE LANE

THE REEF

Epitaph for Mister Wynn

G. P. Putnam's Sons, New York

For Jean, McGinty & Rusty

1

Because his low, wide, handsome bluestone and redwood dwelling basked in the green and gracious suburb of Gray Oak, Amos Wynn did not with his own ears hear the bomb that went off that late afternoon. It exploded beneath the second center pew from the front of the Ebenezer Baptist Church in Angel Creek, a full eight miles away across the gut of the city. However, he heard about it by telephone and in some detail within half an hour of the explosion. For Amos Wynn not to hear about such an event within that span would have constituted an abridgement of natural law as it functioned in the city of Wynnsboro.

The bomb killed a man named Rafe Pullen, a ditcher operator who worked for the city water department. In fact it disemboweled him, for Pullen had been sitting directly above the spot where the infernal device had been taped under the seat, shielded from casual sight by the oaken rack which held the hymnals. Pullen left a wife and seven children, from two to seventeen and a half. The eldest of these, Martine, worked after school and weekends as a domestic in the home of Amos Wynn. A year before the bombing Martine's employer, Wynn's daughter Amy, had promised that she would be seen through college

7

at Wynn expense if she finished high school in the top one-fourth of her class, and it seemed likely that she would.

The explosion also riddled the lower legs, from heel to the bend of knee, of the two men who had been sitting at Pullen's either hand. A fragment of iron, later identified as a piece of the two-inch water pipe from which the bomb had been fashioned, flew forward and gouged away the left eye of a black man, a foreigner named Andrus Thompson. A Teamsters Brotherhood business agent, Thompson had come from Baton Rouge to preach the doctrine of union organization to the employees, almost all Negro, of Wynnsboro's public works department, which held within its franchise water, parks, garbage disposal, and street cleaning.

When he began to recover from his wound, Thompson, a man filled with vanity and a bitter heart, swore to himself that, once he knew the identity of the perpetrator of this frightfulness, he would have his revenge. Since he was black, he assumed that his assailant was white.

Amos Wynn did not hear the telephone, for he was in his basement gun room considering whether it might be profitable to go after bass that late on a Saturday afternoon, meanwhile selecting the lures he thought might be killers if he did go. Amy, who shared with him a house big enough for ten, had to let the instrument ring four times to give herself leeway to stifle an unladylike guffaw down to a level of ladylike decorum before she could answer.

Amy was reading a current best seller, an evilly intentional parody of all dirty novels. Her outburst was provoked less by prurience than by an outrageous image of reproductive organs in a coupling of such hyperbolic lubricity, pulsation, size, duration, avidity, and dextrous juxtaposition that the only possible reaction was mirth. *Wow,* she thought as she dropped the book on her father's desk and picked up the telephone. The voice across the wire was shrill, but she recognized it.

"Just a minute. I'll get him for you," she said and switched on the intercom to call her father.

Amos Wynn came looming toward her in his study, a head and a half taller than his tall daughter, cropped and grizzled where she was shoulder length brown, leathery where she was velvety, alike in direct gray eyes, broad brows, and an owned air of confidence. The Wynns never doubted who they were. He glanced at the novel's garish cover as he reached for the telephone.

"You still reading that pornographic junk?" he grunted. "Who's calling?"

"I read everything, and besides pornography can be funny," she said. "It's Mr. Mayhew."

"What's on your mind, Art?" he said into the telephone. Then he listened without comment while Amy, forewarned by the caller's evident anxiety and now hearing the tinny, high-pitched clatter of voice past her father's ear, stood waiting in curiosity.

Arthur Mayhew, Wynnsboro's Commissioner of Police, was acting entirely within character when he took care to inform Amos Wynn of the bombing even before he made disposition of his forces to contain whatever dislocation of public order that might flow from it. His precaution seems entirely comprehensible when one reflects that Mayhew knew he had been created by Amos Wynn and certainly not by anybody in Angel Creek, which was the city's Negro section, inaptly named for the brown and churlish and beer-can-laden open little sewer which wandered through the area on its filthy way toward the river.

"All right, Art. Get your men out there." Wynn slowly replaced the telephone in its cradle and said, "Damn."

"What, pa?" Amy asked. Her eyes mirrored his frown.

"Some horse's ass bombed a nigger church," Wynn said. He reached for the wide-brimmed stetson which he kept hanging on an old-fashioned clothes tree in the corner behind his desk—incongruous elements both amid the slick Danish modern of Amy's decorating taste.

"Oh?" Amy looked concerned—but not stricken, for she was

a young woman who carried her composure well. "Why on earth?"

"I can guess," Wynn said, pausing at the doorway. "But I want to make sure. They were talking union down there. Damn fools . . . and some worse damn fool blew them up."

"Do you have to go?" Amy asked. "Leave it to the police . . . what can you do?"

"You could better ask what can Mayhew do," Wynn said.

"You picked him, pa," Amy said, mildly malicious. Amy Wynn held her parent in high and fond regard but never in awe.

Amos grunted. "I could have told myself that some red-necked baboon would come up with something like this when the Teamsters first showed on the horizon," he said grimly. "If I'd been brighter I might have headed it off."

"Any ideas?" Amy asked.

"That's what I'm after. It could have been almost any of too many people. We've got our bastards, Amy, ignorant, provincial, superstitious, cruel. Scum is scum. You don't breed it out of the strain just by graduating from mules to station wagons. They can't get it through their thick skulls that the day of running this country by lynch law is done, that the federal government won't let you do it, even if the niggers will. The Teamster thing could have been handled and would have been. Bombing! Of all the blind, stupid, useless idiocies! I'm going to bust somebody's neck. Don't wait dinner for me." He clamped the stetson squarely across his brow and went out into the mild dusk of early April.

Amos Wynn, steeped as he was in what he thought of as tradition but what was in fact recognition of the hard irreconcilables of his world, was not an ignorant man. Nor was he without compassion for those he knew to be his inferiors and, in fact, considered his wards. He accepted responsibility for the essential welfare of Wynnsboro's blacks within his lights, as he would for children. He knew it was no longer the simple world of his grandfathers—perhaps it had not been so simple even then—but he intended to keep it together and functioning the way he believed it ought to function.

Amy watched him go, frowning. She felt no anxiety for his person; she was too long inured to the conviction that her father, in whatever circumstances, would command matters to go the way he wanted them to go and would be obeyed, by anybody in Wynnsboro certainly and probably by anybody in the state capital and some eminent personages in Washington as well. She did, however, quietly resent the way Wynnsboro had, like a somewhat irresponsible teen-ager, of demanding so much of his parental attention.

Returning to the study, she turned on the television to see whether any detail of the bombing had got into the six o'clock news by some unexpected feat of enterprise. *He thinks nothing is done right unless he does it . . . and he's probably right at that,* she told herself.

Wynn got into the jeep—his favorite for fishing and hunting —and wheeled quickly out of the semicircular drive in front of the house. He knew how Angel Creek's potholed streets would manhandle the gentler Wynn cars and, in any case, he really preferred the rugged indestructibility of the jeep. He drove rapidly out of the suburb and headed for the heart of town and —beyond that—Angel Creek. Preoccupied, he did not as he sometimes did spare an admiring appraisal for the steel and glass tower of the Wynn National Building, into four floors of which he had installed the cores of his multitude of interests upon the building's completion only two months before.

He looked upon all of Wynnsboro with a proprietary eye— and knew it and did not consider it weakness or a flaw. Now his city had handed him a new and different kind of problem. He did not intend to permit either homegrown stupidity or meddlesome foreigners to interfere with his handling of it.

There existed no reason why Amos Wynn, or anybody else, should have questioned his authority over Wynnsboro and its region. He had come down in the direct line from Andrew Wynn, the first of his name out of England to hew a way into this wilderness in the early 1700's. His daughter, Amy, of the eighth generation, now stood as the last of the dynasty; this terminal reality was the only canker of real sorrow in his heart. He so deeply hated the thought that the name would die with him that he even had thought of influencing her husband—whenever she might choose one—to foreswear his own name and heritage and accept that of the Wynns. He had abandoned that notion as impractical; he both hoped and believed that anybody Amy held worthy of her for keeps would automatically possess too strong a pride of his own to exchange it for another's. Amy had been born in 1945 in the musty, creaky, roach-ridden, porticoed, columned, white and rotting mansion in which the Wynns had been born, lived, bred, and died, generation in and generation out, for a hundred and forty years. The line was already wearing thin in 1906 when Wynn preceded her, for he was an only child.

By the time of his arrival the town had borne his name for six generations ever since the first Amos, in 1790, decreed that the frontier fort laid down in the wilderness, in turn, by his forefathers had grown into a hamlet of sufficient dignity to bear any formal identity at all.

Now it was a city and it was still Amos Wynn's to have and to hold, to cherish and to discipline. There would be nobody after him. He had, of course, hoped that his first would prove a male. Amy had not, but now he loved her no less for that. He had hoped for more issue, but Amy's mother, who had also been Amy, had proved sickly and barren after her birth. It was because of her frailty that Amos, yielding pride of heritage, had at last consented that the mansion, its acres of lawn long since engulfed by commerce, should be razed. Now father and daughter lived in the wide, low-roofed ranch house he had built for the ailing first Amy in Gray Oak northeastward from the city. The elder Amy had died of cancer thirteen months after realizing her heart's long desire.

Beyond the city's hub, Wynn turned into Myrtle Avenue,

which led from the middle of town into Angel Creek, decaying visibly the nearer it came to its destination. The jeep began to buck.

His way led past Ebenezer Baptist, but he only slowed briefly and did not stop at the scene of the outrage. He saw, as he had known he would see, knots of black people assembled on the sidewalk in front of the church, aimlessly curious, stilled from visible action or outrage by generations habituated to submission. *They're gutless,* he thought, without contempt. *How could they be expected to be otherwise?* Then he wondered if he could possibly have that wrong; gutless the mass of them had surely been for all the generations of the Wynns, but was there a guarantee that they would remain so? Wynn was not insensitive to ferment in the land; it had not yet reached Wynnsboro or so he had thought. But even a year ago would they have listened at all to a union organizer?

Arthur Mayhew's janissaries, he noted, were poking about, not so much officious as bored. *They,* he thought, *are not likely to find out much; after all, it's only a nigger church.* For himself, he sought information, and he was going where he thought he might get it if the stuff was to be had at all. He drove through the main business intersection of Angel Creek where Myrtle met Thirty-eighth Street and four blocks beyond and curbed the jeep where blue and gold coldly flaring neon proclaimed BAR—THE SUDAN—BILLIARDS. Out of habit he left the ignition key in the lock; he knew as well as did any soul in Angel Creek that nobody in his right mind was likely to lift Amos Wynn's jeep.

The six o'clock news broadcast carried no word of the bombing, which did not surprise Amy Wynn since she knew the best single word to describe the news-gathering energies of WYN-TV, which was owned by her father, was desultory.

"I don't exactly know why and I don't think it matters much," Amos had said once when she complained. "Roughly ninety-eight percent of reports on the activities of your fellow human beings wouldn't hurt you if you never did hear them at all. The other two percent would drive you up a wall."

"It's possible your reporters have got hookworm," Amy retorted.

"Girl, I sometimes suspect you spent too much time in the North. It's a matter of latitude. Yankees, I observe, tend to be frantic."

"Y'all prefers Southern comfort, suh?"

"Ah prefers mah uproar and tumult rationed."

Well, they'll get around to it eventually, Amy thought and left the set turned on and the volume high and started toward the kitchen forty feet away. *I haven't any idea when he'll be back,* she reflected, *and it doesn't signify that he said not to hold dinner because whenever he does show up he'll be hungry, and if there isn't something ready he'll make a meal on bourbon alone which, of course, I am not against although I do hold to a belief, probably Yankee, that the liver is happier if it gets some nourishment besides straight alcohol.* She wondered, without irritation, why Martine was late getting home from her afternoon with her family, then thought, *Oh, well, her mother's probably keeping her busy with all those kids, and anyhow it won't hurt me to whomp up a little something for the table.*

WYN-TV did get around to it eventually. She was well into the several ingredients of a Caesar's salad when she heard music breaking off abruptly followed by the urgent voice of an announcer. She hurried toward the study.

". . . o'clock this afternoon . . . The bomb, thought by police to be dynamite in some kind of iron container, wrecked the front pews and shattered and set fire to the altar of a colored church, the Ebenezer Baptist, on Myrtle Avenue in Angel Creek. . . . Commissioner Mayhew . . . One man was pronounced dead at the scene and three others were hospitalized with serious injuries. The corpse was identified as a city employee named Pullen . . . the injured . . . it was not immediately . . ."

Amy gasped and said, "Oh," and then "Oh, no!" and then "Oh, damn it!" and heard no more, for, dressed as she was in linen slacks and a man's shirt, she was on the way out the front door and running toward the carport and her Porsche.

Why didn't he tell me? she wondered as she braked savagely for a red light in the business district and then, recklessly, jumped the light before it turned. *Of course, of course, he didn't know,* she thought, remembering Commissioner Mayhew's penchant for discharging at half cock. *Ah, the poor kid!*

Amy's course, like her father's, led past Ebenezer Baptist. She paused, as he had, noticing a fire department pumper lingering on the scene of a fire long since gone out and, in the bluish-white glare of searchlights, booted firemen standing around with Arthur Mayhew's police, neither visibly doing anything except waiting for the order to pack it up and go back to the pinochle game. They were not to be criticized since, once the bomb had done its work, there was nothing much the functionaries of public safety could do to rectify matters.

She wondered what had become of Rafe Pullen's body but supposed, like nearly every soul who expired in Angel Creek, it had gone to the ministrations of James Dowdy, saloonkeeper, whoremaster, and mortician. She supposed, correctly, that Amos had gone to the same authority for his own reasons.

As a matter of fact, at the moment she drove by, Dowdy had just finished his consultation with Amos Wynn and now in a surgeon's working dress was surveying the dismal task of preparing Rafe Pullen's remains for their penultimate public function.

"You won't need to drain the blood out of him," he told an assistant, peering down in the glare of white light at the wreckage on the marble slab. "It's gone."

Beyond the church Amy turned left into a dark and rutted byway, not quite seeing the packed rows of human habitation on either hand but knowing what they looked like, some neat, some tattered, some upright, some leaning near death but staving it off somehow. She knew, of course, that they were less grand than her own domicile, but it was not something you gave much thought to; it was simply the way things were and had been.

She did not know exactly what she had in mind; she was simply responding to an instinct that said a responsibility existed and that in order to discharge it you had to be where it was. She felt no particular sorrow for Rafe Pullen; she knew him only by infrequent sight as the father of the bright and very dark, skinny teen-ager who had come to her wanting work and whom she had hired—out of pity, mostly—and then had learned to be enchanted and in a way excited by a quick and eager intelligence, entirely unexpected.

No, sorrow and anxiety she felt truly enough, but they were for young Martine Pullen and for the new burdens now brutally descended on those narrow shoulders. She could grieve for Martine, all right, and because of Martine for the savage bereavement of her mother and brothers and sisters.

The Pullen home was one of the neat ones, a stilted, painted, clapboard front room, two bedrooms and kitchen with flowers in front and a wooden stoop that courageously did muster for a porch. Pullen had not been the only breadwinner in the family, for, in addition to Martine, her mother worked cleaning office buildings at night downtown and her thirteen-year-old brother, Eliot, had after-school employment as a carry-out boy in a white supermarket. The Pullens had got along before this Saturday afternoon, and they would get along again, no doubt, although surely under greater strain on thrift and diligence.

Amy did not know exactly what she expected to find, beyond shock and grief and most probably a pathetic need for help. She knew that Martine had adored Rafe Pullen, for, once the shyness of her color and her first job had worn off, she had spoken of him with affection: a man who worked hard, brought home his pay, and was weakly indulgent with all his young except on one unyielding peninsula of parental authority—he would not abide a poor report card fetched home from the teachers.

"He never learned to read until he was older than I am now,

and he wouldn't have learned then except they made him do it in reform school," Martine had once confided. "I guess he doesn't want his children getting their lessons the same way."

Amy's inspiration to see to Martine's advanced education provided the source for a rare but genuine and sometimes acrimonious disagreement with her father.

"Nothing doing," Amos said firmly. "You'll ruin that kid."

"Ruin her! Why, pa, for heaven's sake?" Amy asked, momentarily befuddled by this unexpected intransigence.

"Look where the youngster comes from," he said with some asperity. "Her people are good folks. He's a steady man. There are all those kids. You send that kid off to some college, and she either won't come back or if she does she'll be too good for her own people."

"That's ridiculous" was, for the moment, about all Amy could manage.

"Ridiculous?" he said, his tone coolly disapproving, which was unprecedented in Amos Wynn's relations with his only child. "I've seen it too many times. After God knows how many generations of yassuh, nossuh these people are not geared for it."

"Whose fault is the yassuh, nossuh bit then?" Amy demanded, feeling indignation grow.

"Whose fault it may be doesn't signify. At least it doesn't anymore. You're simply pumping a black head full of notions it's not equipped to understand. Educate her, of course, but high school's far enough. Beyond that you'd simply be condemning her to water too deep to swim in. You've got, I guess, some Lady Bountiful notion about expanding the soul and deepening the intellect. Believe me, Amy, and I know, you'd only make her unhappy in the end."

In totally unjustified anger, which she recognized as unjust even as she did it, daughter accused father of begrudging the money.

In totally justified resentment of the charge, Amos looked her coldly up and down and walked out of the house. "Go ahead," he said, departing. "It'll make you feel good about yourself. It'll wreck the kid."

"You are an . . . an . . . an anachronism," Amy yelled after him, recognizing at the same time the element of truth in his charge that, paying for an education for Martine, she was also indulging a relatively inexpensive wish to approve of herself. *But not entirely*, she told herself fiercely. *Martine deserves it because she's ten times as smart as he thinks she is and I am* not *simply trying to buy myself a bright pet nigger.*

In the end, Amos had yielded as he did to most of his daughter's desires, although he remained unconvinced.

Now, beyond the site of Rafe Pullen's immolation at the church, Amy supposed she would find the Pullen household crowded with the curious and the sympathetic. But the house was quiet. No cars were at the curb and no subdued knots of people stood murmuring on the sidewalk or in the thin strip of front yard, brought together by a herd instinct to pay obeisance to tragedy. Amy had no way of knowing that in places like Angel Creek tragedy carries with it an almost-palpable no-trespassing sign. In such places tragedy emanates nameless threat to the innocent bystander, and both the wise and the foolish instinctively stand well clear of it, wishing not to offer targets of opportunity.

But the house was not entirely deserted. Pale light painted yellow oblongs through the curtains of windows on either side of the stoop. Amy mounted the steps, hesitated, found no bell, knocked softly, waited and when no answer came, knocked again. Then, feeling more of an intruder than a friend in need, she turned the knob and softly opened the door.

They were all in the front room. Mrs. Pullen, a stout, muscular, round-faced woman, still youthful despite or perhaps because of the hard physical labor she performed five nights a week, sat in the middle of an overstuffed, velvet-covered sofa, tearless, staring into the distance, wooden, without expression. She was utterly still except for her hands which were gently, unconscious of her as she was unconscious of them, stroking the heads, the backs of the necks, the shoulders of two small figures huddled on either side of her with their heads in her broad lap. From one of them came repetitious gasping sobs. There was no other sound in the room.

Eliot, the thirteen-year-old whom Amy knew by sight, sat stiffly in a straight-backed kitchen chair. He did not look up but sat as unmoving as his mother; his dark young face was knotted together, eyes squeezed shut, lips pursed, wizened into a grimace of shriveled age. Two younger girls sat scrunched together in an overstuffed chair, holding to each other with desperate, unspeaking urgency.

The only movement in the room was Martine, holding the three-year-old up to her skinny breast, marching back and forth, crooning a wordless, almost inaudible song, her head bent down, lips almost touching the baby's ear.

Transfixed, Amy stood for a moment in the door, unconsciously arrested by and caught up in the quiet tableau Rafe Pullen had left for his testament. In that moment, turning in her silent, soothing march, Martine saw her. In one swift movement she bent and put the baby upon his feet and then stood and stared at Amy. Amy saw the tears spring into the black girl's eyes, and she started toward her wordlessly with her arms out.

Amy's own arms were spread to receive her and she was moving forward when Martine stopped in full stride and came stiffly erect, and in that moment her face was transmuted in a mask of fury.

"Get out! Get out, white bitch! Leave us alone!"

The words rushed out in a spitting torrent, and Amy saw, in frozen horror, that white foam was flecking the girl's purple lips. She stopped dead, and her arms fell dead to her side.

Martine's outburst broke the trance of shock that had held her family. The baby began to howl. Eliot opened his eyes and sat staring dazedly. The two heads came up from Mrs. Pullen's lap and peered in fear and wonder at the white woman standing speechless in the middle of the room.

"My father's dead! You hear, dead. Ain't that enough? You want more? Get out, get out! Oh, get the hell out of here!"

"Martine!" Mrs. Pullen shouted, her dazed face stirred now to angry shock. "Stop that! Shut up! You hear me, shut up!"

Martine was not hearing. From bitter venom the girl's words turned to bitter sarcasm.

"What you want here, white Lady Bountiful? Tell us what you want. Gonna dry the stupid niggers tears? Bringin' us a cake for the funeral? What you want? How can we serve you? You want me back to fix your supper? Can't swing your white ass to fix a meal for yourself?"

For a moment outrage swept over Amy and she started forward again, this time not in pity. But the broken, tormented face stopped her and turned anger into a kind of cold, bemused despair. *Oh God,* Amy thought, *and the poor kid had this in her all the time. And I never knew. And she never knew until now, I'll swear she never knew.*

"You think I don't know what killed my daddy?" The girl raged on. "I know all right. Oh, I know! You think I'm so smart you gonna make me into a bright, educated nigger. But I tell you something. Bright niggers read newspapers. Bright niggers listen to that white radio. Bright niggers see TV, even in your big wide overdone big stone, swimming pool, intercom, electric kitchen, food freezers, air-conditioned, five-toilet, ass-aching big white people's mansion. I know who killed my daddy!"

"Martine! You hear me! Stop that!" Mrs. Pullen shouted.

"Shouldn't be no bright niggers. Bright nigger sees too much. You never should've let that happen. You want a tame bright, white-ass-kissing nigger and I'm it. My daddy was a tame nigger, too. Working his black ass off. Working! Minute he wants a little better for his family, asks a little decency, says he wants to be a man, you kill him. Get! Get out this house! Ain't your daddy's dead."

Amy was still stunned by the suddenness, the total unexpectedness of the attack. She felt impaled by it. But the first reflex jolt of anger was under control and now it was replaced by a flood of pity.

"Oh, Marty," she whispered. "I'm sorry."

"You sorry!" The words came out in a frenzied squeal, and Martine threw her head back and was torn by a spasm of wild laughter out of which rushed the beginning of another tirade. She was gasping now. "Sure, you sorry. Sure you sorry!" She began to laugh again.

Suddenly the girl ran across the room, seized an ornate table lamp and, ripping the cord from the wall socket, ran at Amy raising the lamp base as a club. Amy saw her coming and knew what she intended; she stiffened for the blow, facing the enraged girl, making no effort to dodge. It caught her alongside the face and sharp edges raked her cheek and still she stood. The lamp crashed to the floor. Martine stared at her, seeing the blood start from gashes in Amy's white face and begin to run down her cheeks.

Then Martine collapsed. Amy took her in her arms and felt the convulsed shudder of the thin shoulders and held her closer and crooned, "Marty, Marty."

The girl clung to her, shuddering, her head buried in Amy's breast, gasping. "Oh! Oh! Please." It was a wail of pure anguish. "Oh, Please. My daddy's dead!"

Inside The Sudan, Amos Wynn walked past the bar, nodding briefly but not speaking to the black bartender or the few habitués who looked at him once in curiosity and then away not to be caught staring. They knew of the bombing, naturally, and the sight of Amos Wynn's big, purposefully moving frame did not surprise them. Wynn went through the door into the back room, walked by the row of nickel and dime and quarter slots and, without ceremony, pushed open another door and entered. He did not knock; he never did but meant no discourtesy by the omission.

He was in an oak-paneled office, softly lighted from coves around the ceiling, comfortably furnished, its center being a huge, gleaming walnut desk, its top expanse covered with tooled Florentine leather. A dark man, wearing gold-rimmed spectacles over eyes set in a neatly sculptured, controlled face, looked up as he entered.

"Hello, Mister Wynn," he said. "I sort of expected you." Not even thirty years of knowing Amos Wynn, not intimately as friends but well and in unspoken but thorough mutual understanding, had been able to rid James Dowdy's tongue of the respectful "mister" whenever he spoke to this man.

"Hello, Jim," Wynn said.

"A hell of a mess, Mister Wynn," Dowdy said.

"It is," Wynn said. "And useless."

By stretching the imagination it would have been possible to speculate that Amos Wynn and James Dowdy were partners. They were not in any formal sense, but each recognized that the other had interests in Angel Creek and that these interests were not only compatible but complementary. Dowdy was an entrepreneur, not a land holder. His bar and his funeral parlor, which stood cheek by jowl in Myrtle Avenue, were legitimate, as the slot machines in the back room of the bar and the two whorehouses, Madame Mame's and Miss Paulette's, respectively three and seven blocks from The Sudan, were not. However, all four served human needs which Amos Wynn, the city's liege lord, recognized as universal and possibly wholesome. They were the more wholesome because he knew that Dowdy, in some ways a fastidious man, saw to it that they functioned as quietly, cleanly, honestly, and efficiently as was humanly possible. This business philosophy came easily to hand with the funeral parlor, more difficultly with the other three. But he managed and partly because he managed well, Amos Wynn respected Dowdy and saw to it that City Hall made no waves about Dowdy's concerns and that Arthur Mayhew's uniformed men exacted no tribute from him.

Wynn's traditional interests in Angel Creek were rooted deeper in the soil underneath it. He and his immediate associates held title to perhaps two-thirds of the real estate within the section, including even Ebenezer Baptist and The Sudan and Miss Paulette's. These were practical matters, but Wynn's concern in Angel Creek went deeper and encompassed the people who had their being there. He would not, for example, tolerate other landlords exploiting the necessities of residents who lived in Angel Creek because it was inconceivable and impossible for them to live anywhere else in Wynnsboro. Shylock loan sharks who set up shop in Angel Creek speedily found themselves on the way out of town with instructions, which they were by then avid to obey, not to come back. Discount houses flourished there but high-pressure collection agencies did not, at least not after Amos Wynn had them brought to his attention. Withal, it could not be said that Wynn loved the people of Angel Creek; he looked upon them, by and large, as retarded children unable to care for themselves who did not, under most circumstances, know what was good for them.

He wanted them as orderly as their natures would permit and wanted them obedient. He knew what was good for them far better than they did. What it came down to, in the end, was that what was good for Wynnsboro was what was good for its black population.

If anybody knew most of what was going on in Angel Creek most of the time, that repository of human strengths and weaknesses was James Dowdy. A large part of the reason Dowdy knew was that he was not a blabberer. He was warily selective when it came to giving away information, and probably the only person in Wynnsboro who could have it all, not even including Dowdy's wife, was Amos Wynn.

And so, the relationship between the two men was by no means a partnership; instead it was an odd compound of mutual respect and solid self-interest.

Wynn crossed the room and eased himself into a leather upholstered, old-fashioned Morris chair big enough to hold him in comfort. Wynn, six feet three and mostly cragged bone and sinew and no visible sag despite more than sixty years of hard use, needed some holding, as Dowdy knew. Indeed Wynn's size was the consideration which had moved Dowdy to buy the chair more than twenty years ago. The chair was Wynn's, and Dowdy saw to it that nobody else sat in it in his presence.

"You have any idea this was likely to happen?" Wynn asked.

Dowdy pursed his lips and leaned back in his own chair. "No. Not until it did," he said somberly. "But I guess you could say I'm not surprised. Are you?"

"Nothing much surprises me anymore, Jim. I must be getting slow; I could have guessed this . . . or something like it."

"You think anything is going to come of it, Mister Wynn?"

"I don't know. The Justice Department takes a lot of interest in us these days. The Teamsters could have been handled . . . quietly, sensibly. Now it's hard to say. We could end up with a town full of federal marshals. I don't want that."

"I know you don't."

"What about the people?" Wynn asked. "I took a look at the church. They were there; they didn't seem any different, moping around the same as always. But I wondered a little if they really are the same."

Dowdy pulled at his chin and looked uneasy. "Tell the truth, Mister Wynn, I don't know anymore. The Teamsters didn't just bull their way in here. They must've had some idea that somebody was ready to listen."

"About that," Wynn said, "keep talking to the people that have some say down here. There are some who know which side is up, and you know who they are and how to talk to them. I don't want the Teamsters here and you won't either, but I wouldn't want any other outfit either. It isn't just a matter of people on the city payroll. We could probably put up with that . . . if we had to . . . but it wouldn't stop there . . . and if a union prairie fire gets started, sooner or later it'll hit the plants. And if the plants get hit, they'll get out. If the plants move out . . . considering the payroll . . . Angel Creek will be up the creek. And you know it, Jim."

Dowdy still looked troubled. "I know it, Mister Wynn. But it ain't always easy for people to see that far."

"I know that, and you know the missionaries will talk a hell of a game. Shorter hours, more money, pensions, overtime, time to go fishin'. Screw the bosses and pie in the sky. They wouldn't be the first to buy it; plenty of whites have, God knows.

"But there's another side to it, and they've got the right to know that, too. Hell, more than a right; they've got a duty. We need some missionary work ourselves. The Teamsters come looking like rosy-fingered angels, but anybody who takes the trouble to find out knows they ain't. The record stinks. Working for a union can be a damn sight worse than working for a white man. Sweetheart contracts. Pension funds. Hook-ups with hoods in Jersey, Chicago, Philadelphia, Las Vegas, you name it. Getting the bejesus beat out of you with a bicycle chain.

"You tell them, Jim. I could and they'd look like they were listening, but they wouldn't even hear me. They might hear you."

"I know, Mister Wynn. I've told them. I'm not too sure they hear me right either. Not as clear as they used to."

"This moron thing at the church won't make it any simpler," Wynn said, brooding. "It had to be a white man."

"Don't be too sure, Mister Wynn," Dowdy said slowly.

Wynn looked up at the colored merchant in sudden interest. "What did you say?"

"I said don't be sure it was a white man."

"Why not?" The question was sharp, demanding.

"A white man hanging around that church would be seen, and if one had been seen I'd know it by now."

"At night?"

"That church has been locked nights. I know—I'm a member. Preacher Morgan has been locking it since some kids—white—got in and smeared up the place last Christmas."

"So? So," Wynn said slowly. "Do you know something, Jim?"

Dowdy sat staring down, as though absorbed, at his clasped hands. Wynn was aware of the tension with which the slender fingers were entwined. At last he spoke.

"The name Abel Dowdy mean anything to you, Mister Wynn . . . ? No, I guess it wouldn't."

"Dowdy?"

"My nephew. My brother's son. I had him working here for a while last summer."

"What about him, Jim?" Wynn asked.

"I had to fire him. He was into the till."

"What's he got to do with this?"

"Maybe nothing; I hope so anyhow."

"But I suspect you think otherwise."

"Hell, Mister Wynn, I don't know. I do know he was around this part of town last week. And again today. And that hasn't been usual."

"Where's he been, then?"

"Gervase gave him a job, I heard."

"Oh," Wynn said.

"He's not a good kid, and he's not bright," Dowdy said. "He's driven my brother half out of his mind. I just don't know what ails him."

"Gervase, huh?" Wynn said. "The sonofabitch." He got up and went to Dowdy's desk. "Hand me the phone, Jim." Wynn dialed and waited and then spoke.

"Joe? You're home. Stay there. I want to talk to you." He put the instrument back on the desk.

"Now, Mister Wynn, I told you I'm not sure."

"Neither am I. I intend to find out. So long, Jim."

Joe Gervase, christened Giuseppe, lived in a big, modern, expensive, and heavily overdecorated house—where his wife prudently covered all the costly French provincial furniture with clear plastic slipcovers to let the rich fabrics below show through. The house stood in a less-exclusive residential area than Amos Wynn's home in Gray Oak. When Gervase had, after twenty years of effort, felt rich enough to afford a residence suitable to Marie's desires, he had, naturally, aspired to live in Gray Oak since he could afford it. Because he was by nature wary, however, he had first gone to the trouble of calling on the

chief of Gray Oak's six-man police force to ascertain the probable temper of the welcome wagon thereabouts. The chief, in
turn, asked Amos Wynn and then advised Gervase.

"Joe," the chief said. "Nobody can tell you where to live, and
I won't try to. If you come here, nobody will bother you."

"That's fine," Gervase said. "I just wanted to make sure."

"But I should tell you this," the chief said. "You move in
here, and any time a friend of yours comes to see you he'll get
pinched for vagrancy." Gray Oak's police were not the same
breed of cats as Wynnsboro's larger, more venal force.

Although Marie didn't like it, Gervase wisely settled for less
snooty acreage and expressed his resentment by spending
$150,000 on the house—before furnishings.

Amos Wynn occasionally wondered why he tolerated Gervase
in Wynnsboro at all and considered it a somehow culpable neg-
ligence that he did. Still, Wynn knew that various degrees of
moral turpitude were endemic conditions of the soul of man
and that Gervase probably served these weaknesses as well as
anybody could—except for James Dowdy who served some of
the same needs more discreetly in Angel Creek. Not all the
same needs, for Gervase's interests were more diverse; in some
ways he was a one-man conglomerate. The visible aspects of his
empire were two restaurants and a warehouse on the outskirts
of the city where he functioned as a jobber of auto parts; the
parts business carried the outward insignia of respectability but
not even this was legitimate, for the bulk of Gervase's stock was
trucked in from Detroit, Flint, and Dearborn where it had been
stolen by business associates. Wynn suspected, but did not of
his own knowledge know, that Gervase's trucks freighted more
portable and even less-innocent cargo, including heroin. He
knew it would probably prove impossible to stop that through-
traffic since, if interrupted, Gervase could easily find a way
around Wynnsboro, but he made certain that Commissioner
Mayhew made certain that none of Gervase's deadly contra-
band found a way to consumers in Wynnsboro. Thus Amos
Wynn's stewardship over his namesake city was less than alto-

gether praiseworthy, but he may be forgiven something, if not all, for a realistic recognition that sin was a fact of life and that if it were exorcised in one form it would surely reappear in another.

Gervase, having seen the lights of the jeep turning into his own semicircular driveway, met him at the door, perhaps suspecting that if he didn't he would not be vouchsafed the social courtesy of a knock or a ring.

"Come in, Amos, come in," Gervase said with an effort at the forms of hospitality.

"Did I invite you to call me Amos?" Wynn said coldly. "Come in here; I want to talk to you." Amos led the way across the living room to the door that opened into the other man's study, which was really not a study at all but an office with three telephones and a dictating machine and other devices Gervase was too prudent to put on display.

Gervase felt resentment all right. Very few people treated him cavalierly, but, aware that Amos Wynn was not the multitude, he took care not to show it.

"Take a chair," Gervase said and started toward his desk. He was circumvented because Wynn, knowing that the chair behind the desk was the only one in the room of a size to suit him, was there already.

"What can I do for you, Am . . . ?" he began—but remembered in time.

"You've got a no-good nigger named Dowdy," Wynn said. It wasn't a question and Gervase chose not to suppose it was.

"What about him, Mister Wynn?" he said.

"Get him here," Wynn said.

"Hell, Am . . . Hell, I don't know where he is."

Wynn's eyes were icy. Gervase knew something about that, for those who feared himself, who were many, dreaded his own talent for the basilisk stare, and he knew it. Better men than Gervase had considered challenging Amos Wynn's bleak gray eyes when he was angry—and had reconsidered.

"I'll try to find him," he said, reaching for one of the telephones.

"I said get him," Wynn said.

"Where do you want him?" Gervase asked.

"Here," Wynn said.

"Marie don't like nig. . . ."

"Marie will survive. Get him."

Gervase dialed, waited, dialed again, got an answer, and, speaking quietly, issued brief peremptory orders.

"He'll be here. Fifteen, twenty minutes," he said.

"That's better."

While they waited, saying nothing, Wynn regarded his host with chill lack of expression, but the inner man seethed with sour dislike. Gervase was short, obese, and dark, and gone far toward baldness with a diligently empty face half obscured by a great fang of a nose. The brilliant Oahu sport shirt he wore bulged with the belly that weighed heavy on his belt, hanging over it. *And I endure this, possibly things worse,* Wynn thought. *Damn his soul.*

"How about a drink?" Gervase said.

Wynn grunted his refusal.

At length the doorbell chimes sounded, sounding oddly hesitant, unwilling.

"That's him." Gervase grunted. Without getting up, he called, "Well! Come on in."

The bell chimed again, even more briefly. Gervase yelled, "Come on in, you black bastard."

They heard the front door creak and moments later a dark young Negro, wearing a T-shirt and slacks, a magnificent physical specimen stood in the office doorway. *He'd be a good-looking kid if he weren't so obviously and abysmally scared,* Wynn thought.

"Yes, sir, Mister Gervase." The boy's voice quavered. "You wanted me?"

"I don't—he does," Gervase said, nodding toward Wynn.

"That's him, probably the stupidest nigger out of Angel Creek," he said contemptuously to Wynn.

For perhaps thirty seconds Wynn stared at the young man who in turn, visibly quaked, tongue-tied, unable to utter a word.

At last Wynn spoke. It was more than accusation; it was flat, unemotional, remorseless condemnation. The shadow of the hangman stood behind his words.

"You planted that bomb."

"I . . . I . . . I . . ." The boy couldn't get his voice.

"Sure, he planted it." Gervase's voice was a sneer. "I've known that since five o'clock. How do you like that? Murdering his own people?" He stared at the quivering boy, his own eyes now hard and expressionless. "How many, Abel?"

Slowly, Wynn took his stare away from the frightened boy and turned it on Gervase.

"And you sent him to do it." Wynn's voice was without inflection, and without question. Again it was the hangman speaking.

Gervase threw up a protesting hand. "Now . . . Just a minute . . . Just a minute, Mister Wynn. You can't . . ."

"The hell I can't. You sent him. I know it and you know I know it."

Quickly, Gervase was on the defensive, baffled, dumbfounded. "Hell, Mister Wynn, you know what they were doing down there. What the hell. Niggers. Teamsters. Somebody had to head them off."

"And you had to make a shithouse out of it," Wynn said bleakly.

"You intend to do something about it?" Gervase asked. There was now some recovered defiance in him and, even more, he was genuinely puzzled. He knew, or thought he knew, that Amos Wynn did not want, nor intend to permit, a black declaration of independence any more than he did.

Wynn ignored the question and sat silent.

"There's the kid," Gervase said, flicking a hand toward the black youth. "You want him, you can have him."

The young man expelled an involuntary groan, struggled to speak . . . and could not.

"Of course I can have him. Shut up, Gervase," Wynn said. He fell silent. Minutes ticked away. The black youth writhed. Gervase fidgeted, then tried to hold himself still when Wynn looked up and gazed at him, expressionless. If he was calculating, no flicker revealed it. At last Wynn raised his head and looked at Gervase.

"I can have you, too," he said tonelessly.

"For Christ's sake!" Gervase exploded. "For niggers . . ."

"No," Wynn said. "For being a murdering sonofabitch. And for stupidity. The second is worse."

He sat again without speaking while tension built in the other two men. It was five minutes before he spoke again. He turned to the boy.

"I can let them hang you," he said evenly. "You know that. But I'm not going to, not this time. I want you out of this city tonight. Don't ever come back. If you do, they will hang you. I'll see to it."

The boy began to stammer incoherently, but Wynn silenced him with a gesture and turned to Gervase.

"Give him three hundred dollars," he said.

"For God's sake, are you going to let him. . . ."

"Shut up and get the money . . . now," Wynn said. "I'm not going to hang him for murders you committed. Get the money."

Baffled and sullen, Gervase pulled up a corner of rug, bent over a combination, lifted a safe door and took up a packet of bills. He counted out the money, in ones and fives, a hundred in tens and shoved it into the youth's hand.

"Get! Get out of my sight, you black bastard," he shouted.

The boy vanished.

"I should have counted it. But never mind. At the moment I doubt if you had the guts to gyp him," Wynn said.

"For God's sake," Gervase said. "For niggers." He shook his head in baffled confusion.

"Not because they were niggers," Wynn said softly. "Because they were my niggers."

"That's all?" Gervase said sullenly, hating the man, hating him the more because he knew, of all men, he was the most helpless before this one.

"That's all for now." Wynn said, rising, towering above the lesser man. "If you weren't white and a jury probably wouldn't touch you, I'd hang you." He paused, gazing down at Gervase out of immutable calm. "The day may come when I will."

Gervase shook his head in bewilderment. "Mister Wynn, I didn't know . . . I never would have guessed you'd get so goddamn moral about one dead nigger . . ."

"You misunderstood . . . which does not surprise me," Wynn said. "I am not being moral . . . as you call it . . . about death, even imposed death. But I will not tolerate stupid, self-defeating waste . . . There is one other thing. You will see that Rafe Pullen's widow gets five thousand dollars. Your money."

"Fi . . . ?" Gervase began to expostulate.

"Five thousand," Wynn said quietly, and left.

2

Carver Otis Barton was in Chicago, fighting a school busing case in U.S. District Court and, to his chagrin, not getting very far with it, when the city of Wynnsboro was first brought to his attention. If he had not been at a dead end, at least temporarily, on the school case he might never have got around to going there, for, at this juncture in his career, Barton had more things demanding his attention than he had time to attend to. Of course he had no way of knowing that he would die in Wynnsboro although, of course, even he, despite a healthy arrogance in the vitality of his being, could guess that he was likely to die young and by violence. There were others, fearful for his continued good health or resentful of it, far more than he convinced that his rope was short and that he could soon come to the end of it.

In some ways Barton was an accident of history, a sport from now untraceable genes, but in others he was a perfectly understandable product of the social and technological forces at work in the United States in the two decades after 1950. He was the son of an elevator operator who for twenty years had worked in the Time-Life Building in New York, beginning when the publications had been housed in the Chrysler Tower and so cheerfully popular with the staff that management had insisted on taking him along, as a morale factor, when the corporation moved to grander quarters in Rockefeller Plaza. The flaw in the elder Barton's career, one that not even the highest executives of the Luce empire could forestall, was that his job was steadily being abraded by automation. Instead of coming in out of the muck of a New York morning to a sunshiny greeting from operator Barton, editors, writers, researchers, and editorial auditors came to a juncture where they had to push their own buttons and ascend to their labors in the heavens above to the strains of Muzak. The change did nobody any good, least of all the head of the Barton family. The editorial functionaries went to their work in the same gloom in which they had left Forty-eighth Street, and Barton finally got a job dumping garbage cans into sanitation trucks, in all weathers, in New Rochelle where the family lived in a dank apartment in the decaying heart of town off North Avenue. Not understanding that technical progress, rather than some indefinable white spite, had cost Barton his spruce brown uniform and instead brought him home from work malodorous, a mute resentment seethed around the Barton hearth.

Carver Otis—not even his mother could figure out quite why she had chosen that selection of names for him—sailed through Lincoln Elementary without effort and later, in the rush of events, tended to forget the agony he had needed to adjust to junior and senior high when he had moved on, to his intense astonishment, into student bodies which instead of being all black were almost all white. He had got out with creditable grades just in time to be drafted for service in the Korean War.

This was the first United States war, since the Civil, in which Negro servicemen were permitted the dignity of dying on their feet with rifles in their hands rather than as stevedores in port companies or mess attendants in the officers' wardrooms of ships of war. This upgrading of status came about as the result of an edict, coming from President Truman ordaining full racial integration of the American armed services in 1948. But integration was one thing to the President in his oval office and something quite else to a Marine drill sergeant at Parris Island.

It is axiomatic that Marine drill sergeants, bearing the responsibility of creating Marines out of slew-footed civilians or killing them in the process, are popular with nobody, nor are raw recruits popular with them. Probably one of the least-beloved recruits at Parris Island in his season was Carver Otis Barton, for he discovered somewhere in a previously unsuspected crevice of his soul a belligerent capacity for talking back to outrage. His drill sergeant, a smooth-faced, rough-voiced, ramrod paragon from South Carolina named Guiness, saw that he paid for indiscretion in the brig, in being night-marched in full pack up to his chin in water and, once, in a savage beating that should have taken young Barton to the infirmary for repairs but for an illogical force of pride that would not permit him to admit his hurts. He swore to himself, as had many a recruit before him, that he would survive whatever lay ahead in

Korea for the single overpowering purpose of coming back to Parris Island to kill Sergeant Guiness.

His hatred for Guiness, both racial and personal, became slightly less personal when he was shipped out from San Diego and came first to Pusan and eventually as a replacement in a rifle company of the 7th Marines, First Mardiv, in time to make the hopeful drive northward after the fleeing North Koreans and then to slam head on into the unexpected Chinese only forty-eight miles below the Yalu River. He learned that the fighting Marines, as then constituted, were hardly any more adjusted to the notion of racial equality than Parris Island had been. He got used to the derision of being addressed as a night fighter because heredity had given him the hand and face cosmetics for that duty and to pulling rather more than his fair share of disagreeable duty. He made the bitter winter march— nobody wanted to call it retreat—back from the Changjin Reservoir to the coast at Hungnam and did it every mile on his feet despite a bullet that shattered his lower jaw and reduced him to existing on soup, when even that was available. He did not particularly resent the fact that there never seemed to be room for him in the wretchedly few evacuation helicopters; it was apparent even through his blizzard-numbed sickness that there were worse wounded than himself. He was able to keep moving, but he never did get around to the point of feeling any gratitude to Sergeant Guiness for hammering into him the toughness of fiber to keep putting one frost-bitten foot ahead of the other. Still, he did forget the moral necessity of going back to slaughter him.

He was discharged in a state of mind haphazardly bitter, not against his country, but against the vast amorphous fence that stood everywhere in it bearing a sign, meant for him alone, that translated "Inside," not "Out." Guiness stood abandoned as the goal of his life, but he knew he needed a substitute; the most immediate one that occurred to him was that no dictate on earth would be able to condemn him to a career on a New Rochelle garbage truck; he already had had all the KP he was prepared to endure this side of the grave. By unintended philanthropy, Sergeant Guiness had granted Carver Otis Barton a greater boon than he thought.

And so he took his discharge papers, the twenty-five percent disability the Veterans Administration saw fit to award him and his Purple Heart, and began applying to colleges. Columbia somewhat hesitantly accepted him—there was no graceful way to turn down a GI Bill application based upon his combat record—but four years later found no cause to regret its generosity when he took his BA degree *cum laude* and accepted a Phi Beta Kappa key which he later, in a slightly derisive mood, had mounted as a tie stickpin.

"I do not expect," he said, "that I am going to enjoy the leisure to grow a belly suitable for wearing this as a fob on a gold watch chain."

He came out of Harvard Law in 1958 and was admitted to practice law in the state courts of New York. By 1964—it was only then that he was beginning to anticipate the need—he was admitted to the bar before the Supreme Court of the United States. He had not, until a year or so before, felt much of an impulse toward that august body, for his practice had begun in Harlem where his clients for the first few years were largely muggers, gamblers, dope pushers, car thieves, whores, numbers operators, and other minor dropouts from society.

The thing that altered the direction of his professional bent was his son's graduation from grammar school in New Rochelle; as his father had, Carver Otis and his wife then lived in the Lincoln school district in part because it had not, until then, occurred to him as either possible or desirable that Bartons might live somewhere else.

However it was upon the otherwise joyous occasion of his son's matriculation into junior high that Barton began to discover that his kid couldn't spell, couldn't read, couldn't add or subtract or fathom the new math any more than he could Sanskrit and, in brief, couldn't do anything well connected with education except play hooky, at which he was superb. He had theretofore, proudly but rather absently, thought his son bright. Now his first sad thought was that he had been wrong; the kid was dumb. He called upon the youngster's counsellor and began to learn otherwise. Not only was his son unable to compete with the vast majority of whites in his classes and of his age, but eighty-five percent of the blacks who had come up with him from elementary school were in a similar fix.

"They can't all be that stupid," he told his wife. "Maybe there's something haywire with the system. I think I'll find out."

What he discovered was a phenomenon which was beginning to be called *de facto* segregation in the public schools. His town had not had a legally segregated school since 1889 when the last Negro school had been torn down. Thereafter, so far as the legal situation went, youngsters went to school where they lived —black, white, or yellow. It was called the neighborhood school system and it had a lot to be said for it, chiefly that most kids lived close enough to the nearest school to walk between there and home.

The thing that could not be said for it was not, per se, the fault of the schools. This was that whites, for the most part, lived in certain chosen parts of town and the blacks lived in what was left, generally the old part near the business centers. One thing fitted with another ad infinitum. The blacks lived where they did because very few whites wanted them to live anywhere else. The blacks were generally poorer than the whites because they couldn't get jobs as generally well paying as those the whites could get. Part of the reason that they couldn't get better jobs was that they were generally less well educated than the whites; they were less well educated because they were poorer and because their parents and grandparents had been poorly educated. All this was reflected in the neighborhood elementary school where poor black kids from uneducated and unstable homes competed only with other poor black kids from the same kind of homes. You couldn't blame the school system, really, or at least you couldn't blame it more than you could blame something else. But the fact was, Barton discovered, that when the average black kid got out of neighborhood school and went on to junior high, where he competed against whites, he was licked before he started. It now occurred to Barton to wonder, for the first time really, how he himself had eluded the destiny which had overtaken his son. The only answer he could find was that some peculiarity in his personal chemistry had raised him above the level of average. That explanation did not come hard for him because, all his adult life, he had found it easy to consider himself somehow fashioned of superior clay.

Barton took the matter to U.S. District Court where he argued, among other things, that a white school board had, with malice, gerrymandered the district lines of neighborhood schools to keep the whites separated from the blacks. He knew the argument to be both unfair and dishonest; he knew there were other forces than deliberate ill will at work, but he considered the white mind and white actions so generally inimical as to justify any means of combatting them. And he could show, as a matter of record, that two of the suburb's dozen elementary schools were at least ninety percent black. If that wasn't segregation in fact, what the hell was it?

"They've been screwing us as a matter of habit," he told his wife. "A little judicious screwing, in turn, will help keep them awake."

Barton was lucky. His case was set down before a federal judge who had his eye firmly fixed on the appellate bench and was eager to make a name for himself. The judge ruled flat out in Barton's favor, ordering the dismayed school board to present forthwith, for his honor's consideration, a plan, scheme, or device for breaking up *de facto* segregation and scattering the suburb's black children through all the suburb's schools. The matter became a landmark case, the first public school system north of the Mason-Dixon Line to be forced by federal court order to desegregate. The ruling split the town along a bitter line down the middle. It became more than black against white and resolved itself into white against white, Jew against Christian, WASP against Italian Catholic, Jew against Jew, Democrat against Republican. A half dozen years later, formerly good friends and bridge partners were still not speaking to one another, and PTA sessions were battles royal.

The judge had guessed right. He had made a name for himself. He had also made one for Carver Otis Barton. And Barton had felt the pull of a vocation. At first it was only school cases; after his own town he felt he knew the arena cold and believed he knew how to win in it more often than he would lose.

"They can march up and down until they're walking on their uppers and cold bare feet. They can sing 'We Shall Overcome' till their lungs bleed," he said loftily. "It'll get them exactly where they are already—in the crap. Let me take it to court in front of a federal judge. One man's voice there is as loud and clear as any man's, any school board's, any city's, any state's.

"But let him be a federal. Something happens to a man when he gets on the federal bench. He doesn't owe anybody anything anymore. He has kissed his last ass. And his is there to be kissed. He can be ornery, and if he's a sadistic enough sonofabitch he can enjoy rubbing the noses of lawyers and also institutions in the garbage. Look at the way Judge Skelly Wright put down the Louisiana state legislature. He was New Orleans born, as naturally created segregationist as you could get. But those bastards up in Baton Rouge would pass a law one day ruling the niggers out of bounds and the next day down in New Orleans, Judge Wright would knock it down.

"Set it up; knock it down. He enjoyed it because he was by nature an ornery man. And just possibly getting up there on the federal bench where nobody could knock him down had let enough daylight into his skull to fetch in a little justice with it. Give me a judge, but let him be a federal."

The more he worked on school cases, the broader became Barton's spectrum of interest in the black man's limitations within the American scheme.

"It all ties together," he said. "Education isn't the whole

schmeer, although it's a lot of it. Give a black girl a decent
education and she can get a decent job, not a big job but a decent one. Give a black boy the same thing and he ends up a por-
ter, a doorman, or emptying garbage cans into a sanitation department truck; the driver is white. How come? How come a
black journeyman electrician can't get a card in Harry Van
Arsdale's union and go to work wiring new skyscrapers but has
to make do with piddling patch jobs at twice the hours and half
the price? How come?"

"That's simple enough," retorted another laborer in the
same vineyard, a young, Semitic-faced, bearded, Afro-hair-
styled militant who saw no solution but to boycott all white
society and establish a separate black nation. "From the first days
of slavery, whitey has emasculated the black man, cut his
nuts clean off."

"Nutted him? Man you are nuts," Barton scoffed. "About the
only thing the black man does real well in this country is screw.
Screw and run and leave the little woman and the welfare people to bring up the result. If we can't lick the white man any
other way, we'll eventually screw him into a minority."

"There's more than one way to castrate a man," protested
the militant. "Take his pride; it's as bad as taking his balls."

"You may be right, or partly right," Barton conceded. "But
being right isn't necessarily germane. A question in point is
just how long ago his pride was sliced off—or he gave it up. It's
a little late to ask how today's nigger lost his pride in the first
place. It's fine to suppose his ancestors in Africa were up to the
ass in pride, but it doesn't really signify today. The question
now is how does he get it back? Or can he at all—in the mass I
mean? Some of us have got it, of course . . . accidents of luck or
genetics. But I don't see a lot of the real article in Harlem."

"Whitey ain't about to let him get it back."

"I don't know about that. Why does he have to wait for whitey? The way to get it back is to grab it back. That is, if he's got
the guts."

Barton came to believe that the black man's pride could be

wrenched away from the whites. And he hoped, although he was by no means certain, that it could be done without an unseemly amount of bloodshed. The idea of killing did not appall him, after all he had learned the techniques in Korea, but he thought violence generally counterproductive. Foreswearing bloodshed as a stratagem did not, however, mean meekness. But it didn't mean ignoring the white man either; you couldn't ignore the man who had the cash, held the mortgages, ruled the unions, and sat as chairman of the board.

"I don't believe the white man is entirely impervious to reason," he said. "But, like a mule, it may be he has to be slugged with a two-by-four between the eyes. To get him to listen to reason, you have to get his attention first."

"You reason with him if you want," the separatist said. "I'll go my way."

Barton's generalized concern with the black man's problems did not, of course, exclude himself. Considering, as he now saw, that the place where he lived had disadvantaged his son's education, he decided to live somewhere a lot better. He had his eye on a house in the white North end but, finding that no solidly established realtor would deal with him once the color of his skin came into evidence, he got around the difficulty with a stand-in white buyer, a numbers operator who had reason to be grateful for an acquittal Barton had won for him in Rackets court, and the agency of a professional blockbuster. He moved his family into pleasant suburbia and suffered no distress whatever from knowing that his new neighbors hated his guts. He had expected that.

Meanwhile his preoccupation with clawing away from the white man more and more chunks of place and privilege for the blacks, whom he somewhat patronizingly called "my people," was winning him recognition, not all of it by any means admiring. He made it his business to be known. In half a dozen years he inspired so many sit-ins, lie-downs, marches of mourning or demand, strikes, boycotts, school board picketings and disruptions, voter registration drives, drives for better housing, drives for antidiscrimination legislation, drives for interschool busing, drives for better jobs, better wages, better teachers, for altogether better conditions for blacks everywhere and had done so across the land, north, south, east, and west and in pilgrimages to Africa so diligently that he became known all right. Known not only in the United States of America but throughout the world. Not at all to his surprise, he recognized that he had achieved the status of a messiah. There was no way of computing the fame he had earned against the times he had been in jail and bailed out and had his head thumped by the night sticks of indignant police, but the ratio appeared to satisfy him.

When his attention was first called to Wynnsboro, Barton was in Chicago fighting a dismal battle against Mayor Daley's board of education. The board had failed to produce more than a minuscule gesture toward implementing a project to bus Negro children to white schools. The plan had been, in the first place, a token designed to appease an impatient national administration which, in a fit of righteous pique, had suspended federal aid to education in the city. With a plan at least on paper the aid promptly had been restored. The board now felt no inordinate haste to put the plan into physical operation until and unless—evil thought—the aid funds should be cut off again. Nobody thought that was likely to happen soon considering the reverent awe in which the mayor was then held by the kingmakers of the Democratic Party.

Chicago taught Barton that at least one flaw marred the structure of his theory about the sturdy rectitude of federal judges. The judge he drew there was a former Democratic state Senator who had been brought up politically by the Cook County Democratic machine and had got to the federal bench through the urgent support of the machine, the mayor, and all four of the city's metropolitan papers. The judge, Barton soon perceived, was a monument of virtues—the first of these being an unswerving gratitude to the people who had put him where he was.

"He knows all the appropriate noises," Barton said in disgust. "But let the board bellyache that it needs more time and there's another continuance. He'll continue this case into his dotage—if not into mine."

The board won another continuance for what seemed to Barton an unconscionable two months. Barton was temporarily at loose ends. One hot night he was sitting in his room in a South Side hotel, stripped down to a pair of blue-and-white striped shorts, drinking Scotch with a local activist and his wife, debating whether to go back to New York while he waited out the continuance. The local man had gone down to the drug store in the lobby to repair the liquor backlog and was still away when a girl reporter for the Chicago *American* came to the door and was admitted to ask questions about Barton's intentions. The next day, in the first city edition, he learned that he had been in deshabille alone with an attractive woman guest who was not his wife.

"It was your wife," he told his associate. "And you don't have to know Braille to read this piece in the paper in a way that suggests we were practically screwing, or just finished, or about to begin. Sometimes your town gives me a stomach ache."

"How do you think my gut feels?" the Chicagoan asked.

At this juncture, Barton had a caller who had come a considerable distance to enlist his talents. He was the business agent of the Teamsters local in Baton Rouge and had come to solicit Barton's unique brand of psychic muscle. Barton's fame—or his infame—had fetched him.

The Teamster was a big, bluff, courteously spoken white man who smiled easily but seemed to Barton to radiate such an aura of casually controlled savagery that the black man was immediately attracted to him as one of his own breed. He recognized something akin to his thoughtful capacity for violence—thoughtful because he was by habit ready for it but would neither invite nor employ it unless reason said it would serve his purposes usefully.

"Yes, I'm Barton. What can I do for you?" he asked when they met. The question was not idle. He had, out of learned habit, got as much briefing as was feasible in short order before agreeing to meet the man. He knew, though not in detail, that the Baton Rouge Teamsters had had and still were having difficulty. Trucks had been hijacked, the local's hall had been bombed twice and set afire once and competing locals, both north and south, were raiding the membership. Barton did not see, at once, how any of this had anything to do with him.

"There has been some trouble," the Teamster, whose name was Blaisdell, acknowledged. "That's all in the family and we can take care of it."

"You look as though you might," Barton said. "How does it bring you to see me?"

"Something else does. You know a town—a city—called Wynnsboro in my state?"

"Not much. I know where it is and that's about all. Why?"

"I'm trying to organize the public works department there. Ninety-five percent of the sewer diggers, park custodians, grave diggers, truck drivers, white wings, repairmen, pavers, damn near all the muscle workers they got in the whole department are nig . . . oh, hell, Barton . . . that's the way I've always talked and it wouldn't be natural to change . . . are niggers."

"All right, the word doesn't offend me. Only the way it's most often used."

"I don't use it to make people sore."

"I recognize that. You've got a problem there?"

"You could call it that. These folks are not organized but you could say they think they ought to be. They get the minimum wage and they know other people do better. They get no paid vacation, no hospitalization, no pension plan, no overtime."

"What stops them?"

"They're twitchy, but that about covers it. There are no colored folks in Wynnsboro that ever have been in a union. In fact, hardly anybody in that town belongs to a union. The idea is new and, to tell the truth, more than a little scary; they know the idea of a union around there is about as popular as a bastard at a family reunion.

"But still they know about unions and some of them—mostly the younger—think they ought to go for broke. They're not all that backward; they know about the world outside and they know change has got to come. But forcing it now is something else. The older ones may not be ready."

"It's always that way—even in the North."

"I've got to admit they've got reasons. A church they let us use for an organization meeting got bombed. It killed a man and hurt some others including my man. Nobody thinks it's going to be a picnic."

"Why come to me?"

"Hell, you know that. Just be there. You're the flag black people follow."

"There are others; I'm not the only one by a long shot."

"And I know that. But, for my money, you're the one that makes the most sense."

It was time, Barton thought, to put in the caveat; he was what he was and he did not propose, whatever the urgency, to become something else for the accommodation of somebody else.

"In principle, I'm opposed to rough stuff. Violence gets violence back—most times it's used; not always, but most times. I wouldn't go there—or anywhere—intending to start a civil war."

"There've been a couple of pretty good facsimiles around in places where you were," Blaisdell reminded him gently.

"Not because I pushed it. People get carried away when they've waited too damned long."

"Now and then a skull does get busted. Not only in this race thing. Mine has been—and I've busted some. What business do you think I'm in?"

"Not a quiet one." Barton smiled. He sighed. "All right, I'll take a look. I wouldn't promise anything."

"I don't ask you to. And there's something it's fair to warn you: Wynnsboro's a Southern town, naturally, and that means it isn't anything anywhere near the same thing as the towns where you come from. A nigger doesn't count for much there; everybody else knows it and he knows it, too."

"I've been in Southern cities, Southern pokeys too."

"This one's different. This one's run, lock, stock, and barrel, by a man named Amos Wynn. Wynn's not a red-neck, but in some ways he's more so. His folks invented Wynnsboro . . ."

"The name did strike me . . ." Barton murmured.

"And he thinks he owns it. What's more he just about does. He owns the mayor, the city council, the chief of police, the tax assessor, and the county court. That's a minimum. I wouldn't be surprised if he owns the governor; as a matter of fact I'm sure he does. Wynn is no nigger-hater; he's too used to blacks to waste his time that way. But for him and for people like him— and they are the solid people around there—the Klan and the Citizens' Councils are too far left."

"I guess I'd better see Mr. Wynn," Barton said.

"If he'll see you," the Teamster said.

Blaisdell had driven from Baton Rouge to Chicago, and Barton accepted his invitation to the ride back, a trip which taught him a couple of interesting items about the big Teamster. Dropping his suitcase into the trunk, Barton saw cradled in a rack welded to the deck a Thompson submachine gun.

"Duck hunting?" he asked, concealing the start he had felt at the sight of the weapon.

Blaisdell smiled. "Not exactly. I just feel more comfortable with it there."

The second thing he learned, which kept giving him starts until he got more or less accustomed to it, was that Blaisdell never drove under a hundred miles an hour when he could help it.

"What's the hurry?" Barton asked as they slewed around a truck on a two-lane road south of Indianapolis, zooming back into the right lane with what, to Barton, seemed a suicidally narrow margin between them and an onrushing car. "This Wynnsboro of yours will keep."

Blaisdell's answering grin said the man was enjoying himself.

"Habit," he said. "Long time ago I did a spell as a federal cop shagging moonshiners. They could teach the average Teamster something about driving. You get used to traveling that way. And that reminds me of a story us whites tell in Louisiana; maybe it tells something about us. Likely it does."

"You'd know more about that than I do," Barton said.

"Anyhow this white man was driving fast at night from Baton Rouge to New Orleans. I don't know if you know that road, but it's string straight and flat across the bayou country with only one hump in a hundred miles where it goes over a viaduct. It was dark and this man came up over the hump and hit a couple of colored he hadn't seen. One came over the hood and through the windshield and landed dead in the back seat; barely missed the driver, which he thanked the Lord for. The other kind of caromed off the front fender and sailed about a hundred feet and landed in a field—dead, too.

"This man was a responsible citizen and he wanted to do the right thing, also wanting to get rid of the corpse in the back seat. So he drove to the next town and hunted up the sheriff and told him what had happened and asked what he ought to do about it—if anything.

"The sheriff looked at the windshield and stuck his head in the back seat and felt the body and said he was dead, all right. Finally he scratched his head and said, 'Well, I'll tell you. This dead nigger here, we'll get him for breaking and entering. And that one you tell me about, the nigger back there in the field, we'll charge him with trespass.' "

"Am I supposed to laugh?" Barton said.

"I didn't rightly expect you to," Blaisdell said.

At six in the morning, grainy-eyed and bones and bodies aching, they came into Baton Rouge, drove along the eastern outskirts of the city, pulled off the highway, and took a graveled road to a rough wooden warehouse building set back into a grove of scrubby pines.

"Union hall," Blaisdell said. "I'll check things here and then take you to my place; it might be a little touchy getting you into a hotel, anyhow, this early in the day. Folks are likely to be irritable until they get their sleep out."

"I need to take a leak," Barton said, getting out and stretching. "I'll come in with you."

"Can's just inside the door," Blaisdell said. "Soon's you get a little rest and I finish up here, I'll run you to Wynnsboro. It's only about a hundred and fifty miles."

"That," Barton said, "won't take you long."

Inside the warehouse door, Blaisdell walked toward a window walled room which, Barton thought, was probably his office. He saw several men inside the room in overalls. Looking around, he saw another enclosure and hurried toward it, feeling some sense of urgency after two hundred miles since the last stop for gas. Shortly, with a relieved sigh, he emerged and went to the office. Blaisdell looked up from the desk where he had been going over some papers with a pretty blond secretary.

"OK, Mrs. Walton, that'll take care of it for now. I'll be back late this afternoon. Don't wait for me." He turned to Barton, "OK, let's go over to my place."

As they walked together toward the warehouse door, Barton noticed the sign over the door of the locus of his bladder's recent respite.

"Well," he said, "I seem to have got the wrong john." He gestured toward the sign which said WHITE. "That going to bust up the local?"

Barton grinned at him.

"Don't let it bother you. The other one's over there in the other corner. It's a law, so we've got one of each. But, hell, nobody in my outfit pays any attention to it anymore. When you gotta go here, you go to the handiest or the emptiest."

At two o'clock that afternoon, Blaisdell dropped Barton at a storefront hotel in the Angel Creek section of Wynnsboro. "As I told you," he said, "your man here is the fella named Dowdy. He's a gambler, a whoremaster, and he runs the fanciest colored funeral parlor in town. Don't be put off by his occupations. If the colored in this town listen to anybody, they listen to

Dowdy. Also he's a friend of Amos Wynn—that's saying, of course, if anybody is."

3

Jefferson Stuart could not have been called with justice a misfit in his vocation but it was true that he failed by many degrees to match the stereotype of a Federal Bureau of Investigation agent. Except for other qualities which rendered him useful to the organization, his lack might have been held a serious shortcoming in an agency of government whose romanticized image in the public mind was, rather than a caricature, a close approximation of the truth.

Here was a world of alert young men, conservatively dressed and always well-pressed, closely and freshly shorn, clean-shaven, efficient, wearing always as a badge the appearance, if not always the fact, of anointed intelligence, polite but carrying beneath their good manners an aura of pontifically ordained arrogance, closemouthed to the edge of paranoia. These were thought to be and were in fact relentless fellows who seemed always somehow on the brink of fulfilling the goal their ancient director had spelled out as his own special invention, seizure of all ten of the Most Wanted. Unlike most cops, they tended to shine in the consciousness of their peers, somehow bathed in the effulgence of their sole owner and operator.

Jeff Stuart shamefully violated the rule. Being neat irked

him. Appearing to know something which he did not seemed to
him pretentious. Being clipped and authoritative seemed to
him unnecessarily overbearing. Keeping his trap ostentatiously
shut on occasions when he was short of secrets anyhow seemed
to him a ridiculous put-on in dealing with the rest of humanity.
Worse than any other departure from the norm, probably, was
his almost total lack of the killer drive. The instincts he had
been born with were more protective than punitive.

Now, it is true, though trite, that men are compounded as
much by the absence of forces as by their active pressure. It
could be said that Jeff Stuart had had, at least in one regard, a
disadvantaged childhood. He had been born in a Middle Western hamlet called Lemert, North Dakota, where he was surrounded more by space than by the friction of humanity. There
was nobody around, close enough, to be worth hating for the
color of his complexion or the complexion of his beliefs. The
best his neighborhood could produce in the way of suspect foreigners were a few Catholics and the worst that their neighbors
could think of them was that they might be a little church-
ridden. Of Jews, Greeks, Negroes, Italians, polacks, square-
heads, wops, dagos, greasers, kikes, red-necks, wool hats,
hunkies, or guineas he was totally deprived. In spring and fall a
few hundred Sioux Indians came through his town and stopped
at his father's store or camped overnight in the willows along
the creek bound on the biennial migration from reservation to
reservation, but they failed to antagonize him since they were
peaceful and, anyhow, objects of only vestigial romantic interest. Other than that, he was reduced to the few hobos who followed the Soo Line tracks and his mother fed too many of those
at the back door for him to be inflamed by any apprehension.
In short, he grew toward puberty shorn of an American birth-
right, the inalienable duty to abhor somebody, not for what he
was, but for the likeness in which his ancestors had cast him.
He did not later need to be educated out of prejudice; the poor
fellow had never had a chance to acquire any real supply.

In fact the first common enemy of his class he was able to discover was girls and there, poor puzzled lad, he did not for a long time know where he stood, but eventually he made their peace.

Such a hiatus in a man's soul is difficult to live down and Jeff Stuart never really did succeed, although he grew more sophisticated with time and his years first in the University of North Dakota and later in law school at the University of Chicago which shouldered up against the South Side Negro ghetto closely enough and irritably enough to make him aware that he had a hole in his consciousness somewhere, and that it was possibly too bad he did.

Out of law school he went into the FBI, partly because he did not at once know what kind of law he wanted to practice, except that he recognized that he was not by nature a prosecutor. Nor did he particularly yearn to be a defender since by then he was grown enough to recognize, as a matter of reality, that the purity of the accused human heart was often open to grave question. On the other hand, humanity interested him far more than humanity's torts and civil disagreements. He stayed in the FBI where he became a diligent investigator and, when the Bureau found itself pressed by bewildering psychic vagaries in the personalities of suspects, he proved invaluable as the soft man to play off against the hard one. If he had anything special beyond intelligent attention to detail and a compelling instinct for real justice to recommend him, it was his capacity to get along with almost anybody.

Given what he was—or rather was not—he was the natural selection when the Bureau and even more-exalted sources decided it was time to take a continuing interest in Carver Otis Barton. The conveyance of orders was made by the assistant director, a man named Rembert, who ran the FBI Bureau in New York.

The orders had come to Rembert directly from the director himself who, in Barton's case, had a professional axe to hone and had so managed matters that the Attorney General and even the White House felt obliged to go along with him. Both the director's interest and Assistant Director Rembert's were rooted in deep suspicion. On the other hand both the Attorney General and the White House held somewhat different motives for learning as much as feasible about Barton. It was not unusual that the director on one side, and the Department of Justice and the White House on the other might wish to move in a similar direction for less than identical reasons.

The director had been there forever, through so many administrations that he might have lost count except for the autographed portraits of Presidents which graced his office walls. He had made a lifetime in pursuit of what he held to be the republic's deadliest enemies, Syndicate Crime and Communism, both of which were forever uppercased in his mind. He would not have been astonished to learn that Carver Otis Barton was implicated in either—or both.

The Attorney General and the President, on the other hand, were young and had only less than half of one administration under their belts. They viewed the republic, with whose continued welfare they were now charged, with more hope and optimism than was the director's wont. Still they knew that powerful subterranean currents of unrest, anger, and despair coursed through the land. They knew as well that much of the electorate which had put the President in office believed that these currents, unstemmed, would sunder the country's being. They needed to know what portended and, if possible, how to lead the land safely through it. This meant that they needed to know as intimately as possible the psychological mix of those who expressed and professed to guide the forces of change. Of these, Barton seemed to them the foremost.

And so, although ordinarily reluctant to intrude on other men's privacy, the Attorney General and the President consented to the director's plan which, in simple terms, amounted to domestic espionage.

Assistant Director Rembert, still handsomely crowned with silver hair but wearing flesh which had gone downhill since the era a quarter century earlier when he had first attracted the director's approval by contending, sometimes barehanded, with syndicate thugs, put down his telephone and sighed. He had been listening to the director's gritty voice over the private line from Washington for the last half hour. He pressed the button to call his secretary.

"See if Stuart's in the building," he told her. "If he isn't, find him. I want him."

Found in his office with his coat off, his tie pulled loose and his shirt sleeves rolled up, Jeff Stuart got the summons. He stood up, rolled down his sleeves, pulled up the knot of his tie and reached for his jacket on the hook behind the door. Standing, Stuart was medium tall but looked taller. He gave an impression of gaunt boniness which was deceptive because, at thirty-six, he was physically more sinew than emaciation. He was not a handsome man; prominent high cheekbones and a nose broken in an integration riot on the campus of an Alabama college in 1962 had marred him for beauty. But broadly set, quiet, watchful eyes and a wide mouth that smiled with slow warmth saved him from ugliness.

"All right, I'm coming," he told the secretary and ran the fingers of a big hand through coarse dark hair which tended to grow unkempt. He knew that Rembert preferred his agents neatly barbered—just as he preferred them properly necktied and jacketed. He consoled himself that he was generally clean, if not always neat, but he truly detested barber chairs and the time spent in them.

He took the elevator to the tenth floor of the building at Sixty-ninth Street and Lexington and was nodded past the guard and the blond receptionist, idly thinking of the second that he probably owed it to himself to do something about her and that perhaps he might, or at least try his luck, if the stars seemed right someday.

At the secretary's admitting smile, he knocked and went in. The assistant director was behind his broad desk, his head bent over a file, and he appeared to be studying it. Whether he actually had been studying there was no way to know, for it was one of Rembert's small conceits that he never let an underling suppose that he was not intensely occupied. He looked up with the quick, impatient, rather forbidding frown which, from long exposure to it, Stuart knew very well was another facet of directorial window dressing.

"Stuart," Rembert said without preliminary and without asking him to sit down—he never did, for brusqueness was also a part of the image. "What are you doing?"

"The Carnavalli ca . . ." Stuart began but did not get a chance to finish for abruptness, too, had its uses.

"Drop it. Turn it over to Cavanides. Nothing much to it anyhow."

"Yes, sir," Stuart said aloud, thinking something else, for the Carnavalli matter involved some two million dollars in pilfered cargo vanished from the Jersey docks somewhere into the labyrinth of interstate commerce.

"Now listen," Rembert said. "How much do you know about these black civil rights nuts?"

"Some," Stuart acknowledged, again thinking that the assistant director ought to remember how many times, or at least approximately how many, he had dispatched this particular operative to Chicago, Detroit, Los Angeles, Memphis, Charlotte, and Atlanta on errands having to do with the rebellion afoot within the nation's black population. "Which ones?"

"Most are reds," Rembert said. "Maybe all."

That observation, Stuart thought in private irritation, *stands relevant to almost nothing on earth except the particular set of superstitions almost wholly owned by you, my silver-haired friend, and our mutual boss.*

"I imagine that's possible," he said aloud. "But it would need proving."

"You don't expect them to carry party cards, do you?" Rembert said irritably. "In particular, I mean the local big shot. The one with the double-barreled name—Carver Otis Barton. Why can't he keep it simple? You know him?"

"No. Only by sight. I saw him once, Charleston if I remember. I don't know why he uses all his names. Maybe he likes the whole schmeer. Maybe he thinks it makes his act more impressive. What they call his charisma. I don't know."

"It's one of the things you might find out. I don't think he's just a clown—but it might help to get an idea how much clown there is in him." Rembert frowned. "From now on, he's yours."

"Why Barton . . . sir?" Stuart knew that Rembert cherished the honorific, and he felt no particular pain in using it. "There are others—a good many—who talk a wilder game than he does."

"That's part of it. He doesn't talk as wild, but more of them seem to buy him. He talks nonviolence, but it's tricky talk— and it doesn't keep them from rioting where he is."

"They rioted behind Gandhi, too," Stuart said quietly. "He preached against it."

Rembert looked up sharply. "Don't get the idea this one's any mahatma," he grunted.

"I haven't. I just don't know."

"Look," Rembert said. "I don't know either, but I know what I suspect. This guy's a magnet, I know that. The funny ones, the hard core, are all around him. Maybe they just hope some of his shine will rub off on them." He paused and grunted in sour mirth. "Not bad, huh? His shine. Anyhow, he pulls the wreckers. What the director wants to know is how much the wreckers pull him. Shine can rub off both ways. That's your job, finding out."

"OK, sir," Stuart said. "What's my franchise?"

"You won't be alone."

Stuart was at once wary, but under the constraint of not showing it. In the many ways the Bureau functioned not being alone could mean almost anything.

"Yes, sir?" he said.

"I'm sending Jensen. If he needs help, give it to him. Probably he won't. But he'll keep in touch with you."

There it was. Jensen was a specialist, something close to an electronic genius. There existed no such thing as a secret totally

safe from Jensen, not so long as it was as much as whispered—
and Jensen had been sent to get it. He could get at his quarry
with mikes behind pictures or under rugs or planted in telephones, but these were the simpler tools in his kit, good enough
for the unwary or the unsophisticated. At heart, Jensen preferred a target who was both spooked and sophisticated, for he
was not without sporting blood. The easy ones bored him; he
went at the tough ones with miniaturized tape recorders, spike
mikes planted in outer walls, or shotgun microphones which
could corral one man's asthmatic breath in the roar of a football crowd.

Stuart did not like Jensen. It was not that he had any powerful prejudice against eavesdropping, which he knew to be an in-
dispensable tool in their trade. But he didn't relish it, and the
glee which Jensen took in rummaging through other men's
brains repelled him. Jensen was a scavenger.

"So you want him bugged?" he said.

"Of course. You don't expect him to tell you everything he
knows, do you?"

"No. Where do I fit into this?"

"Watch Barton. Find out who talks to him, who gets next to
him, who he gets next to. Get his confidence."

"I'll give it a shot. But I can't say Barton shows much sign of
trusting white men these days—that is, if he ever did."

"You can be in the open. Admit who you are. Tell him the
government is interested in seeing he gets a fair shake. That's
true—in a way."

Yes, Stuart thought, *a fair shake—with Jensen wiring even
his tail for sound.*

"There's another thing to keep in mind," Rembert said,
looking up and speaking in a subtly changed tone. "The Attorney General will also want your report on Barton. That, I take
it, means the administration is interested in him. At least they
are interested in this so-called civil rights movement and what
it means and what Barton means to it." His tone was careful
now. "I think you understand, Stuart, that a new administra-

tion may sometimes come at the country with preconceived ideas which do not necessarily square with the facts as the Bureau knows them. Keep that in mind."

"Yes, sir," Stuart said, thinking to himself, *at least you're honest, you bastard, and thanks for telling me.*

"We weren't put here—and we haven't stayed here—to be naïve," Rembert said somewhat obscurely, but Stuart knew he wasn't being irrelevant to what he believed—and the director believed—as an article of faith: that organized dissent against what the nation was was the same thing as treason.

"Yes, sir. When do you want me to start?"

"You've started."

4

Because neither Amos Wynn nor Carver Otis Barton was the man to evade an issue, they soon confronted it together. It could not have been otherwise, for the issue was the sole agency which had brought Barton from Chicago to Wynnsboro. And Wynn, already there, was too wise to hope that Gervase's impulsive bombing of the church had killed the issue as forthrightly as it had killed Rafe Pullen. Indeed, if anything, he suspected the bombing had given the issue a shot of adrenalin at a time when, left alone, it might well have expired out of Wynnsboro's generations of habit for leaving bad enough alone to get no worse.

Wynn and Barton came together late in the afternoon of the black man's first full day in Wynnsboro. Guided somewhat reluctantly but politely by James Dowdy, Barton had spent the evening before and most of this day with the elders of Angel Creek and the outspoken few among its more dynamic youth.

It would be wrong to say that Barton was fully pleased by his reception, but he was not fatuous enough to have believed that he could come to a city like Wynnsboro, however famous and even revered he might be, and find a black population boiling to strike off its chains and mount the barricades.

He got a cautious mandate to explore, but that was the word for it—cautious. Sobered by the bombing more than Amos Wynn would have expected, the older and more solidly established men, while sympathetic, hesitated to upset a cart which might very well ruin what apples they did possess while the younger and entirely dispossessed, more avid for change, still hesitated to ram headlong into the odds.

"Look at me," Barton said. "I'm the living proof that it can be done."

"Maybe. You show us how. Maybe we'll go with you!" was the consensus.

Amos Wynn was at home when Dowdy reached him with a message about and, second hand, from Carver Otis Barton.

"Yes, Jim?" Wynn said, picking up the telephone to which Amy had called him.

"Do you know about a man named Barton—Carver Otis Barton is the full handle, Mister Wynn?"

"I know about him, Jim. Nigger from the north, that the one? The rabble-rouser?"

"He's here in my office, Mister Wynn." Dowdy's tone was cautious.

"I can't get exercised very much if he hears me," Wynn said. "What about him?"

"He says he wants to talk to you."

"About the union, I imagine."

"That's what he says, all right."

"Tell him he's got the wrong man," Wynn said crisply—then paused and ran thoughtful fingers through his bristle of graying hair. *Hell,* he thought, *ignoring it won't send it away.* "No, Jim, tell him all right I'll talk to him. Where and when?"

"My office be all right, Mister Wynn?"

"All right, I'll be along in about an hour," Wynn said, hanging up slowly, wondering if that had been just plain relief in Dowdy's tone. *In a way,* he thought, *I ought to be sorry for Jim —he's stuck in the middle between what those people think they want and what he knows is best for them.*

"Who was that, pa?" Amy asked from the door as he hung up.

"Nigger business, hon," he said.

"The union?" she asked.

"It's still with us," he said. "They've got an import now, nigger messiah from up North. I'm going down and take a look at him."

"The times are out of joint, aren't they, pa?" Amy said, smiling at him.

"Don't pull your education on me. They always were out of joint." Wynn grinned at her fondly. "Union! Ninety percent of those people haven't paid their dues in the human race yet."

"When you get mad, you don't sound real human yourself."

As befitted her ancestry, Amy was a big girl, not huge and angular like her father, but sweetly molded over substantial bone. Her hair was the color of an oiled walnut gunstock, her brow smooth over wide-set gray eyes—the color of his but softer—and a wide, full mouth. She was deep in the breast, tall and lithe in movement. After four years in Skidmore and in the North and now twenty-four summers, she had not married. She had nothing against marriage and there had been no lack of opportunity. The delay, she half-consciously realized, was that of all those who had wanted her none had quite come up to her measurement for men. Amos Wynn was a hard man to follow.

It was not that she totally approved of him. She suspected that Amos was a monument to things past, shoring up a present that was doomed, had already collapsed in many places, was still thriving only in sheltered enclaves like Wynnsboro. But if he was the last of his kind, he was also undefeated and incapable of bowing to defeat. This was a whole man and one that could not be scared. She wanted no less in a man she would take to keep. What Amos believed he believed entire; and Amy felt instinctively that indestructible conviction was admirable no matter what the decades had done to declare the conviction bankrupt.

Out in the carport, Amos got into the Cadillac out of some small notion that the occasion called for a little pomp. He was putting the key in the lock when he changed his mind and got out and went to the jeep. *Who the hell do I need to impress?* he thought.

When Wynn entered Dowdy's office without knocking as was his custom, he saw the stranger at once seated on a deep, leather-upholstered sofa catty-corner from Dowdy's opulent desk. His own big, now aging Morris chair sat in front of the desk, facing Dowdy's chair. Now Dowdy, slender and impeccable, was standing with his rump propped on the edge of the desk, facing his guest. His face was carefully impassive as he turned to face Wynn.

"This man here is Barton, Mister Wynn," Dowdy said.

Barton was on his feet, not hurriedly but gracefully and in command of himself. He was compact, quite dark, a little heavy around the jowls and waistband, smiling with lips that were not particularly heavy. He held out his hand.

"Thank you for coming," he said. "I'm glad to meet you. I've heard of you, of course."

"That's possible," Wynn said, taking the offered hand which he found dry and firm. *He ain't jumpy anyhow,* he thought.

"What you want to see me about?" Wynn asked, and thought he was damned if he intended to give the man whatever satisfaction there might be in admitting that he had heard of him as well.

Nor would he betray any surprise at finding Barton not

dressed in a business suit, but wearing a long, loose robe or gown of some rich, colorfully patterned stuff and a small tight skull cap which Wynn automatically thought of as a beanie. *I'll reserve judgment on the rig,* he thought, *but it does look ridiculous.*

"Flashy. This getup." Barton smiled at him, reading his thought. "But it's comfortable in your climate and I don't have to lynch myself with a collar and tie."

"There's that," Wynn said. "It's simpler just to leave the tie off."

"I probably look like a refugee from a missionary roasting," Barton said, still smiling. "But this rig is genuine enough; comes from tribal chiefs in Dahomey. I'll ask you to believe, Mr. Wynn, that while my job is mostly law—and agitation—there's also some show biz in it. It seems to help some to startle the natives."

Wynn smiled thinly. "You'll startle them all right. But I don't know how much you'll impress them. Folks around here are more accustomed to pants and shirts—or overalls. I doubt if many have the time or inclination to look up what an African chief wears."

"You're correct," Barton said. "But I make it a point to tell them—early."

"Well, what you choose to wear is your business." Wynn turned and walked to his special chair. "What do you want of me?"

"I told him how things stand with the Teamsters," Dowdy said. "I guess it's his business to find out and maybe even his right. Or his duty . . . or something. He's talked to some folks, so he knows something—anyhow a little."

This guy has Jim worried, Wynn thought; *he goes careful and formal when he's got something on his mind.*

"It's not just because it's the Teamsters," Wynn said, measuring his words and watching Barton's controlled face for reaction. "Except for the railroad men and the printers, there are no unions here. Never have been."

"I'm sure you're not saying there never will be." It was phrased as a statement and sounded like one, but Barton's brows had a quizzical tilt and his tone carried a faint but unmistakable note of challenge.

"I state the record. I am not a seer. I can't predict the long future and I don't try. But for now it's unlikely."

"Because you're against it?"

"Not that alone, although I am. Because the habit, tradition if you want, of this city and the temper of the people don't want it."

"All the people?"

"The ones who count." Wynn's tone was crisp.

"And that counts out the blacks. My people."

Barton lighted a cigarette, got up with assured grace, went to Dowdy's desk, picked up an ashtray and carried it back to the sofa.

"Mr. Dowdy here is one of my people. He ought to know what blacks count for here."

Dowdy stirred and looked at Wynn before he made a slow reply.

"We count all right. But we live here. We don't want the town wrecked. Mister Wynn knows that."

"You're from the North," Wynn said, "and therefore a little strange to me. But you talk without warrant when you call Wynnsboro colored your people. You don't know them; they don't know you. I don't boast when I say I know them and what they need a lot better than you do."

"Even your South has begun to see light," Barton said equably. "North. South. It doesn't make all that difference."

"Part of what bothers the South is the kind of torchbearers who claim to lead the Negro. Take you. You don't sound insane, but even you, I suspect, might admit that Halloween rig you've got on is a little incongruous for a man who claims to be modernizing the society we live in. That thing is out of the jungles and God knows how many centuries out of gear with today."

"How far out of gear with today are Klan bedsheets?"

"I won't argue that. I left the Klan years ago. Children . . . vicious children . . . but children all the same."

"Why did you leave . . . if I may ask?"

"For its pointlessness . . . and for my own sense of dignity, which is strong."

"You don't concede his own dignity to the black man?"

"The black man, in the South, has his own dignity. It could surprise you."

"And equality?"

"You talk about equality. I suspect it could be easy to misunderstand what the word really means. The only equality that means anything is equality between equals. It is nonsense to preach equality between unequals. White and black are not equals. They never were, never will be. Where did you go to school?"

Barton raised a hand, protesting.

"That was a *sequitur* that didn't *sequit*. For the first, you're perfectly right; there never was equality, sure enough, but I'm optimist enough to believe there can be, and I'll tell you this, I intend to see there is—even if somebody gets hurt in the process . . . As for school, Columbia, then Harvard Law. Why?"

"I'll get to that. To go back to the point I started to make, you . . . and the others of your kind . . . seem to me an odd lot of Pied Pipers to be blazing a trail to utopia."

"I may not have a lot in common with others."

"But something. You're a showman; you admit it. You dress like a clown to prove it. You have been called the apostle of nonviolence. But you were there, you were the prophet of record when fifty thousand blacks went berserk in Detroit. What did that one cost? Mostly in places, I add, where blacks were the big losers?"

"I could quote you that old saw invented by white generals and admirals: You can't make an omelet . . ."

"Don't bother. You all say you want justice for the benighted black. But no two of you chase the same Holy Grail in the same way. One yells—Forman I think his name is—that Christian and Jewish churches have to pony up a billion dollars in reparations.

"Reparations for what? My great grandfather kept slaves; I don't. The parson of the church I go to never did either and I doubt if his grandfather did. And I'm not too damned sure, as a matter of fact, that slavery was a bad thing for the colored."

"You're kidding."

"I am not. All things are relative. When the Belgians more or less turned the Congo over to the natives there were not a half-dozen educated, capable, honest, nonhysterical blacks there to run the country. But you, in your witch doctor outfit, are a product of slavery—and of Columbia and Harvard Law."

"I'm pretty sure you're not suggesting that slavery sent me to Harvard Law."

"It produced you in the country where Harvard is located, conceived, built, and financed by white men. The men who made Harvard also put together the idea that a man should rise to the limit of his capacity. Now you use what Harvard made of you to try to smash the things that made you possible."

Barton was feeling the slow, choking, familiar boil of rage, but he had been through this too many times to let passion betray him. He smiled.

"Mr. Wynn, even Harvard may have got the country's values buggered up in three centuries of wrestling with them. I submit people like you have managed to get them a lot more twisted." He paused for a slow inspection of the quietly grim face across the room. "Although, if we're going to be honest about it, I doubt if the full set of American democratic ideals ever did mean it the way they were written down."

"No. I don't suppose they ever did," Wynn acknowledged. "All the same you'll have to forgive me if I have some doubt about the integrity—good faith if you want to call it that—of you people who set yourself up as the leaders. Who elected you? And let me ask you this, what do you get out of it?"

"For the second, I doubt if you would get it if I told you. For the first, I guess you'd have to call it talent. It's as good a description of the job requisite as any. And I will admit—with blacks feeling their oats and pretty mad—it's a little difficult to stay a leader and still walk soft. Too much competition yelling to burn the place down. It's a little late for moderation."

"So what do you propose to do here in this city? After all, that's the point. The rest is just talk."

Barton stood up, walked across the room and placed a finger against Wynn's chest.

"Organize it," he said quietly. "Just organize it."

Wynn controlled the impulse to strike the black man's hand down. Dowdy looked scared and started to speak, but Wynn cut him off, glanced down at the finger and then stared coldly into Barton's eyes.

"Take it away," he said in a brittle voice. "Now."

Barton stepped back, without haste, composed.

"You need to be reminded," Wynn said. "You're a nigger, all right, if the measure of it is color, and it is. Otherwise you're a stranger. You come from the wrong place. You think you're a black messiah, here to lead the blacks out of a white man's wilderness. You're wrong. They won't follow."

"All right. Tell me why."

"I could let you find out for yourself—maybe I ought to." Wynn paused to study the other man. "Or maybe I ought to tell you, although you may not understand.

"To begin with, Wynnsboro is not a city as I suspect you think of a city. It does have a hundred and eighty thousand people and it is incorporated. Otherwise the resemblance to a city ends."

"The population is roughly one-third black," Barton said. "And they're getting the short and dirty end of the stick—the same as New York or Chicago or Detroit or Los Angeles."

"They may be getting a short end, but it's not dirty."

"Why not an equal end?"

"I'll come to that. But first I intend to tell you what Wynnsboro is. Meanwhile, for what it's worth, I'll admit that part of
the black's condition here goes back to slavery."

"Everything does."

"Not the way you like to think. Now, I said that Wynnsboro
is not a city. It is really a country town that happened to get
big. But it's still a country town. A hundred years ago it was the
place where people traded, sold their crops, bought their machinery, salt, necessary groceries, and came to town on Saturday
nights."

"Did they bring the slaves in Saturday nights, too?"

"Probably not." Wynn was unruffled. "Not often and never
just to rubberneck. Forty years ago it was still a country town.
Thirty, the same thing but growing. The big difference, so far
as the black was concerned, was that slavery was out the
window."

"Technically out."

"No. Actually out. The black man was free by a century. He
didn't have to wait to be asked to come to town on Saturday
night. And a lot did come . . . and most stayed. They got to be
too many for the jobs the town could supply that they were capable of doing. You could say they overburdened the population."

"But they came."

"And kept coming. In some way it was the same thing that
happens in any rural society. Show a boy the town and it gets
hard to keep him on the farm. In another way, I admit, it was
partly the planters discovering machines and the possibly un-
fortunate truth that machines work better and cheaper than
niggers. Also machines are neater. Nobody owes a responsibility
to a machine. He can keep it up or let it go to hell and it matters to nobody but himself."

"At least you're candid . . . or anyhow, halfway candid. It
doesn't change the facts we've got today."

"You're wrong. This is still a country town. It's on the river, on two dying railroads, gets service from one feeder airline. So it has changed some. It had to because it couldn't go on living off the people who came in on Saturday nights. It began to become regional. Now it's a banking town, an insurance home office town, a small manufacturing town. That's mainly what supports it today. I think you can see that banking and insurance do not provide a lot of room for blacks off the farm."

"Maybe that's the trouble. Never let them down out of the trees."

"It's true that ninety percent haven't yet paid their dues in the human race." *Hell,* Wynn thought to himself, *I said the same thing to Amy; I'm beginning to sound like a phonograph.*

"That, Mr. Wynn, is the backbone of what people like me are working on—putting the black man where he can afford the dues."

"Unionizing Wynnsboro will set you back. The opposite of what you say you're after."

"Now, man. You'll have to explain that to me."

"What are you hoping to organize?"

"The public works department to begin. The rest will follow."

"What rest? This is not an industrial town. Never was and, I hope, never will be. You may consider us backward, reactionary, unenlightened. But look at Detroit, Cleveland, Chicago. Cesspools. Do you call that enlightened?"

"You've got a point there," Barton acknowledged. "Man's inalienable right to mess up the place he lives in. It's a right, but it ought to be repealed."

"Here, we don't exercise the right. We need more work for more people, that's true. But we're not about to go ass over teakettle into industry. There are two small industries in this town. One textile plant, came here from New England twenty years ago. The other, newer, manufactures electronic parts. They call it solid state stuff. Do you know what solid state means? Because I don't."

Barton smiled. "Me neither. I admit the language of modern technology baffles me. But you say, after the Teamsters, there's nothing else to organize. What's the payroll of those two plants?"

"Textile, about fifteen hundred. Electronics, maybe five hundred now, but it's growing. But here, so far as you are concerned, is the point: Most of those two thousand people, on the assembly lines and the looms anyhow, are black."

"You're arguing in reverse. They're black; they work, they'll be better off organized."

"I doubt it. The main reason the plants came here in the first place was to get away from fighting with unions. They're light. They're portable. They can move. And if you force them, they will. Then you may have a union, but you'll also have two thousand men and women without jobs. That what you're after?"

"Nope. But to quote the admirals again, you can't make an omelet without busting eggs. Businesses like that, if they move often enough to run away from unions, eventually they'll find they got no place to go."

"Not yet. Not for a long time."

"That's a short haul; we're trying to see further. Tell me, out of curiosity, who owns the plants?"

Wynn was calm about it, knowing anyhow that it would probably not serve much to evade Barton.

"You could say I do. Substantially anyhow. I own controlling stock in both. I'm on the boards of both. My bank finances the capital needs of both. You can't, if that's what you're trying, establish guilt here. Both help Wynnsboro, including the blacks. Together they go a long way toward supplying opportunity to the people you say you're trying to help. We, on the other hand, are actually helping them. That's the difference."

"It still leaves you big daddy."

"So what? Both are general stock companies—over the counter—and both make money. Anybody can buy stock—buy me out if so minded—and well enough heeled."

"Any blacks buy stock?"

"I wouldn't know."

"Aside from clean air and a captive work force what else, would you say, recommends this wholly owned little metropolis of yours?"

"We have a college. Eight hundred students. Well enough endowed to afford the best small college plant in the state and, for its size, the most highly qualified faculty anywhere. And— before you ask—I am chairman of the board of trustees."

"Any black students? Or do I need to ask?"

"Not many. A dozen was the last head count. We're not segregated, Barton. But the admissions standards are high."

"Then what happens to a black Wynnsboro kid who wants to see a little beyond the horizons of a high school education?"

"Most, I believe, go North or to Howard or Tuskegee, places that are easier to get into."

"What happens after they get a degree? They come back here?"

"Not many. A few. Preachers, undertakers . . ."

"The technicians? Engineers, teachers, doctors . . ."

"Some doctors."

"Lawyers?"

"Maybe a half dozen. Shysters, mostly."

"You got any black tellers in your bank? I wouldn't even mention cashiers. Any black foremen in your plants? Supervisors? Electrical engineers? Research scientists?"

"Are there any? I doubt it."

"Mr. Wynn, I think you can see it, all right. There isn't a hell of a lot of use our talking together, enjoyable as it may be. It all ricochets to one side or the other. You want to keep this town feudal. I want it to catch up with the world."

"It is not your town."

"You may have the title, but it's not yours either."

"I suggest you'll discover where the facts of life lie if you try to go ahead with this. You're a nigger, but you're also a foreigner. I don't think they'll buy your bill of goods."

"I don't imagine you want to think about it some more? And then help?"

"No."

"Hinder? Do you think you could stop us?"

"I don't know. But I don't think it will be necessary."

Dowdy, silent, watchful, measuring and worried, spoke up from behind the desk. The tone was placating, politeness overlaying cold warning.

"You know, Barton, I wouldn't do it if I was you. But if you do anything at all, go awful slow. Mister Wynn is right; you're a stranger. This city is going all right; the black man is all right here. You'd see it if you weren't so ready to go off half cocked. These folks ain't ready for you yet."

"I don't think I'm ready to take the word of a house nigger."

Dowdy stiffened and began to rise, but Wynn broke in, coldly, studiously brutal.

"You're a fool, Barton. Try that again here, and you'll get hurt. If I were you, I'd pack and get."

5

Carver Otis Barton and Amos Wynn had talked for more than an hour in James Dowdy's office on Tuesday afternoon, each learning something useful about the other but making no progress whatever toward accommodation. There were here elements of irresistible force and immovable object; it was possible for two such men to respect each other as enemies, impossible for either to be anything except an enemy.

It began to rain Tuesday night in Wynnsboro, breaking a summer drought, flushing some of the garbage out of Angel Creek, washing a stuccoed accumulation of dust from the trees, rendering the land underfoot treacherous where it was not paved. It rained all day Wednesday, steady, leaden, dispiriting. The rain stopped sometime late Wednesday night, and Thursday dawned bright and steamy and the city sparkled as though it had been simonized.

Barton had ignored Wynn's advice to pack and get out and so it was nearly inevitable that they would meet again. The rain, by itself, had nothing to do with bringing about their second meeting, but it did exacerbate the encounter. More than that. Out of human wilfullness and freakish accident, the rain brought them to a level of horror that neither man would forget or forgive.

That summer the Wynnsboro park board, a subsidiary of the grab bag public works department which was Barton's and the Teamsters' target, was building a swimming pool for whites in Bellamy Park in the moderately affluent southeastern reach of the city. For Barton, here was a target of opportunity. It was imperative to him to goad the sluggish rise of black consciousness and the pool could be made to stand as an immediate symbol of the callus on the white soul—all the more so because the muscle labor going into this white playground was black. Barton's stratagem was patently unjust since the department, earlier in the year, had built an identical pool in Angel Creek. Construction of the first had delayed the second deep into the season.

The department had planned the two pools simultaneously, having, in the previous autumn election, successfully floated a bond issue to pay for them. Barton might have been on sounder footing had the board carried through its original intent to build the white pool first. Priority had been switched to the blacks' pool abruptly when Amos Wynn, advised of the board's intent, coldly told Public Works Commissioner David Mayhew, first cousin of the police commissioner, to change his mind.

"The nigger kids need it worse," he said flatly. "They can't go anywhere else and the white kids can. If you get a lot of white foofoorah because of the switch, I'll see that the Gray Oak Club pool is opened to the public. White public. Restricted hours of course. Don't want the little bastards underfoot all the time. Their mothers can taxi them."

"But . . ." Mayhew began to protest.

"But nothing," Wynn said. "Do what I say. It took a cretin in the first place to figure to send niggers to dig a pool for whites before doing the one for blacks."

But Barton had learned long before that an acute sense of fair play was an impediment to his work. If you began being even-minded about the state of the world, balancing one thing against the other, hearing the other man's argument and giving him credit when he had it coming, you ended up full of doubts and talking to yourself, producing nothing. What might be just today was meaningless if you weighed it against the ponderous weight of centuries of injustice.

He went back to such leaders as Angel Creek had and argued the sense of making an example of the Bellamy Park pool. The issue, he said, was not that the whites were getting a pool of their own; that was irrelevant except for the everlasting demeaning truth of white exclusivity, that maddening assumption, made bitterly evident once again by the existence of a pool to which blacks were restricted, that whites were the human beings and blacks were something less.

"But they already built us a pool. We built it, but they, mostly I guess, got to pay for it," protested Cal Eppers, a public works department bulldozer operator. "I skun that cat myself digging the hole," he added, not without pride. Nor was he without apprehension, for he was running the bulldozer on the new job as well, and if what Barton wanted done was done in fact he could see himself losing pay, for the department paid him by the hour.

"All right, they built your pool first," Barton said, purposely letting scorn ride his voice. "The fact that they built the Angel Creek pool first only signifies what these people have always done. They take good care of their cattle; but that doesn't mean to them that cattle are any less cattle.

"And, don't you ever forget this, there's another thing about that black pool being built first. It shows up something they'd rather you didn't know. Down below, buried so deep they probably don't just exactly realize it themselves, they're scared of you."

"Dave Mayhew scared of me? Man, you're crazy!" Eppers said incredulously.

"You can be damn sure they didn't build it first because they love your big blue eyes," Barton said.

The man from New Rochelle had not got to where he was without a capacity for shrewd, often satanic insight into the most hidden wellsprings of human motive.

"But . . ." Eppers was troubled by even worse haunts than lost paychecks although he wasn't sure just what they were.

"But nothing," Barton interrupted brusquely. "The point of stopping that job is a lot simpler and more to the point than who got what pool first. The point we got to make is one even the dumbest white man can't miss. And that is to show that we can stop it. And we can. Without violence. Without a riot. Without a strike. Without anything more than just holding up a hand, like a traffic cop, and saying STOP, no more."

And so it did come to pass as Barton wished. He did not, by any means, win Angel Creek's acclamation. What he got from substantial citizens was mostly doubt and demurrer. But he did get a half-dozen volunteers, none more than twenty years old, two of them girls, one of whom, Lucy Clagget, worked as a file clerk in the offices of Amos Wynn.

"You're enough," he told the youngsters. "Guts belong to the young."

"Tell us what we got to do," Lucy Clagget said.

"I'll be with you. You'll see," Barton said.

Thursday morning was so bright it sang with promise, but twenty-four hours of downpour had soaked the soil, turned clay to grease, and Reed Collins, the foreman on the job in Bellamy Park, found puddles standing in the half-dug pool excavation. He shook his head in doubt and called Commissioner Mayhew to ask if it was really urgent to get on with the pool at once. It occurred to him that the crew could be turned to other work until things dried a bit.

"Damn it, Collins, it's one damn thing after another," Mayhew complained. "I don't see why you can't work; it can't be all that wet."

"It's pretty wet, Mister Mayhew. And I got to get the cat down the ramp first before we can rightly get anything done."

"Why in the hell is the cat out of the hole anyhow?"

Collins was apologetic even though he knew he had been right to be careful. He knew his boss sometimes tended toward petulance and was particularly touchy about the delay in finishing the Bellamy Park pool.

"The forecast, Mister Mayhew. They said it was gonna rain cats and dogs, so I had Eppers pull it up on solid ground quitting time Tuesday night." He was on the defensive which was not an enviable posture when the commissioner was upset. "And it did rain cats and dogs."

"Well, it ain't raining now."

"I know, Mister Mayhew. But it's wet."

"Damn it, do I have to do everything? Give it a try. If you can get the cat down there you can work, can't you?"

"I guess so, Mister Mayhew."

"Well, do it then. Call me if you have any trouble. Goddamned women are driving me nuts about that goddamn pool. Them and their snotty kids."

Collins went back to the job and spoke to Cal Eppers.

"Start her up, Cal, and see if you can edge her down there."

"That ramp's slick," Eppers said doubtfully. "Slick as grease."

"God damn it, don't be always screwing off," Collins exploded, but quickly thought better of it. "Sorry, Ep, I know it's slick. But I just took a Jesus Christ riding from Jesus H. Christ Mayhew. He burns my ass."

"I know," Eppers said. "You still want me to slide that cat down there?"

"Got to, I guess. Start her up. I'll guide you."

Eppers climbed aboard and the tractor belched smoke and settled into guttural, muttering life. Eppers raised the blade and looked for Collins. The foreman stood ahead of him and off to his right. At his gesture, Eppers put the machine in gear; the mutter deepened to the growl of power and the machine began to edge toward the pit twenty yards away.

It did not reach the ramp, however, only to the brink of it. There was an interruption. A small crowd of curious sidewalk superintendents, black and white, had assembled behind the ropes guarding the half-finished pit. From among them, as the tractor moved forward, a half-dozen people sprinted toward the gateway at the lip of the ramp. They moved a few feet down the ramp and stood there, facing the oncoming machine, stumbling as they teetered for footing on the greasy clay incline.

Collins, guiding the bulldozer and with his back to the pit, was unaware of the movement until the tractor stopped dead half a dozen feet from the ramp and Eppers stood up at his levers and, his dark face all astonishment, began gesticulating wildly ahead of him. Then Collins turned around and his mouth fell open.

He stood face to face with Carver Otis Barton and his little band of disciples. There they were facing him, Barton to his right, then a girl, then three boys, another girl, three more boys bringing up their right flank. They made a barrier across the ramp and, *Good God,* Collins thought, *they're handcuffed together, two by two.*

For a long moment Collins was speechless, but when he found tongue it came forth in a bellow of disbelieving outrage.

"Get the bleeding hell out of there!"

Barton was grinning at him, completely self-possessed but delighted.

"Not today. This is a demonstration."

"Demonstration! Demonstration my ass! Get your black ass the hell off that ramp!" Collins' vocabulary on this occasion may have been a fair measure of his indignation since, judging by facial complexion, the ass he himself possessed was probably several shades blacker than Barton's.

"You may as well shut off your toy," Barton said equably. "We're here and we're going to stay here. You're through digging."

"What in hell do you think you want?" Collins demanded.

"Just to put you out of business," Barton said. "The only way you can get that cat down here is through us. Want to try it? I think that's all there is to say."

Whites among the sidewalk superintendents, having recovered, began to jeer, and globs of mud splattered among Barton's army. One struck Lucy Clagget in the mouth and she fell back gagging, scraping at the mess with her free right hand. She lost her footing, but Barton reached and steadied her and then she stood beside him without flinching.

Collins raged and made to start down the slope but stopped and backed up when two youths in the center and the two on the right started to meet him, raising the manacles that linked them threateningly.

Eppers had shut off the tractor engine and Collins went back and looked up at him in baffled fury.

"What the hell do we do now?" he said.

"I sure don't know, boss," Eppers said. "If I was you I'd call the man."

And this, after further yelling at Barton who now declined to answer and merely looked up at him smiling, was what Collins did. He called in deepest reluctance, for he knew, as clear as any vision, that Commissioner Mayhew was going to be upset.

"Mister Mayhew," he said with dragging tongue. "I can't get that cat down the hole nohow."

"Oh, Christ, you again. Why can't you?"

"You ain't going to believe this, Mister Commissioner, but there's seven niggers strung across that ramp in the mud and they won't move. And, I swear to God, they're chained together."

"Wh-a-a-a-t!"

Collins repeated the message and, to his credit, Mayhew got it.

"Jes-us!" he said. "You stay there. I'll be right out."

He put down the phone, shook his head in disbelief, started to get up, sat down again, and reached for the telephone and dialed his cousin's extension. *Damn it,* he thought, *this is a police matter; let him take care of it.* Twenty minutes later when the Mayhews arrived in Bellamy Park in a police car driven by a sergeant, Barton and his people were still on the ramp, still not speaking, and Collins, having ranted himself into voiceless impotence, simply stood on the lip of the excavation and glowered.

Because Bellamy Park was in the white part of Wynnsboro, James Dowdy did not hear of the stalemate at the pool for half an hour after it began; and because Amos Wynn had gone to an early lunch and it took a little time for his secretary to locate him, Wynn did not hear about it until almost an hour had elapsed since the battle was joined. When he did hear, he swore briefly, got his stetson from the checkroom, left his luncheon check forgotten and started for the scene. He arrived ten minutes behind the Mayhews. But for the mischance of Wynn's lateness what happened would not have happened.

The Mayhews had stood in front of the bulldozer, alternately yelling down at the impervious Barton and yelling at each other when they could not get a reply of either defiance or acquiescence. Barton merely smiled occasionally, spoke softly to his troops, and ignored the authorities.

Arthur Mayhew became conscious that the gathering crowd, now nearly all white, had quit jeering the Negroes and were now enjoying the scene. He saw covert smiles and heard snickers and was enraged anew.

"He's making a damn joke out of us," he snarled at his cousin. "Can't you run your damn business, for Christ's sake?"

"Don't yap at me. You're the law, not me. You do something," his exasperated cousin retorted.

"All right, by God, I'll do something," the police commissioner grated. "Hey, you, c'mere!" he yelled at Collins. The foreman, deeply depressed, shuffled forward on reluctant feet.

"Where's your cat skinner?" he demanded. Collins pointed up at Eppers, still in his seat on the tractor.

"Now, listen," Mayhew said. "I've had enough of this. Get that cat started up and tell him to pull ahead slow, right at 'em."

"Oh, God," Collins said, "you ain't goin . . ."

"Listen, you dumb black bastard. I ain't going to hurt anybody, but I am sure as hell going to scare the crap out of them niggers. I want that cat to move in on them, slow and easy, but keep it moving. They ain't going to stay there."

"Look, Mister Mayhew, that ramp's awful slick . . ."

"Can your man drive a cat? Or can't he?"

"He can drive all right. Sure he can drive. But that ramp . . ."

"Screw the ramp! Get him started! Slow, I said slow."

The bulldozer engine was running when Amos Wynn came striding across the soggy turf, but at first he paid no attention to the muttering thunder as he reached the edge of the pit and looked down the ramp straight into the solemn eyes of Lucy Clagget. For a moment he was thunderstruck and then he found his tongue.

"Lucy Clagget, you come out of there! You come up here this minute!"

The girl stared up at him in frozen appeal and then made a half step forward and was stopped by the chain to Barton's wrist. She looked then at the man from New Rochelle, pleading like a disobedient child for forgiveness, but Barton, immovable, looking up at Wynn, did not see her. She tugged tentatively at the chain. But, by then, it was too late.

Wynn became conscious of the bulldozer moving forward beside him, at first in disbelief, then on the instant in black rage.

"Stop the damned thing!" he yelled. But Eppers, high above him, intent on Collins' cautious signal hand, deafened by the engine roar as the machine began to move, did not see him and could not hear him.

The bulldozer reached the end of the ramp and began to tilt forward, infinitely slowly as Eppers' sure hand inched the monster forward in ponderous delicacy.

Calm, unmoving, Barton stared up at the looming machine, absolutely certain in his mind that it would stop, by the sheer force of his will if no other power intervened. The Mayhews, staring down at the Negroes in sick fascination, knew as certainly as Barton did that it would stop.

But it did not. No matter what skill might rule Eppers' head and hand, the rain and the eight tons of steel overruled him. Slowly, with deadly, insensate intent, the machine began to skid. High above at the levers, Eppers fought a sudden desperate battle and lost. The machine slewed sideways and began slipping down the slope.

Wynn saw one girl and five Negro boys turn in their chains and flounder wildly down the ramp ahead of the sliding Behemoth. He saw Barton, galvanized to action, grab at Lucy's left arm and strain to haul her toward the edge of the ramp. But the girl's feet slipped and she went sprawling. The last thing Wynn saw clearly before the machine blotted out the man and girl as it slithered further sideways was Barton on his knees hauling wildly at Lucy. He heard her thin high scream.

The bulldozer did not stop until it hit the bottom of the ramp, sideways, gathering speed, and lurched over on its side, spilling Eppers into the mud. Wynn was down the ramp, not knowing how he skidded and plunged and then he was beside the girl. She lay on her back and—he dimly understood and gave incoherent thanks—she was recognizable as a human being.

Then he saw the blood and then a spike of incongruously white bone sticking up out of the mud.

"Get an ambulance!" he yelled up at Mayhew. He saw that Barton, face down in the mud, was struggling to his knees, the handcuff chain still an umbilical cord to the girl's left hand. Her right arm, from wrist to shoulder, was nothing.

"Give me the key," he yelled at Barton.

At six o'clock Wynn left St. Francis Hospital and stopped at the Wynnsboro jail, feeling all his sixty-two years and decades more.

"Where is he?" he asked the desk sergeant.

"You want to see him, Mr. Wynn?" the man asked respectfully.

"Damn it, take me to him," Wynn said, but without heat.

Barton, still crusted in drying mud, still wearing his half of the handcuffs, was moving as Wynn stopped in front of the cell. He was pacing, three paces to the door, turn, three paces to the back wall.

"Open up," Wynn said to the turnkey. The lock thunked and the door swung open.

Barton turned and looked at him. His face was composed, but Wynn could see the redness of his eyes. *He's been bawling,* he thought; *the world ought to bawl.*

"How is the girl, Mr. Wynn?" Barton said softly.

"She's dead," Wynn said. The guard looked at Wynn questioningly. "Leave," Wynn said and the man walked away.

"Oh," Barton breathed. "Oh . . . I wish . . ."

"You should have wished sooner," Wynn said without heat.

"What can I do, Mr. Wynn?"

"Nothing . . . you've done too much."

The two men stood looking at each other, trapped together in grief, in tragedy, in the aimless death of a child who had made the error of trusting grown men, had obeyed one, had tried to obey the other.

"Are you going to charge me, Mr. Wynn?"

"I haven't. But you've been booked. Negligent manslaughter."

"I know that." A flicker of a smile touched Barton's lips but not his eyes. "They took care of that quick."

"It could be made to stick. Right now . . . with a black jury even."

"I imagine so. I wouldn't fight it. I took her there. I'll take my medicine. Somebody owes her something . . . and it may as well be me."

"You can't pay her anything," Wynn said. "Lucy is the second one dead over this. Did you know that?"

"Second? . . . Oh, you mean the bomb."

"Both niggers. Both killed by niggers. Both with white assists."

"White assists?"

"Commissioner Mayhew this time. You don't need to know about the other."

"Yes . . . I need to know."

"From me, you won't . . . I let the other one go . . . I'm going to let you go. You have to understand this: I told you you would damage this town. You have. There must be no more of it. Wynnsboro can't afford you, can't afford even to have you in jail here. We need to forget you. You can go."

Barton stood silent, searching the other man's lined, cold face. At length he spoke.

"You know, Mr. Wynn, I can't quit."

"You have quit," Wynn said.

But somewhere, deep in his being, Amos Wynn knew that Barton had not quit, could not quit while he lived. *This is a strong man,* Wynn acknowledged to himself, *but in him there is a demon that can't be bought, not with the life of one Lucy Clagget, nor a thousand Lucy Claggets.*

6

Jeff Stuart sat in the second row of the balcony of the Mount Pisga Baptist Church on the South Side of Chicago, on the edge of the black ghetto but not quite all the way into the slums of it. It was Sunday, a day of worship, and this a day of anticipation and apprehension. The Democratic National Convention would assemble the following morning. The city stood ready to call itself beleaguered.

Heat rolled up into the balcony in a stifling tide generated by the August sun smashing down on the yellow sandstone of the church and the grassless concrete of Forty-seventh Street, regenerated by the metabolic processes of two thousand restless, murmuring souls in the well of the church below him. Stuart loosened his tie and unbuttoned the collar of his shirt and longed to get rid of his jacket but acknowledged to himself that it would not be politic to venture further into comfortable impropriety in this sacred place—particularly since the jacket provided modesty for the holster and short-barreled .38 under his left armpit. All the same he could feel the rivulets of sweat, paradoxically cold against his skin, sliding down his rib cage and into the soggy waistband of his slacks.

How do they stand it, he wondered again, looking down across the packed humanity, stirring the hot wet air into languid—and useless—motion with hundreds of copies of the *De-*

fender fanning in hypnotic unison. He looked at his watch; three o'clock, two hours of this gone and no sign visible that it would ever end.

Down in front, under the jutting prow of the pulpit, the picket signs damning the A & P supermarket chain shifted and stirred, the banners of a restless army. The massed choir, all in white and truly marvelous he had thought, finished breathing out the cadence of "We Shall Overcome" and sank back to their benches in sweltering robes. *Hot for me, never hotter,* he thought; *what absolute hell it must be for them.*

Carver Otis Barton had the microphone on the commodious pulpit. It needed to be roomy, for around and behind the civil rights bellwether stood the apostles of the creed here being preached. They were the regulars: a famous woman blues singer, a nightclub comic who was more than half politician, the fat pastor of Mount Pisga, a chieftain of the Black Panthers out on bail pending appeal from a manslaughter conviction resulting from the death of a compatriot, two of the three black members of the Chicago City Council—the third standing in purgatory as a house nigger—the second elected black mayor of a Northern city, a militant lately grown to a personage for his manifesto which demanded one billion dollars from white Protestant, Catholic, and Jewish congregations for generations of proclaimed religious discrimination against black America, a movie star who suffered some embarrassment at functions like this, for everybody black knew his wife was white.

Barton's voice was a rich baritone and passion throbbed in it like a cadenced, controlled alternating current. Stuart had trouble understanding his words, for Mount Pisga's cavern was a place of overlapping echo rather than resonance. Then, too, Barton was speaking in the patois of the streets, a modified English that had never come out of the years he had spent in Eastern universities. *I guess—except for that one other pitiful bastard—I'm the only one here who can't speak black,* Stuart thought ruefully. *They're hypnotized, no question. Of course, he has to be saying what they want to hear, but it's more than that.* Each pause in that imperious voice was punctuated by cries of "Yeah! Yeah!" and "Tell it, man!" and the A & P banners danced and fell in an exalted choreography of scorn.

I don't know if it would help much if I knew for sure what he's saying, Stuart reflected as he reached once again for the sodden wad of his handkerchief. *I do know he's got them and he surely ain't reciting the Twenty-third Psalm. No trespasses are being forgiven here.*

That voice, that's what does it. He plays it like an organ, rich, exhorting, virile, exultant, scathing, conjuring the imps out of hell, calling to the blood more than to the mind. What was it exactly? The summons of a prophet shouting up the slaves—or simply the deep-lunged trumpet of a powerful animal? Sex? He drips the stuff. Then, in the unease of undefined guilt, he remembered the interlude in Jensen's room the night before.

The telephone was ringing when he returned from dinner at the Erie Café. He had dined alone and early, knowing that Barton, after calling on the mayor at City Hall, had returned to his suite at the Hilton. Whatever might be learned there, he knew, was out of his reach. On the other hand, it probably was not beyond Jensen's.

The telephone was still jangling as he got the door open. He left it open and strode across the room and lifted the instrument from its cradle beside his bed.

"Jeff?" It was Jensen's voice. He sounded excited. "Jeff, is that you?"

"Sure it's me. What's on your mind?"

"Jeff, get up here. You gotta hear this."

"Hear what? You tape the Kremlin?"

"Look, no joke. Come on up. You'll split a gut."

"Won't it keep? I'm tired."

"Nah. Come on."

On the eleventh floor, five doors along the hall from Barton's suite, Stuart tapped at the electronic engineer's door. He knew

Jensen kept it always doublelocked. When Jensen called for identification, then opened up, Stuart walked into a room cluttered with fiber salesman's cases which he knew contained not the shoe samples indicated by the company labels they bore but the esoteric gear of Jensen's busybody art. On the dresser squatted a high fidelity recorder, its lights glowing.

Jensen's round face was alight with what had to be satisfaction, and the small eyes behind thick spectacles were bright. No surprises here. So far as Stuart knew, Jensen was a single-minded thief whose only passion lay in what he could lift, undetected, from other men's skulls.

"Wait'll you hear this," Jensen said. "It'll kill you."

"So I'm dead," Stuart said, disliking the ripeness of Jensen's lips and the way he pursed them into a pink bow. "Let's hear it."

Jensen went to the recorder and flipped the switch to rewind, watching the footage meter as the reels spun. When he stopped it and switched to play, he turned toward Stuart, grinning.

"Listen to this!" he said.

No voice came from the speaker, but there were sounds, wordless murmurings, rustles of movement. Then, slowly and quietly at first, a cadenced, slow, deepening rhythm of human sound.

"What the hell is this?" Stuart said. "Sounds like somebody puffing."

"If I turn up the volume, she'll sound like a locomotive going up hill with a hundred car freight," Jensen said.

"She will? Who's she?"

"Just listen."

"It doesn't sound like anything except somebody screwing. Or somebody with asthma," Stuart said. "Where's it coming from?"

"Barton's place, where else? Don't interrupt, will you. Listen to it."

The recorder, more sensitive than humanity, carried in its voice—wordless—a sense of intimacy and urgent blood. The sound of breathing deepened and quickened against a background of movement, of tension. *What is this,* Stuart wondered, listening in spite of himself, feeling—with shamed reluctance—the unbidden stir of his own senses.

There came a word, a single gasped "Oh!" and then, in a moment, a cry of urgency. Then silence.

Stuart sat back, angrily aware that he was, by effort of will, forcing himself to relax from a tension he was sorry he felt.

"When was that?" he said. "Who was it? His wife?"

Jensen got up and took a notebook from beside the recorder, looking at the last open page.

"Ten forty-three. That's when he finished. Began at ten thirty-four. Nine minutes, pretty good, huh? His wife? Wife, shmife. I thought you were supposed to be a detective—of a sort."

"Not a peeper though."

"Wait a minute, there's more," Jensen said, raising a warning hand.

The light began to blink, and he heard the baritone voice, speaking quietly.

"Hand me a cigarette, baby."

"Oh, all right. You shouldn't smoke so much. You shouldn't smoke in bed." A light, fond woman's voice.

"Nor do anything in bed, I guess. You honkies think a bed is the devil's invention—when you ain't in one, baby."

"Oh, no, honey . . . That was . . ."

Through the speaker came a rich, warm chuckle.

"I'll tell you what it was. It was steel cock, black steel cock. It's the secret of my success. Here, put this out for me, will you? You ready again?"

"You're bragging! . . . Oh, no, you're not . . . Look at it!"

A quick stir of motion and the baritone again. "Look out, you're dropping sparks. Turn around, baby." The speaker went dead.

Jensen got up and turned off the recorder. He was grinning. "Rich," he said. "Rich."

"I do not see who the hell's business it is where and by whom a man gets laid," Stuart said, fed up with Jensen, ashamed of himself, angry at his instinctive stirring in the act of electronic voyeurism.

"You can ruin him with this," Jensen said. "She's white. A blonde. I saw her but I don't know who she is. That's your business."

"What makes you think I want to ruin him, and I don't give a damn who lays him."

"I'll bet a week's pay Rembert wants to ruin him."

"The hell with it," Stuart said in disgust. "If you can get screwing off your mind for a minute, what else did you pick up?"

"Nothing useful," Jensen said negligently.

"Well, what? Your idea of what's useful and mine might be different."

"Nothing really. He came in about seven and a little later a couple of those people of his came up and stayed two hours. They wanted something, but he wouldn't go for it. They hung in tight, but he wouldn't buy it. He shooed them out about twenty minutes before she showed up."

"Well, damn it, what did they want?"

"Oh, you know those cats. They wanted him to lead a march down Indiana Avenue to the convention hall."

"He wouldn't?"

"He would not. Said the convention was a white man's beef and there wasn't any sense getting black skulls busted in it."

"Oh."

Now, on the pulpit, Barton stopped with a shout and the hall erupted, roaring, ravenous, transported. He could, Stuart thought in awe, in this moment tell them to go burn down the White House and he'd have two thousand people with matches already lit.

The pastor stepped to the microphone and, voiceless against that din, tried for the third time that afternoon to introduce the only white man on the platform. It was a tall figure, clad like a mantle in goodwill, physically and visibly as drenched as Stuart felt. He recognized the man as a Senator here to pursue his fragile hope of the Democratic nomination. *He sure picked a hard act to try to follow,* Stuart thought with faint, half-amused sympathy. *He won't get any votes here, but he's likely to get some more of his nose rubbed in humility. Whatever this is, it sure isn't a white man's show. All they've got for this poor striving bastard today is the opportunity to be ignored—that is if he's lucky; he could get worse. They've had him swallowing it all afternoon. It doesn't really make any difference who he is; it's the color he is. He should have had sense enough or guts enough to pack it in and get out the first time the preacher started to introduce him and let him get halfway to the mike before he forgot and turned on somebody black. It's his own choice, of course, but wouldn't you think that this, today, here, in this witch's caldron of vengeance, is a lousy place for a white politician?*

Barton had moved aside from the microphone, standing at ease. *Out of two thousand or more,* Stuart thought, *he's the only one not sweating, at least not visibly. Maybe he gets a little more air-conditioning, circulation anyhow, under that wild getup.* Instead of jacket, shirt, tie, and pants, Barton seemed to be wearing only a loose, boldly patterned, capelike blue and white robe. Even silent among his peers, he radiated a kind of sure ascendancy over his surroundings. From the balcony, Stuart saw him beckon slightly; there was an immediate answering stir in the crowd at the foot of the pulpit.

A young man all in black, top-heavy in the gigantic umbrella of an Afro hairdo, talisman dangling on his chest from strings of beads, began to fight a way up the pulpit stairway, elbowing aside protesting photographers, black as well as white. He carried himself in cocksure arrogance, belligerent, scornful. *Must be one of his bodyguards,* Stuart thought; *the man is loaded with acolytes—and they all look tough and maybe they are in-*

deed. Gaining the platform, the young black bulldozed his way to Barton's side.

Barton bent close to the youth's ear to speak. The man in black first nodded, then turned and looked out into the throng. Stuart saw Barton touch his arm and turn to look up into the balcony; the young man's eyes followed Barton's look and Stuart found himself gazing back over the mass of humanity into the faces of both men concentrated on his own.

Barton spoke again and the young man nodded acquiescence, then scowled through space at Stuart. As Barton spoke again, the other shook his head in doubt and reluctance. But Barton touched him on the shoulder, gently but unmistakably propelling him. The young man, frowning, unwilling but obedient, began to shoulder a path back through the crowd.

So now, it's my turn, Stuart thought feeling a small tingle of anticipation. *He had to get to me sooner or later.* He watched the man wedging his way down the pulpit stairway, back through the massed banners, shoving through the crowd at the front of the church, sidling along the wall aisle, in and out of the hot August light through the stained-glass windows. He waited.

Moments later the youth knelt beside him in the aisle. Stuart was aware that this was no obeisance; the kid needed to be heard.

"He wants to talk to you," the boy said.

"Who does?" Stuart said. He had no intention of lending himself to a half-baked deism which substituted pronouns without antecedents for reasonable identification. *He may be God if he wants to be, but not in this precinct,* he thought in half-amused irritation.

"*HE* does."

"Who the hell is he?"

"Remember where you are, whitey," the young man said, turning up at him eyes smoldering with dislike.

"I know where I am. And I don't know what you're talking about."

The youth surrendered sullenly. "Mr. Barton wants to talk to you."

"That's more like it," Stuart said. "All right. When? Where?"

"After this is over. Eight o'clock in the bar at the Blackstone. Men's bar . . . downstairs."

"Why not?" Stuart said. "You going to be there, tiger? Save him from the honkies?"

The boy looked up at him again. *There is a kind of hysteria in those eyes,* Stuart thought. *It's a difficult thing to get really settled in your mind, but I know this kid genuinely hates my guts . . . and, so far as I know, he never laid eyes on me until Barton called him up and pointed.*

"You ain't out of the South Side yet . . . white man," the youth said.

Probably I shouldn't have said that, Stuart thought as he worked his way down the balcony stairway and out into the cooking sunlight where the street in front of the church was filled, down the middle, with squad cars parked bumper to bumper and bored policemen in blue-and-white riot helmets waited for whatever might . . . or might not . . . occur. *Barton must be God to those kids . . . and it must be a hell of a wrench to their souls to let him go off among the enemy without them.* Denial of a sacred franchise to martyrdom.

7

In the hot dusk, Stuart emerged from the Hilton lobby, littered and raucous and spastic in the cacophony of a disunited national political party in uneasy convention assembled, and stood in Michigan Avenue. He turned to the left, giving musing attention to the solid wall of helmeted police standing shoulder to shoulder the full length of the block, their backs toward him.

Across the avenue in Grant Park were the disenchanted, that curious agglomeration of youth—some of whom were in their forties or more—mixed of the unshaven, the intentionally filthy, those helmeted for battle and smeared shiny with vaseline against the anticipated horrors of mace and tear gas, the spanking clean, close-cropped idealists, those with visions of a utopia in which all mankind stood in desperate need and those who only wanted to rip down what mankind already had erected—good or evil, it made no difference.

If there's any common denominator here, he thought, *it's that damn near every last soul in that park is white. No blacks here and I wonder why. If anybody has the right to nurse a beef against the establishment, the blacks probably could bring in more of a case than can the common run of the ones who are here. I wonder what the head count is now: two thousand, five, seven, ten? Who really knows how to count a crowd and if any-*

body does what does the arithmetic signify? Well, these kids are not my assignment, which pleases me just as well. Understanding one man is chore enough for anybody.

He crossed Balbo Street, threading a path among more uniforms, entered the Michigan Avenue door of the Blackstone, turned to the right and down the short stairway, and entered the cool, dark oak serenity of the men's bar. He saw Barton at once, seated at a table in the open center of the room, leaning back comfortably on the solid chair arms, a tall drink in front of him, a cigarette between his fingers.

Barton stood up and extended a hand.

"Thanks for coming," he said. "Have a seat. What'll you drink?"

"Scotch and water. Thanks," Stuart said as he pulled out the chair across from Barton. He had been around and near the man for the last three weeks, generally in the same hotel, often in the same hall with him or on the same street with him, in Los Angeles, Minneapolis, Hammond, Washington, but until now he had never been so close to him, nor had they exchanged a word.

Now he looked him over with frank curiosity. Barton was dark—not black, more nearly mahogany. His body was compact, his manner composed if not exactly serene, his eyes steady and observant. Out of the African robe, he wore a gray silk summer suit, white shirt, a small patterned maroon tie on which, Stuart was surprised to see, the Phi Beta Kappa key served as a stickpin. He wore the blue and gold triangles of the Columbia ring. *The thing that really makes him Carver Otis Barton though,* Stuart reflected, *is composure, that air of pride, just this side of haughty.*

"What was that thing you were wearing this afternoon?" Stuart asked abruptly as his drink came.

"That boogie thing?" Barton smiled.

"No, I didn't mean that. Envy probably. I was sweating like a hog up in that balcony."

"They call it a *dashiki*, that is when they want to be formal about it. I call it window dressing. Part of the act. Comfort is an extra summer bonus. I'll probably freeze my butt come winter."

"Not much business here," Stuart said, looking around the half-empty room. "The Democrats must still all be down at the stockyards."

"It's all right with me," Barton said, sliding a finger around the cold rim of his glass. "It's a pleasant place—without the mob that'll be in here later."

"I remember being here once when I was a kid. Long time ago," Stuart said.

"Yes?"

"I was in law school at the university. Had to work to stay there. Got a job as a spare-time cub stringer for the old Chicago *Times, Sun-Times* now. I got sent here to cover a meeting between Irene Castle McLaughlin and Joe Louis' wife. They were both on the committee for some charity on the South Side, sunshine for ghetto kids, something like that."

"I always thought Irene Castle's bag was keeping medical schools from cutting up stray mutts, not doing anything about stray colored kids."

"It was stray dogs in first place, sure enough," Stuart acknowledged. "Anyhow Marva got here first . . . beautiful woman . . . mink down to here . . . gold lamé dress . . . and ten o'clock in the morning."

"I know she was beautiful," Barton said. "Poor old Joe. Most times beauty is something you buy. And you've got to expect to pay for mink. What about it?"

"Nothing much, I suppose. They were supposed to meet in an upstairs suite. The manager wouldn't let Marva go upstairs until Irene got here. Irene was late."

"Natch."

"Natch which?"

"Natch the first. Naturally they wouldn't let Marva go upstairs alone. She might swipe a towel. Or sit on the can. Who could know?" Barton smiled, and Stuart wondered how a man might manage, as this one did, to compound genuine amusement with glittering ice. "I wouldn't know about Irene Castle McLaughlin."

"She got here finally, but she was more than an hour late and Marva was getting the itch," Stuart said. "Irene came in looking frazzled. Old tweed coat with a tear in it. A tan jersey dress that didn't fit. Ripped stockings. She'd been driving in and seen a dog warden, she said, trying to round up a couple of strays near Lake Forest. She'd pulled up, bawled out the warden, yelled for the SPCA, crawled through a barbed wire fence and caught the strays herself and brought them along in her station wagon."

"You can get mussed up chasing a stray dog," Barton nodded. "What are you proving?"

"Nothing. Except I remembered it."

"My being here have anything to do with tickling your memory?" Barton was smiling again.

"I suppose so," Stuart admitted. "Anyhow, as soon as Irene showed we all went upstairs."

"Maybe you're demonstrating something," Barton said. "I'm not positive what. Something to do with who knows she has to wear gold lamé and mink before noon. And who doesn't give a hoot what she wears because she knows nobody's going to go upstairs until she gets there. And who knows she has the built-in right to tell a dog catcher to go to hell. You've got a parable there somewhere, if you work on it."

"That's about as far as I can go," Stuart said.

"It might be helpful if you knew what became of the stray mutts. Or the black kids, for that matter."

"I couldn't say. But it's a reasonable guess the dogs never got vivisected."

"Neither did Marva, probably . . . Although, for a time there, I imagine she may have felt about the way the mutts did when the catcher was after them with the net."

"Things are different now," Stuart said.

"They look different, that's all," Barton said, and Stuart saw that the black man's protean eyes glittered for a moment with malice.

"No, you're wrong. They are different. And getting differenter."

"Only in degree. Not in kind. How do you think that kid of mine would have done if he'd come in here—with his beads and his bushman haircut—and the brass knucks in his pocket?"

"Some less than welcome, I expect."

"The difference is I'm wearing a suit. And I'll give you this much: Marva's problem was she was born too soon."

"You've got a finger on it. The times have changed."

"I say there's no real difference down in anybody's guts. It's a Supreme Court difference. But that ain't why I asked you here. Just who are you . . . or what?" The question was abrupt, and Stuart wondered why it had not come before.

Well, he had been ready for it. He picked up his drink and took a slow pull at it, looking across the rim of the glass into the black man's eyes. Then he reached into his breast pocket, took out his wallet, and laid his Bureau ID card on the table. Barton looked at it without expression.

"One of the director's boys," he said. "I more than half thought so. But why me?"

"You could call me your baby-sitter—by appointment," Stuart said.

"You mean bodyguard?" Barton's smile carried real amusement. "Man, I'm up to my ass in bodyguards."

"So I notice. That kid you sent after me didn't seem happy at the idea you wouldn't be bringing your mob along."

"They're dedicated, all right," Barton acknowledged. "Most of the time it's a pain, but it makes them feel good. Tell your boss I don't need another bodyguard."

"It's not that exactly, although I expect I might be criticized if somebody knocked you on the head in my presence. The job definition is broader. People are interested in you. You attract a lot of attention. Some people think you're a sort of messiah. And there are others of course," Stuart admitted, "who tend to believe you're a menace. If it can be boiled down to anything in particular, you could say I'm a nonprofessional psychiatric field worker. Reporter would be simpler."

"Would that mean your job is to fix my wagon?"

"No. You do stir things up, though. You're a phenomenon. They want to know what goes on around you—and if it isn't asking too much what goes on inside you."

"What goes on around me is plenty visible," Barton said. "What goes on inside me I may not be much more positive about than you are about what goes on inside yourself."

"You have a point."

"For now, let's just say it's a living"—Barton grinned with genuine mirth—"you've got your way; I've got mine."

"I don't knock it. As I say, I got sent. Otherwise I wouldn't intrude."

"Don't," Barton said coldly. "It's a free country . . . for some. Just don't bug me."

Boy, you just don't know how bugged you already are, Stuart thought, and asked, "Another drink?"

"All right. But these are on . . ." He broke off at a sudden, muffled burst of sound rolling down through the Michigan Avenue door. Whistles shrilled, a siren began to moan and faintly there came the wordless surge of humanity on the move. "Wha . . ."

"Sounds like somebody pulled the pin," Stuart said. "You want to take a look?"

Barton got up, fished in his pocket and dropped a ten-dollar bill on the table.

"I've seen it before, but we may as well," he said.

As they came up the stairs to the marble vestibule below the slightly grand staircase to the lobby, the revolving door to Michigan Avenue was spinning, spewing refugees from the sidewalk. A woman was crying and a man cursed and the faces, Stuart saw, bore the brand of dismay.

"If you could run in a revolving door," Barton said, "they'd be running."

Stuart took Barton's arm and wedged a path through the confusion in the vestibule toward the right. Beyond the whirling door he could see only the surge of movement. They heaved themselves into segments of the door and were flung out to the sidewalk. People were running north. Against the tide the two men worked south the few yards to the corner of Michigan and Balbo.

It was dark now and the block in front of the Hilton was bright against the darkness, a bluish glare of floods mounted above the cabs of police cars, an armored National Guard van, and paddy wagons.

Out in the darkness of the park, rising above the uproar immediately around him, Stuart could hear a hoarse, bull-horned voice insanely bellowing, "Fuck the pigs! Pigs eat shit!"

The close-ordered phalanx of police had been broken up. Stuart was conscious of curses and screams and wordless cries, and somebody yelled, "Tear gas!" The near reaches of the park beyond the avenue seemed to be moving away, and he realized that the mass of youth was in retreat. Retreat from what? It wasn't hard to answer; silhouetted against the glare he could see the rise and fall of nightsticks.

He was jarred from behind and shifted aside and saw two patrolmen stagger by, lugging by legs and shoulders a squirming, squalling, bleeding youth, scarcely identifiable as human, all flying hair and beard and open bloody mouth. At the open rear door of a patrol wagon the police paused, half-upended their cargo and slammed it into the vehicle's maw.

"Stay there, you sonofabitch," one patrolman panted. The youth stared back out of dazed eyes.

Not all fled into the park. Some, like panicked sheep, dashed and dodged and fell and crawled back toward the west, into the police line that stood as a barricade, trying to fight a way to refuge in dark streets and alleys beyond.

He saw a dozen police driving two men against the wall of the Hilton. There were yells and the crash and splinter of glass as the sidewalk window of the bar gave way and the fugitives plunged through falling glass and landed on the floor. One, down on hands and knees, tried to crawl away. The other lay where he had fallen.

Stuart realized that Barton was still beside him and he grabbed his arm and began to press back to the wall of the Blackstone and the door.

"Come on! Let's get out," he yelled.

Progress was nearly impossible; they were being sucked down into a maelstrom. Stuart's eyes were caught by a fat young girl in a loud plaid coat running toward him in a ludicrously awkward, knock-kneed gallop. She stumbled at the curb and went down on her knees and stayed there, submissive. She moaned and pulled the coat over her head, and Stuart found himself illogically wondering why the coat—in this devil's weather. Then a policeman stood over the fallen girl, and a club went down alongside the hidden head and slammed into her shoulder. Stuart was starting toward the girl when he heard a thud and a grunt of pain behind him. He turned.

Barton was staggering back against the wall, one hand up and fumbling at the side of his face. And a club was up, then coming down and the policeman, face contorted in a strange compound of panic and rage, was snarling, "Move! Move, you boogie bastard. You're under . . ." He did not finish, for Stuart's left hand was up seizing the club hand at the wrist and twisting. Stuart saw the policeman's disbelieving eyes turn to him, but by then Stuart's hand was under his armpit and coming out. Then the stub-barreled .38 was pressing against the policeman's throat as widened, scared eyes stared down at it.

"Drop the stick," Stuart ordered, jamming the gun muzzle harder against the Adam's apple. The club fell and the officer's arms dropped at his sides.

"Leave them that way! And move back. Back!"

The policeman stumbled toward the curb, astonished eyes on

the gun. Stuart reached and grabbed an arm, glanced back to be sure it was Barton and yelled, "Get through the door! Hurry up!"

Stuart saw that Barton was reeling. He took his arm and guided him back down the steps to the bar.

"Come on," he said. "If you didn't need that other drink, you do need this one."

The dim lit bar was half-filled with other refugees, now shrill in excitement and relief to be off the embattled avenue, but the table they had had was still unoccupied, and Stuart guided Barton to it. A colored waiter, sizzling with curiosity, appeared at once.

"Double Scotch on the rocks. Johnny Walker black. Twice," Stuart said.

Barton pulled out a handkerchief and pressed it against his left temple, pulled it away and glanced curiously at the blood, dipped the handkerchief in his water glass and mopped the side of his face.

"He hit me a pretty good clip," he said. "How do I look?"

"Raggedy," Stuart said. "At least it wasn't personal."

Barton looked up sharply. "Let's not kid," he said. "It was personal. As personal as the color of my pelt."

"I was out in the park through that mob earlier, before it got dark," Stuart said. "They were almost all white. How was that? I would have thought the blacks would have been there with the biggest, the loudest beef."

Barton grinned crookedly. "I'm going to have a head like a bass drum," he said. "Of course it was all white—or almost. You ought to know the buildup for this convention has been going on for months. Why do you suppose the cops were predicting snipers in those high-rise, black apartments over the expressway to the stockyards? The cops were tailoring a battle their way and ahead of time. They knew they were going to knock heads and they knew which heads they wanted to knock most. But we knew it, too. Why do you suppose nearly every Black Panther and Devil's Disciple out of jail left town a week ago? Simple. A head out of range is a head that's hard to knock. This was bound to be a white man's dispute. We couldn't see much point in getting black heads busted in a white man's war."

"You got yours busted."

"I should have known better than to stick it out there. Getting rapped on the punkin was inevitable . . . under the circumstances."

With inquiring, tender fingers he probed around the wound and brought the handkerchief down again.

"Quit bleeding," he said. "Sign of durability. You know." He smiled, "I knew a *Life* magazine sports writer who once talked to a bunch of anthropologists because he had a theory why blacks are often champion athletes. His notion was that black men enjoy better structural design but got shortchanged on the top end. Like they would have longer, solider bones, more limber muscles, all around better coordination. The other side of it was they would have thicker skulls and less brain.

"Under the circumstances, I hate to admit he could have been partly right. My head is beginning to ease up—although, of course, I may not be giving due credit to the Scotch."

"How did the anthropologists feel about his theory?"

"They agreed. He had his pick of anthropologists."

"Anyhow count your blessings."

"I do, I do. That reminds me, I may owe you some little thing for running that cop off."

"Forget it. I told you I was a baby-sitter."

Barton measured his companion somberly.

"It puzzles me, though," he said. "You're out of character. You're a cop yourself in a way. You could say you were going against your own kind, taking on a white cop for a nigger's thick skull."

"Forget that, too." Stuart was indefinably uncomfortable under Barton's gaze. "I was brought up color-blind; it ain't my fault. Besides, a goon is a goon."

"Tell me this, how come you're a cop at all? You don't look it; you don't really act it. I thought you were a lawyer."

"I am . . . technically. Never hung a shingle though."

"Why not?"

"I'm not sure. I might have . . . if I'd ever felt committed enough . . . one way or another."

"Well, thanks anyhow. I hope the flatfoot doesn't resent you . . . enough to do anything about it."

"He won't. I'm one of the director's boys. But I'm curious about you. Hasn't it ever occurred to you that this hobby of yours . . . or crusade if you want to call it that . . . is the kind of thing that could get you killed?"

Barton grinned.

"Sure, white man. But look at it this way; it's a sign of social progress. Until Malcolm X got it, who ever heard of assassinating a nigger? Lynching, sure. Razored in a crap game, of course. Knocked over in an alley by some crazy hophead, certainly. Nutted for looking cross-eyed at a white woman or gutted in a dispute with a soul brother over a black one, why not? But killed for politics? That's something new under the sun. They're even doing it in the old country. Look at Tom Mboya, squeejeed in the door of a Nairobi drugstore. How respectable can you get?"

"It's your hide."

"Don't think I ain't fond of it. But if you wonder whether us souls are down out of the trees yet, look at it. Both Malcolm and Mboya were knocked off—for political reasons—by other black men. No, assassinating black men for politics is not only new; it's also the black man's own thing. Dignity—for both the knockee and the knocker off."

"You're kidding."

"A little, maybe."

"It isn't merely the possibility of you getting your lumps from a fraternity brother. Probably you irritate enough of them, especially since yours seems to be in a highly competitive trade. But it seems to me the guy you're scratching until he bleeds is mostly the white man. I can't see whites being particularly tender about your hide."

"Probably not. There are plenty of whites who'd be pleased to attend my funeral. But—the Supreme Court again—the honkies are getting taken down with inhibition."

"All right, it's still your hide. Who you going to aggravate next?"

"All right, you got your assignment, and there's no point you not having the itinerary." Barton, from half-mockery, had turned grave. "I'm going back to a place I do not want to go at all."

"Where's that?"

"City called Wynnsboro."

"Oh?" Stuart looked up sharply. "Know about that. Place where a girl got killed? That what bothers you?"

"Yes. From one way, you could say it was my fault."

"Why go then?"

"In this business, you don't not go."

Stuart saw Barton's eyes widen in astonishment and then narrow at him in a warning stare. And just then, Stuart felt the prod of the gun against his neck and looked around at two figures in uniform.

"On your feet. Move slow and careful." The gun muzzle pressed deeper into his flesh, painfully.

8

"I have had it!" Amy Wynn said in vast disgust, and touched the tip of her nose with a gently exploratory finger. "Ouch!"

"What's the matter, girl?" Amos Wynn asked absently, not looking up from the plug which was twitching along the sheeny surface of the water under the lee of a tree-grown bank.

"I'm sunburned. In fact, I'm broiled. And these damned mosquitoes are the size of a North Carolina state fullback."

"Into each life, some rain . . ." Amos began, but his daughter stopped him.

"Philosophy isn't going to heal me, pa. If I wasn't so hungry, I'd be afraid I was a terminal case. Besides the fish wouldn't bite if I was Racquel Welch."

"I doubt if the mind of a bass runs along those channels," her father said. "I guess it's too hot; they'll wake up around sundown."

"Good lord, we're not going to stay out that long, are we? I'll starve."

"Preserve me from the frailty of females." Amos grunted and sighed. "All right, we'll go. Just let me drop one in there in the lee of that log."

With a knowing flip of his wrist, the green and yellow jitter-bug arced out and plopped to the surface inches from his point of aim in the shadow of a fallen tree trunk slanting down from the steep bank. He twitched the tip of his rod, and the plug jerked and made a chuckling sound. The water exploded in silver spray, out of which burst a brief writhing glitter of gold.

"Wow!" Amy yelled. "Don't lose him!"

"Don't aim to." Amos grunted, teasing the fish away from the log where it obviously intended to go to ground and, if it succeeded, would probably snag the line. The fish jumped again and began to run and Amos generously gave it all the line it wanted.

"Hang onto him, pa," Amy pleaded, reeling in fast to get her own line out of the way. "That's our dinner!"

Amos flashed her a quick, craggy grin, and got his attention back to the fish.

"Warm up the fry pan," he said over his shoulder.

The fish jumped half a dozen more times before it came, in exhausted indignation, to the net. Avoiding the snapping jaws, Amos gently hooked his fingers into the gills and held up the green and glittering silver prize.

"Not bad, huh?" he said in a pleased tone.

"Not bad? Wow," Amy said again in admiration. "And I would have gone home. Looks like a three pounder."

"Nary an ounce less," Amos said. "You going to fry him?"

"Pa, your ideas of cooking are back in the last century. Fry a fish like that! I'm going to broil him . . . my way."

"Suit yourself," Amos said, and pressed the outboard starter button and quickly put the boat up on the step into roaring flight homeward across the lake.

Amos came into the pungent kitchen and stuck his big nose down to the bowl in which Amy was mixing a concoction which, clearly, he considered mysterious.

"What's that, for Pete's sake?" he asked.

"Olive oil, red wine vinegar, oregano, salt, pepper, garlic . . . a lot of garlic," Amy said.

"What you aim to do with it?" Amos asked suspiciously.

"For the fish, naturally."

"For the fish? Good lord, you won't taste anything except garlic. It's enough to blow up the house."

"Just wait and see."

"Damn Yankee cooking. I never should have sent you North to school," Amos said warily.

"It's not Yankee," Amy said indignantly.

"What is it then?"

"Wop. Neapolitan," Amy said inelegantly.

"Don't slang people. It's not respectful."

Amy looked at him in elaborate mockery.

"You say nigger, pa."

"That's different. Niggers are niggers."

"So? Anyhow, you'll like this; I'd guarantee it. One weekend in New York a fella took me to a restaurant called Amalfi, and he talked me into trying a broiled striped bass with this sauce. Nobody ever did me a bigger favor; I almost married him."

"With all that garlic, you'd have deserved each other. Served each other right, in fact."

The telephone rang and Amos started toward his study.

"Don't be long," Amy warned. "One thing about wop cuisine; when it's ready it's ready and no fooling."

"All right," he said. "I'll cut it short."

But he did not, while Amy fretted and moved toward exasperated indignation. At last she shouted.

"Pa! Come on! You want to eat ashes?"

Amos came slowly through the kitchen and went on out to the air-conditioned enclosed patio where, when they were alone, they took all their meals, avoiding the stiffness of the formal dining room which had been one of Amy's mother's great prides.

"Who was so long-winded?" Amy asked.

"Jim Dowdy," Amos said. He was frowning, preoccupied, somehow sad, Amy thought.

"What's the matter, pa?" she asked anxiously.

"That nigger's coming back," he said.

"What nigger? What about it?"

"The one that was with Lucy Clagget when she . . . got killed," Wynn said heavily.

"Oh? Why?"

"I don't know why. Well, yes I do. Dowdy says he aims to stage a march. Protest march, they call it."

"Protest against what, for heaven's sake? Is the man insane? After what happened!"

"Apparently still thinks the Teamsters can get organized here. No, daughter, I don't think he's insane; but he's a zealot. And he's trouble. The niggers don't understand how much trouble he is . . . for them, too."

"Can't he be stopped? I just don't understand how he has the nerve . . . after Lucy."

"That shook him. I know that much," Amos said somberly. "But it wouldn't stop him . . . and I knew it wouldn't. Maybe I should have let them try him . . . only I didn't want to be in jail to grow into a martyr. He's the kind of man the niggers would build myths around . . . make him a legend. I had hoped they'd forget him as long as he stayed away. And I think they would have."

"But not now."

"No. Not now. Only if . . ."

"If what?"

"If he can be made not to come back."

"But, pa, you can't make a man do . . ."

"He wouldn't be the first to be kept away from the place that didn't want him."

"But I don't see how. Pa, eat your dinner; you haven't touched a thing."

"Oh, I guess I didn't notice." Absently he took a bite of the bass, then sat brooding down at his plate again. At length he pushed the plate aside, pushed back his chair and got up.

"I'm sorry, girl. You go ahead. I've got to see about something."

"Pa! My wop fish. Don't you like it?"

He sent her a brief, quickly fading smile.

"It's good, honey. Some other time."

He went toward his study and Amy, dispirited now, not knowing why other than that he was and the mood was infectious, forgot her own hunger and left the table to follow him. He was on the telephone as she came to the door, and so she turned away and went to clear the kitchen.

Half an hour later, now into the early night, he came to the kitchen door wearing the stetson.

"I'm going down to the office for a while. I don't think I'll be late," he said.

"Want me to come along?" she asked anxious, in his troubled mood, to offer whatever comfort her presence could lend.

"No, honey, I don't think so. I've got to see some men, and I may be later than I think."

And it was later than he thought. His meeting in the board room at the Wynn National Building with the directors of Wynn Enterprises went on until one o'clock in the morning and accomplished, Wynn reflected when he arrived home and thoughtfully swallowed a double shot of Jack Daniel before retiring to a largely sleepless night, accomplished almost exactly nothing. This was unusual, for the Wynn directorates were occupied by ninety-five percent of the most substantial, wealthiest and strongest citizens of Wynnsboro. They were confident men, sure of position and power and accustomed to getting things down. But not this time.

"Can't he be talked to?" George Abernathy, who was president of the Wynn Assurance Society, asked at large, frowning. "Christ's sake, the man must have a brain. He ought to know nobody wants him here . . . not even the niggers."

"I talked to him . . . when he was here before," Wynn said. "He's not a man you can persuade."

"How about buying him off. A couple thousand, even ten if he's greedy. Hell, it would be cheap at the price," said Harold Ross, cashier of the Wynn National Bank.

"I doubt if there's enough money in town to buy him," Wynn said heavily. "Not his kind of coin, anyhow. I came away with the feeling that that one is not for sale."

"Who the hell does he think he is? Jesus Christ?" Ross exploded.

Wynn smiled a thin and wintry smile. "You might be closer than you think," he said.

"Break his damn legs," snapped Gabriel Jardine, managing director of Wynn Textiles. "That ought to persuade him."

"That's a little unrealistic, don't you think," Abernathy protested. "After all . . ."

"Wouldn't be the first time," Jardine muttered. "Don't we have the guts? Or if we don't, we're sure capable of finding somebody who has."

"Some men are hard to convince," Wynn said. "After the girl was killed, I hoped the niggers would convince him this wasn't the place for him. Looks like they didn't, and, to tell the truth, I'm not surprised. That man has a fire in his belly."

"We will, too," Ross said, "if we let him get away with this swindle. Wynnsboro can't afford that kind of a sonofabitching foul up."

"And that's the only thing we're sure of," Wynn said, rising at the head of the long, gleaming table. "We've still got a week, Dowdy says. We're not getting anywhere except madder here. Give it thought, gentlemen . . . a lot of thought. You're right, Harold, we can't afford him . . . and that boils down to one thing: If we can't afford him, we can't tolerate him."

9

Carver Otis Barton had told Jeff Stuart that he did not enjoy the thought of going back to Wynnsboro. So saying, he understated the case. The larger truth was that he dreaded going back.

It was not, he reflected, that he was intimidated by knowing that white Wynnsboro was hostile to his purposes nor even that much of black Wynnsboro held serious doubts about them. He was used to both white hostility and black reservations and had never hesitated to confront them.

But, for some reason not clear to him, he was haunted by the memory of Lucy Clagget's mouth, wide open in the agony of her scream, just as the bulldozer made its mortal skid across her body. She had been chained to him. Not quite comprehending a wish for absolution, he sought some comfort in the memory that he had used that very chain to try to save her life, and he might have succeeded had he had better footing on the rain-greased clay slope. But the fact remained indelible that he had taken her there and that she had been, in fact, chained to him, a prisoner, unable to save herself. All right, she was merely a victim of terrible circumstance; the world was full of them. The trouble was that an unforgiving crevice of his thought kept reminding him that he had been the circumstance and there was no avenue of evasion around that.

He had glibly asserted to Amos Wynn the proposition of every military commander since Genghis Khan that the creation of omelets entailed the inevitable destruction of eggs. It was true, of course, and if you were in the business of making omelets, you had to subscribe to it as an article of faith. The one difficulty was that, unless you happened to be one of those rare savages who got an orgasmic glory out of carnage, you had to remember now and then that those who got elected to the role of egg seldom were invited to cast the deciding vote or were offered an option to recant just before the frail shell cracked down on the rim of the skillet.

She had looked so fragile, he remembered, and so godawful scared, the poor brave little sacrificial believer.

After Chicago, he decided to grant himself respite before again committing himself physically to Wynnsboro. *I can think up an excuse of sorts,* he told himself, ruefully inspecting his face in the mirror; *the cop that slugged me on Michigan Avenue left a fair-sized dent in this old black skull. There's no real urgency about advertising to the souls in that backwoods town that this game is sometimes played rough. Although I imagine they've got some dim idea,* he remembered, seeing Lucy's face once more.

He returned to New York and three of his ubiquitous bodyguards met his flight at Kennedy International. Left to himself in relatively private moments when he wasn't working at proving his case against the white world, he would have preferred the obscurity and privacy of airport limousines and taxis. But these, as he knew, were jealous men and by habit fearful for his life. They got a kind of fierce spiritual sustenance out of a self-appointed responsibility for seeing that nothing untoward happened to his person and he knew that demonstrations of independence on his part could send them into the sulks. But he was fond of them as men, understood their truculent loyalty and did not quite escape a sly secret pride in the value they placed upon his head. So he rode obediently in the Cadillac and was never quite sure how they had raised the money to replace its factory-installed windows with bulletproof glass.

All the same, he promised himself, *this private army is going to have to stay behind when I go back to Wynnsboro. They won't like it; if there's anything they hate worse than white cops, it's being left out of the action. But Wynnsboro's special and it's touchy. Whatever gets done there has to be done with a lot less bandwagon than works in a place like a Harlem school district. I can imagine how Wynnsboro, white or black, would react to this bunch, all duded up in their Afros, and whiskers and black specs and amulets and beads and God knows what all. I'm probably pretty strange to take, myself; in fact I know I am. But this bunch? Whoa, dad. Not in Wynnsboro.*

The Cadillac deposited him in front of the house. It was a quiet, tree-shaded forty-five-thousand dollars' worth of field-stone and gray shingle shakes, and it was all right so long as Barton's family stayed within their own tall screen of hemlock hedge. Four years after buying the place, Barton understood that anything beyond the hemlocks in that neighborhood was, if not actively hostile, still not friendly country.

Because he valued his family's relative peace of mind, the bodyguards were not encouraged to frequent the place and, understanding this, they did not resent their exclusion.

"You cats make the neighbors nervous," Barton had explained to the disciples. "For me, it doesn't matter. For my wife, it could. Anyhow, there's nothing for you to do around here. Nobody's about to bomb the place. Anyhow, when I'm here I'm not working. OK?"

The disciples privately thought that Barton had been out of his mind to have invaded enemy country to establish his castle keep, although, in this opinion, they did not taint him with the invidious brush of house nigger. His record on the firing line in the confrontation of the races bore no trace of the Uncle Tom; quite the contrary and they knew it. Privately Barton admitted to himself that his, by stealth, establishing himself in hitherto exclusively white territory had been mainly just to prove he could, in the first flush of success after the school struggle.

Later, he hadn't been so sure. It had been, he admitted to himself, a lonely time for Marian Barton. If what he had sought for her in the suburb was secluded privacy, the years had demonstrated that was about the most she was going to get from her neighbors.

Marian met him at the door and kissed him and took his bag and then peered more closely at his face, as concern and a kind of fright came into her own.

"Darling! What happened?"

"Oh, this." He grinned and put an exploratory finger to his swollen temple. "I just happened to get in the way of one of the mayor's nigger-knocking cops."

"Not again!" She was aghast. "I thought you promised to be careful there."

"Honey, I was," he said solemnly. "Well, almost careful. I made the mistake of doing some innocent rubbernecking along with a white man when the cops had their hands full of white kids. Not too full, unfortunately, to take time out to tap me a little."

"It's plenty bad enough—and all the time—without you taking chances you don't have to take," she said. The warning was somber—and familiar.

Marian Barton, now nearing the forties, was a quiet, reserved woman and she would have preferred to be placid of spirit if her husband's occupation had permitted that luxury. They had met while he was in Harvard and she was one of the few resident black women students at Radcliffe, conscious that if she was a student by her own appraisal she was almost more an exhibit by the school's. In her undergraduate days Eastern women's schools still preferred to find their colored students, for the most part, in more far away and exotic places than among the native-born population.

And so she had married the confident young lawyer and life

had developed in fair prosperity, about the way she had thought it might until he had discovered that their son's academic standing was in sorry shape and had set out to remedy matters by forcing the white world to pump a better education into him. Now, she sometimes thought in awe, Carver Otis had turned into a kind of new-century Nat Turner, equally turned on by abrading convictions of injustice but with his vision turned toward more modern methods than the mystic whisperings of a vengeful Lord.

"How about a drink?" Barton asked, easing himself out of jacket and tie and hanging them on the convenience of the newel post at the foot of the stairway to the second floor. "And where's the mail and where's Cary?"

"One at a time, boss," Marian said, smiling. "I'll get your drink. Scotch?"

"With a little ice, hon. The twelve-year-old."

"The mail's on your desk. About two days reading, I should think." She turned toward the kitchen.

"And Cary?" Barton called.

"He said football practice," she said over her shoulder.

"Too doggone hot for football," Barton muttered and went to the small room off the hall which he called his office and scooped up the neatly piled stack of envelopes and looked at it distrustfully.

Half bills and half yells for help and, *to tell the truth, there's not a whole lot of difference,* he thought, carrying the stack into the living room and sinking into a chair where he deposited the load on his lap. *If I was the usual suburbanite, life would be a lot simpler; it would be ninety percent bills. There's a way to deal with those.*

His wife came back and put down a glass, pale amber and tinkling with the ice cubes, on the lamp table at his elbow.

"Thanks, hon," he said, reached for the glass, changed his mind and got up and carried the mail back toward the office. "Pleasure before business," he said. "I'm bushed; I'll read this stuff tonight—or tomorrow.

"What's the idea—football practice? It's the middle of the summer," he said, returning and picking up the glass.

"School opens in two weeks," she reminded him. "He said the coach wants to get things started."

"That kid," Barton said fondly. "He's found whatever it takes. I wish I knew the formula. And I'd like to think he's a genius, but I suspect he only found out what's inside the covers of a book because he also found out if you want to play football you've got to stay eligible."

"Whatever it is, don't complain about it," Marian said. "At least when you're on the first team other people speak to you, no matter what your complexion is."

Barton looked at her sharply, thinking here it is again, feeling the old helpless hurt for her, instinctively half-resenting her for letting herself be hurt because he was helpless to do anything about it, at the same time ashamed of the resentment. But she was safe, she lived in physical comfort and security and a lot of people didn't, and he wished she understood that there were limits to what a man could accomplish. And that thought shamed him, too, because a man should be able to do something about everything that hurt anybody he was supposed to protect. And she probably did understand; in fact, he knew she did and it wasn't her fault that she, in a smaller and less final way, stood condemned to sacrifice as Lucy Clagget had.

"How're things around here?" he asked, keeping his voice light, trying to pretend that he was any other husband home from a business trip, knowing the pretense was absurd. Whatever he was, he wasn't that.

"Nothing's different," she said wearily. And then, for perhaps the thousandth time she reminded herself that it wasn't his fault he was what he was and couldn't help doing what he did. And he was generous and kind and he had given her and Cary everything it was possible for him to give. One man, alone, couldn't change the world or make it generous and understanding, even for his own family. God knows he had tried.

Only . . . she wished . . . she wished . . . oh, Lord, she wished things didn't have to be this way.

"It's all right, darling," she said. "You don't feel hate, not exactly. You just feel that nobody sees you. It's like being invisible."

"I know, hon," he said. "And I don't know when it's going to get different . . . if ever. The trouble for our kind of people is that we've got a life sentence. It doesn't matter whether we like it. We were born to keep pushing."

"You were," she said, a slight reluctant edge in her voice. "Sometimes, darling, I'm not sure I have the stomach for it."

"It might be worse if I wasn't," he said shortly, now with an edge in his own tone. "There are people worse off."

"Yes, but not caught in a nowhere," she said. And she smiled a thin smile. "Doesn't it ever strike you as odd? Guests at the White House, guests of half a dozen Prime Ministers, you invited to speak to the United Nations? And nobody on this block ever has spoken to either of us. In fact, nobody on the whole street ever has spoken to us except the milkman, the meter readers, and the TV repairman."

"Maybe they don't know how good we are at conversation," he said in a feeble effort at jocularity. "Now if we could just persuade a few good Northern liberal Senators and a few African Prime Ministers to move in."

She got up suddenly and came across the room and sat on the arm of the chair and leaned against him.

"Hey," he said, "you're jostling my drink."

"Darling, why can't you quit and go back to your practice?" she said. "You've done enough, more than any other man, more than anybody can ask or expect. It's too much. It's taking your whole life. Away from me, away from Cary. Away from yourself. One man can't do it all."

"Look, hon," he said gently. "I'm not one man. I'm not alone. They're cracking. Even in the South they're cracking. I'm not alone. It's a whole generation. And I know it's rough, but if we take the pressure off, even relax it, everything will slide back to where it was. We can't stop."

"All this hate," she said. "All around us, all around you." He felt the weight of her against him, heavier, as she leaned farther, her head down against the top of his. He felt a drop of heat and moisture and then more and knew that she was crying. "You'll get hurt," she said, "or killed. Oh, darling, quit! Stop now!"

Suddenly, unwillingly, he was angry. Twisting her weight away with a shrug, he stood up, took his empty glass and started for the kitchen. When he returned with his drink refilled, she was huddled in the chair sideways with her arms crossed on the chair arms and her head hidden. He could see her shoulders heave. She was crying without sound, and he felt inexpressibly grief-stricken and, illogically, still angry.

"Marian," he said harshly. "You can't do this . . . every time I come home. You've got to see, you can't. This isn't any fun for anybody, but it can't be turned off like a damn light switch. It's our life, your own life, your kid's life, the life of every poor black sonofabitch in this country."

She did not answer nor did the shoulders stop their slow, agonized shudder. *I can't take this,* he thought, and wheeled and walked back through the house and out through the glass playroom doors and settled heavily onto a cushioned aluminum lounge on the flagstone terrace. *Women!* he thought. *If they had their way, the world would never in God's world move off dead center.*

Simultaneously he felt the grinding weight of his anger, the weight of its injustice and the weight of regret that he had let it come untied. It wasn't her fault; women were conservators; they couldn't help that and they couldn't see, with a man, that in order to have something worth conserving somebody first had to go out and drag it home by the tail. He knew she recoiled from the burden of loneliness, bitter suspicion, fear and naked hatred spawned, like poisonous mushrooms, from the work he did. What she did not know was that he did, too.

It had not been that way in the beginning. At first, in the case of his hometown schools, he had attacked in a kind of exalted outrage. Then, having won, it was for a long time almost fun, a game of proving that it was possible, with enough guts, to uproot the entrenched and to witness the astonishment and, yes, fear of an impregnable enemy brought down. But the weight grew on you. Man was put together as a competitive animal but there came a time of weariness, the sense of mind and sinew exhausted by a struggle that never gave quarter and opponents that, having been beaten, waited only for an opportunity to stamp you back into the muck.

He did not often admit it to himself and never to his wife, but, yes, he was sick of it, sick to the bottom of his soul. Sick of the cost, sick of having to remember the Lucy Claggets. But where, in the name of God, was there a place to say stop, enough, I've done all my spirit and body will bear? Somebody else take it from here. There was no such place.

And so he would go back to Wynnsboro and, he knew after Wynnsboro there would be another Wynnsboro, and another, and another.

"In my business," he had told Stuart, "you don't not go back." And that was about the size of it.

"You'll get hurt," she had said, ". . . or killed."

Well, hell, he had always known that. Not at first, perhaps, or at least he hadn't consciously thought of it. It had been too stimulating then, too exciting, heady stuff. And, in winning, you felt a powerful surge of vitality, impregnability perhaps, a kind of delight in combat, the sense that you were a winner, the absolute inner conviction that you would always roll naturals and never crap out. But that kind of adrenalin in the soul couldn't be asked to run full freshet forever.

Threats, he could truthfully say, had never bothered him half as much as they had worried that bunch of dedicated bodyguards. And Marian had never been told about the threats un-less, despite his prohibition against worrying her, somebody else had blabbed.

All the same no mature man in his right mind got through life without recognizing his mortality and speculating, in con-templative moments, upon the manner and time and place of its arrival. He knew he had.

And he could say truthfully, he thought, that he did not fear death. That was true. It was also true of course, he admitted, there were ways and times it could come which he would prefer to avoid. He wouldn't want to be dragged through a mire of pain that unmanned his spirit and he wouldn't want it to come tomorrow if it could sensibly be avoided. After all he was still full of juice.

But in these morbid considerations, he reflected, he held a certain small advantage over most men. He had been almost there once on the trail out of Changjin when the bullet had gone through his neck including the carotid artery. He had been even more full of juice then, full of all the sap of being twenty years old—and he had looked the proposition in the face and felt some awe, yes, and some regret, but no terror. Only a vast concentrated curiosity to stay conscious until it all went out.

But he was sensible and sensible of his obligations. He felt a sense of security and gratitude and comfort in knowing that that quarter million dollars in life insurance meant that, what-ever her fears, Marian would never be going back to the slums.

10

In his teens, Peter Higgins had been the victim of a recurrent nightmare so overwhelming that sometimes, when some other sense warned him of its loom, he would wage a despairing battle against sleep—and would lose and, once more, be swept into the horror. The weird part of it was that, in the midst of it, he would know it was only a nightmare and that, sooner or later, he would wake up. But knowing was one thing, believing quite another. Sometimes the grip of the dream set itself upon him so powerfully that even after he had gasped himself awake he could not believe that he had escaped.

The dream that haunted him was that he had slain another human being. He did not dream the act itself, nor even how it had been done. He would only know in the fever that the deed had been done and that he had done it. Sometimes he would fight to absolve himself by manufacturing a collateral vision that somebody else had done it. The attempt was foolish, and he knew it, for the nightmare would never accept a scapegoat.

It always took him into the depths of a quaking regret, not remorse, for the dream never spelled out the identity of his victim. All it told him was that he had killed and that he must now struggle to escape the consequences. But, bound fast, he would know that no escape was possible. No matter how he might twist and dodge and lie and claw for an alibi, his mind would know it was all transparent. And, caught, he would be dragged to retribution.

He experienced that punishment only in anticipation, for the nightmare never carried him to the point of actual capture. Sometimes he almost wished that the dream would run itself to its conclusion before he woke up so that he might get through the hanging or the electrocution or being drawn and quartered and reach the refuge of oblivion beyond it. But the dream never granted him that mercy, if mercy it was. But he was sure that quailing from it must be even worse than enduring it.

Now the dream was come upon him real, in this day, in this hour. He was here to kill a man. Without warning, nausea swept up into his throat. He let go of the shotgun. It clattered against the wall and slid to the stone floor with a clanging thud. He grabbed and missed and stood with his heart hammering, certain that the noise must have been heard, though he knew it could not have been. He was sick, cold, and sweating.

He remembered something he had forgotten and, though it was a simple thing, the oversight compounded his terror. The jacket, that wretched thing that had disguised his disguise which in turn stood for his best hope of safety. He wrenched himself out of the red and green sports jacket bought for him for this purpose by some emissary he had never known and would never know. It had, it was to be hoped, effectively camouflaged the blue trousers, the gray shirt, and the gold and crimson shoulder patch of the Wynnsboro traffic police. If he had been noticed, God forbid, he would not have been taken for a police officer—which he was not—but was intended to resemble one if anybody noticed him from this point forward.

What he would do, he had been told, would bring police in hordes. He would be one of them, one of many, no more blamable than any other man in uniform.

But he knew he had to look like one and was afraid he did not. And indeed, he did not in these dragging moments. The gray shirt was wet and stained dark halfway from his armpits to the belt. His long and thick brown hair, in whose appearance he had always taken pride, was wildly tousled from the times he had dragged sweating hands through it. Peter Higgins was too near collapse to recognize how near he was. He only knew that he was here in this impossible place—and could not get away.

It was not the vision of the man he was to kill that racked him. Beyond seeing him on television news shows in a prison day room he knew nothing of the prescribed victim. The identification pictures he had been shown—to insure against mistake—brought the man no closer to reality. The other man, as a man, did not create his present agony. It was what the nightmare of childhood had done to him, the utter conviction that a murder done by him could not be hidden and that now he would have to live the dream through to its end.

It was unbelievable. But he was here in this dank gloom, in a cemetery, behind a bronze door, with a gun, with sentence already pronounced on him, face to face with the doom that he had been taught in sleep had to be his.

He was here to kill the man, and he knew he would kill him. There was no escape from knowing it, scurry as his nerves might trying not to believe. He had to kill him. The price of not killing him would be himself killed.

He hated Gervase with helpless loathing. And the worst of it was the helplessness. Gervase, in this moment, he could gladly wish dead, though he knew he could not, out of his own will, do it himself. Gervase, he knew as a certainty, simply would not permit that kind of disobedience.

It did not occur to him to marvel that Gervase had trapped him. Most of his life he had expected to be trapped and more often than otherwise the expectation had come true. He had learned long since that he was one of those born to be wrong—and to be caught at it.

Peter Higgins—that was his real name though he had used so many others that reality no longer seemed much different from alias—had drifted into Wynnsboro three years before on the run from an aggravated rape conviction in Kentucky. He had won the shaky perquisite of a fugitive by mousetrapping his unwary keeper while awaiting sentence in a leaky country jail. He was both broke and scared—chronic conditions with him— and yearned with all his soul to keep running. But he had to eat, and when he had slunk into one of Joe Gervase's roadhouse saloons on the edge of the city to beg a handout, the bartender had moved to throw him out. But he had relented and put him to mopping the floor and cleaning an unkempt toilet. It was humiliating work but really no worse than the jobs he had been required to perform in the jails in which he had spent a third of his forty years. Higgins had been a misfit so long and so abjectly that he expected nothing better.

Gervase noticed him one day when he came to the saloon to cast an eye on things and check the take from the slots in the back rooms. Gervase made it a rule of his professional life not to trust anybody and to be suspicious of any circumstance until it was proved either useful or harmless—both if possible. He called the bartender into the small office off the back room.

"Who's the punk?" he asked. Heavy and slow moving and big in the belly, Gervase looked placid and harmless until attention was paid to his quiet eyes. They were unwinking, expressionless, and, the bartender always thought, menacing. Mean as a snake, he had told himself.

"He came in. Hungry, dirty, hangdog," the bartender said. "The last one had taken off and we needed a swabby, so I put him to work. Probably won't last. They never do."

"He looks scared. You can smell it."

"There's that," the bartender said thoughtfully. "I don't know if he's too bright. But he keeps his mouth shut, don't raid the bar, and he does what he's told. Fact, I think he's on the lam."

"What makes you think so?"

"He's got no social security card . . . and he's jumpy . . . like now."

"We'll see," Gervase said.

Gervase got it out of Higgins. Not easily by any means, but Gervase was an impossible man to lie to. Better men had found it impossible to stand up to the understated menace contained in him. Driven by it, Higgins retreated, lied, was cornered . . . and confessed.

"So? Rape? And assault?" Gervase said out of wooden calm. "What'd the judge hand you?"

"I don't know. I left before he did it. The DA was hollering for life and the way the judge'd acted all through the trial I wouldn't have been surprised."

"Neither would I. In Kentucky. White woman?"

"Yeah, she was white. But no count white," Higgins said in feeble defense, not counting on it for much help. "You going to send me back? Please, I'll . . ."

Abruptly Gervase made up his mind. He could not yet see how, but it seemed likely that this one—with his built-in social vulnerability—could be useful. It wouldn't hurt to see. It was the virtue of the scared and helpless; they couldn't talk back and they couldn't refuse.

"Stick around," he said. "I'll see you ain't bothered—so long as you do what you're told, keep your nose clean, and keep your trap shut."

"How . . ." Higgins began to ask and dreaded asking and had no confidence in refuge in any case. But he was helpless not to ask; Gervase, he dimly understood, now held him between thumb and fingertip and he cursed himself for caving in. *I should of run,* he told himself bitterly.

"In this town I do what I want," Gervase said coldly. "Or put it another way; this town does what I want. Just don't give me cause to regret it. It'll freeze your balls how fast you're back in that Kentucky jail."

"God! Thanks!" Higgins gasped. "It scares a man shitless— like me—run out of chances." He was feeling something which might have been gratitude if that emotion had not been impossible to him.

"Forget it. You'll earn your keep. And you'll earn every day you're out of jail."

And so Peter Higgins became a bond servant in Giuseppe

Gervase's vineyard, forever in jeopardy. He learned his duties and performed them with humble efficiency. His were small jobs, generally sordid, required by Gervase's multiple business interests. He tended bar when he was needed in one or another of Gervase's establishments. More regularly he was sent to make the collections from the slots. The sight and heft of all that money made him sick with hunger and dreams of freedom. But he never tried to hold out so much as a nickel; that, he knew, would take more courage than he could spare. Four times, in the three years, he was called upon to drive a pickup truck at night to the lake a dozen miles beyond the city limits where others of Gervase's servants—voiceless and to him un-recognizable—disposed of burdens which, in the little he glimpsed of them, seemed heavy, awkward, and bundled in shapeless wrapping. He desperately wanted not to know what the bundles contained. Even the thought of guessing left him in icy sweat.

On a few occasions he was directed to discipline unruly whores. Gervase disliked being inconvenienced by fractious em-ployees. Higgins did not really like the idea of beating a woman, but the assignment did have certain terminal satisfac-tions when, having got the girl into a suitably contrite frame of mind, he could take out his distress between her remorseful thighs.

Gervase never gave Higgins anything really dangerous to do —like the truck runs to Detroit, Chicago, and New Orleans. It was not compassion that spared him; Gervase recognized that anywhere across a state line or even much beyond the city lim-its of Wynnsboro rendered Higgins a danger to him, as well as to himself.

And so, when the blow did fall, Higgins could not believe what had happened to him. He did not really believe it even yet, here in the cemetery, behind a bronze door, in a police uni-form, with a shotgun. And, indeed, Gervase had not nominated him to this horror without hesitation. He could have preferred a stouter vessel, for Higgins' fundamental lack of spine was no secret to him. He knew that killing in cold blood required a certain amount of resolution and even a taste for it and he could have called upon men he knew who owned these qualities, which Peter Higgins did not.

But he chose Higgins because, first, the man could not refuse and, second, he would not dare fail once he understood the penalty for failure. And it was not ignored by Gervase that Higgins would cost less, for Gervase was, in his heart of hearts, a thrifty man. Moreover, he had confidence in his operations plan which was, he reflected, a little complex but foolproof. Foolproof if Higgins didn't panic and screw it up somewhere along the line. If he did, it was still foolproof; as for Higgins, well what of Higgins? He shrugged.

"Don't be stupid," he told his thunderstruck servant. "You're not, repeat not, going to get caught. It's greased all the way, from start to finish. You'll have money, identity, a passport, a clean bill. You can start over, home free."

"But . . ." Higgins began, forced to give tongue by the cloud of sheer dread now descended on him.

"But nuts. Just don't fuck it up. Now listen, I'll go over it again."

And so now, with the hopefully unidentifiable sixteen-gauge Winchester automatic lying on the stone floor at his feet, Peter Higgins was waiting where Gervase had arranged for him to wait to do Gervase's bidding. The place did nothing to soothe him for it was cold with a chill ancient and oppressive. The obvious truth, as Gervase had taken care to impress on him, that this was an ideal ambush did nothing to assuage Higgins' dread. He knew that nothing less than Gervase's steel will could have forced him to jimmy the bronze door the night before and now wait here in this dusty mausoleum, generations more enduring than the proud planter's family who had erected it before the Civil War. Higgins' recurrent shudder was nothing he could control.

Beyond the door, he knew, lay a short downward slope of unmowed grass, blotched with plantain and dandelion, to its verge against the rusted iron of the cemetery picket fence. The pickets were planted in the top course of a granite retaining wall whose bottom stones, four feet below the cemetery level, were flush with the sidewalk of Myrtle Avenue, the main thoroughfare leading out of Angel Creek and into the white regions of Wynnsboro.

Once more, for a time grown countless, Higgins lifted his wrist and stared at the illuminated dial of his watch. Three twenty-five. Pretty soon he would have to force himself to the necessity of opening the door. He shuddered again and did not know how he could do it, but the time was almost upon him and he knew he had to do it. He knelt and got the shotgun and, fumbling, got the safety clicked to off. He stared at the watch again. Three twenty-six. Any minute now the niggers would be coming out of Angel Creek and in the lead would be the man he had to kill.

He was beyond thinking about it now, trembling on the taut high wire of desperation over the abyss of his despair. In the days before this moment he had longed for the impossible boon of hating the man he had to kill. But even that little help was beyond his reach. Peter Higgins in an inchoate way hated the world that had given him birth and never let him stop suffering for being alive. But he lacked the passion to hate any one living being in it, except for that new and helpless loathing for Gervase.

He disliked niggers and held their color contemptible and beneath his station, but he had born with that vague conviction and there was no real heat in it. It was merely the way you were if you were white. Once in the Cook County jail on a bad check charge when he was just out of his teens, he had thought briefly that he would learn to hate. It had begun the night a half-dozen colored prisoners had cornered him in the dormitory washroom, forced him to kneel head down into a toilet bowl, ignoring the moans of his humiliation, calmly raped him six times. Having done that, they hammered at him again until, in dumb obedience, he mouthed them one by one.

He had wished that the earth would open. It failed to oblige him. But the word, as it had to, got around that corrupted jail and within weeks he was serving a regular custom of the arsonists, rapists, drunk drivers, burglars, con men, killers and wife beaters who made up the dormitory population. Cook County, not having cells enough for its malefactors, practiced communal living. It had come to him at last, in blinding astonishment, that he had learned to enjoy his immolation.

Just across the undefined border of Angel Creek, which anybody who lived there knew exactly by the condition of the street if nothing else, Carver Otis Barton had marshaled his demonstration.

It was less impressive than he could have hoped, but he was satisfied. A thousand, he reflected. No, to be honest with himself at least, nearer seven hundred. And mostly kids. But there were some from the public works department, including Cal Eppers whose conscience would not let him up after letting the bulldozer slide on that ramp. That had been the day of revelation for Eppers; he would not again let a white man, a fool white man, shove him beyond the bounds of reason.

"When we cross over," Barton told his parade marshalls, gathered loosely around him at the head of the small throng, "there'll be the whites. Not important people. The bums, the red-necks, the bottom of the town. They don't matter. They don't make the decisions. They make the noise, that's all.

"Don't yell back. Don't throw anything back. Five across and keep your arms linked and—if you can, which I doubt, keep in step. You hang onto each other and you're a little less likely to get mad or scared.

"This girl," he said, gently touching the shoulder of sixteen-year-old Audrey Clagget who stood beside him, wearing a look caught somewhere between pride and panic, "will be with me. They know her. She gave her sister to this."

"Let's see we don't give her," Eppers muttered.

"What we're going to give her is a college education," Barton said. "Let's go. And let's keep it dignified . . . whatever."

The time was on Higgins. Beyond the bronze door he could hear the swell of human noise, a voiceless, almost toneless hubbub above the sounds of traffic. It was now. He went down on his knees and, for a moment, could not decide which hand to take from the shotgun to push against the door. He pressed his forehead against the metal and willed himself to lean forward and the door budged. The creak of the hinges ran across his nerves, a saw blade.

He had earlier, while still in some possession of his faculties, thanked God that the door was hinged on the left so that, opening, the aperture would face toward Angel Creek. The target would be coming from that direction, leading the march into white Wynnsboro. He would not need to expose himself; he could do the job with the door cracked only enough to get the shotgun muzzle out and give him vision.

He could not see his side of the street below the wall but on the other he was conscious of police spaced along the curb facing into the street and behind them a smattering of whites. The whites were yelling; that would take attention from him as Gervase had said it would.

Through the pickets he could see them coming. They were fifty yards away, moving ahead, arms linked, five abreast. Long afterward he remembered that they were silent, looking straight ahead, refusing to acknowledge anything other than themselves.

They were closer and now he recognized the man. He knew the face, but he would have known anyhow for Gervase had told him the man would be wearing some kind of crazy jungle cape or whatever. Like neon, he thought.

Barton marched in front, in a row of five. At his left, nearer Higgins, his arm was linked into the elbow of a girl, maybe a teen-ager, and *what in all the hell is she doing there,* Higgins thought. The girl, of all the goofy things, was skipping. On Barton's right, also with elbows linked marched an adult man. Higgins did not know him.

They were twenty yards away and Higgins knew he would have to do what he had come to do before they came abreast. If he waited too long, the man in the cape would be closed off by those on either side.

Higgins got the gun up to his cheek and jerked at the trigger. He was not ready for the weapon's vicious kick and reeled from it, eyes jerked shut. When he could look again, the girl who had been beside Barton was down in the street and Barton was leaning down to her. Barton went down to his knees beside the girl. The cape was a brilliant blotch of red and purple above the girl's white dress. Higgins fired again and the man fell across the girl.

Higgins bolted. He did not know in that moment that he still carried the shotgun, dragging it by the barrel so that the stock banged along at his heels. He had been told what to do down to the last detail, but now he ran in blind panic.

Jeff Stuart could never afterward remember precisely how it was that he had seen Higgins go. Perhaps it was the noise and an instinct for the direction of the shots. He had been watching Barton come out of Angel Creek into the street, sunken on the other side below the level of the cemetery.

He had seen the girl go down and Barton drop beside her and then, with the second shot, he had raised his eyes and had seen the man in blue and gray break out of the mausoleum and crash away into the depths of the cemetery. The man was twenty yards away, not more, across the street and he had seen the wildly frantic face full on.

He jerked at the gun under his armpit, but the rushing figure was already gone among the headstones. Stuart ran into the street and knelt beside Barton, who had fallen back from the girl and lay twisted onto his right side. The cape, already colored fit for a funeral, was now awash with blood somewhere on the left and the stuff was pumping out. Stuart felt for the wound and found it and pressed his fingers deep into the flesh, hoping to stem the arterial pressure. It wasn't going to be much good, he thought, not much good at all.

Barton grunted, then yelled and twitched over onto his back and opened his eyes and looked up at him.

"Baby-sitter," he said.

"Don't talk," Stuart said.

"White man?" Barton asked.

Stuart was ready to answer but then remembered and shook his head.

"That's what I told you. Knocker and knockee. Just us souls."

11

Carver Otis Barton was truly dead, a lump on the neglected cobbles and streetcar tracks—never uprooted though they had not carried a trolley for twenty years—that took Myrtle Avenue over the frontier out of Angel Creek into white Wynnsboro. You don't need to wait for a coroner's report to know it, Jeff Stuart thought as he got up from his knees beside the two bodies, the man and the girl, the second innocent who had made the error of cleaving to the man from New Rochelle. He's dead, all right. And dead with him is that peculiar juju of his, whatever it was, that conjured black hearts to a kind of exalted savagery. The question now is what kind of legacy the juju left behind—if it left any. Looking down at the blooded huddle, he found it difficult to comprehend that all it stood for had been brought to an end so simply, so quickly, with such finality. Half-listening, he heard around him the stunned beginnings of human grief and shock, muted sobs, unbelieving moans and cries and a shattering feminine scream.

He turned away, slumping a little with a burden of weariness he would have found hard to define. He walked toward the frontier into Angel Creek. He had, without conscious thought, come to a decision. He had lost his man and here, standing over this lump, now ready for a silenced grave, there was nothing left to do or to be learned. Lost his man? There was no real truth or justice in that; he had been given Barton as something to study, to understand if he could. Protecting the specimen was no part of his duty; Barton himself had snorted at the idea of yet another bodyguard. Still, he was lost. Just or not just, Stuart felt an overpowering sense of failure.

The trouble was that his job had gone dead along with the beating of Barton's heart. Whatever was left to do, it seemed to him now, was almost total futility: the vain picking over and sorting out of a dead man's spiritual baggage. Had he left behind anything worth the effort of appraisal? He had carried a torch and called its flame his own; had its light gone clean out with his? In those moments it seemed to Stuart that the place to find out whether Barton had heirs or merely mourners was among the thousands in Angel Creek who had been, mostly with dragging feet, working up the nerve to follow him. The people who paid Stuart had wanted to know, first, what Barton was up to and with whom he was in cahoots and, second and more important for the long pull, what he really signified to those he had called his people.

There will, naturally, he thought with some bitterness, *be hell to pay for this. And, since I was present, Rembert may find it handy to let some of the hell slop over on me.* You could not let a man who had dined in honor with the President be gunned down on the street and not expect trouble to come. He wondered, as he had before, just what this flamboyant and arrogant man had meant to the young President who, to tell the truth, had a fund of flamboyance and arrogance in his own right. Had the two men been friends? Was that even possible when most of what the one represented threatened one way or another to alienate much of the electorate which had sent the other to the White House in the first place? He was pretty sure that part of the reasons which had taken Barton as a guest to the White House was a politician's intelligent curiosity to take the measure of things which caused him trouble in his job. There might well have been more to it than that, he thought; Whatever you might have thought of him you had to admit that Barton had been a compelling personality and, whatever you thought of the President, he was obviously more than a mere package of crafty expediency.

For that matter, he wondered, what did I think of Barton myself? I scarcely knew the man: looking at him from a distance, listening to him practice his witch doctor art, a couple of head-to-head talks and, of course, that little dust-up among the Chicago cops in Michigan Avenue. Scarcely the material for an intimate appraisal. He felt a sudden and completely unexpected stab of grief and loss. *Good Christ,* he thought in the amazement of revelation, *I'm going to miss him.* Cynical he may have been, cocky, chip on his shoulder, a cocksman proved (and who shall blame him for that?) but—it had to be recognized—all the same a soul on fire with conviction and more sheer physical guts than most men ever dreamed of. Like him? Who could like him? It could in time have come, he realized now in the sudden crystal glimpse of truth, to something akin to love for the outrageous bastard.

He wondered at the impulse which had led him, with Barton dying practically in his arms, to deny that the killer had been a white man. A futile, foolish, pointless thing to do, but what did it matter? Barton had made that almost gleeful point of blacks, in a time of growth and awareness, killing other blacks for motives loftier than mere back alley passion. He couldn't really have believed that Barton could get much comfort from the thought of being killed by a soul brother—but on the off chance that he could he had let him believe it. Why not?

For himself, he knew he would not forget the white and distorted face which had burst from the mausoleum twenty yards away. Nor the sight of that absurd, deadly figure bounding away among the tombstones, with the murder weapon ridiculously banging at his heels. And, he thought of it only now, hadn't the sonofabitch been in uniform? By God, he had! A cop! But Barton's killer a cop? And in uniform? Impossible! There could not be that much stupidity abroad in the world. He shook his head in disbelief. It was incredible. All the same he would not forget the face. Nor would he suffer it to escape.

He did not recognize it at once, but some alchemy was at work in the generally mild soul of Jeff Stuart. He had never been the hunter, the pursuer; he had been instead the lustless, standoffish bystander among the wolf pack with which he ran. But then he had never before stood by and watched a murder committed. But now, unbidden, there rose in his throat the sheer thirst for vengeance. He would get this one. He saw again, as though photographed on the retina of his mind, that white face, the dark panic-ridden eyes, even the tousled brown hair.

He was meeting people as he moved deeper into the dismal streets. They were few at first, some running, more walking, woodenly wearing faces gone blank, a few crying and all coming to meet him and going beyond, scarcely noticing him as they passed. Gradually they became more, and he saw that expression was coming into the faces with knowledge. Now their faces were set in anger and those who noticed him did so in enmity. *I guess I can't blame them a hell of a lot,* he thought.

He walked on and as he began to thread through humanity clotting the corner at Thirty-eighth Street he heard glass crashing and looked in time to see the last shards glittering down from the frame of a pawnshop storefront. The feel of rage was growing palpable.

In his preoccupation it had not occurred to him that he might stand as a catalyst to crystallize the inchoate passion accumulating in the street. It began to dawn on him at Fortieth Street when he came, of a sudden, against an obstacle. A man stood in front of him, feet apart, knees bent, staring at him out of malevolent eyes. He moved toward the curb to walk around the man who, he noted automatically, was burly but unsteady, grimacing but unfocused. The man lurched and was in front of him again.

"Where you goin', white man?" the interceptor asked.

"None of your business," Stuart said. "Get out of the way."

"Not so fuckin' fast, white man. Wha' you doin' here?"

"I told you. None of your damned business," Stuart said, moving this time toward the building line. The man moved with him and closed in and Stuart let him have one with the hatchet-edged palm of his left hand against the neck under the right ear and the man sagged and went down. Stuart stepped around him and walked on.

All right, he told himself, *you're learning something but I don't know what use it is. Barton's dead and they're upset about it and why wouldn't they be? But what's it prove, if anything?* The grief and outrage of partisans against the wanton destruction of heroes had been going on since man began, but what had it ever in history really accomplished or changed —except, of course, in the case of Christ. Christ's murder had changed the world ever since but any comparison had to be ridiculous; whatever he was, Barton had been no Christ. This had to be just another gut-wrenching but fruitless venting of futile rage and grief. What would it come to, what could it come to? Nothing. Given a cat's allotment of lives—even in fractions—Barton himself might have done something with it. But, without him, nobody was going to do much but get drunk and smash some store windows. *Grief,* he thought, *is the ultimate expression of man's helplessness, and his helplessness is his ultimate grief.*

He turned in at The Sudan where, this night, the gaudy neon

had gone unlit. He had some half-formed notion that, in an expedition which had to be fundamentally useless, he might as well talk to James Dowdy. He knew the saloonkeeper and Angel Creek's doyen but slightly. He had gone there once with Barton when Barton was seeking, but not getting much backing. He had no idea that Dowdy would have anything to offer, but at least he knew him and no other soul in Angel Creek unless he counted the stranger he had minutes ago left unconscious on the sidewalk.

One dim light burned behind the bar and only two people were in the room. One was the night bartender, almost invisible except for the white shirt with sleeves rolled above the elbows; the other, on a stool in front of the bar, Dowdy himself.

Stuart crossed to them and, though he could see little of their faces, was conscious that the two men had turned toward him. He was aware of tension as he crossed to Dowdy and stood close enough so that he knew Dowdy could see his face.

"Mr. Dowdy, I'm Stuart. FBI. You remember I was here with Barton?"

"Yes, I know," Dowdy said. "What can I do for you?"

"Probably nothing," Stuart said. "I was there when Barton was killed. I don't know; I thought I ought to see how people are taking it."

"That was foolish, Mr. Stuart," Dowdy said.

"Foolish? How?"

"Did you come in a car?" Dowdy asked, without answering.

"No. Walked," Stuart said.

Dowdy pulled himself erect on the stool and his voice was low and intense.

"Even more foolish, Mr. Stuart. How are you going to get out?"

"The way I came," Stuart said, suddenly irritated.

"You had better go then. Or maybe it would be wiser to call a police car to come get you."

"I don't need cops," Stuart said impatiently. "I'm able-bodied."

"I'm not positive anybody is able-bodied enough to get through tonight, Mr. Stuart," Dowdy said heavily.

"Oh, for God's sake," Stuart said.

"*HE* ain't likely to be around much," Dowdy said. "Look, Mr. Stuart, I'm serious. This going to be a bad night. You could stay here, but it wouldn't do either of us any good if a lot of drunks bust in and find you hiding out with me. I'd go and I'd go careful. Use the side streets. You'd better think again about me calling the police to get you."

"No," Stuart said. "I'll be all right."

And he really believed he would be.

12

Three days later, assembling the statistics from its bureaus east and west and north and south, the Associated Press distributed a box score, more or less accurate, on the carnage which flowed from the assassination of Carver Otis Barton.

The semifinal returns of tangible result—semifinal because the repercussions could never be circumscribed by any finite period of time and tangible because the intangibles bit deeper into the nation's soul and were impervious to measurement—came out thus: riots in seventy-nine American cities; property damage from burning, smashing, and looting, two hundred and thirty-one million dollars; cities to which the National Guard or federal troops were summoned, sixty-two; persons arrested, two thousand nine hundred and forty-six; persons hospitalized, one thousand four hundred and sixteen (those treated at the scene, at home or released after first aid in hospitals were not counted); persons killed, eighty-six, mostly blacks under twenty-five but including eight white policemen, one National Guard second lieutenant and three white youths who committed the foolhardiness of driving into the Oak Lawn ghetto of Chicago for backlash purposes and were incinerated in their own vehicle by a Molotov cocktail. Clearly Carver Otis Barton was a person of consequence, and he did not die either unmourned or unaccompanied.

Disorder in Wynnsboro may have been less wild and fierce than, for example, Detroit where the dead totted up to twenty-four, including an eleven-year-old girl whose demise provoked an additional dispute between the police and the black community so bitter that even more bloodshed appeared imminent. Nobody who would admit it had seen her die, but the blacks found all the evidence they really wanted in an autopsy report that the instrument of her death had been a slug from a .38 police special. But the police replied, reasonably enough, that their access to this particular weapon was not exclusive: Almost anybody could get one through the mail. They added in further support of official innocence that the child had been shot in the back which, they declared, was contrary to police practice.

But the trouble in Wynnsboro was bad enough considering the city's relatively small population of one hundred and eighty thousand and, even more, considering that the blacks who made up roughly a third of that number had only just that summer begun to unlearn the habit of ten generations of circumspect behavior.

According to the official police report which differed from the wildly various recollections of eyewitnesses, Barton had died at 4:14 P.M. and the burning had begun, in a kind of spontaneous combustion, two hours later in the gloom of dusk. The first fire broke out in a brick-fronted, frame building on Oak Street in Angel Creek. The building was leased by a Jewish merchant named Falstein who dealt in discount electrical appliances and did a large time-payment business among his clientele. The building was owned by Amos Wynn's real estate firm.

The men on the first fire department pumper to reach the scene encountered no opposition, but they were astonished to glimpse shadowy figures sprinting out of the burning store and others staggering along the street and into alleys, bent under the burdens of television sets and stereo hi-fi equipment. They did suffer some hindrance getting to the hydrant in front of the building because a pickup truck was backed to the curb there, tailgate down, while three men wrestled with the stubborn bulk and weight of a king-size refrigerator-freezer combination.

"Get that goddamn truck out of there!" the division chief squalled as he leaped from his red sedan drawn up alongside the stymied pumper.

Two men paid no attention as they continued to heave at the loot, but one turned a sweating dark face toward the chief and spoke equably.

"Take it easy, man. We leavin' in a minute." He was quite accurate for, just then, a misjudged heave by one of his colleagues sent the freezer crashing into the street. The speaker paused for a brief inspection and shook his head.

"It's a wreck," he said with no evident grief. "Let's go. Git the same thing over to Empire Discount."

"Don't that beat hell?" the chief said to himself as his men began laying out and coupling up hose. "What is this . . . anyhow?"

Later, as grief sank the iron deeper into the ghetto and found no better outlet than avarice and directionless hate, the firemen began to encounter more opposition than their familiar enemies of flame and smoke. Hoses were slashed and stones and brick came down on the firefighters from the roofs. Then the shooting began and one fireman took a slug thirty feet up on a ladder and fell dead on the sidewalk. Chief Melvin Davis called all his men and equipment out of Angel Creek.

"Let them burn themselves down," he told Amos Wynn in weary anger.

"Maybe we ought to, but we can't," Wynn said. "For now, keep your men out of danger, but close. We'll clear it for you."

Chief Davis looked at Wynn speculatively but without astonishment. Blazing a path for firemen was a police job, but he was accustomed to the thought that whatever of consequence was done in Wynnsboro was often the doing of Amos Wynn.

Amos Wynn had known Angel Creek all his life and well he should since he owned much of it. As owner, he felt a proprietary concern for its real estate, but—and he would have been hard put to define this—he felt just as much responsibility for the essential well being of its community of human beings. He would see to it that they were not cheated and this prohibition included their not cheating themselves, which was always a possibility when you had to contain the excesses of children.

Wynn had left his home and gone to the Wynnsboro's command center as soon as he knew what was breaking loose. He had his stetson set square across his brow and was heading for the jeep parked between the Cadillac and the Porsche in the carport when Amy came running up on the other side and climbed into the seat.

"Where do you think you're going?" he said.

"Along," Amy said.

"What for, girl, for Christ's sake?" Amos said, taken aback.

"Because I want to."

He grunted. "You're a woman."

"What's that supposed to mean?"

"It's supposed to mean you stay here. Out of the way."

"When I get in the way," Amy said doggedly, "I'll know it and I'll go and you won't have to tell me."

Amos, from long experience with his daughter, suspected he might be losing this one.

"I'm only going to city hall," he said.

"That's where I'm going."

"Godalmighty, girl, I still wear the pants in this family. I ain't in any wheelchair. When I am, God forbid, you can run things. Until then, kindly beg an old man's pardon."

"Hush up, pa. And start driving."

To Wynn it was a source of both pride and occasional despair that his only heir considered herself, in most ways, his equal. She fished with him and hunted with him, and she had killed a Kodiak bear in Alaska which he had not—he slightly but only now and then was resentfully embarrassed by the fact that she had had the skin dressed and tanned and backed for a rug on his study floor. Withal she indubitably was, as he had just reminded her, a woman and with graces whose eventual bestowal upon some man as yet unidentified fired him with prescient jealousy. She sure wasn't a son and by that token wasn't an equal. But, on the other hand . . . he sighed and stepped on the starter.

Now his city—their city, his and hers—was being cruelly mauled in a way that he could not have foreseen, had no way of anticipating. Amos Wynn was still a long way from acknowledging even to himself that Angel Creek could ever fumble its way into the danger of forgetting essential obedience to himself; he was an intelligent man, an observant one, in most ways a sensitive one, but the concept of Angel Creek's dependence on the Wynns had been handed down to him untarnished through seven generations which had never, until now, found any warrant to question themselves.

Now, here it was. There was yet no way of telling how far this might go, nor what direction it might take beyond aimless destruction and thievery. But, for now, the imperatives were clear. It had to be contained and extinguished. He left Fire Chief Davis, turned abruptly in the dark and dank old first floor hallway of city hall and strode toward the door lettered COMMISSIONER OF POLICE—PRIVATE. Silent, but watchful, his daughter was at his side—not behind him, beside him.

Arthur Mayhew sensed the loom of Wynn's great bulk, cradled the telephone into which he had until that moment been screaming, and stared at the two figures filling the door-

way. That damn girl, the thought popped into his mind unbidden, why in the name of all that's holy does she always have to
tag along? And her damn eyes, just like her old man's, boring
holes in you.

"Amos," he began. "Now they're . . ."

"I know they are," Wynn said shortly. "We should have seen
this coming. We didn't. You didn't. I didn't. Now we've got to
stop it. I want you to come with me . . . now."

"Where, Amos?"

"Where else? I want to talk to Jim Dowdy."

"Amos, you can't. Every street is blocked. On the outside by
us, on the inside by them."

"That's why I want you along. Your badge."

"Now, look, Amos . . . for God's sake, I got my hands full
here."

Mayhew was aware that Wynn's gray eyes were inspecting
him, that the inspection was calm and that, just under the surface of it, lay a stratum of contempt.

"Maybe you're right, Art," Wynn said without heat. "It
would be better to have a man with me. You're about as much
use as tits on a boar. Where's Kelley?"

"Amos, you hadn't ought to go in there." Mayhew's voice was
going shrill, and he knew it and hated knowing it. "They've
gone crazy."

"All right, they're crazy. Where's Kelley?"

Mayhew retreated. "On the way. Couple of prisoners."

"I'll go back with him."

"Look, Amos." Mayhew was pleading. "I don't think . . ."

"I know you don't, Art."

Damn the contained old sonofabitch, Mayhew thought in
private anger. *Damn the overlording bastard. Who did he
think he was anyhow?* Mayhew's problem was, in part, that
like it or not he did know who Wynn was and he knew that he
would always knuckle under.

Him on top of everything else and everything else was way
too much. Two hundred and twenty cops and a quarter of

those niggers and therefore unusable. And sixty thousand thiev-ing firebug maniacs to herd back into line.

Wynn had turned and was starting out, but then he wheeled and came back into the doorway, big hands on either jamb, leaning forward.

"You got anything yet on the other?"

"Wha . . . What other, Amos?"

"Oh, shit, Art. What other is there? The guy that killed him."

This, too, Mayhew shuddered. The whole city falling apart and he was supposed to be out baying after some unknown will-o'-the-wisp with a shotgun.

"We lost him . . . That is, if the one we thought might be him really was him. Then everything blew up. I've got two men on it. They think they got a line on the car. Amos, you know I can't spare any more."

"Clean away, eh?" Mayhew didn't have to look at that cast concrete face under the shadow of the stetson to know there would be a thin smile on the wide mouth. "Maybe he had a good idea what he'd be up against. You're going to have to put up a better show than that, Art. Else we'll have Washington on our necks."

"Maybe they were on our necks before it happened," May-hew said resentfully. "I didn't have a chance to tell you before. But we found out the Justice Department had a man with Bar-ton when he got here."

"They did, huh?" Wynn's eyes had narrowed and were now slits gimleting at his police commissioner. "Where is he?"

Mayhew spread his hands.

"Amos, I don't know . . . he's gone . . . somewhere. Hasn't been in his hotel since noon."

"Find him. And run him out."

"Amos, how in God's name do you think I can run the FBI out?"

"I don't know. That's your business. Do it."

Wynn and his daughter walked away. As they entered the

squad room, a slender, almost slight, cold-eyed man entered the outer door following two sweating, scared Negro youths hand-cuffed together. One held his right hand to a bleeding mouth and the other was reeling drunkenly.

"Take care of them, Butch," the slender man said to the officer at the desk.

"Right, Lieutenant. What's the charge?" the desk sergeant said.

"Doesn't matter. Forty-two ten. That'll hold them until I think of something better."

"Hello, Kelley," Wynn said.

Lieutenant Kelley turned toward the big older man. *He looks beat,* Amy thought, still listening, not liking the way things seemed to be going, feeling a slight cold shiver of dread.

"Oh. Hello, Mister Wynn," Kelley said. "We've got a mess, but I think we can handle it."

"I want you to take me to see Dowdy. Maybe he can help put a damper on it."

The lieutenant studied Wynn a moment before replying.

"I don't know, Mister Wynn. I'm not sure we can get there tonight. But maybe he could help . . . that is, if we can get to him. You sure you want to try?"

"You ready to go?"

"Soon as the car's gassed up. And I need a new tire. Some sonofabitch—oh, excuse me, Miss Wynn—used a knife on my left front."

While the tire was being changed, Amy Wynn decided that she had been quiet long enough and too submissive. She got her father aside in the graveled, floodlighted parking lot.

"Pa, you don't make sense," she said coldly. "If what they tell us is what's really going on, Dowdy can't do anything . . . not tonight certainly. You get the nutty idea that you're the only one that can do anything here . . ."

"Well?" Wynn said, looking down at her angry face and reflecting, in an unoccupied corner of his mind, that temper sat handsomely on his daughter. Today she blazed—which was a contrast, he remembered, to the tantrums of her childhood when she had merely squalled and kicked and turned bright red.

"You can't possibly do anything in Angel Creek except get yourself beat up—or killed."

"Who? Me?"

"Yes. You!" Amy felt like squalling and kicking. "If you go in there, I'm going with you."

Wynn looked down at her in monumental calm.

"You are not," he said. "I take more from you than I should, possibly because I'm fond of you, but there are limits and this is one of them. You take the jeep and go on home and I'll be there before long."

"I'll . . ." Amy began threateningly.

"No you won't. You'll do as I tell you."

Wynn's tone was even, and Amy had to recognize that it was inflexible now and she got ready to sputter and decided against it and snorted "Idiot!" and turned away and climbed into the jeep behind the wheel.

"Ready, Mister Wynn?" Kelley came up to ask and, at Wynn's nod, climbed behind the wheel of the squad car while Wynn jackknifed himself into the other seat. Before starting the engine Kelley leaned to the glove compartment and dropped a heavy pistol into Wynn's lap.

"Know how to use it?" he asked as he turned the key and the engine coughed and caught.

"Yes . . . But I don't particularly want it . . . I'm not hunting anybody," Wynn said.

"Hang onto it anyhow," Kelley said. "If you do need it, the glove compartment is going to be too far away." The car moved off.

Amy watched it go, swore aloud and half-decided to follow and then decided against it. *I am damned,* she swore to herself, *if I am going to let him wallop me right in front of that . . . that cop. Besides he's probably right; he's so used to the idea that nothing can touch him that everybody else believes it, too.*

Kelley drove carefully, stopping for red lights, leaving the car's siren silent and its red flashers turned off.

"You don't believe in advertising," Wynn said.

"Only when necessary."

"Quiet," Wynn mused as they drove westward through the city's business hub, passed under the railroad viaduct and moved on toward a flickering glow that said Angel Creek lay ahead.

"It'd be pretty quiet now anyhow. It's two A.M. or after. We slapped a curfew on around ten; it'll be six to six until we get this under control."

"Any trouble with whites?"

"Not since we sealed the streets. That was around eleven. Before that a few cars full of bone brains tried running in and out. We shagged 'em—not before one damn fool got himself killed."

"Who was he?"

"Fool kid. He had a shotgun and thought he was going to get some nigger meat, I guess. Instead they got his meat."

A flashlight flagged them down and Kelley flipped on the flashers and drew slowly up to a wooden sawhorse barricade. An officer stepped out of the dark and turned a flashlight beam on their faces.

"Oh. You, Lieutenant," the policeman said. "Who's that with you?"

"Mister Wynn," Kelley said. "Open up."

The barricade was moved aside and Kelley drove by, switched on the radio transmitter, and spoke quietly.

"This is Kelley, Car Twelve. Going to Dowdy's place on Myrtle."

"You alone, Lieutenant?" the speaker crackled.

"So far. But I want another car with me. How many inside now?"

"Fourteen. Byrnes had to come out; his partner got hurt. Jones and Allen are on foot; their car got burned."

"All right. Tell Gillen to pick me up at Myrtle and Twenty-seventh and follow from there."

"Right," the speaker acknowledged.

The cruiser rolled on slowly. They passed a store burning on their right. Now and then a swiftly furtive shadow moved along the sidewalk or ducked out of the beam of the cruiser's headlights.

"Not much down here," Kelley said. "Most of it's right in the guts of things around Thirty-eighth."

"What's it add up to?"

"Six blocks burning up there. More stores busted into. We've got, oh I guess a couple hundred locked up. Six cops hurt, none too bad."

At Twenty-seventh Avenue, Kelley brought his car to a careful stop in the middle of the street and turned on the flashers.

Suddenly, lightless and unseen out of the dark, a car roared by and a rock crashed through the left rear window and a high, hysterical voice came above the snarl of an unmuffled engine. Kelley sat impassive.

"Pretty wild," Wynn said.

"Yeah. They're upset."

Flashing red lights moved slowly toward them out of Twenty-seventh and a second squad car cut in behind them and stopped. Kelley slid from under the wheel and went back to the other car, returning in moments.

"OK," he said. "We go."

The two cars rolled up the street, sirens silent but the flashers now going. The sky ahead of them was redder and flames leaped and fell away. More people were visible now and Wynn was conscious, in the glow of fires, that the cruisers were being stared at from the sidewalk. The silence was eerie.

"They're not likely to start anything unless we shove into a crowd," Kelley said. "We might have to at Thirty-eighth. That's why I called Gillen in; one car could get hit; two and the chances they won't move are four times as good."

At Thirty-eighth, stores were burning on all four corners. A car lay overturned in the middle of the street, a police car, Wynn noted. The intersection was full of humanity and the deep-throated grumble of a thousand voices.

"This where we find out?" Wynn asked.

"Probably. If anywhere," Kelley said calmly. He slowed to a crawl, turned on the siren, and inched into the crowd. As the car crept ahead and the black faces staring in at the driver and his passenger slowly yielded, Wynn found himself musing back to the beginning of all this, Barton's first coming to his city and his undeniable impact upon it. But who in all hell would have thought he'd got this deep into them, a Northern nigger, a foreigner, a black carpetbagger? He had thought he knew these people, knew the compliance bred into their souls. Grief? Well, perhaps, but if it was grief they'd had to learn to love the man in a terrible hurry. Maybe it wasn't the man they loved, but some mysterious, racially forgotten quality they read into him. Anger? He knew that Wynnsboro blacks got angry like anybody else, but, by and large, they kept it under their belts. Or went out and got drunk and knocked up their wives again or anyone else they could get to spread her legs. But this mass outpouring. What had there been about Barton that could inspire this rupture of a pattern fixed for generations?

"Whitey! Goddamn murderer!" The faceless voice out of the throng was a squall of rage.

"We're about through," Kelley said. "Can you see if Gillen's coming?"

Wynn looked through the back window, now clouded by a spider-webbed splinter of safety glass where a rock had struck. Right behind them, almost bumper to bumper, giving the crowd no place to squeeze between and separate the cars he could see the repetitive burst of red light as the flasher revolved.

"He's there," he said.

"Good," Kelley grunted, then said, "We're out. Wasn't bad." Slowly the car picked up speed.

There were occasional fires on either side. The street was littered and figures could be dimly glimpsed frozen in doorways or moving against the brick walls, but there was no more interference. The two cars pulled to the curb before The Sudan, a white brick building with a darkened marquee over the sidewalk.

Wynn started to get out, but Kelley laid a restraining hand on his sleeve.

"Wait a minute, Mister Wynn. I want to talk to Gillen."

"For what?"

"Tell him I'm going in with you."

"That's not necessary."

"I think I'll go anyhow," the lieutenant said, getting out.

Kelley came back and Wynn got out and together they went to the dark doorway. Wynn fumbled for and found a bell push and pressed it. The door, on silent hinges, swung open against a dark interior and a controlled hard voice came at them out of the blackness.

"Who is it? What you want, man?"

"Police officers. Put on the lights," Kelley said crisply.

"Police?" The word was drawn out into what sounded like three syllables. "Didn't call no police here, man." The door began to swing toward them.

"Wait a minute," Wynn snapped. "Is Dowdy here?"

"Who Dowdy?"

"Never mind that. Tell Dowdy it's Amos Wynn." Wynn's voice was low but imperious.

"All right. Wait." This time the door swung all the way closed and the lock clicked loud in the stillness.

The door opened again and the same voice told them to follow. A pencil flash snapped on, turned downward against the floor and Wynn followed it, conscious of the scissoring movement of legs and feet against the light.

"He's in there." The light flashed on a doorknob. "Go on in. Light's on the right. Switch it when the door's closed."

Following Kelley, Wynn stepped through, feeling, rather

than hearing the door swing shut behind him. He heard the latch click.

"Dowdy?" Wynn called. There was no answer.

"Where's the damn light?" Kelley muttered and, as he did so, Wynn heard another scrape and click seemingly from the door behind him.

"Here," Kelley said. The switch clicked and the room sprang into subdued light. A man sat leaning forward, head on the hands outspread on the sheen of the desk.

"Dowdy," Wynn said again, more sharply. "Jim, wake up."

"Wait a minute, Mister Wynn," Kelley said. Swiftly he crossed the room and stood behind Dowdy. When he raised his head, the lean face had gone entirely expressionless.

"He ain't going to wake up. He's dead."

With a grunt, Wynn whirled and reached for the door. The knob was frozen, locked from the outside. He tried it again, nothing.

"We're locked in," he said and crossed to the desk and stared down at the dead man.

"What did it?" he asked. Death, as such, had no power to intimidate Amos Wynn. This dead man, brown-skinned, expensively and conservatively dressed, was something else. *Barton's legacy*, he thought grimly; *it's getting to be too much. It was too much the first day he came here.*

"Shot," Kelley said. "Here, look. In the back of the neck." He took up the desk telephone and dialed, frowning. "No answer," he said at length. "Line's dead, maybe cut."

"I told you we're locked in," Wynn said. "Now what?"

"Shoot the lock out," Kelley said. He returned to the corpse, lifting the head by the curled, thick, neatly barbered hair, then let it fall.

"He's still warm. There was somebody wasn't his friend."

"Barton called him a house nigger," Wynn said thoughtfully. "By Barton's lights, I suppose he was. Not by mine. Not by most of Angel Creek; they know better."

Kelley slid a careful hand inside the dead man's jacket and withdrew a wallet and opened it on a thick edge of currency. He fanned out the bills, several hundreds, more fifties and twenties and two tens.

"Wonder what he did for small change?" he muttered.

"Maybe you'd better count that," Wynn said. "Anything else?"

"This." Kelley held up two sheets of notebook paper closely written with figures and hieroglyphic symbols.

"Numbers drops—and the take. Probably just today's."

Well, Wynn thought, it was of course possible that Dowdy had died in a contest over Angel Creek's flow of gambling money. It was chickenfeed if measured by the customer but important money measured in the mass. And that was the way Dowdy had measured it all the thirty years Wynn had known him. Perhaps he had died for that, but Wynn doubted it. Dowdy had been the shrewd overseer of Angel Creek's dependable peace and obedience. Both had disappeared with Barton.

Damn his black soul, Wynn thought without emotion. *I told him this town couldn't afford him. It can't even afford him dead.*

"We might's well get out, Mister Wynn," Kelley said. "I'll leave Gillen here until homicide shows up. You get any idea about that monkey met us at the door?"

"Nothing but the voice. I got the notion he was skinny, but I don't know. I should have paid attention, but I wasn't thinking about him—then."

Kelley went to the door, took the .38 from a shoulder holster and, holding the weapon muzzle diagonally down, shot out the lock. The shot reverberated in the room. Kelley switched off the light and eased the door open as footsteps came pounding across the outer room. A flashlight beam punctured the dark and caught them in the doorway.

"Hold up! You're covered," a voice grated behind the light.

"Gillen! It's me," Kelley called. "Take it easy."

"I heard a shot," the officer said.

"That was me. Somebody locked us in. Did anybody come out the front?"

"No. Not a soul. Why?"

Kelley's voice was dry. "We didn't lock ourselves in. Swing your light around."

The flashlight beam swept the room and stopped. At the end of the bar a door stood open and beyond it the light picked up the rough texture of brick.

"Naturally," Kelley said disgustedly. "There's a stiff in the back room. Call homicide and stay and keep an eye on the place until they get here. We're leaving."

"Right," Gillen said, and returned to his car.

Wynn and Kelley were back to Fortieth Avenue, approaching the jammed intersection at Thirty-eighth. There were more fires now and more people, fitfully illuminated by the flames. Many were burdened but hurrying to get whatever they carried quickly out of sight.

"Just like a nigger," Kelley said. "Stealing more than he can tote."

Ahead the crowd milled in an amorphous mass but just beyond the car a smaller knot of people swayed and struggled over something down in the street. Kelley slowed to a crawl and flipped on the flasher and siren. A wordless roar went up around them.

"Here we go, dippity, dippity," Kelley said.

Then out of the thrashing group before them one figure heaved itself upright and kicked out at the crotch of a man clawing to pull him down. For a moment the man's face turned into the headlights.

"Stop!" Wynn shouted. "That's a white man."

As Kelley braked the car beside the struggle, Wynn slammed the door open and leaped out with the pistol in his big fist. He saw the white man go down again and fired into the air, reversed the pistol to make a club and slashed his way into the melee. A black man started for him and he swung the weapon and heard the thunk of steel against bone. He kicked another

man backward and reached down into the tangle, got the white
man by one arm and pulled him up.

"Get in the car! Move!" he shouted. The man stared at him,
vacant-eyed and reeling. "Move!" Wynn yelled again. The man
stumbled toward the car. Kelley had swung the right rear door
open and now he reached across through the opening, got the
cloth at the white man's shoulder and heaved. Wynn moved
swiftly backward toward the car, facing the mob, swinging the
pistol by the barrel. He felt Kelley's hand guiding him and slid
backward into the car and slammed the door.

"Get going!" he said.

The car began to move, but out of the gloom, seemingly all
at once and from everywhere, came a rush of dark figures. Close
up, Wynn could see the faces, sweating and eager, inches from
his own. The car began to rock.

"God damn it, they're tryin' to flip us," Kelley snarled.
"Grab that . . ." The sentence ended in a grunt, and Kelley
slumped down against the wheel. Turning toward him, Wynn
saw an arm being withdrawn from behind Kelley's shoulders
and beyond it a black face with teeth white in an open mouth.
Wynn's arm came up, and he jerked the trigger and the face
vanished in a gout of blood. The shot and the man falling back
pressed the crowd into momentary retreat. Wynn reached and
hauled Kelley's body across his lap, shoved it against the right-
hand door, squeezed his own bulk across the seat and under the
wheel. The siren was still squalling. Wynn slammed the car
into gear and drove straight at the crowd, his foot all the way to
the floor. The crowd began to yield slowly, then, lusting, gathered itself and surged back toward the car. Wynn grabbed for
the pistol on the seat, shifted it to his left hand and pointed it
out the window and into the air and fired until the hammer fell
against an empty cartridge. He could hear screams and now the
crowd rushed back in panic—or most did. Twice he felt the
wheels run into yielding bulk and then over it. He kept going
and then the street ahead was, all at once, clear.

He remembered and slowed before he reached the barricade

at the border but left the siren howling and the flasher turned on. *Hell,* he thought, *I don't know where the switches are anyhow.* Kelley, beside him, had rolled over with his knees on the floor and his upper body face down on the seat. Wynn risked a glance at the man in the back seat. The man was silent, his body inert and lolling. *Out cold,* he thought.

Then, still driving fast with his left hand, he felt over Kelley's upper body. *I can't tell,* he thought, *damnation, I can't tell.* He could feel no breath, nor detect any sign of a wound. But that didn't mean anything; he may be dead . . . or he may not. Barton, Barton, he's getting his price. *This man, this Kelley, he's my kind.*

He stopped as the flashlight signaled at the barricade and an officer came to the window.

"Kelley?" the man called. Then, he said, "Mister Wynn?" as the light came on his face. "Where's Kelley?"

"Hurt. Maybe dead . . . I don't know . . . and I got another one in here. Whistle up an ambulance . . . on the double." He paused. "No, don't do that. Call St. Francis and call headquarters. Say I'm coming in to the emergency entrance. Get moving."

With siren and flasher both going, driving faster than he really dared, he punished the cruiser through the deserted streets, rocketed through the center of town and swung between the stone gateposts. He rounded the front of the hospital with the tires squealing and pulled up at the ambulance entrance. White figures trotted toward the car, wheeling stretcher tables.

A police car braked to a stop beside the cruiser. Commissioner Mayhew got out and hurried toward him.

"Amos! What happened?"

"Get somebody to turn off those damned lights and that whistle," Wynn said. "I don't know how."

The lights and siren died as Mayhew's uniformed driver went to the cruiser, and the commissioner grabbed Wynn's arm and asked again.

"I don't know exactly," Wynn said wearily. "We got stopped.

They had a white man down—the damned fool—and we went to get him. We got him. Then a bunch came at us . . . mostly kids . . . and they were trying to tip the car. Somebody got halfway in the car and Kelley flopped. I shot him."

"Shot who, Amos, for God's sake?"

"The guy in the window," Wynn said. "Who'd you think? Kelley? Come on, I want to find out."

With the commissioner at his heels, Wynn hurried into the emergency receiving room and to a nurse at the desk.

"How is that man?" he demanded. "The officer."

"I don't . . ." she began.

"Damnit, woman, find out!" Wynn snapped.

She reared back, automatically preparing to register indignation, but a man in a white jacket with a smear of blood on his right sleeve came toward them.

"Sir," he said, addressing Wynn, the size and posture of whose presence automatically left the commissioner out of things. "The man . . . the one beside you . . . who is he?"

"Police officer . . ." Mayhew began but Wynn interrupted.

"Not who, how?" Wynn demanded.

The man in the white jacket had a straight, grave, young face.

"Serious," he said. "He was stabbed. Into the left lung. I don't know yet. It may be too much. Can you call his family?"

"Don't think he has one," Wynn said. "He's Catholic." He wheeled on the commissioner. "Art, get a priest."

"It could have been an ice pick," the intern said.

"Get back to him," Wynn said peremptorily. "Art, God damn it, get moving."

He went to the nurse at the desk.

"That man's name is Lieutenant John Kelley," he said. "Spelled with two *e*'s. Find out about the other one."

The emergency nurse made a beginning toward bridling again but looked up into the cold angry eyes soon enough and got down off her stool and disappeared. She was gone for five minutes, then returned, now restored to businesslike crisply professional composure. If she was still angry at Wynn's cavalier disregard of protocol, she had her feelings under control.

"He was beaten," she said. "He was unconscious. But he's coming around. Who is he . . . sir?"

"I don't know . . . except he has to be an idiot," Wynn said. "Where is he? I want to talk to him."

"Sir . . . you can't . . . the doctor . . . I'll call . . ."

"He's alive, ain't he?" Wynn said. "Take me where he is."

The nurse led Wynn, with Mayhew at his heels, to an emergency booth. There, behind the curtain, another nurse and an intern were working over a battered face which groaned when it was touched.

"Who are you?" Wynn demanded.

The man muttered and tried to sit up.

"Just tell me," Wynn said.

"Stuart." The man grunted, reeling.

"Stuart what?"

"Stuart, FBI . . . wait . . ." the man mumbled. He felt toward his chest, grunted again and fumbled more urgently. "Where's my . . . where's my jacket?"

"You said FBI?" Wynn demanded.

The man nodded woodenly.

"Oh, for God's sake," Wynn said, staring down at the battered figure in brooding dislike.

"I . . ." the man tried again.

"Never mind," Wynn snapped. "I'll see you later . . . you're luckier than you know." He turned to the commissioner.

"Art," he said. "Get somebody to take me home."

At five A.M., Amos Wynn walked up the broad, shallow bluestone steps, pushed open the unlocked door, flopped the stetson onto a peg of the hall tree and crossed the living room and went down the long hall to his study. He went behind the bar, brought out a quart of Jack Daniel, found a tumbler and poured it half full. Raising the glass, he was aware of weariness, a sour grief, and, for once in his life, confusion.

Coming into the room, fresh and fully dressed, Amy looked at him, her first alarm giving way to a slow smile of affection.

"Well," she said. "He made it back. You look as though you needed that."

"I did. I still do," he said, putting down the empty tumbler and reaching for the bottle.

"You also need some breakfast. The coffee's ready. I'll hustle the rest."

"I damned well don't want it," he said.

"But you're damned well going to get it," she said.

13

Peter Higgins was on the run again—a familiar condition—and moving as fast as an unfamiliar set of circumstances and harassments would permit. He was running in terror from a real life nightmare, but strangely, in a layer of consciousness beneath his dread, he was experiencing an exhilarating sense of freedom. It was, he dimly realized, the sure and certain knowledge that, at last, he was out from under the malevolent presence of Giuseppe Gervase. In this appraisal of a blessing, he was in error, which he might have understood had he been less scared and more intelligent. He would not, in fact, have needed to be very much more intelligent, for Gervase's presence hung palpably all around him as he fled; it was indeed the wide extension of Gervase's presence that made his flight possible at all. Had he known it, Higgins might well have been even more terrified, for it would be many months before he finally escaped Gervase and he would come close to death before he did.

Gervase, of course, well understood Higgins' weaknesses of intellect and courage. These qualities were factors in a mathematical exercise which Higgins represented to Gervase. Other things being equal, he would have had the killer killed with as much dispatch as possible after he had done his work. Higgins dead and disposed of, to Gervase's mind, would have been a sight neater—and cheaper—and by all odds safer than Higgins on the run, eating money and carrying with him a potential blabbermouth. Higgins owed his continued life—whatever it was worth—to the other half of Gervase's equation. For the time being, Gervase calculated, Higgins alive represented a form of insurance. He would let him live as long as he stood for a potential profit.

The soundness of Gervase's estimate of Higgins' qualities was demonstrated clearly enough as he ran. His way, as Gervase had promised, was well greased beforehand but Higgins, reduced by panic to a jelly, left small but telltale traces of his passage, beginning in the cemetery itself.

Becoming conscious that he still carried the shotgun and feeling that it advertised his guilt, he simply let go of it as he ran. The weapon was found the morning after the riot and was turned in to the Wynnsboro homicide bureau. It might well have ended there in anonymous obscurity except that a loose-lipped property custodian let slip the fact that it had been found to Jeff Stuart who—when he got out of the hospital two days later—went to inquire on the well-founded suspicion that the first thing the killer would have wanted to do was get rid of that damning evidence.

With all the weight of the Bureau behind him, Stuart commandeered the weapon from the possession of the protesting Wynnsboro law. It took the FBI, with its facilities, just ten days to trace the gun to its seller, an international ordnance dealer in Arlington, Virginia. The dealer, more accustomed to selling tanks and submarines to the armed services of Israel, could scarcely be expected to remember the purchaser of one used, nineteen-dollar sixteen-guage Winchester double, and he didn't. His sales records did, however, reveal that the gun had been bought by mail, paid for with a postal money order, and delivered to a general delivery box in the main post office on Canal Street in Chicago. That trail petered out there, for the box no longer had a renter and nobody could be found who could identify the indiviudal who had been its renter briefly in the period during which the gun had been mailed. And so the gun, itself, accomplished nothing but to provoke a new flurry of outrage against the mailing of deadly weapons across state lines. There were, once more, outcries against the traffic in Congress, but the lobby of the National Rifle Association soon silenced these.

Higgins had remembered, according to his detailed instructions, to mop the gun free of fingerprints before abandoning it. But he had done an unworkmanlike job even of that. The FBI, subjecting the gun to a scrutiny whose intensity was justified only by the use to which the undistinguished object had been put, found a smeared palm print left on the cheap varnished stock by a sweating right hand.

In the end, the print contributed to Higgins' undoing, although not immediately. Through some slipshod bureaucratic oversight by the numerous law agencies which had had Higgins in their custody at one time or another, his prints had never found their way into the millions stored away in the FBI's library of malefactors. Nevertheless, after his capture, the print did help, for it went to establish that this, indeed, had been the hand that had been upon that gunstock in a position suitable for firing the weapon at least once in the past.

Otherwise, Higgins' escape went according to plan, which was the usual way for illicit activities to go when they had been engineered by the resourceful mind of Giuseppe Gervase.

Across the width of the cemetery from Myrtle Avenue ran a

street bearing the proper Southern name of Magnolia, a secondary thoroughfare, not heavily traveled, and bounded on the side opposite the cemetery by scrubby trees bordering the meander of Angel Creek. It had been chosen precisely because it was thus unfrequented and even more likely to be so now, fifteen minutes after Barton's death, for the word had run like quicksilver and the morbid-minded—as who is not?—were now aimed with mankind's unerring instinct for calamity toward the other side of the cemetery.

Higgins came plunging blindly among the tombstones and topped a little rise thirty yards short of Magnolia Avenue—and balked. A police car was parked at a cemetery side gate directly in front of him. Higgins' instinctive abhorrence for anything in any way connected with the law was, in this moment of horrid crisis, multiplied many times over. He wheeled, ready to bolt again, before he remembered. And then, even though he now recognized that this was exactly according to plan, he approached the cruiser on numbed and dragging legs and in mortal dread.

The side window of the car had been lowered, and the driver now leaned out and called to him.

"Hurry up! Get the lead out. You think there's all day?"

Higgins walked woodenly through the gate and attempted to approach the car, but the driver sent him back to the gate.

"Latch it behind you!"

The driver leaned across and swung open the right-hand door and snapped, "Get in!"

Then, suddenly galvanized, Higgins ran the last few feet to the police cruiser, literally dived through the door and slammed it after him and sat trembling. The driver regarded him with distaste and put the car in gear and drove off at a sedate speed.

"Hurry, for God's sake," Higgins contrived to blurt.

"Hurry, my ass. You want to put up signposts," the driver said coldly and fell silent.

"What'd you do with the gun?" he asked at length.

"Gun? Gun?" Higgins couldn't seem to get his faculties to functioning. "I don't . . . oh, it's back there."

"Where, for Christ's sake?"

"In the cemetery . . . I didn't want . . ."

"You're a stupid sod," the driver said. "Where in the cemetery?"

"I . . . I'm not . . ."

"Forget it," the driver said. "I'll go back tonight and pick it up. Why in hell do you suppose they picked you for this?"

"I . . . I don't . . ." Higgins' tongue felt petrified and his brain dead.

As it turned out, the driver had no opportunity to recover the gun that night, for, by the time he had delivered the killer where he was supposed to be delivered, all Angel Creek had erupted and every man in uniform was on riot duty.

The car was a new, clean Chevelle painted an undistinguished medium blue, the kind of automobile one sees without attention. It was parked in the rutted lot behind Gervase's farthest roadhouse. A sign on the highway, if you were heading toward Wynnsboro, encouragingly said FIRST DAMN CHANCE, and on the other, if you were leaving town, enticed the wayfarer with a terminal message, LAST GODDAM CHANCE. The driver wheeled the cruiser around the low quonset building and into the lot, out of sight from the highway.

"There's your transportation," he told Higgins, nodding toward the Chevelle. "I expect you know how to drive."

"Sure," Higgins said earnestly, not quite aware that he was being insulted.

"Well, then," the driver said, giving tongue to both distaste and impatience. "Be about it. I'm sick of the sight of you and I don't want anybody to hang me up playing footsie with you."

"Wh . . ." Higgins began.

"Cut it," the driver said rudely. He leaned toward the glove compartment and opened it.

"Here's your map. Burn it when you're there." He unfolded the map and spread it in front of his passenger. "You ditch the car in this junkyard in Atlanta. Drive it around in back and leave it out of sight from the office. Nobody's going to find it for a week; that's been arranged."

"Is it . . ." Higgins began again and was again interrupted.

"Of course," the driver said. "It's hot. But the guy that owns it hasn't reported it swiped. He doesn't even know it has been. You're doing business with an old established company—if you didn't know it."

"But," Higgins said. "The money?"

The driver reached into his breast pocket and handed Higgins an envelope.

"It's in here. Five hundred bucks."

"Five hundred?" Higgins protested, alarm and outrage beginning to find root in him. "It's supposed to be fifty thou . . ." Once more the driver did not permit him to finish.

"I don't know what you thought and I don't care. Whatever you're supposed to get, you'll get in Mexico City. Not from me. This is walking around money just to get you there. And your tickets are here. So's your passport. Your name, for now, is Phil Henning; try not to forget it. Now get out of this car and haul ass. I don't like you."

Higgins drove all night, not even stopping to eat, and in the dawn found the automobile graveyard on the outskirts of Atlanta and, as instructed, left the Chevelle there. It was another ten miles from the junkyard to the airport, but he walked every yard of it, terrified at the thought of exposing himself to curious eyes by taking a taxi.

To the airlines, Atlanta is approximately what Chicago once was to transcontinental railroads; everything stops there and most passengers change planes there and, burdened by the density of traffic, most planes are late.

Higgins boarded his nonstop Eastern DC8 for Mexico City at one thirty, two and one half hours behind schedule, and, airborne at last in the three abreast economy section, first looked covertly at his neighbors on either side, and at last permitted himself a sigh of the deepest relief.

These first welcome feelings of security ran out on him two hours later when the pilot, unusually closemouthed for one of his calling, came on the address system and said, "Ladies and gentlemen, there is no, absolutely no cause for alarm. But an overheat problem has developed in number three engine. It is not serious, but we will be landing at Brownsville."

Oh, Christ! Higgins thought, *Brownsville . . . still in America.* He began to sweat again and by the time the flaps were down and the DC8 was in final approach he could smell himself and was in a new panic of fear that his seat mates could not mistake the stink of guilt coming out of his armpits.

Still, in Brownsville he had an inspiration and was thankful for the mishap. If the plane had gone through on schedule to the Mexican capital, he thought, he might have been subjected to some unwelcome scrutiny by the customs people. But, as he had learned in his long career of vagabondage about America, it was possible for a tourist to walk across the rickety international bridge over the muddy little Rio Grande at Brownsville without anybody giving a damn or even noticing. He took the airport limousine into town and walked over the border to Matamoros. *Safe,* he thought. He was wrong.

The forces that would run him down had not yet begun to flex for the pursuit. The Wynnsboro police constituted little threat to him; Angel Creek still smoldered that day in the aftermath of the nightlong riot; Mayhew's forces still had all they could manage and more and were adequately excused from looking very hard for a murderer who had no identity. Jeff Stuart was still in St. Francis Hospital, bruised and dazed and only fitfully remembering that he and probably he alone had actually seen the killer almost in the split second of the killing.

But the forces would gather and they would be formidable. Barton had been eliminated, but his elimination had no chance whatever of being speedily or expeditiously forgotten. If not exactly a friend, the man had been a guest and a confidant—in his field—of the President of the United States. His slayer would need to take account, not of a provincial police department, but of an aroused federal administration bent, if not exactly on vengeance, at least upon the urgent necessity to erase the mark of Cain from the forehead of the whole nation.

Higgins was, of course, not yet aware of the challenge his fear confronted. He felt better already as his feet topped the humped arch of the bridge and started down the slope into Mexico. Mexican customs and immigration took only the most cursory glance at his new passport and casually waved him on. Spring had come back into his stride and the black curtain was lifting from his mind as he walked on out of the bridge plaza and into the broken streets of Matamoros.

The strain of murder done and escape had, nonetheless, left its mark on him in both spirit and body and he thirsted for forgetfulness and relief. He found them in a seedy bar where he ordered a margarita and then another and so on and on. If forgetfulness was what he needed most, he got it in full measure, and by nine o'clock in the soft evening air was woodenly drunk.

He woke up with a dreadful retching hangover, conscious of oppressive sunlight beating through a window and the maddening buzz of flies around his head. He stretched in agony and felt some vague stir beside him and heard a soft rough voice saying, *"Buenas dias, señor."*

He rolled painfully onto his side and found himself staring into the liquid dark eyes and pockmarked face of a pudgy Mexican nymphet who, he realized with a touch of sick revulsion, couldn't be much over twelve years old.

Although every thought and movement hurt, he found his way to a bus station and that afternoon, with his stomach in rebellion against every sway and bump and filter of acrid dust through the floorboards, was on a tatterdemalion bus for Mexico City.

He reached the capital in three days and, remembering his orders, called upon a Señor Diaz who ostensibly ran a Ford agency but actually made the bulk of his considerable income by serving as a pumping station in the long pipeline that kept the Giuseppe Gervase enterprises in the United States supplied with heroin which had begun its journey as crude opium from the mountain poppy fields of Turkey. Higgins' directions were, in essence, to follow the pipeline in reverse until he reached sanctuary with Gervase's business associates in the Middle East.

"You are late, señor," Diaz told him when he was satisfied with Higgins' identity.

"I know. I got offloaded in Texas, and I thought it might be better to take a bus."

"It wouldn't have made much difference," Diaz said. "You leave here tonight with Cubana. I have your visa—printed separately outside your passport. You'll be in Havana by midnight. You know what you are to do there?"

"Yes."

"Excellent. It is better not to delay." It was as well for Higgins' peace of mind that he did not know that Diaz was thinking how easy it would be to get rid of him permanently and was wondering how it could be explained that Gervase seemed to be going soft in his advancing years. Oh, well, he thought, it was none of his affair. Only that his instinct favored keeping messes cleaned up, with all sloppiness eliminated.

Higgins thought anxiously of the money again and because Diaz seemed an amiable and obliging sort dared to ask about it. He might have nerved himself to ask anyhow, for he was now approaching and hurrying deeper into an unknown world and who could foresee what lay ahead? Being broke and on the bum —and even on the run—in America was one thing; trying to endure the same condition among probably hostile foreigners was another.

"You have the money for me?" he asked.

Diaz's friendly face underwent a subtle change, becoming wary and somehow hard and threatening.

"Money, señor?" he said. "You expect money? From me?"

"I was told fifty thousand dollars." Higgins persisted because he had to.

"Incredible, señor. Incredible," Diaz said. "There are no

such resources here. The sum is fantastic. Out of the question. I have been told to arrange for your further passage and I have done that, as you see. But money? Fifty thousand dollars? Incredible."

"But I can't go without money. To strangers."

"Perhaps," Diaz said musingly. "And you cannot go back either, eh?"

"No. No! Of course not," Higgins said and shuddered against his will.

Diaz fell silent, reflecting. Of course he can't go forward without money. And that led to the inevitable next thought: Perhaps Gervase hadn't told him everything; perhaps the man hadn't gone as soft and mad as he had suspected; perhaps it was being left up to him to arrange that this fugitive should go no farther. For a few long minutes Peter Higgins, without knowing it, stood in terrible danger. But Diaz pursued his musing further and Higgins was saved. If Gervase hadn't specifically told him, it was Gervase's fault. Why should he take on even a small extra risk for his customer across the border? He could give Higgins money, and he could, he knew, collect from Gervase easily enough; a delayed shipment would be sufficient persuasion when Gervase's customers, in turn, would be crying for supplies. If giving Higgins money was not what Gervase had intended, the misunderstanding was on Gervase's head where it belonged.

"Of course, señor," he said. "You must have money. Impossible to survive without it. I can give you two thousand dollars. That will take you to your final destination and by then, most possibly, Señor Gervase will have arranged for your further support. But fifty thousand dollars? Incredible! I, myself, would kill the Pope for that." Diaz smiled broadly and added, "A joke, eh?"

"But, good Christ, I got to live," Higgins blurted.

"Of course, of course. Probably it only slipped his mind . . . in all the haste," Diaz said soothingly.

The gnawing, unrelenting necessity for money never spared

him more than brief intervals of freedom from anxiety in all Peter Higgins' months as a fugitive. Added to the outright terror of his condition was the slow growth of conviction that he had been cheated. The money, after all, had been promised. Against his will he had done what he had been forced to do. The money was his and his choking, resentful loathing of Gervase grew while he suffered under the burden of intolerable injustice. In his condition of repetitious fiscal extremis it was perhaps not surprising that he did not remember that his bondage to Gervase lay so deepseated that, forced by Gervase's iron will, he would have done the murder for nothing.

And so it went. Cubana's Flight 465 to Havana and the sullen, shambling guards at José Marti Airport. An unexplained, fear-filled night in the airport lockup there until, in the dawn, a man who spoke no English, but whose efficiency was clearly not diminished by that defect, appeared, got him released, shepherded him through customs, handed him tickets, and herded him aboard Iberia's weekly Flight 941 to Madrid.

Thank the merciful God that is done, the Cuban told himself in Spanish as he watched Cubana take off. *I dislike doing the dirty work passed on by North Americans because they are too lazy or too arrogant to do it for themselves. And it would not have been possible at all if Fidel did not love American dollars even more than he hates Americans. For me, the satisfaction is dollars alone; I personally do not hate Americans enough to share Fidel's pleasure that the commerce he allows to pass through here is efficiently ruining the brains of young Americans. But, of course, I do not love them either. The dollars are sufficient. It is only that I wish they would do their own dirty tasks.*

Madrid was not particularly difficult for Higgins. In a way, his lack of the language helped. Merely to be stupidly uncomprehending, he was discovering, was enough to provoke official impatience. And that quality, which of course could have led to jail, instead had a way of settling problems and misunderstandings by waving him impatiently on. He was discovering the one great virtue of a transit visa; if you did not plan to stay in a country, its functionaries were well pleased to get rid of you as expeditiously as possible.

He nearly enjoyed the bus trip down to Barcelona on the Mediterranean Coast and along the precipitous shore, between brown headland and sparkling sea, all the way to Marseille, where he arrived six days after he had discharged the shotgun from ambush in the mausoleum.

A brisk, conservatively dressed, middle-aged businessman who spoke clear, if somewhat sibilant English took him in charge when Higgins reported at the shipping agency address he had been given in the heart of the city.

"What am I supposed to do now?" Higgins asked, already wondering how he might weasel further funds out of this cool customer. Until now he had spent very little except for meals on land, one night in a modest seaside hotel and bus fares. He still had most of the original five hundred dollars given him by the driver of the squad car in Wynnsboro and all the two thousand from Diaz. But it wouldn't last forever; in fact, he told himself angrily, it wouldn't last forever if he had actually collected his full, rightful fifty thousand. He had earned it.

"To Beirut," the businessman, who gave his name as Cuirasse—which was not his real name—said. "Beirut is splendid. There you can disappear forever."

"That's an Ayrab place, ain't it?" Higgins said. "What am I going to do among a bunch of Ayrabs?"

Cuirasse chuckled.

"Live, my friend. Live and enjoy. It is, as you say, Arab but almost only in name. Most of the people—the shopkeepers, the innkeepers, the how you say whores will speak your language. Even more will speak French which you should learn particularly since you will find time on your hands. Beirut is a civilized city. And it has advantages much greater than mere civilization. It is a city of understanding of problems such as you have. It is a place to hide, many have done so. Have no fear, you will learn."

"Understanding what?" Higgins asked in perplexity.

"Understanding money. What else?" the Frenchman said.

Higgins got another three thousand dollars—in Lebanese pounds—out of the Frenchman whose line of reasoning followed a direction similar to that taken by Diaz. A body sloshed up on the waterfront? Why not? It would be simple. But, then again, why not let Gervase sweat a little, paying the bills of Higgins' pilgrim's progress. It was a fact well known all along the pipeline from eastern Turkey, to Beirut, to Marseille, to Havana, to Mexico City, to Wynnsboro, and almost all the way to the eventual consumer that Gervase was a compulsive tightwad. Having from time to time suffered from his thrift, his business associates took a certain spiteful pleasure in running up his bills payable.

Two days later Air France began letting down over Cyprus. Forty minutes later the big plane circled in the high mountain pass over the Lebanon, sliding down above the many hairpin turns of the high road to Damascus, dropped down over the myriad greens of banana, palm, pine, and almond trees, racing its shadow across the dust-yellow city and set down on the long runway whose far distant end ran up against a mountain wall.

Because Higgins' passport was American—and not because it was phony—the immigration officer who boarded the plane at the terminal ostentatiously shifted it to the bottom of the pile. In Beirut the placement of passports from any planeload whose passengers included Americans always reflected the current state of Lebanon's capricious feeling about the United States of America. There was nothing personal about it; it was simply that when Arabs were put out with the U.S. State Department, which was often and frequently for a whimsical reason, American passports went to the bottom of the pile and were processed last.

Thus it took Peter Higgins two hours to clear the Khalde International Airport and suffer himself to be picked up by a swarthy man who said his name was Khalil, drove a taxi and confided he had been sent to meet him. It did occur to Higgins to wonder how Khalil had known so surely which American he was but he did not ask, which was just as well since if he had the only answer he would have got would have been a cheerful grin, a shrug, and an observation that Allah was to be praised. Higgins was feeling abused at what he correctly took to be discriminatory treatment by customs and immigration.

"What's wrong with those jerks?" he demanded. "Damned foreigners."

"Don't be nervous," Khalil said sympathetically.

"Who's nervous?" Higgins retorted. "I'm pissed off."

"In Arabic English that is what 'nervous' means," Khalil instructed him. "Pissed off."

14

Amos Wynn, who had been broodingly mulching the still-juvenile plantings on one of the several back acres of his suburban homestead while subconsciously mourning the two-hundred-year-old oaks which had surrounded the dynastic mansion the first Amy had persuaded him to raze, walked up onto the patio and came upon his daughter. Amy, oiled from tip to toe and clad in a pair of knotted handkerchiefs, was taking the sun on a plastic air mattress.

"When I was young," he said, pausing to regard her with slight disfavor, "a young woman would get arrested for the way you look."

"Nobody's looking, pa," Amy said reasonably.

"That is to say, of course, that I'm nobody. In fact I'm not looking. On purpose. Looking at you in that rig—or lack of a rig—below the chin embarrasses me."

"I am doggoned if I know why," Amy said, grinning lazily and hoisting herself on one elbow to squint up at her father against the sun. Her left breast slipped over or the cloth slid away from it enough to bare an edge of the deep pink areola.

"Cover up," her father grunted. "Every night when you say your prayers you ought to give thanks that I am constitutionally opposed to incest. Why don't you get married?"

"You are a dirty old man," Amy said equably. "I know plenty of panting dirty young men, but the reason I don't or haven't got married is that I haven't yet found a dirty young man enough like you." She grinned at him. "Of course, that puts the onus of being against incest on both of us. Terrible burden to put on an only child. Where're you going?"

"As soon as I get out of these clothes and sluice the barnacles off me and get dressed, I'm going down to St. Francis."

"For what?"

"The doctor said I could see Kelley this afternoon. I intend to."

Amy doubled and got onto her knees and rose to her feet, tall at least to his shoulder and toothsome in spite of the simonize coat of suntan lotions.

"I'm coming with you. I can get ready as fast as you can, probably faster."

"You don't need to, and they might not let you. And I don't know that, even with clothes on, you'd be what the doctor ordered for a man who's had an ice pick through a lung and a quarter inch from his heart."

"Pa, you know I know how to behave."

"All right, I know it. But why should you want to see him?"

"Bawl him out. And then thank him."

"He's still too sick for either. And you've never met him so far as I know."

"I met him, all right," Amy said with some grimness. "That is, I did if he's the one you went ratting off with and came back a pair of casualties with a hitchhiker."

"He's the one," Amos said. "But where do you fit in? I don't follow much of this, daughter."

"I do. Going into that riot was his business. It wasn't yours. Even if he only took you because you bullied him into it, he ought to be bawled out. A man your age."

"What's wrong with my age?"

"Nothing except you won't admit you've got it. Besides I want to thank him for bringing the remnants home."

"He didn't bring my remnants home. I brought his. Hasn't it ever occurred to you that a woman constantly butting into men's work is likely to wear out her welcome?"

"Nuts," Amy said and moved toward the door. "Same old get nowhere. I'll be ready in ten minutes."

Wynn shrugged and went to his shower. Fifteen minutes later they were in the Cadillac with Amy at the wheel, moving out of the drive and into the five-mile route to the hospital.

"Pa," Amy said thoughtfully as she drove. "You're an autocrat, but I can understand why you don't even know it and couldn't if you tried. The Wynn family has operated so long on the theory that everything—big or little—has to be their doing."

"There's such a thing as responsibility," Amos said mildly.

"My foot! You don't even let this city blow its own nose." There was genuine asperity in Amy's voice. "I have loved you as long as I can remember, but I just wish you'd get it through your head that you are not God and don't have an obligation to be God and you are not going to last forever."

"There's some mileage left in me," Wynn said patiently. "Daughter, I am not trying to be a deity. But it's a fact that *He* does need a little help around here."

"And after you?"

Wynn grunted. "I don't know," he conceded at length. "I

wish I did. This has been a Wynn responsibility through more granddaddies than I can count, but we're out of Wynns."

"I hate to say it, but maybe it's a good thing in the long run," Amy said soberly. "Us Wynns never gave the place the right to grow up."

"It's going to be a bad time to start," he said heavily. "Something's happening. Something I don't exactly understand—but something I don't like."

"You mean the other night?"

"Of course." Heavy-lidded, his eyes were on the street ahead but not seeing it. "This city has been getting along with itself, dealing with its own problems, since it was nothin' but a trading post—not even a crossroads town because there wasn't but one road. Not perfect . . . nobody ever said that. But at peace with itself. I know what goes on in the North, but, Amy, I tell you God's truth, I never would have dreamed our colored could have run crazy over one dead foreign nigger."

Amy shuddered. "I don't know, pa. How could I? But maybe it's time to consider not calling them 'our' colored. You ever think of that?"

He looked at her strangely.

"Not often. I admit that. Maybe it does sound pretentious . . . or patronizing . . . but damn it all, Amy, people that can't look after themselves have got to be looked after."

"Are you sure they can't, pa?" Amy's tone was gentle. "Maybe we're too . . . too . . ." She took her right hand from the wheel and touched his arm.

"Hell," Wynn said tiredly. "There wasn't but one man in Angel Creek that knew enough to come in out of the rain . . ." He sighed. "Jim Dowdy . . . and somebody killed him."

"Why?"

"I don't know—" He stopped and glowered at a delivery truck which broke past a red light and cut them off as the Cadillac lurched under the brakes. "Crazy nigger kid . . . well, that's not quite honest . . . I really don't know, but I did think maybe Dowdy got killed because he talks . . . talked to me."

"That man you picked up," Amy said, changing to the subject which was something she had begun to contemplate the night before when she couldn't sleep. "The FBI man?"

"Damn idiot," Wynn said shortly. "Had to be an idiot . . . in there afoot . . . and alone . . . He asked for it."

"I don't understand why the government was following that Barton man," Amy said. "Do you?"

Wynn snorted.

"Don't ask me to understand Washington. It starts with the Supreme Court, I guess. And the so-called liberals that don't really know their butts from first base . . . that's another thing. The FBI was with him when he was alive . . . And I am damned if I can guess what more they're going to prod their fingers into now that he's dead. There'll be some . . . and it'll probably make something worse that's too bad already."

"I think you ought to talk to him," Amy said.

"Why? He's a cop. Only that, a cop with a different kind of badge and what in the flaming blue hell does he know about a place like Wynnsboro?"

"I don't know. Maybe nothing . . . if you're right. But maybe he knows something about Bar . . . the dead man . . . or why the government was tagging around after him. Or what they thought they wanted here."

"I know what Barton wanted," Wynn grunted. "He wanted to wreck these people . . . in the name of something he called their rights. Well, he damn near did—and got some people killed besides himself. I've been wondering, ever since I first talked to him, how he managed to live this long."

"He's dead, pa . . ." Amy said in a troubled voice.

"I know he's dead . . ." Wynn said shortly. "It would have been better if he'd died sooner . . . before he brought us a corruption . . . a corruption—I don't know. He's dead . . . and somebody's going to be a long time paying for his funeral."

"Look," Amy said as she turned the Cadillac between the gateposts into the hospital grounds. "You're going to see Sergeant Kelley. Why don't I see the other man and . . . if he's all right . . . well enough, I mean . . . bring him out to our house?" She smiled at him. "If you're going to have to live with the damn Yankee federals it might pay you to know what they're made of."

Wynn looked at her through a moment of astonishment. Then he grinned.

"So?" he said. "Not only a daughter—but a crafty one."

"You've done it like a noble, so far," Amy, who was stacking plates into the dishwasher, said with approval as her father entered the kitchen. He took a new bottle of Drambuie and one half-filled with Metaxa *grande fine* from the stock in a cabinet, an array of many labels and colors and a hundred bottles deep.

"Noble?" Amos said.

"You talked about bass and you had your opinions about bill fish. You laid a curse on the man who will use a glass rod. And you talked about shooting . . . about which he seems to know something himself. But you didn't say word one about shooting colored Civil Rights people . . . or what business of his he may think that is. Restraint, I call it."

"Not restraint at all," Amos said. "You don't pick on a man while he's eating. Bad for the stomach." He turned back toward the patio where they had eaten dinner in the soft dusk. "You got a good hand with a steak, young lady," he said over his shoulder.

"Oh, I know that," she said. "What now? Do you want me to get lost?"

"No," he said. "Stick around. You might learn something I might miss. They're supposed to be a closemouthed lot. But I've seldom known the man that didn't open up better with a good-looking woman to hear him."

"A put-up. A put-down," Amy said. "A put-on."

"That Yankee gibberish irritates me," he said as he left.

"It would me, too," Amy called after him. "If it didn't you even more. I'll be out in a few minutes."

Jeff Stuart started to get up as she stepped onto the patio in a short, white, almost miniskirted dress that accented the long brown velvety sheen of her legs. She smiled and gestured him down.

"Don't," she said. "I'm not against politeness, but you still look rickety."

"Some," he admitted. He turned the slow, warm smile toward her. "If that dinner doesn't heal me, I'm beyond hope. You're a great cook, Miss Wynn."

"Thanks. But it takes talent to spoil a good steak."

"The other way around, I suspect." He sat back and rolled the dark, aromatic brandy in the goblet cupped in his palm. "Pure gold," he said. "Cops don't often get the likes of this."

"We suffer slight tinges of civilization, even here in the boon-docks," Amos Wynn said. "I don't remember how I happened to discover that the Greeks know more about brandy than any-body else, but I'm happy I did."

"I ought to admit I'm a little surprised," Stuart said. "This is a big house. And this is the South. Do you do everything here, Miss Wynn?"

She giggled. "Pioneer stock. Draw the water, chop the cotton, milk the cows, bake the bread. You'd be surprised."

"Not after that steak, I wouldn't."

"The truth is I don't—not normally. But I can make do. We have a girl"—she went remote and somber—"she'll be back. Her father, a man named Pullen, was the first one killed in all this . . . this . . . whatever you call it. I sent her home to help her mother—there are six more kids—until the family gets straightened out."

"Oh," Stuart said. "I knew about that one. But I didn't know anything about a family. There are always things you ought to know, but don't. Come in in the middle of the second act . . . you don't really know what went before."

"That's one of the things the matter with bureaucracies, par-ticularly federal bureaucracies," Amos Wynn said coolly. "Op-erate in a vacuum of ignorance . . . and mistake it for divine guidance. I don't particularly intend to be offensive."

"I'm not offended . . . yet," Stuart said.

"I'm a little curious to know why you went charging into Angel Creek," Wynn said.

"That wasn't too smart," Stuart acknowledged. "But Barton was dead. I wanted to see how people were going to react."

"They came close to reacting you into a funeral," Wynn said.

"I know, and I don't remember whether I said a decent thanks for saving my hide."

"Thank Kelley." Wynn grunted and swallowed the liqueur in the slender tulip glass.

"Yes. I will. How is he?"

"He'll make it. It ain't easy to kill Kelley."

"I would like to ask—that is if you can say," Amy said, "what your interest was in this man . . . why you were there."

Stuart thought about it briefly, considering his orders, and then smiled at her. No breach of security here and, besides, he thought, it was pleasant here and he owed something to hospitality. On the other hand, he was aware that he was not here out of hospitality alone, but it wasn't surprising that these two, father and daughter, could be reserving judgment about him, might even stand together in opposition, united in an as-yet unspoken hostility, not necessarily against him, but against unknowns that had wracked their settled world. But he was a guest here and he held no real secrets to betray and, moreover, she was an attractive woman.

"It's simple," he said. "He was my job; I was assigned to him."

"Why?" she asked.

"Because the people who pay me wanted to understand more about him, the reasons he had such an extraordinary influence with blacks. It wasn't only here; you know that, of course."

"You mean you were sent to spy on him?" Wynn asked abruptly.

"No," Stuart said it slowly, remembering Jensen and the tape recorder. "He knew I had been most of the places he's been going—at the same time."

"Then, are you saying that where he went he went with FBI sanction?" The cold edge in Wynn's voice was beyond mistaking.

"Not that either. Barton went where he wanted and why he wanted. I went to watch. Look, it's not so hard to see; Barton's . . . Barton was a phenomenon."

"So is a hurricane," Wynn said. "You've seen what he did to this city."

"Mr. Wynn, I'm not so sure you can charge it to Barton." Stuart kept his voice even, but now there was an underlying edge as cold as Wynn's.

"Why not? He came here . . . an outsider . . . uninvited . . . unknown. And tried to spellbind the niggers into something that could wreck this town . . . and them at the same time."

"Don't be too damned sure—sorry, Miss Wynn. Your man—Pullen, is that his name?—was killed before Barton ever set foot here."

"I don't condone stupidity," Wynn said shortly. "That's what killed Pullen, haphazard, pointless, useless stupidity. Barton getting killed was something else."

"Why? They're both dead—apparently for more or less the same reason."

"No. Pullen died by the accident of sitting down on top the place where some cretin had put a bomb. It could have been anybody else in that church." *I wonder,* Wynn thought grimly, *what this cop would say if I told him what I know about Rafe Pullen planting his tail on top that dynamite.* "On the other hand, whoever killed Barton intended to kill him, just him."

"Killing is a sloppy business, Mr. Wynn. It wasn't just Barton . . . nice and clean and just like that. That little girl got it, too, remember."

Wynn got up and walked to the edge of the terrace and stood, stiffly erect, staring out into the night. After a while he turned.

"I know," he said. "Damned shame. Her sister, too. Another one on Barton's record."

"He told me about the sister. It bothered him," Stuart said softly.

"If it bothered the man so much," Amy said, angry now in refreshed memory, "why didn't he stay away?"

"I think he thought he couldn't," Stuart said. "Whatever you people may think about Barton, I think he was sincere believing he had a mission and had to keep on."

"Mission!" Wynn said. "He was a wrecker. Let me tell you, you people, you in the North, you in this administration particularly, seem to get a lot of sanctimonious satisfaction out of sneering at us for trying to maintain a way of life.

"But let me tell you something: Way of life is not just a handy old Southern cliché, another way of saying keep the niggers in their place. We have a society to keep going, an economy to make function and it has taken us a hundred years since the end of slavery to evolve a way to make it function. It is not a way to denigrate the nigger; he has his rightful place in the way things work. And it does work . . . and will continue to work if we're left alone."

"Here in your town—this town that has your name hung on it, Mr. Wynn, I suspect you mean that the only way things will work right is the way Amos Wynn says they should work. I'm not trying to be offensive either."

Wynn stared at the younger man, measuring, challenging.

"I don't know anybody better qualified," he said coolly, then added, "Don't worry, I don't offend easy."

"I honestly haven't a clue who is best-qualified to run things," Stuart said. "Maybe you are the best, the big daddy to all you survey. And it isn't my business to screw up what anybody chooses to call a way of life. But I do think your kind of people are going to have to recognize sooner or later that this country is in the middle of a revolution. It's here and, like it or lump it, I think you're going to have to figure out the ways to live with it."

"It's possible. If people like you are going to wet-nurse the revolutionaries. Tell me, what side are you on?"

"Nobody's . . . when I can help it. If it doesn't sound too childish, I guess I'm on the side of justice. I'm a cop, not a crusader."

"All right, I'm not against justice . . . if anybody knows what it is," Wynn said. "You say there's a revolution and you may be right but it's also possible—hell, certain—that you look at it bass ackwards.

"Take your blinders off and look at this town—the way it was—the way I think it'll be again. Provincial, sure. One-third colored. The whites in control. The decisions in white hands—and if you want to make something of it, mostly my hands and my family's hands before me.

"What kind of a town is it? I'll tell you. Clean? Only as much and the kind of industry that it can support without pollution. Prosperous? All right, I admit that most of the prosperity is in white hands and all of it in white control . . . where I believe it should be. The niggers? Working and getting paid at the kind of work they can do. Sometime compare our unemployment record with, say, New York's. Crime? Of course, but it depends on what you mean by crime. People gamble, they whore, they drink: they do anywhere else, too. There's a man who runs dope through this town, but if it didn't move through here on U.S. 165, it'd be going through Meridian on U.S. 59 or somewhere else northbound. But I promise you, none of it stops here. We haven't had a forcible rape in five years and the only two killings in six have been Rafe Pullen and your man Barton . . . not counting a white man who shot his wife two years ago, and I'm not sure he wasn't justified, from what I heard."

Wynn had been walking back and forth across the slate terrace. Now he sat down and took up his liqueur glass.

"That's how much revolution we've had here . . . until this. Now look at where the revolution really is. The North. Where the niggers are emancipating themselves with the eager, blind bleeding-heart cooperation of the liberals, the courts, the Urban League, the Panthers, and God alone knows who else.

"And what is the country getting for it? They yell, 'Burn, baby!' and what does that come to? Courts jeered and judges called pigs and a judicial system gone to hell. Colleges and universities occupied like enemy towns; fifty niggers say they have to have black professors and a curriculum of black studies. I cannot for the life of me think what black studies might be except possibly voodoo, cannibalism, how to shuck a coconut or slit a man's gut with a razor. And so the university administration—paid by white men in an institution built and financed by white men—folds like the erection of a scared stallion. Excuse me, Amy."

"Go ahead, pa," Amy said. "You're in full tongue."

"Elementary school systems gone to hell because the niggers scream so loud for local control that they get it. What's that come to? Niggers fighting niggers, and when they get together a little bit they fight white Jewish teachers. Windows busted, fires in the waste baskets, kids gone over the hill, and white teachers beat up by overgrown, overmuscled, underbrained dolts. Schools burned to the ground. I read the papers.

"Niggers—people to the degree that they walk on their hind legs and possess a seemingly limitless reproductive capacity— fill up your cities to get on the welfare rolls—and produce more kids to increase the take. It's easier than working—and often more profitable because they run strikes of the unjobbed— plenty of spare time for picketing—to get more pay for not working than a journeyman cop gets for working. And if he is foolish enough to try to keep some order among them, they screech about police brutality. Give them time and they'll tear you silly, conscience-driven liberals up by the roots. And they'll do it, totally oblivious to the clear fact that when they do there'll be nobody left to pay for their free ride.

"Crime? We have a President who got himself elected largely on his pledge to get law and order back into the streets of this country. And, by God, if he wasn't up to the ass in armored limousines and helicopters and Secret Service bulls standing by even when he has to go to the toilet, he wouldn't dare walk outside the White House fence for fear of being mugged.

"I am not bragging, Mr. Stuart, when I say that I elect two Senators and four Representatives and they go to Washington charged, in part, with the job of running that town. If any town in this state was run as incompetently they'd be fired out of hand.

"Revolution! Are you people totally blind? Or plain gutless? Which side are you on, Mr. Stuart? You said it was a revolution. If you mean that, pick your side. Nobody sits out a revolution."

Wynn sat down.

"Amen," Amy said. "Mr. Stuart doesn't have to take sides. Not yet, anyhow. I was born with mine."

"You see half of it," Stuart said calmly. "But you're bat-blind when it comes to the other."

"What other?"

"I don't have to go through all the clichés with you. I'm sure you've heard them until you're sick of them. Only, I guess I ought to remind you that clichés get to be clichés because they generally have a truth content of better than fifty percent.

"So I'll be specific. You say that blacks are ignorant savages and, in Northern cities at least, vicious, freeloading hoodlums. Do you think your definitions apply to the case in point, a man like Barton?"

"Barton was a sport. A freak."

"Freak? Columbia? Harvard? A man maybe three or four million people in this country—and not all blacks—thought of like the second coming of Christ? Freak, Mr. Wynn? Sorry, I don't buy it."

"Pied Piper would be closer to it than Christ," Wynn said grimly. "I said Pullen getting killed was a brainless, brutal accident—there are whites as ignorant and vicious as the worst blacks. Maybe Pullen's death was worse than an accident, because I suspect it was the bait that pulled Barton here. Anyhow, he came. I talked to him and I know he wasn't stupid. He had to know what he was doing, and he chose to do it anyhow— drag the niggers into it with him. Believe me, ignorant as they are, most of them knew he wasn't their cup of tea."

"Then," Stuart said, thinking as he did so, *I've got to keep the facts rubbing up against his nose because he will not see what he doesn't want to see,* "Then, if they were so set against him, why did they riot? Why did blacks riot all over the country when he got killed?"

"I confess I don't know," Wynn said wearily. "Why do babies throw tantrums? It doesn't add. What does add, is that Barton knew exactly what he was doing. He was handing down an ultimatum, a challenge, and he knew damned well it was a life or death challenge. He could have predicted it himself. Barton was executed."

"Executed!" Stuart stared at the older man in disbelief. "Mr. Wynn, I don't know what you mean by executed," he said at last, softly. "Barton was murdered, bushwhacked from that cemetery. I saw him killed. I saw the killer."

The silence that fell then, Stuart felt, was eerie, nearly tangible. At last Amy spoke.

"You saw him?"

"Yes. He came out of a door of a tomb. He had a gun. He ran."

"Why didn't you do something about it?" Wynn asked harshly.

"I made a stab at it. He was behind a tombstone before I could get my gun out."

Wynn stood quietly, somberly regarding Stuart. At last he sighed and walked to the table and picked up the Drambuie bottle, uncorked it and started to pour, then changed his mind and put the bottle down. He turned to look at Stuart again.

"I wish you'd got him," he said.

Stuart looked up quickly, puzzled.

"I don't understand that," he said. "I thought you just said

Barton was executed. I suppose you meant he got what he had coming."

"I meant it, all right," Wynn said. "He came here. A clear threat to everything this city is, has been for generations. He knew it. But I wish you had got him. As it is they'll be tagging us another Dallas."

Christ, Stuart thought, *what inconsistency!* Defending a murder and blood lust for the murderer. A town's good name the only issue. What in the name of everything didn't he understand about these people?

"What are you going to do now?" Amy asked. He looked at her and saw that her face, so vibrant with life, wore a look of strain.

"Follow my orders, whatever they are," he said. "That's what I think I'm going to do because I think I know what my orders are going to be."

"What?"

"Find the man who killed him. Bring him back. See him tried."

"What if your orders turn out to be something else?" Wynn asked.

"Then I'll quit the Bureau and find him anyhow."

"Why?"

Stuart took his time answering because he had to probe his own thoughts which, he knew, were strange to him, foreign to what he had always taken himself to be.

"I didn't know Barton very well," he said at last. "Not really well. But there was something about him. A kind of purity. A kind of incorruptibility—whether you agreed with it or not. I know you didn't."

"No, I didn't," Wynn said. "But I know what you mean. Yes, I saw that."

"Anyhow, I'm going to find the killer. I never saw a man murdered before."

"You look like a man who'll do what he thinks he has to do."

Wynn sighed. "I wish you had got him when you saw him. If you had, this city could start getting back to something like normal."

"I wonder if you aren't being optimistic," Stuart said. "In his way, Barton was big medicine. No place he went ever got back to what people liked to call normal. He might do the same thing dead."

"I've thought of it," Wynn said.

"You said he was executed. By that I suspect you could be saying the town decided he had to die and so it killed him."

"Something like that. Yes."

"Then it must have been somebody from the town."

"Not necessarily," Amy put in. "Don't killers . . . executioners . . . sometimes get hired?"

"Well, yes. But he could have been from Wynnsboro. Would you like to see him?"

"See him? How?" Amy asked in a puzzled voice.

"Like this," Stuart said. "Remember, I saw him. What I saw has been put on paper. It's here. I brought an envelope with me. You put it somewhere. Could I have it please?"

"Of course," Amy said, getting up. "It's in the hall. No, I'll get it," she added as he started to rise. "But . . ."

In a moment she returned with a manila eleven-by-fourteen envelope. Stuart opened it and laid a glossy print on the table.

"That's him. Practically to the life," he said.

Amy leaned over the portrait of a man's face, frowning. Wynn got up and walked around the table and stood beside her, brooding down at the picture. It had been painfully extracted from Stuart's memory.

"How'd you get this?" Wynn asked at length.

"They sent a man down from New York," Stuart said. "He spent most of yesterday digging it out of my skull. It's good. That's the man."

Wynn turned back to the portrait, absorbing it line by line and shade by shade. At last he turned to Stuart and slowly shook his head from side to side.

"No," he said. "Never saw him. It's one man's face, all right. I'd remember him if I had. Amy? Girl?"

Amy straightened up and turned to the two men.

"It's a strange thing . . . looking at a murd . . . at a killer. You're sure?"

"I'm sure," Stuart said.

"No, I think . . ." she began and then shook her head decisively. "No, it's nobody I know."

"It's time I turned in," Stuart said. "I still feel a little raggedy. I want to thank you for asking me. If this is Southern hospitality, you ought to patent it. I wonder, Miss Wynn, if you'd be kind enough to call a taxi?"

"Taxi? If this is Southern hospitality, don't abuse it. Taxi, nothing. I'll run you down. Do you want to go to the hotel or back to the hospital?"

"Oh, the hospital for tonight. It's hardly worth it checking into a hotel. I'll be going to New York tomorrow. But I'd like to see Lieutenant Kelley before I go. Do you think they'll let me, Mr. Wynn?" he asked, getting up.

"I doubt it; he's still pretty sick," Wynn said.

"You know, you're the first FBI man I ever met," Amy said as she drove the red Porsche through the quiet, dark streets. "You surprised me."

"Surprised you? How?" Stuart said.

"Oh, I don't know exactly. I think I had a picture, maybe from television: young, lean, pretty boys all smiles on the outside but with a meanness so close under the surface it shows through. You don't fit the picture."

"Well, I'm lean enough. And I'm not quite an octogenarian."

"That's not what I meant. Oh, I don't know. You seem, well, almost gentle. That is until you said you were going to follow that man. Did you really mean that?"

"I meant it. A little out of character, maybe, but I meant it. I think I began meaning it the moment I saw him."

"Why?"

"You may have me there. Or I mean maybe I can't explain it. In a funny way that man, Barton, was beginning to mean something to me. I tried to say it to your father: a kind of purity and that doesn't say it right. Force. Sheer bloody will. And—this is screwy—but I think he was pretty sure he would die the way he did. And then I saw the man that wiped it all out, all at once, just like that. So much less a man than the one he killed. So plain, damned, barbaric. Oh, blast, I know I'm not saying it right."

"I think possibly you are," Amy Wynn said softly. "I think you are. I think I understand. But have you thought what getting him might do . . . now?"

"No, only getting him. Why?"

"Well," Amy said slowly, considering whether she should say anything and, if so, how to say it. "Well . . . if my father is right, that he was executed . . . then, if you do find him, where else could it lead to? The city lived a long time before there was a man called Barton. Well, I guess this: Is he more important than the city?"

"I can fumble around somewhere toward what you mean," Stuart said. "And to tell the God's honest truth, Miss Wynn, I don't know. Maybe he was killed for the city's sake, as your father suggests, but the man I saw was the one that pulled the trigger."

"I think it's time to eliminate the 'Miss Wynn.' Call me Amy. I don't know whether to wish you good luck . . . or bad luck."

"Your pop is a man of strong opinions," Stuart said irrelevantly.

"All the Wynns are," she said. "They always were. Counting me, that's eight generations. The Wynns don't have whims, they have convictions."

"They can also cook," Stuart said, as the Porsche whispered between the stone gateposts and stopped at the hospital entrance. "Thank you again . . . Amy."

Unknotting his tie and shucking his way out of his shirt, Stuart went to the bathroom and scowled at himself. *The face still looks quite a lot like hamburger,* he thought. *Strange man, that Wynn: powerful, it comes out of him like electricity. Charming girl, a dish, in fact, and still there's her old man's force in her. Too bad, I'd like to see more of her; that's the trouble with being a cop. I wonder, now, if I should have showed them that picture. I'd swear he never recognized it; but I wonder about her. Something strange, something not to put a finger on. I'm tired, so damn tired. All right, so you get hell beat out of you and what do you expect to be? Bright-eyed and bushy-tailed?*

15

One of the reasons why malefactors on the run often head for the border is that an international boundary, at least technically, offers less of an impediment to the pursued than it does to the pursuer. There results a temptation to breathe easier once across the line. This sensation of security can be a dangerous illusion, however; if the predators can locate the fugitive and if they want him badly enough they are likely to get him sooner or later, as witness Eichmann shanghaied out of Argentina to be hanged in Jerusalem.

The killer of Carver Otis Barton was wanted by the United States government as urgently as any evil-doer who ever committed a murder and got away. Peter Higgins on the run was neither forgotten nor forgiven merely because, for the moment, nobody who really wanted him caught even knew who he was. As a human entity he existed nowhere except in that brief image engraved forever on the retina of Jeff Stuart's mind. That was all and it wasn't nearly enough.

But it was a place to start. Stuart was still in the hospital when Rembert dispatched a portrait illustrator to his bedside. The artist, whose name was Parker, was no Rembrandt, but he did possess an uncanny knack for capturing and transferring to paper the essence of a face, both structure and spirit. He was often employed by newspapers and magazines to limn the principals of trials or executions where cameras were *verboten.* Here he confronted a handicap; he had to wrench an image out of another man's memory, not from life.

Though bandaged and lame, Stuart was sitting up when Parker arrived late in the afternoon of the day following the killing. It was only that morning that Stuart had repossessed enough of his faculties to advise Assistant Director Rembert by telephone that he had actually seen the killer.

They shook hands, which brought a painful wince from Stuart.

"You look pretty bunged up," Parker said, pulling up a chair and unlimbering a sketch pad and pencil. The tools of the artist's trade constituted baggage of ultimate simplicity; as the callowest of art students, he had once anxiously asked a Pulitzer-Prize winning cartoonist what esoteric supplies he should lay in. He had never forgotten that august personage's advice that if he had any talent at all he could draw with the grime from under his toenails.

"OK, pal, let's get started," he said now.

Stuart shook his throbbing head and muttered, "Christ, I can see him now."

"But I can't, you know," Parker said. "Let's see if you can unbutton what you see. What color was he?"

"All right, I see. The essentials." Stuart tried to rub away the ache above his eyes with his undamaged left hand. "White. Be-

tween five ten and five eleven, guessing against the height of
the door he busted out of. Weight? Put it between hundred
and fifty and hundred sixty."

"How old?"

"That's harder. I have an impression of young, but there's
something wrong with that and I don't know what it is. Maybe
it's that you see somebody you know and he looks younger than
you know he is. That doesn't make sense, does it?"

"Yes and no. Maybe more than you think. How do you want
to say it in words?"

"Old thirty, young forty-five. That's even stupider."

"No, you're reaching, and that's what I want. Hair?" Parker
had been doodling with light strokes of the pencil. He ripped a
sheet from the pad, crumpled and dropped it.

"At the moment, messed up, which doesn't surprise me. He
had it long, clear down the back of the neck, and flopping
around the sides of his face, long sideburns, down past his ears.
But that doesn't help any, I guess. He's probably crewcut by
now."

"I wouldn't bet. Some of those hairy ones are so up to the
hips in vanity they'd go to the gas chamber before the barber."

"It was darkish, brown I guess. And it was so sloppy I
couldn't tell if it was curly or wavy but it probably was."

"Come to a peak in front or recede around the temples?"

Stuart screwed his eyes in painful thought. "Got a cigarette?"
he asked and waited until Parker shook one from a pack and
held a lighter for him. "No, neither. Came pretty well down on
his forehead and full all over."

"Eyes?"

Stuart grunted, something which might have been mirth but
wasn't.

"I'll bet they never looked like that before—or will again.
Wide open, stretched open, scared crazy."

"I'll rest 'em for him. Color?"

"I don't know. I'm colorblind. Kind of medium, that's the
best I can do."

Parker snickered, but the pencil was busy.

"How about that? Blind leading the blind. Scars?"

They kept at it. Brows? Straight and dark, medium heavy and scarcely broken. Nose? Long, just a little bulbous at the tip, off course in the middle, an impression of being out of kilter, maybe broken. Mouth? Open then—gasping actually . . . or gibbering . . . but if he shut it it might be straight and thin, hard to tell. Chin? Came down to a sort of triangle . . . and, oh yes, it had a cleft in it.

The floor was littered with discarded wads of paper when Parker put the sketch pad in Stuart's lap.

"Anywhere near it? Within, say, a thousand miles?" the artist asked.

Stuart squinted at the drawing, picked it up, turned it left and right, scowled down at it a full minute.

"Maybe," he said at last. "Generally, that is . . . but . . ."

"Nobody thought it was going to be easy," Parker said, unruffled. "I know you see it, but I can't see inside your skull."

"Give me the pencil a minute," Stuart grunted. Very carefully, doubtfully, he held the pencil above the sketch.

"Go ahead," Parker said. "Show me what you mean."

"Well, right here," Stuart said, touching the pencil down just below and outside each eye. "A kind of bony look."

"Gimme," Parker said, reaching for the pad. Swiftly, lightly, he penciled in curving lines, almost like question marks and handed back the pad.

"That help?"

Stuart studied the drawing again and smiled. "Sure does." He frowned at the drawing. "And there's something else . . . hard to put a finger on."

"Go ahead," Parker said. "Take your time. This isn't a one-man show."

It was near midnight before they decided that they had gone as far along that road as they could travel together. In some ways, Stuart thought, it was remarkable. In others it somehow just missed in a way that defied definition. Nobody could be expected to duplicate the stark madness he had seen, but some-how, and he couldn't guess how, Parker had contrived to imbue this paper face with things that went beyond skin and hair and eyes and bone. This, in essence, was the man he had seen and—he swore to himself—would see again.

"If he could see himself, he'd sweat," he told Parker. "I still don't know how you did it."

"When you find out, you'll get my prices." Parker grinned and looked at his watch. "I can catch a two o'clock for New York. I'll have prints of this down here tomorrow—air express."

Higgins might have sweat indeed had he seen not only his portrait created out of another man's memory but also the mass of forces, still functioning in total confusion, massing to pursue him. Moreover, he had left some mismanagement behind.

The Chevelle was discovered in the Atlanta junkyard on the fifth day after the shooting, two days earlier than Higgins had been given to understand that it would be permitted to be found. This slip was not the fault of the junkyard owner who happened to be a distant relative of Giuseppe Gervase and had discreetly gone fishing for muskellunge in Wisconsin to avoid getting anything uncomfortable on his conscience. It was found by two teen-aged boys who had taken advantage of the owner's absence to go ragpicking for a usable carburetor for their ja-lopy. Astonished to come upon something so showroom shiny amid all the sorry debris, they first tried to start the car but, failing, told one of their fathers and he reported it to the police.

They, in turn, were puzzled when they could find no aggrieved owner to whom to restore the car, which carried Ten-nessee plates. These turned out to be no help when it was dis-covered they had been lifted from a car in Chattanooga. Even-tually the car was traced to a reputable Memphis distributor who knew it was missing from a shipment but couldn't for the life of him tell why or how.

Recovery of the car went out on a routine stolen auto report. And because—such deeds as the spectacular ambush of John

Dillinger in Chicago in 1936 excepted—a full half of the FBI's crime-busting reputation was based on the tracing of stolen cars across state lines, the report came routinely to that federal agency. Perhaps it was some bureaucratic instinct—plus the fact that the Chevelle had been ditched only four hundred and thirty-eight miles from Wynnsboro—that moved the FBI to pay a little more than routine attention to this one. By then, some one hundred and eighteen hours after Carver Otis Barton's death, federal sleuths were in full cry from coast to coast and border to border and every remote possibility that came their way was going under a microscope.

There should have been no reason why the abandoned Chevelle should betray anything useful whatever. The whole point in stealing a brand-new, ownerless, and thus unidentifiable automobile and equipping it with somebody else's license plates was to prevent it becoming a mindless Judas. But it did, through no fault of its own.

As earlier with the shotgun, it was not carelessness but anxiety that had caused Higgins to fall short of perfection in erasing the spoor that proved that he had once been inside that particular automobile, hitherto occupied only by the professional who stole it and the assembly-line workers who built it.

Higgins had followed instructions and meticulously polished the steering wheel, shift lever, dashboard, cigarette lighter, inner and outer door handles, and all other surfaces he suspected he might have touched before deserting the car. Also, according to instruction, he had thrown the key away, aiming it somewhere into the fathoms-deep jungle of rust which surrounded him. But, in the final relieved instant, he had not remembered to wipe away the prints of his thumb and forefinger before he wound up and threw. It should not have mattered. The key should have vanished forever inside the charnal house of iron corpses but, by random chance, it wedged itself point forward into the decaying radiator of a 1938 Chrysler Imperial.

The glint of sun on new metal, where nothing else was either new or bright, later caught the eye of one of the two FBI agents who came to comb the scene of the car's recovery. But not even this find wrought any immediate harm to Peter Higgins, for, as has been reported, his prints were not then anywhere in the possession of the FBI.

But he made a far worse error, one which all by itself suddenly changed the manhunt from an amorphous monster of scrambling anywhere and everywhere for clues which did not exist into an entity with direction as well as purpose. Nothing was proved; nobody knew yet who Higgins was and nobody knew where he had gone. Nothing was certain, but one circumstance surrounding the Chevelle carried enough credibility to make it seem worth pursuing.

Higgins had been told to burn his road map and he had obeyed. It was his final act before sneaking out of the junkyard and wending his cautious way toward the airport. But anxious to be gone and trusting fire to accomplish what fire was supposed to accomplish, he did not wait to see it all consumed and to scatter and trample the ashes. The map was folded and he set fire to it as it was instead of opening it up and crumpling it loosely, which was foolish.

Most of the paper was gone when the FBI arrived on the scene, but charred stubs and some fragments of unburned paper remained, enough to identify it for what it was. But for that, Peter Higgins might have safely disappeared forever, leaving no trace but his image floating just behind Jeff Stuart's eyes.

A curious agent scooped up the lump of char with care, just as other agents all over the United States were then scooping up material, however trivial, which they hoped—very remotely—at one time or another might have been with or near the unknown murderer.

To his ultimate cost Higgins had not been aware what miracles can be transmuted from burned ashes when they are subjected to microscopes and chemicals, and he might not have worried had he known. The map committed no such folly as tracing a direct route from Wynnsboro to Atlanta. It was not even a regional map which would have included both states and both cities. It was only an oil company road map of the state of Georgia which carried on the reverse side enlarged sections detailing the street plans of the state's major towns, of course including Atlanta. That had been its only purpose; the only extraneous thing on it was a cross-hatched mark to pinpoint for Higgins the exact location of the junkyard. Nobody had added anything more incriminating than that—except for one deadly imprimatur which was the fault of neither Higgins nor the person who had supplied the map.

Road maps, given out free by filling stations everywhere, are by nature as anonymous as grains of sand and bode no ill for anybody. This one was different. The Gulf Oil dealer from whom the map had been picked up had the habit, in the hope of reaping some small free advertising thereby, of stamping the name and address of his filling station on the maps he gave away. He had had the rubber stamp made to identify the bills he sent out once a month to credit customers and saw no reason why he shouldn't get this extra use out of it.

The dealer's mark was in the charred but not-yet disintegrated corner of the map. And the FBI's esoteric tools found it and brought it up, faint and wrinkled by heat, but loud and clear.

All at once the manhunt, which until that moment had nothing more tangible than purpose, acquired the priceless asset of a probable direction. Somebody who had been in Wynnsboro within recent memory had also been in Atlanta and in a stolen car.

It was as clear to the FBI as to anybody else that if a man wanted to leave Atlanta his means of egress were limited. He could take a train or a bus or he could buy another car or steal one or he could walk. And then, too, he could fly. Only the first two and flying seemed probable, although none of the other possibilities was neglected in the ensuing burst of activity. But, because any fugitive was presumed to be in a hurry and because

Atlanta was the hub of all air transportation through the southeastern United States, the clear point for concentrated attention was the airport and every passenger who had boarded there for anywhere from the day of finding the Chevelle and backward in time to, say, no sooner than twelve hours after the death of Carver Otis Barton.

Within twenty-four hours, Eastern turned up a circumstance which, if by no means proving anything, at least seemed worth further inquiry. Flight 905, leaving Atlanta late for Mexico City the afternoon following the murder with one hundred and three passengers, had developed minor engine trouble over the Gulf of Mexico and the captain had decided to land at Brownsville for inspection and repair. The passengers had been off loaded while the bothersome engine was inspected. Three hours later when the plane took off again, one passenger was a no-show and had not since been accounted for. Although the cabin crew had paid no particular attention to the missing passenger, one stewardess in tourist class recalled him vaguely as male, Caucasian, medium-sized and on the preferred side of middle age.

Now, airline passengers have been known to cancel or abandon for reasons persuasive to them when an aircraft comes to earth unscheduled because of a mishap in the sky. In most cases, however, passengers who chicken out because they happen to distrust airplanes are more likely than not to demand their money back. This one had not, then or later. Such slight unorthodoxies have betrayed smarter men than Higgins ever was.

The manhunt did not immediately abate elsewhere, for none of this really had proved anything more than a reasonably credible possibility, but Brownsville now became a focus of concentrated study. Within hours the city swarmed with spruce, polite, neatly dressed youngish men full of questions. However the FBI had to be aware that harrowing Brownsville in the hope of turning up a fleeing desperado was likely to be a barren occupation. Brownsville is a small, pleasant, prosperous, open city where nearly everybody knows nearly everybody else. As a place for a fugitive to go to ground, it seemed as unlikely as any place in the United States, especially with Matamoros lying just across that sickly little Rio Grande.

Matamoros, even smaller than Brownsville, much more poverty ridden, a warren of broken streets and sleazy tourist traps, hospitably full of sin for the wayfarer weary of gringo puritanism, boasts a civic asset of incomparable magnificence: it lies beyond the jurisdiction of the U.S. Federal Bureau of Investigation. Or at least it seems to.

The spruce young agents, therefore, looked across the river with longing eyes. They did not yet know what they were chasing, but whatever it was they did not confidently expect to find it on their side of the bridge. To charge across in force, they were aware, would seem a frightful breach of international decorum, egregiously impolite.

Not that that would have stopped them had they been sure of their quarry. But they were not sure, a blight upon their ardor. Higgins held the temporary trump of good manners.

However, along a border as long, as friendly, as mutually troublesome as that between the sister republics, the Bureau and the *Federales* had long since worked out a full set of resourceful alternatives for skinning each other's cats. Instead of converging on Matamoros over the international bridge, the FBI reversed its course and moved in from the south, still directed by Rembert in New York but now under the immediate tactical command of a man named Josh Clements, whose ordinary working title was legal attaché in the Embassy of the United States in Mexico City.

The main difference between the agents at Clements' disposal and those on the north end of the bridge was that his failed to exude that aura of polite and well tailored deadliness which distinguishes the FBI within the territorial confines of the United States. His looked more at home in Matamoros, but they were just as deadly. And Clements could count among his assets the eager cooperation of the *Federales* who enjoyed a good manhunt as much as anybody else.

And so, very soon, Matamoros was as full as Brownsville with questions for taxi drivers, bartenders, bus company ticket agents, hotel room clerks, rooming house proprietors, auto rental agencies, dancehall girls, young men selling their sisters, pimps and whores and their relatives. The *Federales,* meanwhile, set about cultivating their special garden of stool pigeons and the entrepreneurs whose known occupation was the growing, processing, and smuggling of marijuana and imported heroin across the river and into the United States. It was one good measure of the value the United States placed upon the head of Barton's slayer that the Mexican authorities were for this occasion empowered to guarantee Uncle Sam's conditional amnesty to dope traffickers in return for useful information.

Despite all this effort it took three more days to turn up the pockmarked teenybopper tart with whom Higgins had spent his night of margarita-induced oblivion. They found her at about the same time that the fugitive was coming to earth at Beirut, eight thousand miles away.

News of her discovery, while not definitive, was enough for Rembert, in New York, to order Stuart to suspend trying to find somebody in Wynnsboro who could—or more important would consent to—identify Parker's ouija-board portrait of the killer, and get himself and the portrait to Matamoros in a hurry.

With the aid of an interpreter, a captain of the *Federales* named Hernandez, Stuart interviewed the girl in the bar where she sometimes danced, quite often drank more than was good for a child not yet thirteen, and always hung around between customers.

"How is it she remembers a particular American?" Stuart asked, not really expecting this expedition to pay off. Captain Hernandez relayed the question to the girl in liquid, friendly syllables. Her brow furrowed, she made a face of distaste and spat angrily on the floor and answered, and the captain turned to Stuart.

"First, he was no good. As you say, he couldn't get it up?"

"Where was this?"

"Her room. She took him home with her," the captain translated.

"Why did she think he couldn't, as we both say, get it up?"

The girl made another face and the captain grinned.

"He was drunk as a skunk. Blotto."

"Can she describe him?"

She could and did with voluble disdain. Slender, dark, long wavy hair, a pest in bed because, in addition to not being able to get it up, he threw up in her slop jar and, what was worse, yelled in his sleep. Like a cat making love.

Stuart grinned. It was clear that his quarry, if indeed, the moppet's customer had been he, had done little for international relations.

"I suspect she didn't like him much?"

The relayed question brought on a tempest which, while weathering the storm, Stuart thought must when translated boil down to a full dossier.

"He didn't pay her," Captain Hernandez said, turning a solemn reproachful face to Stuart.

"So maybe I'd better pay for him," Stuart sighed. "It's a bad thing for gringos to run around leaving unpaid bills behind them. Gives the country a bad name. How much?"

"Three pesos—a buck fifty," the captain said.

"Tell her I want her to look at a picture, a drawing," Stuart said. "Tell her it's very important to be sure—either way. I don't want to harm an innocent man—even if the bum doesn't pay his bills and goes around cheating little girls."

He removed Parker's portrait from a slender leather folder and laid it face up on the table. The child stopped spluttering and took one quick hard look at the picture and screeched.

"Este es el! Pig!"

"I doubt if you need that translated," Captain Hernandez said.

"No," Stuart said. "But there are two questions left: Who is he? Where is he?"

16

Jeff Stuart's view of his boss was, for the moment, restricted to the marcelled sterling silver crown of the assistant director's head. For some three minutes, all of them frowning, Rembert had been bending over his desk studying the original of Parker's reconstruction of the nameless face of Peter Higgins. At last the assistant director looked up, still wearing the frown which deepened subtly as he regarded his operative. He tapped an authoritative forefinger on the portrait.

"This a good likeness?"

"It's the man."

"You're sure of that? Most of these drawings from eyewitnesses are useless; you know that."

All right, you bastard, Stuart thought, *so I'm a lousy witness.*

"It's the man," he said again. "I confess I don't know how Parker brought it off—but he did."

Rembert grunted and went back to studying the picture.

"We've run it through the picture morgue, of course," he said at length. "There are people who look vaguely like him.

Same general types. The longer I live the more I recognize that people aren't nearly as various or unique as everybody would like to think, especially about himself. Still, I only say look vaguely like him. There's nobody I'd swear was him. I've had the possibilities sorted out; you go through them after we finish here. You may see something the rest of us have missed, although I doubt that."

I guess you just can't help being a bastard, Stuart thought, and said aloud, "Yes, sir."

"Too bad you didn't plug him on the spot," Rembert said and added a sixteenth of an inch to the depth of the frown creases.

Stuart grunted. "That's what Amos Wynn said, too."

"Who is Amos Wynn?" Rembert demanded sharply.

"I guess you could call him Mr. Wynnsboro," Stuart said. "He owns about half the city and, the way I hear it, runs all of it. His family has been there forever and, as you've probably guessed, the place is named for them."

"Oh, yes. I see. Why did this Wynn want this man shot? Did he say?"

"I gather he's jealous of the town's reputation. Thinks if I'd shot the man, the mess would be all cleaned up now and the town wouldn't suffer."

"He's probably right. It's too bad you didn't and why didn't you?"

"I'd have shot him, all right. I didn't get the chance. He was gone like a flushed pheasant. But maybe it's better I didn't."

"Better?" The frown which had been relaxing, tightened up again. "What do you mean by that? Now, we've got to chase him."

"If I'd killed him, we'd never know why he did it."

"Well, there's that. Still, I don't know that the why is so important. If he was dead and on hand we'd know by now who he was and from that, if we're any good and I submit we are, we should have been able to figure out why. Probably just a Southern nigger-hating nut anyhow."

"I don't know, sir. Wynn said something that struck me as strange."

"Wynn? What's what he says got to do with it? What'd he say?"

"Said Barton wasn't murdered so much as he was executed."

"Executed? I don't get it."

"I don't know that I do—exactly. If I interpret him right he meant that, by his lights, Barton was committing an offense against the way things are done there, and it was so bad it was intolerable. That Barton knew it, and went ahead anyhow."

Rembert regarded Stuart quizzically, then smiled thinly.

"You think this Wynn had anything to do with it? If he's such a big shot?"

"That would be stretching things. All I say is I don't think he's mourning Barton. Just the fact that he was killed on his turf. Wynn is a very big man, not only at home but right through the state and into Washington. I can't see a man like that making a mess like that—practically on his own doorstep."

"You never know. But I can't either."

"I showed him that picture and I'd swear he didn't recognize the guy." Stuart paused, now frowning in his own right. "But . . ." He paused and shifted in his chair, reached for a cigarette and thought better of it, knowing the assistant director had quit after thirty-five years as a three-pack man and consequently harbored the reformer's contempt for the moral weakness of the unreformed.

"But what?"

"Well, his daughter saw it, too. She's pretty near a beauty, by the way."

"Keep your mind on your work. What about her?"

"Nothing really. Except the way she stared at that picture . . . and kept going back to it. I had a funny feeling she might have seen the guy sometime . . . or was wondering whether she had . . . Oh, I don't know . . . nothing to put a finger on."

"Well, that's possible, of course. If the man was a local. She might have seen him somewhere. Half-remembered him, maybe. You better work on her some more. Prod her memory."

"Work on her? Where, sir?"

"You're going back tonight. I've got the country covered, but so far we haven't a damned thing to go on except where it happened—and this"—Rembert tapped the portrait again—"for whatever it's worth."

"It's a good likeness," Stuart said doggedly.

"Well, I hope so. You understand, Stuart, we want this one."

"Yes, sir."

"It isn't just the Bureau," Rembert said, sighing heavily. "Although, of course, we'd go after him anyhow. But now the White House is in it—seems this Barton was some sort of half-assed consultant to the President. So he's raising hell. Not to mention the blacks ripping the country apart over this. So we get him."

Stuart nodded toward the picture.

"I expect I'd better start with that. Comb the town. Somebody may make him. Then . . . the girl."

"You say yourself you haven't got anything there . . . except maybe half a hunch."

"That's all," Stuart admitted, "maybe less."

Rembert frowned again.

"You know, I can half-sympathize with that man Wynn's feeling. Black troublemaker coming in and busting open a city. You can't blame those people for not liking it. But this assassination thing won't do."

"No. I'm sorry I lost him, really sorry."

"Lost him? Lost who?"

"Barton."

"You weren't his bodyguard. It was up to the city to protect him—for their own good."

"I know. Still . . . I was beginning to like the guy. And it happened right in front of me . . . and a lot of people in this country put a lot of faith in him."

"I don't know about that. Wrong kind of faith. Wrong kind of people. Wrong all the way around. I don't mourn him any more than your friend Wynn does. But we got to get the guy that killed him."

"I doubt if the local police are going to be much help. They seemed to me to be just throwing up their hands."

"Naturally. What would you expect? Southern cops. They're probably glad he's dead. Well, go through the pictures. Then get back down there."

Rembert reached toward another file folder waiting on a corner of the otherwise immaculate broad plain of desk. It was dismissal and Stuart got up to go.

Stuart's meeting with the assistant director took place on the third afternoon, some sixty-eight hours, after Barton's death and fifty-eight before discovery of the Chevelle gave the first solid clue to the direction of Peter Higgins' flight.

Leaving Rembert's presence, Stuart stopped at the blond receptionist's desk to ask her to make a plane reservation for Wynnsboro, to order up the assistant director's selection of photographs of reasonably possible look-alikes of the Parker portrait and to ask her to send a telegram in his name inviting Amy Wynn to have dinner with him the same night in Wynnsboro. The last request brought an arch smile so concocted of silver-pink lipstick and dark-blue eye shadow plus mascara that Stuart wondered how she kept her face from splintering.

"So-o-o-h!" she observed on a rising inflection.

"So," he said. "Business." He took a final appreciative glance down into the cleavage as she obligingly leaned forward in an obligingly low-cut blouse.

I really ought to do something about that—sometime—maybe, he thought as he turned toward the elevator. *Fool's gold, though, most likely. You'd have to scrape her first before you could get anywhere near the girl underneath. She's a yale lock with tits. But—some tits.* For no reason whatever, he found himself remembering Amy Wynn with eagerness.

*   *   *

"Hello, cop. Welcome back . . . I think." The smile, as well as the voice, was warm and open. Amy Wynn was waiting outside the gate, on the concrete apron where lesser mortals were forbidden to tread when Jeff Stuart left the airplane at seven thirty. He saw the figure standing in the dusk, leaning against a column of a Southern airport's rain-roofed boarding wing, and, although he really was still too far away for recognition, he felt a small quick stir of the senses as he walked toward the gate, and that, he told himself, was nonsense. It stopped being nonsense when the tall—for a woman—figure came up to him smiling.

"Hello. But why? This wasn't in any blueprint I drew. Just the same, thanks. Thanks very much," he said. *She's really lovely,* he thought; *Stuart, if you've got to be a cop and badgering people is a cop's business, please Lord, make all the badgerees to these measurements.*

"You offered to feed me and I'm hungry," she said. "I'll figure out your motives later—after I'm fed."

"Even if they're as lousy as you probably suspect, you could probably lick me with one hand tied behind you. I'm still over on the frail side." Stuart smiled. "I'm hungry too, and it's your town and what or where do you suggest?"

"Amos wouldn't object if I fed you at the club . . . even if you are a Yankee. . . . But to tell the truth the club is dismal on week nights. Besides you invited me and so there's the matter of your pride . . . if Yankees have any. There's a place called Wong's if you can abide Chinese . . ."

"Chop suey Chinese? Or Chinese?"

"Chinese Chinese. I know the difference, although in this case the owner is a wop. But the chef is from Peking by way of Hong Kong. And stiff with pride and talent."

"You said the owner's a wop. How come? I never yet heard of an Italian *tong.*"

"He's one and, I often think, a neat little *cosa nostra* all by himself. As for owning a Chinese restaurant, he owns most of the things that my father doesn't. But there's no conflict in that.

Pa owns the blue chip things; Gervase owns the playthings, the grown-ups' toys."

"Such as?"

"Slot machines, nightclubs, loose ladies, and Chinese restaurants, things like that."

"He sounds busy."

"He's a busy crook, but the food is honest. He'd lose Wong in a minute if it wasn't and he's too smart to let that happen."

The restaurant was set in a grove beside a lake well beyond the city limits. It was thatch-roofed, dimly lighted inside, hung with fishnet, blown glass Japanese net floats and models of outrigger canoes. Tropical fish circulated languidly in lighted tanks against the walls.

"Chinese?" Stuart asked as they were seated in a booth.

"Oh, you know. I guess there was a time when a Chinese restaurant looked either Chinese or like a restaurant, or both. Nowadays, from here to Hawaii, they all look like Trader Vic's. I warn you, it's expensive, for here anyhow."

"It'll take some doing to beat Pearl's on Forty-eighth Street in that department."

Two hours later, beyond the ribs and the *dem sen*, well into the lemon chicken and beef with lotus roots and beginning to feel succulently stuffed, Stuart grinned at her.

"You're right. I surrender. It's superb, wop or no wop, crook or no crook."

"I told you," Amy said contentedly. She lifted a silver cover from a serving dish and looked at him accusingly. "You forgot a mushroom. That's sinful."

"All yours," Stuart said.

"I can't," she pleaded. "And I promise not to repeat any sorry gags about Chinese food. Now, tell me what you're here for, as if I couldn't guess."

"How about if I say girl chasing?" *That was pretty feeble,* he thought, *but the fact is I don't know how I ought to go at this girl. There are three possibilities, the least satisfying being that she never in her life laid eyes on the guy, which is what she said*

the other night. The other two are, one, that she saw him some-
where, some time and it kind of tickles her memory or, two,
that she saw and remembers but has some reason why she
doesn't want to say. But what reason could she conceivably
have? A relative? It seems to me I heard somewhere that she
and her old man are the last of a breed. A boyfriend? A lover?
Some local hotshot that she knows, out to save the country, and
she doesn't want to turn him in? Well, she's certainly a girl who
would have boyfriends. A lover? Well, of course. He found he
disliked the idea.

There was skepticism in her smile. "That's flattering, of
course. But you'll have to forgive me for doubting it. With a
fresh murder on your hands, I can't see the boss cops giving you
time off to chase a backward Southern girl around the bushes."

"There's such a thing as mixing pleasure with what would
otherwise be nothing but business."

The smile was warmer. "That's a left-handed way to go
about it, but sounds more honest than your first try—and quite
a lot more flattering."

"It was meant to be. This is pleasure. And don't ask me to
swallow that backward Southern gal guff; it doesn't become
you."

She grinned at him. "All right, I won't ask you to. The fact is
I was pretty well Americanized once."

"Americanized?"

"By Yankee standards. You Yanks don't admit that anybody
south of the Mason-Dixon Line really belongs to the republic."

"That's parochial, a local prejudice and not true."

"Don't be too sure about that. I can remember a President
who went around complaining it was impossible to shoehorn
anybody from the South into the Supreme Court."

"All right, I remember him. He was an incompetent picker
—and a worse loser. But I don't know why we should talk politics. What was this about you getting Americanized?"

"Pa wanted me to go to school at the University of Alabama.

I wanted to go North. He thought I could get corrupted, but I won. I went to Skidmore long enough to get a degree."

"Did you get corrupted?"

"No, but in the winters I froze. There wasn't anything else around, much, to get corrupted by—except money. And since I had plenty of that already, the corruption didn't take."

"Skidmore a rich place?"

"The dean said it wasn't and she didn't approve of girls having a lot of money—not more than eight or ten dollars a week. She just didn't know where the shovels were kept. Most of the girls—not all—had money to burn."

"What was there to spend it on?"

"Clothes, mostly. That's a girls' school. Males were a scarce commodity."

"Miss them?"

"It was a long time ago, but I don't remember that I did. I'm normal enough in that respect and I got my share of such as there were."

"I would expect that."

"Thanks again. But if I felt deprived then, I don't remember it. I know they say that girls go to college mainly to get in on the open season for husband hunting. But, honestly, I don't think I was on safari."

"Fastidious maybe."

She chuckled. "That's a big, fat, pretentious, silly word. Picky is what Amos calls it. I think he's afraid I'm going to ripen into an old maid."

"With just the two of you there, I would think the thought of you marrying would scare him some."

"Oh, maybe it does. At least he'd raise hob if he didn't think the man was good enough. And if he thinks I'm picky, he is twice as much. But he's also generous—and honest with himself. He knows he isn't going to last forever, and I'm sure he's bothered now and then by the idea of me being left to wither alone . . ."

"He struck me as being an extraordinarily solid human being."

"Oh, he is. Most of the time." She laughed. "While I was up North in school, he got a wild idea and talked me into the college beauty contest, the idea behind that being to get elected Miss America. Honestly. He was serious about it, some harebrained notion about the flower of Southern womanhood and showing the damn Yankees."

"You weren't?"

"Nope. It seemed sort of silly to me. Anyhow I got beat, nosed out by a five-foot-ten flautist."

"Huh? What in God's name is a flautist?"

"Girl who plays a flute. Where did you go to school, anyhow?"

"The sticks. University of North Dakota and Chicago. What did her being five-feet-ten have to do with it?"

"Maybe nothing, although that was a year for tall girls."

"But you're tall."

"She had three inches on me. Amos almost blamed himself for that; thought perhaps if he'd been a little more ardent when I was conceived I might have made the height. But mostly he was sore at the judges. He thought they had jobbed me because I was a Southerner. That still isn't telling me what you're really trying to do here."

Stuart caught the eye of an alert waiter and ordered stingers. *Damn it,* he told himself, *you should have been thinking while she was gabbing; instead you were thinking about the dame and you still don't know from first base what to do.*

"This is where the man got killed," he said slowly. "And, to be honest with you, Amy, that's just about everything we've got to go on—that, and my memory, and the picture I showed you."

"It isn't much, is it?"

"Not nearly enough. If we get him—and we will—I'll know him."

"Why are you so sure you'll get him—if that's all you have?"

"The Bureau has tools to use. And it's persistent."

"Are you sure you don't mean relentless? Or vengeful?"

"It's fair to ask." He paused to consider and decided to order another drink and Amy accepted. She drank with grace, he thought. He waited until the tall stemmed glasses of frosty amber were set down. "I don't think you can say that of the Bureau. Cold-blooded, maybe, but not vengeful. But maybe in this case I could be charged; it's an unusual feeling."

"Charged? With what?"

"Barton was murdered. I saw the man who did it. I want him. It's a personal matter."

"Manhunt." She turned puzzled eyes toward his own somber look and shuddered. "It seems so . . . so savage. What if you find him and then find out he was absolutely, morally convinced that what he did was right?"

"Oh, Amy. Murder is not right to begin with. And if he was so sure he was right, why should he run?"

"That's naïve. Of course, he had to run."

"There's another thing . . . and it involves you . . . everybody here. Barton was killed here—in Wynnsboro—and not anywhere else. He had been everywhere else and everywhere he went he offended somebody, usually many, just as bitterly as he offended Wynnsboro. But he was killed *here*. It puts an awful strain on your city."

"So did he by being alive and here; remember that," she said. "I wonder if you people understand how much of a strain he did put on us. Not only what he was trying to do which the people didn't want done—not even many of the colored people wanted it." She remembered Martine Pullen's face contorted with hate and shuddered again. "He brought the violence and bitterness and death, not somebody else. He brought it, and it turned and killed him."

"All right, I admit it; Barton wasn't a gentle man. He was what he thought he had to be to get done what he believed had to be done. And, whatever people think, there was a lot of justice in what he stood for. Look, he was a leader. Maybe he was the most important leader of something that is becoming—has become—an enormous power in this country. Powerful and I admit—scary. Look what happened after he was killed—how many more died, how much destruction."

"Insane!" she said. "Insane! The colored run crazy because of this one man. What's admirable about that? Death, fires, bombing, looting! The colored themselves paying the biggest price!" Her eyes were blazing. "Why couldn't he have left us alone?"

"He couldn't. Not and be what he was. Amy, if you could, would you help me?"

"I? How could I possibly help?"

"I don't know. Probably you can't at all. But it's a reasonable assumption, at least as reasonable as any we can make now, that the killer belonged here."

"How can you assume that?"

"Because Barton was killed here—not anywhere else. If he came from here . . . well, you might have seen him somewhere, sometime. And if you saw him, you might remember."

"Jeff, I don't know . . . I really don't know. Jeff, I swear I'm not a racist. I'm no red-neck reactionary. I don't believe in murder."

He laid his hand across her forearm, and she did not draw away.

"I wouldn't think that even if I knew you were," he said.

"But I don't know if I'd help you. This is my city, my place. I grew up in it, I know its ways, and I know what it stands for. I know it has been badly hurt, and it wasn't the city's doing. No, I love this place and because I do love it, I don't know whether I would help."

She was silent, brooding, and Jeff watched her, still wondering, still nagged by a conviction that somewhere deep in her mind, known to her or not, lay a memory of the face of the still-nameless man who was Peter Higgins.

"It's late," she said at last. "I'll take you to your motel. And thanks for the dinner."

"You didn't oversell the wop Chinese," he smiled.

She was silent on the drive back into the city, and, abstracted, Stuart did not try to get the talk started again. As she drew to the curb in front of the cubist modern glass and redwood entrance, he asked, "Will I see you again?"

"Of course. If you want to." She leaned across from the steering wheel and kissed him lightly on the lips.

"Good night, cop."

17

Amos Wynn was a contained man and he endured most of life's impositions with fortitude. But there were certain hardships he abominated and before which he felt helpless; among these was packing a suitcase, even an overnighter which did not demand much beyond clean linen and shaving gear. Passing his bedroom, Amy overheard him blaspheming in a low-pitched growl. *I knew it,* she thought, and entered without ceremony to find him huge and baffled in front of the tall old cherrywood chest which had belonged to his father and grandfather before him and had been ordered from a famous English cabinetmaker by his great-great-grandfather in 1820. Amy admired its scarred beauty and had not resisted when he had refused to part with it—or let her do away with any of the antique artifacts with which his bedroom was furnished—when she had done the house over. Drawers were open up and down the tier of eight, and oddments of haberdashery dangled.

"What can't you find?" she asked. "Socks?"

"Anything." He grunted. "It seems to me either you or that kid Marty must deliberately ball things up."

"None of that," she said crisply. "Here, let me do it. Where're you going—and for how long?"

He stood back in half-resentful gratitude. "Washington," he said. "Just overnight, I hope. Two days at most."

"It'll be hot," Amy said and began expertly laying out thin white open-weave shirts and underwear and went to his closet to find two crisp cotton drip dry suits.

"You won't be the best-dressed rube from the sticks," she said. "But you won't wrinkle much in these. By the end of a Washington day you may not feel any better, but you'll look cooler than a lobbyist in a hundred and seventy-five dollars' worth of sodden silk."

"I saw Gabe Jardine in one of those the other morning," he said, feeling more like conversation now that he had got the suitcase ogre onto another back. "I told him he looked a real dude in that two-hundred-dollar finery. I thought I was flattering him, but he looked hurt. So I asked why and he petted his lapel and said it cost two hundred and seventy-five."

She turned from filling the suitcase and grinned at him. "Born diplomat, that's my pa. The directors are snappy dressers and the boss looks like a hayseed. I think I prefer it that way."

"So do I," he admitted and grinned back.

"You're flying?"

"I called Zeke and told him to get the plane ready. You want to fly me over?"

"I would—but I have a date."

He looked at her with quick interest, knowing that no usual man could keep her from the controls of the twin Bellanca where, almost more than anywhere else, she felt supremely sure and content.

"That FBI fella?" he asked. "Again?"

"The FBI fella," she admitted. "I think he thinks I'm a clue."

"You getting sweet on that one, girl?" The question was casual, deliberately so, but he knew a quick sense of foreboding and hoped no somberness of expression betrayed him.

"I don't think so," she said, wondering whether that was strictly accurate. And she was aware of the shadow that had fallen across his face. "But he asked me. And he's interesting. Why're you going?"

"Partly to run him out of town," Amos said, hoping the tone was joking but knowing it hadn't come off.

She stood up from the suitcase and gaped at him, disbelieving. "Because of me?"

"No, daughter," he said, gravely now. "You know better than that. When did your old man try to run your life for you? You like the man; that's enough for me. No, not because of you. Not even because of him. Because of his job."

"Would it make any difference, pa? If not Je—Mr. Stuart, wouldn't they send somebody else? Or more of them?"

"That's the point. I'm not trying to get rid of Stuart. I intend to get rid of the FBI."

"How, for heaven's sake?"

"That's why I'm going to Washington. Mose needs some talking to by hand. He's not earning his keep, not in this."

Amy shook her head doubtfully. "The Senator? What can he do?"

"He represents the state. I want him to start representing."

Amy's smile was slight but mischievous. "Pa, it would be a little more accurate to say he represents you and you represent the state."

"Either way you want it, daughter." Amos grunted. "It comes to the same thing."

"Just a minute," she said and walked from the room and came back smoking a cigarette and frowning in thought. "I don't think I understand what the Senator could do . . . or how. I always thought the FBI was . . . well, a law by itself . . . independent, I think I mean."

"They act like it," Amos said. "They do indeed. But the country has been putting up with too much of that sort of thing for too damn long. But, get down to cases, they live on government money too, which is to say tax money, and where do you suppose tax money comes from?"

"Yes, but when did anybody ever ask any of us what they could do with our money?"

"They didn't. But they have to get it from the Congress, and if Mose's four terms have been worth a damn for anything, they've given him enough seniority to be chairman of the Judiciary committee. And that committee says whether the Justice Department can have any money and how much and what for."

"But my civics courses, I seem to remember, said the money comes from the House, not the Senate."

"It does," Amos said. "But the beauty of it is that after the House gets through ladling it out, there stands Mose and his committee with the right and duty to say yes or no. What I intend to do is to give Mose Kirkwood a short hard lesson in the art of nay-saying—loud and clear."

Amy said, "Whew," and took the time for a long, thoughtful sigh. Amos recognized the look his daughter was giving him as complicated. It was mixed of parts of admiration, awe, and alarm. "Tell me," she said, "because I think I ought to know. Is there anywhere any size or type or degree of bobcat you won't take on?"

"I don't think so, daughter," he said gravely. "Not if it's necessary."

"I know you've told me that some day I'm going to have to take over for you," she said solemnly. "So I think I have the right to know. How many things like this do you propose to leave for me to deal with?"

"I won't leave any loose ends, girl. Not if I can help it."

She left the room again and came back with a freshly lighted cigarette and stood with one elbow planted on the highboy, gazing absently down at the open suitcase.

"I wonder if I put in everything you need," she said aloud and, with one corner of a brain most of whose parts were dealing with more troublous considerations, mentally counted off shirts, handkerchiefs, shorts, T-shirts, ties, shoes. "Oh, your razor and things," she said suddenly and started toward the bathroom.

"Pa, I don't think you ought to do this," she said, returning with both hands full of toilet articles and coming to a stop before him.

"Why?" he said. Amos had never abridged his daughter's right of free speech or her freedom to disagree, and he did not expect to do so now. But he was genuinely puzzled. He knew that she, like himself, held the welfare of the city that bore their name something near to sacred. It had not occurred to him that they might differ on what constituted Wynnsboro's welfare.

"Oh, it's mixed up in my head. But, pa, I know it's wrong. And what may be worse, I've got this funny feeling that it's dangerous."

"I don't follow you," he said.

"I don't know that I do . . . not entirely. But won't it look strange . . . maybe even guilty . . . in an odd way . . . for Wynnsboro to try to stop the law from trying to catch a murderer?"

"It's not Wynnsboro—it's me."

"That's the same thing. We're Wynnsboro . . . besides . . ." She fell silent, brooding down at the suitcase without really seeing it.

"See here," he broke in, "it's not a case of Wynnsboro not wanting a killer caught . . . although, there may be some of that around, too. The thing is that by butting in, without any kind of a by-your-leave, the carpetbaggers make Wynnsboro look ridiculous. It's just one more of the same—moving in, taking over, shoving home government over to the side. Schools, elections, killings, it's all the same. I've seen it happening all through the South and I'm not about to put up with it here."

"But . . ."

"The federal government can't even claim a jurisdiction. There's no federal law against killing. Say they catch the fella; they can't charge him with murder or try him for it; the only federal case they can make is that silly makeshift that he screwed up the nigger's civil rights by killing him. The killing was done here; the jurisdiction belongs here. If the killer's to be caught, let local law catch him and a local court hang him."

"Damn it!" Amy said in sudden asperity. "That's begging the question. You know yourself that Arthur Mayhew couldn't catch a cold . . . and I'll bet Je . . . Mr. Stuart knows it as well as we do."

"It's not a question of Mayhew's competence," he said, more coolly this time. "The issue is whether this community—or any community—can any longer manage its own business. In 1954 —if you want to pick a year, but the pressure has been on us longer than that—the Supreme Court began to say we can't. I say we have reached the limit of tolerance; the buck stops here, to quote one of the people who took his turn at diddling us."

"I don't know," Amy said. "Sometimes I think I don't know how to talk to you anymore, pa. It's all mixed up. I agree with you and I couldn't be prouder of you and I couldn't love you more than I do. But I wonder, sometimes, if you aren't hanging on, out of sheer splendid orneriness, to something the world has left behind."

"The world can get stupid enough to leave the wrong things behind, girl," he said gently. "Washington wants us to throw away all our past as excess baggage, like cleaning the junk out of an attic. I say the past, our past, wasn't just an ornery white man's accident, nigger-whopping for the fun of it. It has been a kind of evolution. It grew the way it did because it had to; it suited our needs. It still does."

"Pa, we still say 'nigger,' not only that, we say 'our nigger,' but you don't have to look very far to see that they aren't ours any longer, if they ever were. Look right here in the house, a youngster as bright and eager as Marty. Do you think she belongs to anybody anymore? Either to whop or to take care of?"

"To take care of, surely. To encourage her to try to be something she is not and never can be, that's another matter. That's doing her harm, not good."

"Oh, pa . . ."

"Or get back to Barton," he said. "God knows he didn't do himself any good here. But something a lot more important than him, he did this community an absolute wrong. I told him what made this place work—both socially and economically. He understood; I'll say this for him, he had a brain. But, even after understanding, he had to go ahead, and that, of course, was what killed him."

"Maybe, if you're going to talk abstractions, that was what killed him," Amy said. "But the thing that killed him dead was a load of buckshot and the thing that pulled the trigger wasn't any abstraction. I said when I came back in here, pa, that what you plan to do in Washington is wrong. And that's what's really the matter with it. A man got murdered here and now you're trying to keep him from getting caught."

"Not that, girl. I'm trying to keep this community from getting hurt any more than that man Barton has hurt it already."

"I believe you," Amy said tiredly. "But it won't work because it won't look like trying to save the town. It'll look like trying to shield a killer. And I swear, pa, that's something that doesn't become you."

"Amy, I can't stop to think what it looks like," he said. "All I can do is what I believe has to be done."

"It won't be the town that'll be blamed," Amy insisted. "They'll blame you. I don't mean Wynnsboro will blame you. But the world outside will look and say that Amos Wynn is just a nigger-hating, Southern, red-neck."

"As long as you don't believe that," Amos said stiffly. "I do not give a good goddamn what anybody else says or thinks."

She ran the two steps toward him and buried her face against his chest and clung to him, and he put his arms around her shoulders and did not know that he was crooning soothingly as he had when she was little and sleepy or bruised.

"I love you, pa," she said, shuddering away what had come close to tears.

"I know, girl, and I love you," he said and released her. "Now, I've got to go. I'll be back tomorrow night—if not, by noon the next day. Don't worry about this and have a nice time with your fella."

She stood back and laughed a little shakily. "All right, pa, you go get him fired if you want to."

One of the things Zeke Appel liked moderately well about his job of flying the Wynn Bellanca was that he was not expected to entertain his employer or talk down to him about the esoterics of airplanes and weather and turbulence or go through the motions of teaching him to fly or flatter him when he inexpertly tried to do so. The truth was that air travel—even in private luxury—tended to bore Amos. It didn't scare him or excite him or exhilarate him or fascinate him or give him any of the other emotional jolts that airplanes did for many people; an airplane was simply a way to get from one place to another—when it became necessary to go—with greater neatness and less bother. He had bought the Bellanca partly for that reason but more because a hundred thousand dollars seemed to him only a modest price to bring to Amy's cheeks the happy flush of exuberant excitement which the airplane gave her while inexplicably leaving him cold. Amy had become a skilled pilot under Appel's tutelage after he had once been assured, by Amos, that he wouldn't be working himself out of a job by teaching her.

So now Appel sat in the left-hand seat and quietly monitored his instruments at 9,500 feet and a heading of 060 and occasionally spoke quietly into the microphone which was the Bellanca's umbilical to the dark earth below and he did not wonder that the big man beside him in the right-hand seat sat in quiet, crag-faced composure in the dim glow of instrument lighting. Amos did not appear to be paying any attention to the man beside him, the airplane, the instruments, the radio, the weather without or the earth below and, to tell the truth, he wasn't.

If Amos Wynn was a fatalist, it was only in the sense that he never railed at fate. But neither did he accept it on terms of blind chance. Instead he tried to anticipate it and shape it to the mold he wished it to take. More often than not over the span of sixty-two years he had succeeded, not always perfectly but close enough. Now and then he had failed entirely but did not on those rare occasions consume himself in futile recrimination.

Now he would have recognized even without Amy's genuinely tormented doubts that he was dealing with disparate elements of chance whose probabilities were anything but susceptible to precise reckoning. The basic fact, as he saw it, was that as long as the federal government—which meant the Department of Justice, which in turn meant the FBI—kept up its active pursuit of the killer of Carver Otis Barton, his city and all it meant were in danger. He genuinely did not feel the danger was personal beyond the degree with which he identified himself with Wynnsboro and Wynnsboro with himself. To Amos, Wynnsboro was a living entity which had been created out of Wynn blood and brain and loin and to which the Wynns, each generation of them, owed a responsibility of parenthood.

It did not seem especially incongruous to him—only a known if not happy fact of life—that that sense of parental responsibility and authority could be reckoned—by carping minds—to be rooted in something more real than mere sentiment. Amos Wynn knew he had blood relatives in Angel Creek. Kinfolk of as many kinds and degrees of kinship as there had been generations of Wynns. The Wynns had been mostly proud and lusty men and not always fastidious. It was possible for a man of Amos Wynn's qualities of mind and heart and authority not to think of these people as blood kin even though his mind coldly acknowledged the fact that they were. He even knew who some of them were, but he did not think of them in terms any different from those he used for any other inhabitant of Angel Creek. They were wards, to be looked out for.

Carver Otis Barton had been something else, an alien, a danger. By his arrogant daring, his challenge, his confidence that weakness could be found and exploited there, Barton had revealed a hitherto unsuspected flaw in the fabric created by generations of Wynns. Left alone, not interfered with, Barton might very well have succeeded in what he had set out to do. And his intention had certainly implied more than the considerable injury of establishing the first black labor union in seven generations of history. It implied more than the real possibility, which Wynn had set forth to Barton, of driving away the city's industrial base.

For all those generations, Wynnsboro had grown, had prospered, and had had all its being based upon a known and accepted order of life. Amos did not consciously think of that order as based upon white domination and black servility. He did not begrudge peace or prosperity or individuality or even pride to the least of the city's black citizens. It was simply a fact of Wynnsboro's history that the blacks were a part of the living corpus and that entity was a responsibility given to and laid upon the line of Wynns. It was not a responsibility which could be entrusted to other and untried hands, no matter whose they were, nor how eager to take over a job vested exclusively in the name of Wynn.

Barton, he recognized, had been an accident of history. But Wynnsboro's vulnerability which Barton had disclosed was not an accident. He couldn't know whether it had been there all the time, but the seed must have been and Barton had found it and fertilized it. It had sprouted without Wynn recognizing it immediately and probably even without the canny awareness of James Dowdy. He missed Dowdy now more than he had expected, for Dowdy had been his true agent in Angel Creek.

Now he thought it was essential that Barton be forgotten as swiftly and thoroughly as possible. He would not be forgotten while the federal government remained in full cry, baying literally across the face of the world in pursuit of his killer. No matter what doubts Amy might feel about the right or wrong of murder going unpunished, the important thing was that Wynnsboro get back its wholeness.

After Zeke Appel had landed the Bellanca at Washington National, Wynn took a taxi into the city and the Sheraton Carlton where he kept a two-bedroom suite for two reasons: He did not like new hotels, and he did not like the last-minute uncertainties of making reservations.

He telephoned Senator Moses Kirkwood at his unlisted number at the Watergate and said he wanted to see him in the morning.

"Of course, Amos. I'll be in the office by ten o'clock," the Senator's rich and assured voice said.

"Better be there at eight," Wynn said crisply. "I don't want to waste half the day."

"Of course, Amos, of course," the Senator said, sounding somewhat less assured. "I just thought, well, I do have a breakfast meeting."

"Cancel it, Mose."

"I will, of course." The Senator knew that getting out of his early morning meeting would be a simple matter since the conferees he had planned to meet were the hundreds of brilliantly hued tropical fish he kept in a battery of softly lighted, meticulously regulated tanks he kept in his office in the Old Senate office building. He loved the fish and found that an hour spent in the morning caring for their needs and admiring their languid iridescent beauty somehow seemed to soothe him for the rigors of the legislative day ahead. "I'll be there at eight. Amos, can you tell me what's on your mind?"

"I'll tell you in the morning. You might guess if you've been doing your homework."

"Oh? Oh, maybe I see."

"I suppose that's possible," Amos said. "G'night."

It was five to eight and the sun was already threatening its worst when Amos, with difficulty, uncoiled his great frame from all the annoying protuberances and narrownesses of the taxi and mounted the sun-glaring steps of the Old Senate. He took the SENATORS ONLY elevator to the second floor, ignoring the disapproving stare of the boy who ran it, and marched down the long echoing corridor until he came to the door bearing Kirkwood's name and their state seal. He opened without knocking and stood for a moment, huge even framed in the vast tallness of a U.S. Senator's office entrance.

"Still playing with your toys, I see," he said.

Kirkwood was standing in front of the fish tanks, gazing solicitously at his pets. Startled, Kirkwood turned, then came toward him with his hand outstretched.

"Amos! You're early. Yes, my vice. A man needs something to take his mind off this nutty town now and then." The Senator was a portly man with a shiny balding head and a big, florid, affable face. He did not look dangerous but he was a powerful man—partly through seniority but partly also through canny political guile and partly from knowing the sources of his strength, perhaps the most important of these being the support of Amos Wynn through twenty-two years in office.

"Come and sit," the Senator said, nodding toward the massive chair which he—like the dead James Dowdy back in Wynnsboro—had had installed years ago because he knew that when Amos Wynn sat he liked something big enough to enclose his bulk. "What's up? That murder?"

"Execution, Mose," Amos said softly.

The Senator looked up sharply, then rocked back in his own chair and nodded his head and spoke carefully. "Yes. I know what you mean; the man would have first torn Wynnsboro to tatters, then the state. But using that word *execution* around here is dangerous, Amos. It's fashionable around here, these days, to look on the man as a kind of nigger Jesus Christ. Execution? I suppose, in those days, people thought of *that* as an execution."

"Maybe. By their lights at the time. But this was different," Wynn said thoughtfully. "Barton was a wrecker. Even dead he turned out to be a wrecker. He'll keep on being one until they forget him."

"People have taken a long time to forget Christ," Kirkwood said thoughtfully.

"Come off it, Mose. This was no messiah, not in Wynnsboro. Even the niggers knew he was no good for them. The first time he tried to raise hell—and got a dumb little girl killed in the process—he had only half a dozen people that would buy him. The second time—when he got still another little girl killed along with himself—he didn't have more than maybe a few hundred."

"But after he was dead, Angel Creek blew up," the Senator said softly.

"There was that," Amos nodded. "I wouldn't have expected that. I've tried to figure it out since. Maybe it was just blowing off steam, mostly young ones, and the chance to steal—but I'm not sure. I have a feeling Barton left a ghost to haunt us. We've got to get rid of the ghost."

"How?"

"By forgetting him—and settling down. The Teamsters are still poking around, I know that. Nothing much right now, but I know of some. If they made a hard try again, there could be trouble. They'll feed off Barton's ghost if it seems to offer much nourishment."

"Amos"—the Senator's big round face had gone entirely solemn—"why are you here? How do you think I can help?"

"I want to get the federal government's nose out of the thing. As long as they keep prying into it, it keeps the whole country stirred up—and some of that is bound to rub off on Wynnsboro. Newspapers, radio, TV—they keep chewing on it. The federals have no jurisdiction. They just come in and grab it. It's a local case and I want local law left alone to work on it—as it has the plain right to do."

"I don't know, Amos. I doubt if it's possible. Maybe you don't know how bad this town got stirred up by that killing. Even the White House. It's fierce."

"Nevertheless, facts are facts," Amos said softly. "Don't underrate your own muscle, Mose. You're a heavyweight in the man's party." He nodded his head in the general direction of 1600 Pennsylvania Avenue. "You run a heavyweight committee —singlehanded, as I know. Money is a fact—probably the biggest one—and you can put your foot down on the money. It might be the roughest job I ever handed you to handle—but I —we—want the FBI to get out of town and leave us to handle our own affairs."

Senator Kirkwood sat up abruptly. "Good God, Amos, the FBI won't even take orders from its own boss. Hell, they don't even report to him, he might just as well not be Attorney General for all the say he gets to say. You just don't know!"

"It's what I'm trying to find out," Amos said implacably. "And what I'm telling you to find out."

"I know already," the Senator said with a certain desperation. "Around here monkeying with the FBI would be like trying to abolish motherhood—or Santy Claus. I wouldn't stand a chance in hell next election."

"You may not anyhow, Mose," Amos said softly. "Meanwhile, since you're disinclined, I might take a crack at that sacred institution myself."

"I wouldn't if I were you, Amos," the Senator said. "You can't touch them, not even you. They'll just ride you harder. The director is the only hunk of suet I know of that's made out of solid granite."

18

On a Sunday morning, feeling wearily frustrated and futilely pensive enough to let himself drip dry in the shower before stepping out to scrape the dark shadow off chin, jowl, and throat, Jeff Stuart inspected himself in the motel bathroom mirror without enthusiasm and decided that he needed a haircut. *That again,* he thought. *If I can't or so far haven't been able to deliver anything professionally useful I guess I ought to go through the motions of at least pretending to look something like the image of what the director is morally convinced all of his agents ought to look like. That is to say, to put it a little more succinctly—neat. But no matter what a barber can do to my hair, I am damned if I can think of any trade or profession that can do anything similar for my head.* Neatening *that, to quote my five-year-old niece in Minneapolis, presently seems beyond the reach of modern technology. What is it now? A month? Six weeks? No wonder I need a haircut.*

With the doleful indolence of a man who suspects that even if he hurries he is not likely to accomplish much, he got into fresh underwear and socks and then, remembering that even the most feckless of men enjoy some small recourse against the vicissitudes of the world, decided to take a look at the weather. He shut off the hum of the air-conditioning, drew back the blinds, slid open the ceiling-tall door, and stepped onto his balcony and drew in a lungful of material that felt like a chemical compound of mug, mush, and the emanation of a dank, wet hell. Like that again, he thought, and went back in to search the hangers behind the curtain wall of his closet for the lightest, most porous, most transparent, least-confining apparel which he thought might permit a fully grown adult male to appear on the streets without being jailed for indecent exposure. He left the room and walked across the grassy court, circled the apron of the swimming pool in which three kids were splashing and yelling with youth's blessed indifference to a berserk sun and a fat brunette in a bikini was recklessly exposing everything but her buttocks to its doubtful mercies, and went on to the coffee shop. The air-conditioning there was turned up to the top and on overdrive, and he suddenly felt as though he had somehow inadvertently stepped onto the polar ice cap in his BVD's.

He shivered his way through tomato juice spiked with pepper and worcestershire, two scrambled eggs, which came out steaming but had congealed by the second forkful, grits which were tasteless to anything but a Southern palate but absolutely unavoidable at any breakfast table south of the Mason-Dixon Line, three cups of black coffee. He signed the check with a quaking hand and stepped back out into God's untampered inferno with something close to gratitude.

Back in his room, he fiddled with the air-conditioning until he hoped he had won a reasonable compromise between the Equator and the Arctic Circle and wondered what to do next beyond the necessity of confessing to Rembert in New York that he wasn't getting anywhere. He remembered, with thanks, that Rembert disliked having his weekends in Connecticut interrupted—especially with negative news—and that confession could wait until tomorrow. Meanwhile, what about today? He gave a few moment's moderately pleasant reflection to the thought of calling Miss Amy Wynn who, he suspected, might be an attractive object to observe even in this weather, but he gave it up. The reason, he acknowledged to himself, was funk;

since the girl was intelligent as well as attractive she was likely to recognize instantly the bumpkin insolence of having thrust upon her the companionship of a dolt who couldn't find his ass with both hands.

He went again to his locked briefcase and got out the rendition of the face he had seen in the cemetery and which had been extruded so painfully from his memory by the artist Parker. He stared at it for what could have been and probably was the thousandth and fourteenth time. That bush of lank hair, the wild eyes, the long cleft chin, the undefinably askew nose. There had to be a flaw in this somewhere, he thought, and if there was a flaw it had to lie somewhere in his ability to communicate what he had seen to Parker's skills. Back to that, eh? A flaw—and whose else could it have been but his own? This was a recognizable face, a face belonging to one man and no other. And he had seen it, he would swear, as it now looked back at him from the drawing board. But he must have goofed or else neither eyes nor memory was worth a damn. For if he had seen that face so indelibly in that moment, others must have seen it thousands, nay hundreds of thousands of times, though in moments of less stress. And so, then, how conceivably explain that nobody else could recognize it? The only possible explanation with any claim to credibility was that he, Stuart, had goofed, and this thing on the drawing board was not at all what he had seen in fact. How in the name of even the most farfetched logic did he have the gall to offer the split-second photography of his fallible eyesight and even more fallible brain against the sane and unprejudiced memories of a city of one hundred and eighty thousand souls? On the other hand, although it was not a particularly encouraging thought, who was to say that they were all that unprejudiced?

The only detectable ray of optimism penetrating this black tarpaulin of gloom, he suddenly remembered, was that enraged, undersized, underaged, and underpaid Mexican tart. Out of all the world known to him, she was the only living soul willing to swear she had seen the same face he had seen. On the other hand, you could scarcely describe her testimony as free of prejudice because who was likely to get madder than an unpaid whore?

His telephone chose that moment to ring, something which it had not often done in the weeks recently past. His first and not exuberant thought was Rembert. But on Sunday? Not likely. The second, far more optimistic, was Amy Wynn. He picked up the instrument in a spirit of illogical hope and said, "Hello. Stuart."

The voice which came back belonged to neither of his diametrically opposed hunches. It was male, it was baritone, it carried a quality of courtesy, and it was flavored by the South but not saturated by it.

"Mr. Stuart, my name is Blaisdell, Ed Blaisdell. I would like to talk to you—whenever it's convenient, of course, sir."

Blaisdell? At least that was recognizable enough out of his unfruitful gleanings to suggest that his mind and memory had not both gone AWOL forever. Interest quickened within Stuart's skull which, until then, had spent this Sunday morning in one of those minor purgatories which every man fashions for himself upon occasion. With his head working back toward order, Stuart not only felt the stir of something beginning to happen but his profession's elementary requirement to mind his tongue when using public instruments of communication.

"From Baton Rouge?" he asked.

"That's right, sir," the baritone came back, somehow managing to sound melodious in a speech of only three words.

"I'll be glad to see you," Stuart said. "Where are you now?"

"In the lobby, Mr. Stuart."

"Do you want to come up here?"

"I could. But I wonder if you might like to take a drive. My car is here—air-conditioned, of course—and it's a nice day—so long as it's air-conditioned."

Cautious bastard, Stuart thought. *But it's reasonable, even if it is fundamentally comic. Here's a guy calling the FBI, and he'd rather not come here because he suspects I might be bugged which is, on the face of it, a contradiction since we are supposed to be the bastards who do the bugging. And, I admit, not merely supposed to be.*

"Sure," he said. "I'll be down in a minute. How'll I know you?"

"Don't matter, Mr. Stuart. I'll know you," the baritone advised him.

The man who rose to meet him as he opened the lobby door gave, first, an impression of enormous and powerful stature and, second, an impression of controlled, catlike grace of movement as he came forward and, smiling warmly, offered a hand.

"A pleasure," he said. "A pleasure. The car's outside. I'll apologize for what you have to go through between the front door and the car. There's a little weather today."

"I noticed," Stuart said, setting about the professional business of appraising this huge human being and his purposes. Stuart was an old hand in his business and had long since learned that snap judgments are likely to be shot through with faults at first invisible. He would not make up his mind in anything like a hurry but, offered an offhand choice, he thought he would not enjoy meeting this man in a dark alley at a time when he had reason to feel less than friendly. On the other hand, as he knew, there are such things as cowardly lions, even tigers, and bull rhinoceroses. In either case, he doubted if this particular encounter was going to be a test of either.

The car was long and heavy and black, road-stained and unpretentious except, he noticed, the tires were oversize, glass-belted, expensive as he knew, and designed not to yield to abuse. They got in and moved off smoothly, with well-ordered efficiency and, he noted without surprise, the transmission was manually controlled and not a mindless automatic turbo drive.

"Quite a wagon," Stuart said conversationally.

"Supercharged," Blaisdell said. "I don't like to dawdle."

Soon after they swung into the belt highway circling the city and from that to the interstate six lane going south, car and driver were consuming an effortless, undramatic ninety-five miles an hour.

"The cops ever object to this?" Stuart asked, more out of curiosity than concern.

"Some have, I expect," Blaisdell said. "I don't generally wait to find out what they have on their minds."

They rode in silence for a few minutes, and Stuart found he was enjoying the ride for its own sake as one enjoys assured competence in any endeavor from symphony to sin.

"You suggested this," he said at length. "I suppose you had a reason—beyond the fresh air, of course. And of course you know that I know who you are."

Blaisdell chuckled. "And, naturally, I know that you know why I preferred the car to your room."

"I'm not offended," Stuart said. "A man gets into certain kinds of habits. I can appreciate that."

"I thought it was possible I may be able to help you—or that is show you somebody who might be able to help you," Blaisdell said after a while.

"Why?"

"That ain't too hard to explain, Mr. Stuart. You probably know that when Barton first came to Wynnsboro I was the one that brought him—and why I did."

"Yes, I knew that, and I've meant to talk to you sooner or later—once I get through with poking around in this town. I don't quite understand why you might want to help me."

"You could say I feel kind of responsible, which would be true in a way. And you could say that, although I didn't know him very well, I kind of admired Barton, which is also true in a way. For a colored fella, he had a lot of stand-up guts."

"For a colored fella—or any other fella," Stuart said. He still wasn't making any judgments, at least not any he would be willing to go bail for, but the huge man seemed to be approaching whatever he had in mind with more openness than Stuart as a rule found usual in the course of his work.

"I guess you could probably also guess," Blaisdell said, "that I have more reasons than I've gone into so far."

"Seems logical," Stuart said. "You want me to guess?"

"Go ahead. But I doubt if you'll be guessing."

"So do I, but I'll take what chance there is: You still intend to try to organize this town."

"Almost right, Mr. Stuart. Almost. I don't intend to *try* to organize it—I intend to organize it."

"I suppose that means you've figured what trying has cost so far. And made an estimate of what finishing the job could cost."

"I have."

"It's worth it?"

"Mr. Stuart, I guess you'll have to believe me. The union is my business. It's not only my business, it's a business I believe in. Put it simple: I can't afford to let this one go down the drain. Let one go and others will go."

"I don't have to tell you the town doesn't want it."

"No, you don't. But not the whole town. Not the folks we intend to organize. They may be scared, but they want it all right."

"You could be overreaching, Mr. Blaisdell. This may be, anyhow partly, an ordinary town. But Amos Wynn is not an ordinary man, not even partly."

Instead of answering immediately, Blaisdell took his right hand off the wheel, reached across to the glove compartment, punched the release button and reached inside. Under the big hand, Stuart saw a glint of dull metal which to a man in his business was instantly recognizable as a Colt .45. *Now what the hell*, he thought in puzzlement. Blaisdell's hand came out engulfing two long aluminum tubes, and as he flipped the door shut, he asked, "Cigar?"

"Thanks," Stuart said, taking both tubes. "Want me to open yours?"

"That would be kindly," Blaisdell said, adding, "They're from Havana. They still seem to get to me."

"I wouldn't be idiot enough to ask how," Stuart said. He unsealed one tube, delicately slipped the corona out of its aromatic protective wrapper and handed the smoke to Blaisdell who bit off the end while Stuart touched a match to the wrapper and let it get well alight before offering the flame to his companion.

"Respect a man who respects a cigar," Blaisdell said, while Stuart went about opening the other tube. "Now, you were saying about Mr. Wynn?"

"I said he's an uncommon man and that, by definition, makes this an uncommon town."

"Believe me, Mr. Stuart, I don't downrate Mr. Wynn. First place, when one family owns a town for maybe two hundred years, it's likely to be habit-forming. Second place, I expect all of Mr. Wynn's granddaddies down all those years would think highly of the one Mr. Wynn that's left—as you say, he's an uncommon man. But if you look at it another way, he's a man . . . and I have dealt with men."

I would bet a year's pay on that, at short odds, Stuart told himself.

"It'll be interesting to watch," he said aloud. "I don't question your right to try to organize Wynnsboro. And I don't question Wynnsboro's right—which means Mr. Wynn's right— to try to keep you from it. It appeals to me as a spectator sport, but it's none of my business. What I'm interested in is a murder and a murderer. Aside from that being my business, I have a personal interest in it. Like you, I feel partly responsible. Also, I think Barton was too much of a man to get plugged the way he did."

The speedometer needle, he noticed over the bulk of Blaisdell's right arm, was sitting comfortably on one hundred and five. Despite the air-conditioner's conscientious expulsion of the gray fog of smoke the car's interior smelled luxuriously of two two-dollar cigars.

"You're right about Barton," Blaisdell said. "That may sound strange to you coming from a man where I come from, and maybe it is strange at that. Around here we are likely to tell nigger stories that would probably interest those high-priced brain doctors you got in New York.

"Take this one, for example: Somebody fished a body out of the river one day and so as to make it strictly legal he called up the sheriff and the sheriff came out to look when he got around to it, which he was duty bound to do anyhow. This body had one peculiar thing about it: It was wound up in log chain with the ends padlocked together. So the sheriff came and looked and kind of toed the body over and walked around it a couple of times and he finally said, 'Ain't that just like a nigger —stealin' more chain than he can swim with?' As I say, that's a local joke, but likewise as I say, your New York head doctors might think there's something peculiar in our heads about niggers. Troublesome conscience, would you say? Whistling past a graveyard, maybe?"

"I'm damned if I know," Stuart said. "You told it, I didn't. I wonder why."

"Maybe I just wanted to see if it would rile you."

"It didn't, but it didn't give me a belly laugh either."

"Didn't think it would. But to get back to business, you got a copy of that picture you've been toting around all over Wynnsboro the last few weeks?"

"Not on me," Stuart said. "Back at the motel, of course. Why?" He couldn't have defined it and didn't know what it was, but he felt that quickening of the blood that comes, but comes rarely, to the patient hunter.

"I said before I thought maybe I could help you," Blaisdell said carefully. "And I expect you know by this time that I wouldn't be likely to do that unless, some way or other, I thought it might help me too."

"Sounds reasonable," Stuart agreed. The hunter's instinct was sharpening, and if something was going to come of this, he had no intention of blowing it by crashing through the underbrush.

"You mentioned that Wynnsboro is an uncommon town. And I agree with that. One of the things that's made it even more uncommon lately is that it's had an uncommon killing."

"You're understating that," Stuart said. "That murder was so uncommon that the whole country is still talking about it. And the black part of the country, which already has exploded once, stands more than ready to blow even higher over it, any day, any night."

The car was slowing perceptibly, and Stuart looked across Blaisdell's arm again and saw that the needle was down to eighty.

"Would you guess," Blaisdell said and paused to inhale a lungful of luxury, "that it would take a little of the uncommon out of Wynnsboro—make it a little more natural, say, a little more like just any other little old town—if you knew who the killer was?"

"I don't know what it would do to the town," Stuart said. "Help it? Hurt it? I don't know." He paused, measuring his own excitement, curbing it, considering. "It would most likely stir up a lot of hell, at least at first," he said at length and paused again. "But what it would do in the end I honestly don't know. And I say again, it's not my business, but the murderer is."

"You mind going back to your motel and picking up a copy of that picture?"

"Of course not."

"And then taking another ride with me—down to Baton Rouge? It ain't too far and I could have you back tonight."

"The way you drive," Stuart said, with admiration, "you can probably make it before sunset. Why Baton Rouge?"

"If you'll oblige me, I feel more at home there."

"I'll oblige you then."

The big car rolled off the interstate at the next interchange, circled back under the expressway, and came up on the other side headed back toward Wynnsboro at an even hundred.

"You're not only obliging me," Blaisdell said as the car settled down to quiet and competent violation of the laws of the state. "Anyhow, I can't identify your man. That's not right—I can but I never saw him in my life. But I'll take you to somebody that did see him and wouldn't want to even remember it while he was inside the city limits of Wynnsboro."

"I'll accept that—even if I don't know why," Stuart said.

"You'll see why," Blaisdell promised as the car got back up to a hundred and five and then more.

Two hours later with the brown manila envelope containing Parker's drawing lying across Stuart's lap, Blaisdell rolled the car off the expressway and onto a gravel road and stopped at an unpainted building that looked like a warehouse incongruously located in a setting of dark pine woodland.

"Union hall," Blaisdell said. "Come on in."

Inside the hall itself, Blaisdell led the way to a separate glass-walled office, through it past file cases and empty secretarial chairs and hooded typewriters, opened a door and stood aside courteously for Stuart to enter ahead of him. As Stuart did so, a slender Negro wearing a patch over his left eye socket stood up and put down a half-smoked cigar whose costly bouquet was immediately recognizable. *I don't know how thriving this union may be,* Stuart thought, *but if they're doing as well otherwise as they smoke I wonder why they think they need Wynnsboro.*

"This is Andrus Thompson, Mr. Stuart," Blaisdell said. As the two shook hands, he went on, "Andrus knows Wynnsboro pretty well. In fact, he knows it better than he wishes he did in some ways. He lost that eye up there when somebody blew up a church he was talking union in. But he's been back since—off and on ever since he got out of the hospital."

"What can we do for you, Mr. Stuart?" Thompson asked. Stuart was aware that he was being measured for height, weight, color of hair and eyes, and for something less definable but far more important in the Negro's system of values.

"Mr. Blaisdell is in a better position to say that than I am," Stuart said cautiously, thinking, *he isn't going to tell me thing-one or even the time of day unless Blaisdell wants him to and not even then unless he trusts Blaisdell, which I suppose he does.*

"Mr. Stuart and me have been talking, Andrus," Blaisdell said. "I wouldn't say we want the same thing, but I don't think anything you might want to say to him about what goes on up there would hurt us any. He's been spending quite a lot of time in Wynnsboro—more or less like you have."

Thompson grinned. *It isn't malicious, necessarily,* Stuart told himself, *but neither is he unhappy at the idea that he knows something I haven't been able to find out.* He waited.

"You know the Gray Oak Country Club?" Thompson asked.

"In a way. I have a guest card," Stuart acknowledged.

"Know that fat bartender, the one the members call Gus because they never bothered to find out his real name?"

"I've had drinks at the bar, yes," Stuart said, thinking this time the bastard *is* being malicious. "I know who the man is."

"Ever ask him anything about whether he ever knew or guessed or had any ideas about Barton and what happened up there?"

"I would have liked to," Stuart acknowledged. "But I was a guest, you understand, and I've never been there except as a guest, along with a member. Not a very handy situation for trying to cross-examine the bartender."

"Just as well." Thompson grinned, and this time there was no doubting the malice. "He wouldn't have told you a gawdamn thing, mister."

"Does that mean he doesn't know anything?" Stuart asked, beginning to feel scratchy in spite of himself but resisting any temptation to show that he resented being taunted only, evidently, because of the color of his skin.

"Mr. Stuart didn't blow out your eye, Andrus," Blaisdell said gently. Threat? Reminder? Stuart didn't know.

"No," Thompson said, without looking at Blaisdell, keeping that one good right eye fixed on Stuart's face, a gaze at once bright and teasing and fired with a searing rage. "But he's white, and I don't need many guesses to understand that nobody black blew it out. I got to keep that in mind—and I do."

"I'm sorry about the eye," Stuart said. "But he's right. Wearing a white hide doesn't necessarily mean blowing up blacks."

"I'll accept the fact," Thompson said, not relaxing the stare. "But I don't think I accept the sorrow. White grief over a gone black eye? I doubt it."

"You got off the track," Blaisdell said, still gently. "Leave color out of it for a minute. This is work."

Thompson nodded grimly, reluctantly. "All right, so let's get on with it. What I meant was you got to understand something that a lot of whites don't," he said to Stuart. "That's this: A black man just naturally would rather not know anything about anything that white men get into a sweat about." He wasn't apologizing, Stuart knew, but just as clearly he had decided to relinquish for the moment whatever pleasure he might have been getting out of making a white man dangle. "It's just that they know there ain't any percentage in it. Not down here anyhow."

"Barton wasn't a white man," Stuart said.

"That's right. But Barton's dead," Thompson said reasonably. "Getting mixed up in white men chasing around in circles over who did it ain't going to bring Barton back to life. The way a lot of people think, even thinking about it is something they'd rather not do and knowing about it ain't even healthy and talking about it, specially to a white man, could get somebody else dead. Even messing around with Barton at all—colored or not—wasn't too healthy. You can see that by just counting the headstones. So, even if you and Gus had had the bar all to yourselves all day, he wouldn't have told you anything except hello and good-bye and the price of your tab. But he'd have been polite about it."

"Would he have had anything to tell me if he hadn't felt that way?" Stuart asked, feeling that whatever he might get was now going to come anyhow and the less talking he permitted himself the better.

"No, Gus wouldn't have known anything that you could use

to get a rope around anybody's neck, most likely," Thompson said thoughtfully. "But Gus did hear something before Barton was dead that would have interested you after he did get dead."

"Yes?" Stuart was willing to wait, all afternoon if necessary, or longer. Maybe he wasn't going to get anything more than a crumb, but he knew that if you had enough crumbs and eventually got them sorted out properly and stuck together you stood a chance of assembling a loaf.

"One thing you need to know is about bartenders," Thompson said. "Any bartender, black or white but specially black."

"Yes?" Again. "I think I know where you're going."

"Probably. In your business you ought to. People generally don't think about bartenders, and if they did, they'd think they were deaf anyhow. Practically anybody will say practically anything in front of practically any bartender—specially if the bartender's black and even more specially if the guy on the stool side of the bar is gassed." Thompson stopped abruptly and looked to Blaisdell, who nodded without saying anything.

"You understand, Gus ain't to get into any trouble because of anything I say," he said, turning back to Stuart. It was not a question, Stuart knew, and knew as well that the low voice carried both suspicion and menace, and he knew that, but for Blaisdell, he wouldn't be hearing it at all.

"Not if I can help it," Stuart said quietly, but he was thinking that if Gus knew anything really significant, whether Gus liked it or not or Thompson liked it or not or whether Negroes deliberately steered clear of white affairs or not, Gus was likely to find himself someday on a witness stand.

"Sometimes you got to take a chance," Thompson said in resignation. "About a week before Barton got back to Wynnsboro the second time—on a Saturday night at the club—two guys were at the bar getting loaded on Gus' martinis, and around that time everybody in town, black or white, knew Barton was coming back and he was going to put on that march for the Teamsters.

"Gus ain't deaf, no matter what drunks think. He heard

them two talking about the march, and one laughed and said there wasn't going to be no march. The other one wanted to know how come that was and the first one laughed again and said he knew all right," Thompson said.

"These two were members?" Stuart asked.

"Members," Thompson said.

"It's interesting," Stuart said. "But you said it yourself—it doesn't put a rope around anybody's neck. And maybe it doesn't mean anything at all. Drunks talk a lot. Did Gus know who they were?"

"Maybe the members can't remember Gus' name, but he remembers theirs, all right."

"Who were they?"

"I'll be damned, Mr. Stuart, if I would tell you if you had me hung up by the thumbs, FBI or not."

"Would Gus tell me?"

"Not if he could help it."

"Then why the hell do you have the guts to put him on a spot?" Stuart demanded, angry now and willing to let it show. "You know damned well he's going to be asked. It's not evidence. It doesn't prove anything. It can't be used in a court. It's hearsay and probably doesn't mean one blasted thing. And you've got the guts to stick it in front of me and you sure know I'm going to ask him about it because I've got to. I promised he wouldn't get hurt if I could help it and he won't—if I can help it. Christ! You drag me down here two hundred miles to feed me that crap! What are you, anyhow?"

Thompson was unruffled, and Stuart was aware that Blaisdell was smiling slightly at the sudden display of temper.

"Just testing, Mr. Stuart, just testing," Thompson said.

"I asked you to bring that picture along," Blaisdell said.

"What's this crap got to do with the picture?" Stuart demanded.

"Nothing," Thompson said. "And I guess old Gus can stand a few questions. That's all hearsay, like you said. What you really came down here for is to see a man you seen once already. Didn't do you much good that time, I know that. This time, a little different, maybe. You mind waitin' here with Mr. Blaisdell a little?"

"He's my transportation," Stuart said. "I'll wait." Now what the hell, he wondered. It wasn't much of a Sunday anyhow, and there's the odd chance this junk about old Gus isn't as dry a hole as it sounds like. If somebody really was getting ready to fix Barton's wagon a week before he showed up, and if a couple of drunks knew even a little about it, there's the possibility some other people knew about it as well. But they sure aren't going around talking about it now, drunk or sober. Gus is going to have to stand a few questions, all right, maybe a whole lot of questions.

"Smoke?" Blaisdell was resting comfortably with his elbows on the scarred desk. Now he reached into a drawer and proffered another of the slender cylinders designed to pamper the minor vices of the rich.

"Thanks," Stuart said, accepting the cigar absently. "How much of that was simple shit?"

"I don't know," Blaisdell said. "As far as it went, which I admit wasn't very far, I expect it was true. You're going to put Gus on the pan of course."

"Of course." Stuart went thoughtfully about the ritual of firing up the corona. "But not to fry him—not if I don't have to."

"I'll tell you something," Blaisdell said. "It's true what Thompson said—the average nigger wants no part of white men's fusses, and he'll go a long way to stay clear. But I swear this time it's different—that Barton meant more to these folks than they're ready to admit. You don't think Thompson would've said Gus' name out loud unless Gus knew he would and okayed it?"

"It occurred to me," Stuart admitted.

The man who entered behind Thompson five minutes later, stocky, big-shouldered, heavy-lipped, a broad, quiet face, was one man Stuart remembered out of the dozens, or was it hundreds who, over the last weeks, had met his questions in sullen or infuriatingly stupid silence and negation. The man stopped halfway across the office and stood looking at him calmly but now with nothing left of the submissive but impregnable armor of silence and denial which he had shared with every other black citizen of Wynnsboro with whom Stuart had come face to face in week after week of futility and frustration. Stuart got up, put down the half-smoked cigar, and came across the room and offered his hand. And now the hunter's instinct was entirely alive, alert, ready.

"You've met Clagget before," Thompson said abruptly. "He has decided—he decided by himself—he ought to talk to you. He couldn't talk to you in Wynnsboro. I guess you understand why that would be."

"I do," Stuart said. Then, on an impulse he would have had trouble explaining, he put his right hand gently on the man's shoulder.

"I'm sorry about your girls, Mr. Clagget."

At first Clagget returned his look with steady eyes. They were still steady on his own when Stuart saw tears start from under the lower lids and slide down the black cheeks, ignored.

"Maybe they were foolish to be near Barton," he said quietly. "But I guess I know why they did."

"Show him the picture," Thompson said to Stuart.

Stuart started toward the desk where Parker's drawing waited inside its envelope.

"He don't need to," Clagget said. "He showed it to me before. The man was called Pete Higgins. That's about all I know about him except he worked sometimes for a white man named Gervase. I don't even know if Higgins was his right name."

19

"You hungry?" Stuart asked out of a long silence. The big car had been rushing north for more than an hour at the velocity which appeared to make Blaisdell feel most at home behind the wheel. Stuart had long since decided that he might as well resign himself to comfort too. *As a law officer it might be embarrassing to get pinched for speeding,* he told himself, *but I'm pretty sure nobody's going to catch this laddie.* Blaisdell seemed to have settled into the quiet pleasure of fracturing the all known speed limits and Stuart had been turning the day's events over and over, trying to decide what to do with what he had. Dusk had come down on them and Blaisdell had turned on the lights.

"I could stand a snort and a steak," Blaisdell said. "You too?"

"Two snorts and the steak," Stuart said. "Know a good place?"

"About ten miles up the road, and about the same this side of Wynnsboro. Good bar and prime meat." Blaisdell allowed himself a rich, warm baritone chuckle.

"What's funny?" Stuart asked.

"The place. It just struck me you might get more than a steak. If you do, I'll let you buy the dinner."

"I was going to buy it anyhow. My expense account is in your debt. What's the extra I'm going to get beside a prime tenderloin and about three martinis?"

Blaisdell chuckled again. "Let's wait and see if you get it." The car rushed on at undiminished speed for another five minutes, the white beam of its lights stiff-arming the night into retreat ahead of them. Then the speed eased and the car peeled off into an exit to the right.

They drew up and parked among other cars before a long, low, stone building with dim lights showing through curtained windows. There were no signs visible but, as a uniformed doorman swung a massive wooden door wide for them Stuart saw the words THE ROOKERY carved into the oak.

"Roadhouse. Probably the best in the state," Blaisdell said.

A handsome brunette, wearing black net tights, a minuscule ruffle of skirt and with her breasts pushed up improbably to swell out of a spangled bodice, smiled and said, "Good evening, gentlemen," and led them to a table in a corner. "I've seen you before," she said to Blaisdell, "haven't I?"

"Often," he said. "Your memory's good—this is the usual table."

"When they come your size, they're easy to remember, sir," she smiled again, archly this time.

"M-m-m-m," Blaisdell murmured and sat down.

"Would you like a drink?" she asked. Blaisdell looked inquiringly at Stuart who said, "A martini please. House of Lords, ten to one, straight up, no vegetables, thanks."

"Pinch bottle, double on the rocks, please," Blaisdell said, smiling at her. "The boss in tonight?"

"In the office I think," she said, turning away and walking erect, although fetchingly undulant.

"He hires 'em for looks—plus other qualities," Blaisdell said, looking after her in appreciation.

"Who's he?" Stuart asked.

Blaisdell chuckled again. "If I see him, I'll tell you." Serious again, he asked, "Make any profit today?"

The drinks came and the brunette waited.

"Give us a little time to get the dust out of our throats, dear," Blaisdell smiled. She smiled in return and left.

"Some, of course," Stuart said. "I don't know how much yet, but I'm ahead of where I was. Having a name to go with that face is a profit, even if the name is phony. And knowing he's a local is even more. You know that picture has been seen and turned down by maybe five hundred people. I've got the list. Some had to be liars."

"Probably more than some," Blaisdell said. "The colored wouldn't say boo because to them any white man is bad news, like Thompson told you. If any whites you showed it to knew who he was they wouldn't be likely to admit it either—for a different reason. I guess you probably don't exactly realize how much the federal government ain't appreciated down here."

"I'm finding out," Stuart said.

"And you'll keep finding out. It'll amaze you."

Stuart sipped at his drink and lighted a cigarette. "That man of yours, Thompson, interests me," he said. "He had me wanting to take a poke at him."

Blaisdell, looking grave, waited a moment to answer.

"He's not my man, hardly any more than he's yours," he said. "If he belongs to anybody he belongs to the Teamsters—and himself, mostly himself. Don't mistake me—he's a good man in our kind of work, and he believes in it. But he's proud . . . and he's stuck on himself . . . and he hates hard. That business of his eye, it eats on him . . . never lets up."

"Generalized anti-whitey?"

"In a way, yes. But he really wants to know *who* did it. I'm not sure I hope he finds out."

Stuart changed the subject. "This Gervase Higgins worked for? What was Higgins' job? I've heard about Gervase—some—and it sounds like he's not likely to be elected man of the year by the Junior Chamber."

"Nope. He isn't," Blaisdell smiled. "All I know now about Higgins with Gervase was he was suppposed to be a kind of hanger-arounder, a slob, an errand boy."

"I'll have to talk to Gervase."

"Don't make any appointment ahead of time," Blaisdell said.

"Gervase is the kind of man, he makes an appointment with the law and you get there right on time, and you find out he's gone to Canada fishing."

"Shy type," Stuart said.

"That's a kindly way of putting it."

The brunette appeared, balancing a tray that seemed several sizes too big and too heavy for the way she was constructed. But she put it down on a serving table with grace and without disaster.

"Say-y-y!" Blaisdell said, giving the attention of admiring nose and eyes to the great, crusty, aromatic, dripping, charcoal-blackened lump of meat on the plate in front of him.

"Steak sauce?" she asked.

"You're a kidder," Blaisdell said. "How'd you know what I wanted?"

"It's that memory again," she said. "And what you look like wanting." She turned to Stuart with a smile only half-apologetic. "I took a chance on you, sir," she said. "You looked like the same thing."

"You're a cautious gambler," he said. "If it's just a little beyond dead rare and there's butter—not sour cream—for the baked potato and the salad dressing is just a little more than half blue cheese, you're in the money."

"I'm in it," she grinned and began putting down the rest of the dinner.

"Now, Mr. Stuart," Blaisdell said. "I'll ask you to look at that—and also you can pay for the dinner."

"I told you . . ." Stuart began, then, puzzled, "look at what?"

"That," Blaisdell muttered and nodded his head almost imperceptibly.

Following his gaze, Stuart saw a short, fat man, half bald, wearing a shimmering electric-blue suit and a yellow shirt and broad blue tie standing near the entrance, talking to the woman in tights. As an example of sartorial ingenuity, the man was arresting enough, but what gave him genuine distinction was the flamingo beak of nose, a feature so commanding as to diminish all competition, whether pendulous flesh or outlandish fabric.

"Our host?" Stuart asked curiously.

"Our host," Blaisdell said. "Worst crook and best restauranteur in five hundred miles, any direction. Giuseppe Gervase."

"So?" Stuart said slowly and studied the man. *He's outrageous enough, the Lord knows, and it'll be interesting to chat with him no doubt, and I've got to do that but I'll bet, if what I hear is anywhere near accurate, I don't get damn all out of it. I wonder if a review of his income tax returns over—say the last ten years—would make him any more gossipy. I'll suggest that to Rembert.* "So," he said aloud, "Wynnsboro's answer to Jimmy Durante. Kind of gone to gut, isn't he?"

"It's excusable," Blaisdell said. "He eats from his own kitchens."

"If that result is inevitable, I'm going to quit right now," Stuart said. So saying, he cut and forked another generous mouthful and chewed it without effort and felt it slide richly across his tongue and down his throat and cut another piece and spoke. "No, I'm not. Let the gut take care of itself. What do you know about that man?"

"What everybody knows," Blaisdell said. "He'll buy anything if the price is right. He'll sell anything, including close relatives. Some other things I don't know but believe. People who are said to bother him tend to disappear. They say he knows where nine bodies are buried because he picked the burial sites. I believe it—it's in character."

"I'll talk to him."

"You'll probably waste your time."

"It works out that way sometimes. About the bartender? Gus?"

Blaisdell shrugged. "I don't know except that Thompson had quit funnin' you, that I know."

"Do you know who the people were, the drunks he heard shooting off their mouths."

"Only in a general way. They're members. They're important businessmen in the town. I do know their names, but I'm not going to tell you. That's up to Gus. He put his neck out a piece as it is now. I'm not going to stick it out any further for him. Maybe he will—maybe he won't. That's up to you to find out."

Stuart took another mouthful of steak and let it melt.

"You level with us," he said. "I appreciate it. I imagine you know it's not the usual thing."

"Probably not. What do you do next?"

"See Gus and Gervase. Snoop. Tell the boss that the picture has a name—of sorts. You said you're still going to organize Wynnsboro. When?"

"Even the coffee is good," Blaisdell said, draining his cup and using his napkin with deliberation. "That depends. I would rather do it after you get your man. My idea is that getting him would soften the place up some. Especially since now you know he's a local. Like it or not, that puts the town on a spot that's not any more comfortable than an afternoon in hell." He paused and signaled the hovering brunette and pointed to his coffee cup. "On the other hand, you haven't got him yet, and you may never get him. If that's the case we'll go ahead cold turkey."

"We'll get him. Now that he's got an identity we'll get him," Stuart said seriously. "But I can't promise tomorrow."

It took the big car and its master just over seven minutes from the restaurant to the motel. Entering the lobby, Stuart was greeted by a raucous wolf whistle from a caged mynah bird which, plainly, looked upon the lobby and all who crossed it as a private fiefdom.

The nutty bird only whistles at men, Stuart remembered. *Queer as a set of purple teeth.* He got his key, went to his room, thoughtfully removed the picture from its envelope and studied it. *So you've got a name,* he told it, *now let's find you a place. The hell with Rembert's peaceful weekend in the country,* he thought, as he picked up the telephone and asked for the long-distance operator.

"I found out who it was," he said when Rembert's voice came on the wire, rather querulously.

"About time," Rembert said. For a moment the line was silent except for the faint crackling hum of a thousand miles. "*What* did you say?"

"I said I know his name, or anyhow a name. It could be a phony, but I know within limits who he is."

"Who is he?" Rembert's voice had gone tense with excitement. "No. No. Code it, put it on the wire. Do you have an open Western Union?"

"I think so," Stuart said. "No, I know so. There's an all nighter down the street."

"Move it, move it," Rembert said impatiently. "To the office. I'll be leaving here in ten minutes."

"No need to rush," Stuart said cautiously. "It's still full of holes."

"Everything is always full of holes," Rembert said oracularly. "And everything needs a hurry. Move all you know, now."

Stuart typed and coded the short telegram, sent it himself, returned to the room and told himself to wake up no later than seven and, having faith in the mysterious processes which went on inside his skull, stripped and got into bed and allowed himself five minutes to consider the possibilities, agreed with himself that they had improved but on the whole were still bleak, and went peacefully to sleep.

His skull did not fail him. He was awake at five minutes before the hour, showered, shaved, reluctantly put on a tie and lightweight sport jacket. *The way that man dresses,* he told himself, *maybe I even ought to go formal.* He breakfasted in the frigid igloo of the coffee shop, returned to the lobby, absently repaid the mynah's indecent proposal in kind and asked the man at the desk to call a taxi.

Finding Giuseppe Gervase at any given time, Blaisdell had advised him, was a catch-as-catch-can proposition. The likelihood was that daylight would not discover him in any of his several restaurants since they were costly rendezvous for Wynnsboro's affluent and opened late, or even at the numbers drops or the taverns which, so far as Blaisdell's information went, he did not often visit personally.

"He has runners. Higgins probably was one," the Teamster had said. "Likely your best bet is that auto parts joint of his. I've been told he gets a certain amount of good, clean, harmless fun out of giving nigger customers a hard time. Hobby of his, the sonofabitch."

Stuart could have spared the effort he put himself to during his twenty-minute taxi ride to the tarnished cinderblock and corrugated-iron cavern of a warehouse set amid the pennant-decked bargain counter of Wynnsboro's long row of secondhand car dealers toward the edge of the city.

"Gervase in?" he asked of a sleepy-eyed man in stained dungarees and skivvy shirt leaning back in a scarred wooden swivel chair with his heels comfortably aloft on the surface of a rolltop desk.

"Nope." The man, reluctantly awake, turned his attention to the gatefold of a *Playboy* magazine, which had been separated from the publication and pinned to the wall above the desk.

"New one," he said. "Just picked it up last night. Some tits."

"Sure are," Stuart said. "You expect Mr. Gervase?"

"Nope," the man said. "Not soon. You know, that's a darn good magazine, better all the time."

"Sure is," Stuart said. "If not soon, how soon?"

"T'mara mornin'. Went to N'Orleans. Could be back t'night, but I ain't sure. Y'all wanta see him?"

"When he's here," Stuart said.

"Ya'll come back," the man said, closing one eye and letting the other, half-closed, rest ruminatively on the gatefold.

"Sure are some tits," he said. "G'bye now."

"Sure are," Stuart said. "Be seein' yah."

*　　*　　*

Back at the motel, Stuart gave the mynah another dishonest promise, picked up his key and an urgent summons to call the assistant director's straight-through line.

"You see that man?" Rembert demanded as soon as he was on the line.

"Nope," Stuart said.

"Where've you been then?"

"Tryin' to see him, boss."

"Where is he?"

"Gone. N'Awlins. Back t'mara. Ah'll see him, sure will."

"If you're trying to be funny, I am not repeat not amused," Rembert said dangerously.

"I'm sorry," Stuart said. "This place is either giving me hookworm or the heebie jeebies."

"How about that colored bartender?"

"He's next."

"All right, keep me informed. Incidentally, we've got a trace —as far as Mexico City."

"From there?" Stuart asked, fully alert.

"Havana," Rembert said in a tone of total disgust.

Stuart sat and contemplated the telephone and, making a decision which he assured himself was logical and possibly cold blooded, dialed the number of the Wynn residence and was uncomfortably aware of inner tumult as he waited for an answer.

Martine answered on the fourth ring and obligingly agreed to call Amy from the terrace and the sunshine.

"Hello cop," she said. He hoped the easy welcome of her voice meant genuine pleasure as well as politeness and felt the tumult getting worse.

"I'm getting a little more sophisticated about your town," he said. "You know it, naturally, but it's new to me. I've found a great place to take you to dinner if you'll be nice enough to come."

"I should have better judgment—but I'll come," she said. "I'll pick you up. Seven all right?"

"Sure is, ma'm. But wait a minute. Would you mind taking me out to your club for a drink first?"

"You're broke?" she asked suspiciously.

"No, but you did invite me. I'm just calling your bluff."

"It wasn't a bluff," she said. "But it sounds sneaky."

She was in white again. It was crisp and short and gleaming above the long, lovely brown curve of leg and below the rosy-golden upper swell of breast revealed by the deep cutout of collar line.

"Why the club?" she asked as he bent over, negotiated the tricky backward twist and settled into the right seat of the Porsche.

"The Stuarts go first-class," he said. "For example, look at you. You didn't come from steerage."

"Maybe not. But I'm sophiscated too—the club does not have the best drinks in Wynnsboro."

"All right, I know it. I'm taking advantage of you. I can't go there alone on a guest card, and I want to ask one quick question there and then I'll take you where the drinks are better."

"What kind of a question? Who?"

"Listen, Amy." He was at once deadly serious. "Gus. The bartender. He may know something I need to know. If you don't want to, all right, we'll skip it. But if you can put up with my being nosy, will you go in and order a drink and then go to the girl's room for a couple of minutes?"

"You get Gus in trouble and I swear I'll shoot you," she said.

"I'll shoot myself if I do," he said.

"All right. But I ought to have my head looked into."

They crossed the spacious veranda which surrounded the Gray Oak clubhouse on three sides and entered the softly lighted bar and took a small table. White-coated and silver-haired and somberly genial, the bartender whose distinction was that his real name was unknown to the membership wrapped his portly figure around the end of his mahogany domain and came in deference to the table.

"Evenin' Miss Wynn—sir," he said. "What can I do for you?"

"Evening Gus," Amy said. "You can make my friend a drink if you will. Nothing for me, thanks. Excuse me." She got up and left.

"Yes, sir?" Gus said.

"A martini please," Stuart said. He wondered whether he ought to call him Gus as the members did but, now that he knew better, decided against it. The drink came, and the bartender started to move away but stopped at Stuart's gesture.

"I talked to Andrus Thompson yesterday," he said. "In Baton Rouge."

"Yes?" the word was politely inquiring.

Stuart said, "He mentioned you."

"Oh." For a long moment the Negro looked down at Stuart who was acutely conscious, once more, that he was being weighed, measured, and evaluated. "I knew he would," the bartender said at length. "I told him he could—after I made up my mind about it."

"I want to talk to you—if you will," Stuart said.

"I thought you'd want to. But not here. Only one thing, Mr. Stuart—I know your name—what's this likely to do to me—in the long run?"

"Nothing if I can help it, and if what Thompson told me is right, nothing even without my help. You heard somebody say something, he said. They call that hearsay and nobody can make you testify to it."

"I know that, sir. I've got a lawyer too. In Angel Creek. But I mean what can it do that's not in court? I need this job, Mr. Stuart." The voice was low, carefully modulated, and Stuart was thankful that the only others in the bar were a man and woman entirely absorbed in each other.

"I'll keep you out of it," Stuart said. "But the names of the people you heard talking could help me."

"I see, sir. Excuse me." The bartender moved to the other table, went back to the bar and mixed two juleps and delivered them and returned to the bar. When Amy returned, he brought a check for her to sign and handed her a pencil. Amy signed and started to hand the check to him and stopped as she saw a folded slip of paper under it.

"What's this, Gus?" she asked.

"For your guest, Miss Wynn. Thank you." He took the check and moved back to the bar. Amy handed the paper to Stuart and looked at him inquiringly as he slipped it into his inner breast pocket without opening it.

"What's that?" she said, frowning slightly.

"When I can I'll tell you—if it turns out to mean anything," he said.

"You and your cop games," she said half angrily. "You promised me dinner, remember?"

"Just a minute, lovely, I forgot something." Stuart arose and went to the bar and grinned at the older man. "I thank you," he said. "What's your real name?"

"Augustus," the bartender said and grinned back.

It was a Monday night and The Rookery had only a few cars in the parking lot.

"We've practically got the place to ourselves," Stuart said as Amy expertly nestled the little car into a parking space.

"Well, you do know how to pick a diner," Amy said with approval. "Another one of Gervase's places. If he wasn't such a bum, I would be tempted to adore that man."

The brunette met them, smiling her professional welcome, and led them to a banquette along the wall. Stuart gave her one quick, startled, all-seeing look, for, this time, it was almost all-seeing indeed. The tights and ruffles and sequins had given place to a plain deep and sultry red body stocking which reached from toes to neck and concealed almost nothing at all because it was transparent.

"Wynnsboro's reply to topless," Amy said after they were seated and the brunette had gone toward the bar with Stuart's order for a Rob Roy and a martini.

"I ought to say wow, and I would if you weren't with me," Stuart said.

"Go ahead. Don't mind me."

"I didn't mean it the way you think. The difference is I'd rather say wow at you. You're beautiful, you know, Amy—you do tricks with my insides."

"By intention," Amy said.

It was absolutely true, he thought, looking at the deep wide-set gray eyes under heavy dark lashes, the generous mouth, and the chestnut luxury of hair that glinted red here and there in the long rich fall to her shoulders.

It's a good thing she's business, he told himself, *because otherwise my conscience might be deviling me for goofing off. This is only the fourth time I've been with her, counting that first dinner with her old man, and, my lad, you'd better watch it because you're getting into quicksand and you certainly never intended that. Probably few things anywhere would look sillier than a twenty-thousand-dollar-a-year cop with his tongue hanging out over a girl whose old man owns an entire city, probably a state, too, for all I know.* He was acutely aware of how conscious of her he had become.

And it was vaguely disappointing, therefore, that for the moment she did not seem conscious of him at all. She wore a puzzled speculative frown and, he became aware, was watching the brunette, now approaching from the bar.

"What is it?" he said. "Thinking of calling the Watch and Ward Society? Or if it's jealousy, which I doubt, forget it—she's not even in your league."

Amy flashed him a preoccupied smile. "Neither," she said. "I was just wondering . . ."

"Wondering what?"

She shook her head. "I don't know. She looks familiar."

"Well, you're seeing it all. If she's familiar, she'd have a tough time hiding it tonight. Steak interest you? I ate here last night. They're superb."

"I know. I've been here before. Steak? Of course."

She took her eyes away from the brunette and gave them wholly to him. *I don't know what it is except that it has to be nutty,* she thought. She looked at the lean, scarred, unhandsome face under its untidy thatch of coarse dark hair, graying a little around the edges. *I wonder how old he is,* she thought, and found herself unaccountably stirred. *Foolish,* she told herself, *he's a cop and why should you find yourself getting more and more interested in a cop, especially a United States cop, a buttinsky by trade, the kind of man whose work Amos automatically abominates? I certainly don't know what it is, except that for some insane reason he's exciting and the eyes and that slightly crooked mouth are so gentle, and how in the world does gentleness go with being a cop?* She found herself looking with approval at the square, brown, strong hand lying idle on the whiteness of the linen handy to his drink.

They ate and when a three-piece combo began to play at ten in an adjacent room, they rose without discussing it and went to dance. She was light and sinewy in his arms despite her height.

"I quit learning anything in my teens," he said. "That stuff they do now, I wouldn't even know how to approach. I'm sorry."

"Don't be," she said, grinning. "I'm no Watusi type either. I can tango, I can rhumba, I can waltz, and I can even fox-trot. That's the repertoire. When I want a workout, I play tennis or swim."

"If you weren't so obviously rich, I'd ask you to marry me right now," he said. *And, you goddamn idiot,* he told himself, *you more than half mean it, maybe more than three-quarters.*

"It's an interesting idea," she said. "But what has my being rich to do with it? I didn't earn it. Neither did pa, anyhow not all of it. The breeding stock was there before he started."

"That's it—it's there," he said. "I probably couldn't keep you in perfume, much less Porsches. The one you're using smells like Replique, is it? A double sawbuck the quarter ounce.

You see what I mean? And you couldn't keep me because I'd make a lousy poodle."

"I don't keep poodles—they're too antsy-pantsy. Yes, it's Replique."

"I thought so. Besides I'm a cop."

"You might outlive it."

The tone was light, but they were both a little uneasily and a little breathlessly aware of something deeper and stronger and that neither was yet willing to acknowledge aloud. Like it or not, they both knew, the barriers were there and they were formidable.

It was two o'clock and closing time when they left the roadhouse and were struck, as though by a physical blow, by the heavy summer sultriness of the air.

"Whew!" Stuart grunted. "I thought New York was hard to take in the summer, but . . ."

"But nothing," she interrupted. "At least we've got air that isn't half exhaust pipe."

"But it's half water, steam I mean."

"You gave me an idea and anyhow I'm not sleepy. Do you swim?"

"Yes. Why? But I haven't any trunks with me."

"That's no problem. If you want, let's go home so I can change. You can wear a pair of Amos'."

"*His* trunks? I'd look like a cub scout in a carnival tent."

"Who cares? It's night. Besides you're not exactly a midget."

"I'm no dinosaur either. But, all right. There's nothing wrong with the idea. It's splendid."

The Porsche took them to the one-story mansion, and Amy handed him a pair of tan trunks and pointed out a bathroom.

"They have a drawstring," she said. "Give me five minutes. I'll be back, Replique and all."

He was standing in the living room, feeling foolish but thanking providence for the drawstring, which was his only salvation, when she returned, tall, sweetly formed, deep of breast and smiling at him in a tight, brief, black, strapless suit.

She looked at the bundle of cloth around his middle and grinned. "When does the balloon go up?"

"Don't pick on me, please lady. Where are we going? The pool?"

"Pool nothing. The water would be practically scalding. Wait and see. It's about ten miles. Just a minute, I'll take a couple of robes."

The moon was long set, but the sky was without cloud and there was no wind and the little lake lay blackly calm, a faithful mirror for a million stars. They got out of the car and walked hand in hand, confiding in the night, down to a narrow strip of beach. It felt like sand and the starlight called it possibly white. Stuart took a deep breath and unconsciously squeezed the hand he had. It squeezed back.

She took it away and said a little breathlessly, "Last one in's a nigger baby." Then instantly contrite, "Watch your fat mouth, Amy."

He chuckled. "I don't think that's going to start a race riot. OK, let's go."

They hit the water together in long shallow dives and came up together, getting rid of the splash in quick shakes of the head and, without consultation, settling down shoulder to shoulder into the smooth fluid rhythm of an easy crawl. They did not speak, but he was acutely aware of her nearness, the soft gurgle of water, the momentary flash of her arms as she rolled and they came up in turn and dug through the starlit sparkle of disturbed water. The water was cool and exciting flowing along the length of his body and he was conscious of great well being.

After ten minutes straight out into the black lake, they pulled up in unspoken agreement, treading water.

"Why isn't it hot?" he asked.

"It's over a hundred feet deep, that's why. I'm glad to learn you can swim."

He laughed aloud and then grinned at her in the starlight.

"What's that all about?" she said.

"Sheer, undeserved contentment. I bellow when I'm happy; it's a rare thing and needs encouragement."

"So am I," she acknowledged. "Grand? Isn't it grand?" Her hand touched his and without further preliminary and without accounting for it he had her in his arms and their mouths came together and held. They sank.

They kept going down a long time and a long distance of which neither one was acutely conscious since their full attention was otherwise engaged. They came up just in time and did not speak since their lungs were busy pumping oxygen into the space where it was needed for more than one reason.

Silently, thoughtfully, they turned together and began swimming slowly, almost lazily back toward the beach. Both were subconsciously aware that some profoundly important crisis awaited them there and neither was consciously willing to guess exactly how it would be.

They came out of the water together and stood close to each other on the warm white sand. Without either needing words, he reached for her and she came to him, raising her arms. The kiss was long and slow and searching, and the wet bodies melted toward each other in a gentle sort of savagery. He felt his flesh rising urgently inside the bundled envelope of Amos' shorts and was aware that she must feel it as well. Jeff Stuart had lived thirty-six years and had not been a hermit, but he knew he had never felt a sexual compulsion so demanding as this. There was nothing casual about this—it hurt with an exultant agony of physical pain.

She took her mouth away and bent backward and looked up at him and he could see, even in the faint light, the questioning in her eyes. He bent his head and kissed her throat and then put up his left hand to the top of her black suit and began gently to draw it down from her breasts.

"No," she said and stepped out of his arms. "No, and I mean no."

"I'm sorry," he said, not meaning it, feeling illogically resentful. He made no move to touch her again. Instead for a long time they stood looking at each other, examining, testing, and suddenly, they both knew, loving. At length, she nodded her head.

"No," she said. "I didn't mean no."

Deliberately, not taking her eyes away from his, she reached both hands to the bathing suit and slowly rolled it down, down from breasts and belly and hips and legs, unafraid, baring the dark triangular tangle of the pubis in pride and willing submission. "No," she said again. "I didn't mean no."

Amos Wynn's bathing trunks lay in a sodden bundle around his ankles. He stepped out of them and knelt where she lay on the sand, looking up at him. Without otherwise touching her, he bent his head to kiss her breasts and felt the nipples rise to the summons of his questioning tongue. She sighed and reached for him and pulled him down to her and her thighs opened.

"There," she whispered and he felt himself invading the warm, wet darkness of her and felt her hips rising against him and was conscious of the seal-sleek wetness and response of the vibrant body beneath him. The friction of the pubic hair where their bodies were joined carried its own strange electrifying excitement.

She murmured something he did not understand, and he muttered and did not understand that either although he knew in some dim corner of awareness that whatever he said must have been maudlinly idiotic. For both it was a gulf without any standard of measurement. It was both endless and ended in a moment when they drew apart and opening his eyes to look at her again, to examine the loveliness suddenly and unaccountably his he was at first aware that he could see her more clearly. He looked upward from her face, now painted rosy against the sand.

"It's daylight," he said in total surprise.

"And us jaybird-naked," she said shakily and went up on one elbow to kiss him again, tips of her breasts caressing his chest lightly, yet with an electrifying awareness in both of them.

She stood up, tall and graceful in her nakedness. She

scratched an arm urgently and then slapped with vigor at her right rump.

"Damn the mosquitoes," she said. "Savages. Love among the cannibals. I'm one vast lump and it itches. Why didn't you warn me?"

"I didn't know. This is your state, you know," he said innocently, wanting to have her in his arms again and, then, acting on the desire and added as she turned her mouth up to his and came closer, "They didn't bite me."

"Cop's blood," she said bitterly. "Not even vampires would . . ."

Driving back toward the city, she took her eyes from the road and studied him with grave curiosity. "How much does it matter I wasn't a virgin?" she asked.

"None," he said and knew he was lying since he was, knowingly without any logic, savagely jealous.

"I'm sorry I wasn't—I wish I had been," she said, somberly. "Even if the other was only one and only less than nothing. I should have had it all here for us."

"Don't talk like that, Amy," he said roughly, meaning it. "I tell you it doesn't matter." *And it won't*, he told himself, *it won't and what the hell do you expect you could ask of her anyhow.*

"Do you want me to tell you about it—so you'll know it was nothing?"

"No!" he nearly shouted.

"All right, I won't," she promised. "Just believe me—it was nothing and I wish it hadn't even been that."

"Shut up! I'm in love with you," he said.

"You'd better be," she said.

At six o'clock in the morning of a day that promised early to be both lowering and scorching, back in his clothes, he stood at the door of the Wynn house with Amy in his arms. He put two fingers of his left hand gently under her chin to tip her mouth up to his, but she drew back and looked at him, frowning.

"Just a second, I think I'd better tell you something and I don't know whether I ought. Probably I hadn't ought, but I'm going to anyhow."

"Don't," he said abruptly.

"It's not about me," she said, reading his mind. "I remembered where I saw the girl before."

"What girl?"

"The naked one in the red nothing. At The Rookery."

"Why? I don't get it," he said puzzled.

"I saw her there about six months ago. She had more clothes on. I was there for dinner, and we were having a drink and I heard something loud and there was a man standing beside this girl near the door and he was cussing her. Dirty language. Then he slapped her. It was the man you've got on that silly cop picture of yours."

"Thank you, dear," he said after a while and drew her back to him.

"Probably shouldn't have told you," she muttered and raised her lips.

By eight thirty, shaved and showered and dressed again, he was back in a taxi heading toward Gervase's tatterdemalion warehouse and wondering what small chance the day offered of intercepting Wynnsboro's virtuoso of free enterprise—free-wheeling would be closer, he reflected.

He had had trouble persuading his mind to get off the subject of Amy Wynn and the unbelievable night just past. The difficulty was that every time he thought of her, his insides had insisted on swelling into a huge lump of satisfied delight with the world. But, with effort, he had got his mind back on business and was now dutifully pursuing it.

You're still a cop and her old man still owns a city and probably a state, he had warned himself. *Who the hell do you think you are . . . anyway?*

He walked in the door of Gervase's dismal headquarters, tapped at the door of the office, and walked in without waiting for an answer. Gervase was there, wearing slacks and a loud sport shirt, moodily inspecting the *Playboy* gatefold which still held a place of worship on the wall over the desk. He turned at the squeal of hinges and Stuart's footsteps and directed at his caller past the great divide of his nose a black-eyed stare pregnant with the lack of hospitality.

"Who're you?" he grunted.

"My name's Stuart, and I'd like to use a little of your time if you don't mind."

"I mind. Why? I asked who you are, not your name. I don't give a shit about your name."

Stuart reached for his wallet, fingered out the Bureau ID card, and laid it on the scarred desk top under Gervase's nose.

"FBI, Mr. Gervase."

"So what? I got nothing to do with the FBI. Whaddya want?"

"You know a man named Higgins? Pete Higgins?" Stuart's voice had turned cold and his dark eyes were on Gervase's, direct and now wintry.

"Higgins? Who's he? Never heard of him." Gervase was glowering. "Don't waste my time."

Stuart took the manila envelope from beneath his right arm, drew out the print of Parker's work, and, first picking up the ID card and returning it to his wallet, laid the portrait on the desk.

"That refresh your memory?" he asked. "He worked for you. Your hired man."

"Never heard of him. You're fulla shit," Gervase said. Then he looked at the picture. "Oh, him. Yeah, I know him," he said with no discernible trace of embarrassment. "He owes me money, the shit."

"Where is he?" Stuart asked in a brittle voice.

"How should I know? If I knew where he was, I'd get my money."

"When did you last see him?"

"About"—Gervase's stare was surly—"I don't know it's any your business, whatever your name is. What about him?"

"We want him."

"Why?"

"Murder."

Gervase sneered. "You got to be full of shit. The slob wouldn't have the guts to kill a cockroach. Strictly a nothin'."

"When did you see him last?"

"That again. How'd I know? Month ago, two, three, he took off, that's all I know."

"Hear anything from him?"

"Nothin'. I told you he owes me money. You think he'd be sending me postcards?"

"You're not killing yourself cooperating," Stuart said.

"No. And I don't aim to be," Gervase said.

"That can be changed. If it becomes necessary," Stuart said.

"Try it, cop."

"If it gets to be advisable," Stuart said, picking up the portrait and sliding it back into the envelope. He turned to go, then paused at the door and spoke over his shoulder. "By the way, the chow in those restaurants of yours is first-class."

"Yeah. First-class," Gervase grunted, turning his gaze back to the gatefold.

20

The summons reached him at the Wynn summer home under the pines on the shore of the lake where Amy and Jeff Stuart were giving exultant fleshly acknowledgment to the mutually realized truth that, without either being able to blue-print the process in precise detail, they had become lovers and were glad of it.

They were lying on the skin of Amy's Kodiak bear—which she had given to Amos for his study but which he had sent to the lake so that he might be less painfully reminded that she had shot the beast and he had not—in front of a fire snapping redly and comfortably in the fireplace, defense against the air-conditioning. They were less than exhausted but for the moment, enormously pleased with what had transpired, they were content to muse upon what they had discovered in each other while they waited for the tidal wave to regenerate itself and sweep over them again. Jeff rolled and propped himself on one elbow and looked down, inventorying from less than a foot a face that he had often inventoried from vaster distances and even in its total absence. There it all was, lustrous chestnut hair, now indecorously tumbled, smooth broad brow, wide-set gray eyes now luminously drowsy, full wide mouth faintly smiling up at him.

"You're strong," she murmured.

"You're incredible," he said back. "Also I suspect you're permanent."

"You had better be permanent," she said.

"I didn't think to ask or to do anything sensible," he said half-dubiously. "Did you use anything?"

"Anything?"

"Oh, hell. I mean take any precautions."

"Of course not."

"Isn't that a little reckless?"

"I don't think so. Not since I decided you're going to marry me."

He bent and kissed her lightly and arranged a spurious frown.

"You have? You didn't tell me."

"I didn't think it was necessary. Will you light me a

cigarette?" She waited until she had drawn the smoke into her lungs and exhaled, watching the gray haze curl upward in the firelight. "Anyhow, it may be the only way I can keep you from wrecking my town."

"That again. Practical, of course. Nothing foolish—like love?"

"Oh, that too. An enormous lot in fact. What you might call a bonus, something extra. Tell me, do you want children?"

"I hadn't really thought about it. It seemed a little premature, considering everything; but if you do, of course. I was one of seven so I imagine there's a certain amount of fecundity somewhere in me."

"To tell the truth, I don't know about me. I was an only child and so was Amos before me. But I know I want more than one. I grew up alone and it would have been hell if it hadn't been for pa."

"You're fairly gone on your old man, aren't you?"

"I always have been. Now there are two of you. I hope you get along together."

"I will if he will. Out of gratitude if nothing else." He ran a gentle finger across her forehead and the thick eyebrows and down to the tip of her nose, let it pause on her lips, then moved it down to her throat. She reached up and took the whole hand and put it on her right breast and held it there.

"M-m-m," she said.

He felt himself rising again and bent to kiss her, the right hand now curving around her waist to draw her toward him. She rolled to him and twined her legs into his, and the telephone began to ring.

"Damn it!" he said.

"Damn it," she said and, as the ringing continued, untangled herself from an embrace which had begun to get complicated. She got to her knees and slid upright in supple curves and walked toward the summoning bell. He watched her go, exulting in the firelight picking out velvety highlights on breast and flank and long leg and movement. *She's all of a piece,* he thought, *all of one tall and graceful and lovely, beautiful, beautiful piece. And how could this happen to you?*

The ringing stopped, and he heard her voice, low and clear, and then she was coming back toward him and the instantaneously returning surge of his desire for her. But the smooth brow was frowning and her eyes were puzzled.

"It's for you. What . . . ?"

"I left the number with the hotel, darling. It's a regulation."

"Oh, that's all right. You know I told you to. But this call is from New York . . . somebody called Bert something . . . no Rembert, that's it. Who could that be?"

"The boss," he said, getting up, hearing somewhere inside himself the old, by now instinctive, sense of the call to action.

"Hello. This is Stuart," he said into the instrument, feeling obscurely silly to be standing naked at attention before the silver-thatched, impeccable martinet and monitor of his professional life, no matter how far away he might be in the flesh.

"Rembert. Where the hell are you?"

There could be several answers to that, you bastard, Stuart thought, *and it would serve you right if I told the truth.* He didn't have to think of an alternate because Rembert wasn't waiting.

"Can you get a plane tonight?"

"For where, sir?"

"For here, of course."

"There's a two A.M. I should be able to make."

"Well, make it. And come direct to the office. This could be it." Rembert's voice carried a thin overtone of excitement, and Stuart felt it too. Instinct, instinct, and long training. When they called you like this . . .

"Anything I should know right now, sir?"

"No. It'll keep until you get here." Stuart knew Rembert's professional aversion to saying anything significant over a telephone he did not certainly know was secure.

"All right, sir."

"Where's your passport? Got it with you?"

"No, in my apartment. Top right dresser drawer. Somebody could pick it up."

"Somebody will. I'll have a bag packed for you. You'll be leaving here at eight. Don't miss that plane."

The line went dead and Stuart thoughtfully cradled the phone and turned and found her beside him, her eyes questioning and at the same time full of sad knowledge. He put his arms around her shoulders, and she came to him unresisting for a moment. Then she shook her head and drew back and looked at him.

"The manhunt, isn't it," she said. It was not a question.

"Yes." He nodded. "I'll have to go."

"I know. I heard. The last plane. We'd better get dressed."

It was thirty miles to the airport, and for all but two of those she drove in silence, abstractedly expert with brake and clutch and curve. He sat beside her equally silent, glum in the knowledge that he could feel her unease and her hurt, aware that between them lay some unsaid but fundamental difference, afraid to plumb it for the fear that it could mar the great thing that they had only now begun to find.

"That comes first, before anything else, doesn't it?" she said as the airport floods brightened the black horizon ahead of the car.

"You know the work I do, Amy," he said. "It has nothing to do with us."

"I wish that was even half-true," she said in a low and bitter voice. "And I wish now, more than half-wish, that I had never told you."

"One: I love you. Two: Don't make trouble for your conscience. I'm glad you told me, but you have to believe I'd have found out anyhow . . . sooner or later, I would have found out." *One thing she'll never learn from me, if we live to be a hundred and live all but five minutes of that together, is that I knew before she told me. But it's true that I'm glad she did. If this woman does in fact love me, which my gut knows is true*

*but my head holds to be impossible, the absolute, final, and
utter proof of it is that she did tell me—when she not only did
not have to but passionately did not want to. The fact that her
reasons for holding out made absolutely no sense in my eyes has
nothing to do with it. The point is that she did tell me.*

*Now, it is obvious without being told very much, I am about
to be sent to lay hands on him. I have known for three days
who he is. Now they think they know where he is. And if
they're right, I am going to get him pretty soon. The strange
thing is that I wonder now if I feel the same about getting him
this minute as I did three days ago before I knew who he was—
and before she told me.* In a strange sense now he owed Barton's killer a debt of gratitude as well as the one of retribution.
*Do I want him as badly as I did? And if I do, what difference
does it make? If they're right, if they are, I am going to get him,
of course. Even if it does hurt this woman I cherish, even if I
hate the thought of hurting her whether her reasons are illogical or not.*

"What did he tell you?" Amy asked in a voice in which he
could hear the strain as the Porsche turned off the highway
into the airport approach. "If I can ask a cop."

"Don't, Amy," he said. "I can't think of anything I know I
wouldn't willingly tell you." *You stand convicted a liar,* he told
himself in shamed anger. "But he didn't tell me much—he
never does—on a telephone." *That at least, you phony, is the
truth.* "He just said to get there and I'm going to be going
somewhere else. Somewhere outside the country. That's all I
know now."

"It couldn't be something else, could it?"

"Something else? Like what?"

"Some other case. Something else than this bad dream."

"I doubt that. Amy, I can only guess, but my guess is they
have a reason to think they know where he is and they want me
to go and make sure it's him."

"Treed, is that it?" She stopped the car at the entrance. "And
now you go to shoot him out of his tree. Poor hunted thing."

"Amy, try to remember, he's a killer."

"Oh, I know, darling. I just wish you weren't a bloodhound."

"I'm not. It's a job."

"I wish to God men would think up some other excuse for justifying every damned thing they do!" she said. Then she turned and kissed him and said, "Oh, darling, I'm sorry. I wish I hadn't said that. Come on, you've got to hurry. I'll go to the plane with you."

"What about the car?"

"Let it sit. They know it's mine—nobody'll touch it."

"You Wynns," he sighed. "I'm beginning to understand what it's like to own a city."

"I think I would rather own you."

"I gave you the deed, remember?"

She walked through the terminal with him, her arm linked in his, pressing close against him. They went on out the brightly lighted boarding wing and out to the jet, its offside engines aleady whining, and came to the foot of the ladder.

"All right, tiger. Go get what you're after," she said, turning to face him, putting her arms over his shoulders and pressing herself against him in such long, taut curves that, half-embarrassed, he knew his body had sprung to its instinctive, urgent reach for her flesh again.

"They'll arrest me," he said. "I love you." He broke away and started up the ladder, stepping awkwardly, toward the conspiratorially smiling stewardess in the doorway.

At six thirty A.M., as quickly as a taxi could hurtle him along the still deserted Van Wyk Expressway and over the Triboro and downtown to Sixty-ninth Street, he entered the building on Lexington and took the night elevator to the tenth floor. A uniformed guard got up from the blond receptionist's desk, leaving a half-eaten pastrami sandwich and half-finished coffee that smelled unpleasantly of the waxed cardboard which contained it, and led him along the corridor to Rembert's office.

The assistant director, needing to get rid of the gray stubble on his chin and looking puffily all of his age, came erect in his big swivel chair in which he had been nodding away the night's impatience.

"Not any too soon," he said sourly. "You won't any more than make the flight."

"I still don't know where, sir," Stuart said.

"Naturally." Rembert frowned, an expression which went with whiskers no better than it did with clean shaven jowls. "Now, listen. There's no extra time for details."

"Yes, sir."

"You've got the man made. Now, careful, any reason, any at all to doubt the identification?"

"I don't think so. I got verification from another source since I notified you."

Rembert looked up sharply. "When?" he demanded.

"Tonight . . . last night, that is."

"Where from?"

"Wynn's daughter. We guessed right; she had seen him and half-remembered it." From long habit, Stuart knew that Rembert would prefer to have any perceptive guess accomplished in the plural.

"So that's where you were." Rembert grunted. "How was it she remembered?"

"Yes, sir," Stuart said, fairly certain that he hadn't blushed. "She had been in a local nightclub six months or so ago and had seen a man hit a cocktail waitress. She remembered the incident but only just now, I think, connected the face."

"Why 'just now'?"

"Because I'm not absolutely sure. You know, the atmosphere down there. Nobody really wants to remember. It's instinct. They're town proud; they wish the whole business would go away."

"I know about that. Did you know Wynn went to Washington and tried to throw weight around and get the Bureau out? Damn fool thing to try." Rembert picked up a heavy envelope and tapped the edge impatiently on the immaculate surface of his desk. "Let's get to it. Your ticket and passport and money and most of what you'll need to know are in here. Your bag's there in the corner. You're on Pan Am 2—tourist class."

"For where, sir?" Stuart asked while, even in the surge of anger, realizing that the assistant director probably simply assumed that if he didn't know where, he ought to.

"Beirut, of course," Rembert said impatiently, confirming Stuart's diagnosis without saying so.

Stuart kept himself in hand, aware that this was requiring some effort. Then, without conscious thought other than that he was due on an airplane, he decided against it. "God damn it, I don't know thing one about any of this," he exploded.

Rembert's eyebrows shot up in astonishment, but, just as outrage was about to set in, he shook his head and grinned. The grin was totally without precedent.

"That's right. You don't. I'm tired. All right, listen. There's a chance—maybe as good as fifty-fifty—that your man is in Lebanon. But we've got to be sure."

"In custody?" Stuart asked, unconsciously leaning forward to listen and to remember. So far, nothing new; he could have guessed this much as soon as Rembert had uttered the name of Beirut.

"No. That's why you're going. We've got a protocol problem, or perhaps I should say a diplomatic one. We can't bust the guy, naturally, and the Lebanese won't unless we're positive."

"Why not?"

"You probably know, or maybe you don't, that most of the raw stuff that gets turned into heroin in France and then comes into the States for our junkie population comes through the port of Beirut."

"Yes, I know. Starts in the poppy fields of Turkey. Somehow gets into the hubcaps of automobiles and airline stewardesses' brassieres."

"Yes. The Lebanese national police—the Sûreté—cooperate pretty well with our narcotics people. As a matter of fact, what we've got here was relayed to us from the Sûreté by the Bureau of Narcotics." Rembert's fundamental distaste for this intelligence was mirrored on his face, which did not surprise Stuart in the least, for he had long been aware how little love got lost between any two sets of United States lawmen.

"As I say, they cooperate, after a fashion. They stop some of the traffic. Obviously they don't stop it all, otherwise our junkies would have to go straight. Truth, I sometimes suspect they stop just enough to make a showing. Lebanon has lived on trade ever since the Phoenicians—and opium and morphine are trade. But that has nothing to do with us.

"What does have to do with us is that the man they think may be our man seems to be hooked in somehow with the drug traffic. He's not big, but he is known to and they believe he works for people who are. That's the knotty part."

"How so?"

"The Sûreté knows who the wheels are. They and the narcotics people, naturally, want to bust the wheels. And they don't want to spook them by grabbing your man for us unless they're absolutely sure he's him. So that lets you in."

"All right. Can I ask how they made him?"

"You got to go. You'll get that there. The first thing you're to do is see the director of the Sûreté. I don't have to warn you to be diplomatic about it. In the first place he's head of a national police force, piddling as the nation may be, so he's a big frog in that puddle. Moreover"— Rembert paused and shook his head incredulously—"the narcotics people tell us he's an authentic prince. Emir, they call it. Most likely up to his ass in royal dignity."

"What's the prince call himself?" Stuart asked, getting up, taking the envelope from Rembert's hand and starting across the room to pick up the waiting suitcase.

"The Emir Mohammed Abu Riche," the assistant director said solemnly.

Because the Bureau had forehandedly greased the machinery for him, Stuart was propelled through customs and immigration like a missile and boarded the 707, whose engines were already muttering, and went to his seat, ignoring the admonitory frown of the stewardess who met him in the cabin door.

21

The city had surprised him, blazing sun and glittering sea beating against sand and bare-boned cliffs, the bright *flambuoyants* in the mall separating the rutted pavement of the Corniche. Then, all at once, the glassy and glossy new hotels with their feet in the surf and the guests toasting in bikinis or less and then the plunge into the stifling heart of the old city. A cacophony of auto horns and the curses of outraged pedestrians, bent porters carrying pianos on their backs, dark men in *kuffieh* or *tarboosh,* women in black, fat-tailed sheep on the drive to the abbatoir, fierce men swaying far beneath their rumps the deep black pouches of pants seats tailored thus because they knew that when Jesus came the second time he would be born to a man and, since nobody knew when the blessed event might occur, it was only prudent as well as reverent to provide room for the delivery. And noise: the horns, the yells, the agonized bleating of streetcar bells, and over everything the everlasting raucous duel between wailing *muezzin* in the minarets and pealing Maronite Catholic bells in the church towers.

The Sûreté was exactly in character, yellow sandstone pockmarked with the bullet scars of revolutions, ancient and modern, high stooped from the narrow cobbles of the street, dispirited bougainvillea trying doggedly to bloom on the iron pillars. Inside, open, red-tiled space, and ancient wrought-iron staircases rising steep to the offices above.

Either the setting or the emir, chief of police of this Oriental maelstrom, was out of place. He got up from a desk piled a foot deep with documents, and came across the dusky, high-ceilinged coolness of his office, smiling urbanely. Salt and pepper tweed, complete with vest, portly figure but a strong one, gray-flecked black hair, smoothly barbered aquiline face, horn-rimmed spectacles on a black ribbon, an air of friendly interest combined with total self-possession.

"Mr. Stuart, I am happy to see you," the director said, holding out a strong dry hand to Stuart's. He nodded at the khaki-uniformed guard who had brought Stuart to the door. Moments later, the guard was back with aromatic jigger-sized cups. "You will take coffee," the emir said.

Stuart wondered how to go about dealing with a princely cop and how, if it came to that, he was to get his man away without formal extradition and unmeasured reams of red tape. He need not have worried. In the next forty-eight hours, he was to discover that the emir was not only a suave cosmopolitan but also an extraordinarily competent and almost unbelievably tough law officer.

"You want to know, of course, whether we have your man," the prince said. "And if we have, you want to know how best to deal with the affair."

"Of course, sir," Stuart said. "First, naturally, whether he actually is the man we want."

"I believe he is," the prince said. "I am almost certain. But, you understand, we must be entirely certain."

"I would like to ask, sir, how you got onto him."

The prince gestured toward the stacks of paper on his desk.

"There. And the drawing you circulated through Interpol. You understand, in a country like this, small as it is but with a difficult role in disturbed lands, a seaport, technically at war with Israel just across our border, theoretically half Christian and half Arab, the sluiceway of tradition for all manner of adventurers, spies, agents, political fugitives, desert oil princes, and the merchants of yellow diamonds who haunt them, oil men, smugglers, thieves, murderers, confidence men, money merchants, plotters, always plotters of a thousand kinds—in such a milieu there are many faces to watch and remember.

"It is, I suppose, a hobby that I spend much time watching them myself—Lebanon is small enough for that—although properly that work could be delegated. But I watch, hobby or duty or some of each I do not know.

"I saw this face and I remembered the poster and I wondered. In the end, curiosity became conviction. I spoke to your people—and now you are here—and now we shall see." He went to the desk and handed Stuart a form filled out in Arabic and French, bearing a small, blurry passport-size photograph.

"That is a *carte d'identité*. We require it of any foreigners resident here. If you cannot read the Arabic script, he has been here just more than three months."

Stuart studied the muddy little picture and at first felt only the sag of a dead end. The back of his mind had been printed so indelibly with that face; he had told himself that if ever he saw it again—and he swore to himself that he would—it could only be with the instant electric shock of recognition. But this? He didn't know. The sideburns, the bush of hair down the sides of the neck were gone; so much, he thought, for Parker's convictions about the fanatic devotion of the hairy ones. The eyes did not have the look of madness he had seen in the cemetery. The photograph was enough out of focus and badly enough printed to conceal any indefinable deformity of the long nose. But the thing that bothered him most was that failure of instinctive, instantaneous leap of knowledge that this was the face, indeed.

"I don't know," he said at last, handing the document back to the prince. "I honestly don't know. It could be the man. And it could be someone else. I ought to apologize, I was certain that I could say, immediately, yes or no."

"Of course." The prince was undisturbed. "These photographs are, for practical purposes, useless. You must see the man. It has been arranged."

By no overt signal which Stuart could detect, the oak door, twice the height of a man, opened. The man who entered was tall, stooped, swarthy, mustached, handsome, of middle years. The eyes were dark and glinting, half-hidden by heavy lids, and Stuart was aware that they were being used to take his measure in minute detail. *Rough customer,* he thought, in quick appraisal.

"Lieutenant Haddad," the emir said. "He will guide you."

"Yourself? You are standing clear?" Stuart asked.

"For me to be seen where the man can be seen would be unusual and would cause comment. For Lieutenant Haddad to be seen there will not. They know who he is, of course, but they are accustomed to seeing him."

Well, I'm in the dark anyhow and maybe I ought to get a little out of that and if I have to be rude to do it, I guess I'll have to be.

"But I don't know who Lieutenant Haddad is," he said.

"He directs that part of my force which deals with drug smuggling," the prince said. "Of course, Mr. Stuart, you would want to know with whom you deal. I am sorry—you are a stranger here."

"What do we do about this, Lieutenant?" Stuart turned to the thin man who had not yet spoken beyond a curt nod when his name was spoken.

"The man you want to see—here he goes by the name of Philip Henning, which is possibly not his own—appears fairly often late in a nightclub on the Corniche," Haddad said. "He has a girl there, one of the bar girls—she is not Lebanese— none of them are. He drinks more than a man should who wishes to keep his wits or his life."

"No, Henning is not his right name. But probably neither is the name I want him under. When will I see him?"

"Probably tonight—late. I will call for you at your hotel. You are at the St. Georges."

Stuart nodded, knowing it was not a question, knowing without resentment that they would of course have made it their business to know where he was, and probably much more as well.

"If he is the man, then what?" Stuart asked. "I was told this could be . . . well, delicate for you. Of course, we are anxious not to jeopardize your other cases."

"Of course. We are grateful," the prince said.

"The gratitude is on our side. If he is the man in fact, are we to collar . . . to take him immediately?"

The lieutenant sat forward to speak but sat back as the prince answered.

"I think not. It is, as you say, delicate. There, in a crowded place, the disturbance would be seen. This man has associates—no, I amend that—he, by himself, is of no importance to us, but we know that he is known to—and probably works for, in some illicit capacity—people who are known to us for other reasons. These people alarm easily and we wish not to alarm them more than is necessary. It is better to take him later—discreetly. If it is done well, as it should be, nobody needs to learn what has become of him."

"All right," Stuart said. "I am in your hands. And you have our thanks."

"For the actual arrest, I intend to be with you," the prince said, rising. "More coffee? No? I cannot blame you. It is our habit in the East and I fear our hospitality often abuses the nervous systems of our guests." He came around the desk and took Stuart's arm and walked him toward the tall door. "A driver is waiting to take you to your hotel. I suggest a rest. All Arabs sleep through the afternoon anyhow, and I recommend the custom to you for this day, at least. It may be a long night."

*   *   *

The stairway leading down into the din smelled of old urine and new whiskey and salty-oily harbor air. Up the steps rolled and pounded, almost palpable against his nerves, the beat of a rock 'n' roll band. Stuart followed the lieutenant, now out of his elegantly cut green uniform and into a pin-striped, double-breasted suit whose high pinched waist and flaring skirts somehow made him look, from the rear, absurdly like an Oriental potentate.

A fat, bald young man with cold inquiring eyes met them at the foot of the stairway, greeted the lieutenant by name, and took them through a curtain and into the deafening blare of the band, led them around the edge of a frenetic dance floor and back through tiers of tables to a small table at the back of the room. Stuart thought he saw lights shimmering on water and when the music stopped abruptly realized that they were on a concrete balcony only a few feet above the harbor. In the sudden silence, he could hear small waves slapping against the pilings beneath his feet.

"Who was that?" Stuart asked as the bald man moved away.

"The owner," the lieutenant said. "He breaks many laws."

"He seems to know you," Stuart said.

"It is a small country."

"And the laws he breaks?"

Haddad shrugged. "It is not important. He knows which laws not to break."

"It's blacker here than the inside of a witch's brassiere," Stuart said. "If this Henning hangs out here, how am I supposed to see him? Braille?"

"Pardon?" the lieutenant said.

"I'm sorry. I don't make jokes—rather I make an idiot of myself," Stuart said. "But this place is crowded. It's dark. It's noisy. And if the man is here, where is he? I will need to get close to look."

"Oh, excuse me. No, he wouldn't be here. If he has come, he will be in the bar, not here. Tell me, Mr. Stuart, does this man know you?"

"No. No, I don't think so. He has no reason to know me. And I saw him only once when he was . . . busy elsewhere. No, I do not think there is a chance in hell that he would know me."

"How is that . . . in hell? No doubt I will grow accustomed to American speech in time. I get accustomed to many things."

"There is no reason for him to know me, lieutenant. None at all."

"How, then, if I bring him to this table?"

Stuart hoped his jaw stayed in place. True, the murderer he pursued was being chased eight thousand miles from home base and in a strange country and in strange circumstances and company just as strange. But, since when did the law invite the murderer to sit down for a drink—or the murderer accept—in order to make things easier and more sure all around?

"You know this man?"

"As I said, it is a small country. And it is my occupation to know the people in it. Particularly strangers."

"It would make it simpler," Stuart said. But he thought at the same time that it would be an insult to any man's sense of fairness, provided he had one. *They taught me as a kid,* he reminded himself, *that there was something faintly lousy about shooting a pheasant out of a car window or blasting a duck on the water.*

The lieutenant, meanwhile, had been brooding into the tiny glass of Scotch which had been set before him.

"No," he said at last, sighing. "No. The director would not be happy with it."

"Not happy with what?" Stuart asked. "I'm sorry, Lieutenant Haddad, you leave me a curve or two behind . . . I'm sorry, I'm afraid I do not follow you precisely."

"He would not want me to bring Henning to this table. It would attract attention, not much, but any is too much. Henning knows me, of course, but to be seen with a stranger—and then to disappear—no, I think not."

"All right. It did sound bizarre. What else then? Is the man in this room?"

"Probably not. Almost certainly not," the lieutenant said. "At this hour." He held his watch up close to his eyes and shielded the dial in a cupped hand to read the luminous dial. "After midnight, he will be in the bar. He will be half drunk. He will be here to watch the woman and, of course, to be with her. Excuse me." The lieutenant rose.

"Where are you going?" Stuart asked.

"Into the bar. In five minutes you will come through that curtain"—he pointed across the noisy gloom—"the door to the bar is just beyond. This part is for tourists; the bar is the place for serious drinking—and for making rendezvous. It is dark there also, but not so dark as here. It is small; there are booths and tables and it is divided into three small rooms. The man is a regular and so, out of courtesy to the dollars which he carries, he has a regular place. Pass beyond the bar itself and step to the left. The man and the woman will be in the small booth at the end. You will know; I will be sitting with them."

"You really do make it your business to know the strangers," Stuart said. "Doesn't this man fear you?"

"I believe not," the lieutenant said with formality. "I, too, sleep with the woman. It is a convenient arrangement. He pays the rent." He strode away, threading a pathway among the crowded tables, a picture of dignity, while Stuart looked after him in quizzical awe.

Stuart sat alone, watching the second hand of his wristwatch perform its unhurrying march, looking up only to brush off— politely—an overdone blonde who wanted to trade her company and possibly body for drinks. When the watch had ticked its deliberate way to his appointment, he rose without haste. His feelings, to his surprise, were unemotionally clinical. He was doing what needed to be done, making sure. And he was finding the errand slightly distasteful; he found no zest in this, though, damn it, there should have been.

He parted the curtain and passed through, crossed a stone-paved hallway, once again assaulted by the smell of urine, opened a door and instead of rock 'n' roll, found himself coming up against another solid wall of sound, this time emanating from an accordion, a violin, and human lungs. The air was nearly opaque and rank.

He moved slowly by the bar, remembering directions, and immediately had to stave off a boarding party of another blonde and a red-haired competitor. Murmuring thanks and apologies and politely prying away clutching tentacles tipped with impossibly iridescent nail paint, he moved through the eye-smarting pond of smoke. He saw the lieutenant first, then the girl. She was, he saw with some surprise, pretty with a heart-shaped impudent face, dark hair long to her shoulders, and, even more surprising, without the lacquer and simonize finishing coats of her colleagues.

There were the three in the booth, with a bottle of Black and White on the table in front of them, and the man in the shadow at the back of the booth had his head down and Stuart could not see his face. But Haddad, he knew, was aware of his coming and then Haddad did something to raise his companion's head to attention. Awkwardly, he let his right elbow slide on the wet table top so that it jammed against Stuart's leg and forced him to miss a step. Instantly Haddad was on his feet apologizing loudly and Stuart, ignoring the deliberate assault for what it was, kept his eyes on the shadowed man.

The head came up, curious at the interruption, not particularly alert or wary, looking at them. Stuart found himself staring, from not more than five feet, directly into the face and into the eyes, then insane, now slightly clouded with alcohol, that he had last seen beside a decayed mausoleum on the other side of Myrtle Avenue in the city of Wynnsboro.

There was no question, none at all.

Where was the exultation? He felt nothing but cold certainty. Accepting the lieutenant's apology in curt politeness, he moved back out of the bar, fended off another assault from the bar girls, and went back to his table in the big room and waited.

Ten minutes later he saw the lieutenant's tall, pinch-waisted elegance returning and waited without excitement.

Haddad, who was aware that he had been unexpectedly and extraordinarily tense as Stuart had entered the bar and he himself had created the diversion to raise Henning's face for inspection, sat down again as Stuart moved away into the fog of smoke. *He'll wait for me,* he reflected, *because he wouldn't know what else to do. He'll wait long enough for me to do the private business which I now must do because, having thought of all the possibilities, this seems to me to be the neatest and surest. And that is what is needed now: neatness and certainty and no undesirable consequences.*

Under the table, he pressed a knee urgently against the girl's leg. She looked up quickly and he, making sure that Henning's head was down again contemplating the whiskey in the glass in his hand, looked directly at her and deliberately completed the closing of his hooded right eye, the one on the far side of Henning. The gamin face began to tighten in anger, but then she shrugged. Haddad had the answer he wanted. He picked up his drink, finished it in a gulp and spoke to Henning.

"I go now, my friend," he said. "Duty. The job, you know."

"OK, OK," Henning said in tones only slightly thickened, for, if Peter Higgins was a mortal of few positive virtues, one he did possess was a set of entrails highly resistant to the assaults of alcohol. "Goin' out 'n shag crooks, huh? Good man."

Haddad grunted something that might have been mirth.

"You know, they can't all be allowed to run free," he said.

"Have n'other drink," Henning said.

"Not tonight," Haddad said and got up and climbed the fetid stairway to the street and moved around the corner of the building into shadow and waited. She came in three minutes, and she was angry.

She came to him cursing, in low-voiced hissing amalgam of bastard Arabic, pidgin English, and fluent Italian.

"*Halas!* Enough. Sonofabitch, take it off my back! You know I can't come tonight. *Basta!* You theenk you make finger, I run. I'm weeth heem tonight. You can't wait, no?"

"Shut up," he said in Arabic. "*Halas!* This is business. Listen to me, I do you a favor, you and your sot of an American."

"Ha! I wait the year you make a favor."

"Shut up and listen. Remember, I can cancel your visa tomorrow and back you go to starve in a Naples crib."

"Aha," she hooted. "You cancel a visa! I hear that before Reedicolos! Not while I got these . . . and this, I theenk not." She put her hands under her breasts and pushed them up until the nipples came out the top of the low-cut blouse and then, with deliberately inexpressible vulgarity, grabbed his hand and pressed it into her crotch while she spread her legs apart and violently jerked her pelvis forward.

He slapped her hand away and glowered, whirled abruptly and began to stalk away, then as abruptly turned back and slapped her hard across the mouth.

"Listen! Get that man out of here . . . Tonight! Send him away! At once. If you don't, he is a dead man."

"Ha!" she began to spit again but looked at him, and some quality in the fury on his face stopped her.

"Now," he said harshly. "Go back to him. Tell him I said he has to run, tonight, right away! How drunk is he? Can he drive? Answer me."

"I don't understand," she muttered.

"He will. The man who bumped me in the bar, remember?" She nodded.

"American. The FBI. He is here to take Henning. Tell him this. The man is here to take him for the Negro he killed in America. Now, do you understand?"

She nodded woodenly, her eyes now wide and fearful.

"But . . . but . . . where can he go?"

"He has a car. There is only one way to go. Damascus, over

the desert to Iraq, down the river and into Kuwait. After that, I don't care. He can hide forever in Kuwait."

"But why? . . . Why?" Disbelief was growing on her face again.

"Tell him, he'll know. Why? A favor to you, my Italian whore, just a favor."

He turned and walked back to the stinking stairway. She stood frozen for a moment, staring after him, and then, galvanized to action, she ran toward the bar.

"You are certain, Mr. Stuart?" Lieutenant Haddad asked, taking his seat at the little table over the water.

"Yes," Stuart said, feeling none of the elation he knew he ought to feel. It was all downhill now. "And now?"

Haddad looked at his watch, scowling, calculating.

"It is a quarter after two. If he follows his usual pattern, as I am sure he will, he will leave here about half after three. The woman's employment keeps her until after four, and it will take her a quarter hour to get to his apartment. For about one hour he will be alone. He will be quite drunk. We will take him then, discreetly, so that she will know nothing—only that he is gone."

"I suppose discretion is necessary, but why can't we just collar him on his way? Keep it simple."

"The taxi driver would know. They are notorious for talking. Other matters are concerned here, as you know."

"I know. As I told the prince, we are grateful for the cooperation. And we do not want to make anything else difficult for him." *All the same,* he told himself, *I'll feel easier when I've got the bastard under lock and key. I can't say I care much for this playacting—even if it's necessary to keep from goring his highness' other ox.*

"You are satisfied, Mr. Stuart?" the prince asked, having sent another emissary for the thick Turkish coffee. It was a quarter to three and Lieutenant Haddad had brought him back to the Sûreté where Stuart was not astonished to find the director, pipe in mouth, shifting through his deskload of documents. *I guess he does have a lot of people to keep in mind,* Stuart thought with sympathy, *bastards and nonbastards, they all needed watching.*

Haddad spoke to his chief in Arabic and the emir stood up. "Time to go," he said. "Shortly, Mr. Stuart, your quest will be over."

"It will be a relief," Stuart acknowledged.

But it was not. It had begun to rain when the three men emerged from the darkened Sûreté and got into the back seat of a big Lincoln sedan. Two uniformed officers occupied the front seat, and against the glare of the headlights, Stuart could see the upthrust snout of a submachine gun held by the man on the right.

Fifteen minutes later the big car drifted in to the curb, and all but the driver dismounted silently to the narrow sidewalk.

"This way," Haddad murmured and led them to a heavy doorway, half seen against the rain-wet rough stone wall. The lieutenant did not try the door but, with a familiarity which wryly amused Stuart considering Haddad's acknowledgment of the target of his carnal activities, took a key from his pocket and inserted it in the lock without needing light. The door swung open on rasping hinges.

Haddad led the way along a dark hall and stopped on the lock side of a door. Stuart thought, *Does every hall in this bloody city smell of piss?* Haddad motioned the uniformed officer to the other side of the door. Stuart carefully put a hand inside his jacket, comfortingly close to the butt of the .38.

Haddad tapped softly on the door. He waited and tapped again, more loudly. Nothing. He looked toward the prince and whispered, "Drunk." He looked questioningly at his chief, who nodded. Haddad tried the door, slowly, silently. It swung open. The uniformed officer turned a flashlight beam into a single large room and drifted the beam from right to left and uttered a loud, angry exclamation in Arabic.

Stuart looked in over the shoulder of the policeman with the torch. Beyond lay hurried chaos. It took only moments to demonstrate that the recent home of Philip Henning, né Higgins, was desolately empty of everything except the disorder of swift departure.

The bedlam which ensued was all in Arabic and thus a closed book to Stuart although the general drift was clear enough when the uniformed officer shepherded in a shambling unshaven figure in pajamas who first appeared resentfully rubbing sleep from eyes but soon awoke entirely into terror when Haddad took him by the throat while the uniformed man prodded both his memory and verity with the muzzle of the machine gun in the ribs.

Coldly impassive, the director listened to the terrified concierge's protests and, when the man was released to cower against the wall, to a spurt of talk from Haddad. At length he turned to Stuart.

"The concierge says he arrived at ten minutes before three. He says he knows because the man made an unusual degree of noise and wakened him. He was usually quiet. He left again, carrying two suitcases at"—the emir raised his wristwatch to the now illuminated hallway lights—"ten minutes after three. It is now thirty-three minutes after three. He cannot be far ahead of us."

"But . . . where could he go?" Stuart asked.

"That simplifies things for us. The ways he could go are limited. South is Israel . . . out of the question. North along the coast, Syria, but that is unlikely, for beyond Syria lies Turkey and he would not find hospitality there. That leaves east, over the Lebanon and the Anti-Lebanon, then Damascus and beyond Damascus. It is certain, I think."

"What are the chances of catching him?"

"Reasonable. The road to the top of the Lebanon climbs all the way. The car he drives is an old Renault. Also, he is not expert here, although we know he has been over that road more than once. And it is raining. I think we will catch him, but it is necessary to go at once."

With his quarry fled, the strange apathy which had gripped Stuart when he had understood that the long chase after Barton's murderer was likely to end as prosaic routine evaporated and he was on edge again as the big car, headlights blazing, bored eastward through the dark street and began to rise perceptibly.

The hiss of tires on wet pavement sounded louder than the surging purr of the engine as the driver smoothly swung the car into and out of the first of so many hairpin turns doubling back on one another that Stuart could never afterward reckon whether they totaled twenty or fifty or a hundred. They were, he was aware, rising quickly but there were neither any slackening of speed or signs of labor from the big engine. The headlights stabbed into a solid silver curtain of rain and nothing else was visible. *This guy can drive,* he thought.

"I think Americans are sometimes amused that we prefer big powerful American cars," the prince said. "Now, perhaps you understand. This road, if you could see it, you would recognize as dangerous. It goes up to the top of the Lebanon, over two thousand meters, and drops almost as swiftly into the Bekaa Valley.

"You cannot see, of course, which may possibly improve your peace of mind. We skirt cliffs to the right, an abyss to the left, inches beyond the verge. The drop, in places, is more than a thousand feet, nearly straight down."

"I have decided to trust your driver," Stuart said.

"Your confidence is wisely invested."

"What chance do we risk that he will leave the main road?"

"You know the man," the prince said to Haddad. "What do you think?"

"None," the lieutenant said. "He is frightened. He will run. He knows his only chance is the border."

"I keep wondering what scared him," Stuart mused. "It is the next thing to impossible that he knew me."

"Who knows?" Haddad murmured. "The man is a rabbit."

"I doubt if rabbit instinct carried him that far," Stuart said.

"The people with whom he has associated here enjoy an excellent intelligence network," the prince said calmly. "If they did not, they would be less successful."

"There's that," Stuart acknowledged, but the question continued to nag.

The driver grunted an exclamation in Arabic and then spoke rapidly over his shoulder.

"So!" the emir said with satisfaction. "He has caught a glimpse of light higher up. It could be the man, for it is very late and in this storm it is unlikely for others to be on the road. In any case, we shall soon see."

The rain, Stuart realized, had turned to snow, a wet, white, wind-torn drift against the headlight glare. The big car lurched in the tight hairpin turns, lurched but recovered swiftly with more than two tons of steel and rubber solidly planted on the pavement.

"He will not be having this enjoyable a time of it," the prince said. "Not in that small machine."

A moment later the driver exclaimed again and this time Stuart saw it, a quick flicker of light. He knew it was higher, but in the drive of the storm it was impossible to guess how much higher. Now he was feeling the tension again and then he thought, however much willing cooperation he was getting, he did not know the philosophy of these Levantine huntsmen toward fugitive prey.

"It is necessary to take him alive," he told the prince.

"If you are certain he is your man?" The director's voice, polite and calm, was faintly questioning. "Of course, if possible. But we do not yet know how he will react."

"It is politically necessary to take him alive," Stuart said. "The situation in our country . . . if something should happen to him so that he could not be tried for the murder . . . there would always remain questions."

"Of course," the emir said. "He will not be harmed—more than whatever is necessary to win his cooperation."

"I don't mind a few lumps on him . . . if it's necessary," Stuart said. "How do you prefer to handle this?"

"The driver knows what to do—and he is competent. With his small car it is no problem. We will merely crush him against the cliffs on the right. He will be effectively trapped there."

"I'll want to be out in a hell of a hurry."

"All of us . . . except the driver."

The big car rolled into another tight turn, and this time, instead of a lurch, the rear wheels lost their grip and skidded to the left where, Stuart remembered, there was nothing but that long drop. The driver cursed under his breath as he fought the skid and the limousine found its footing.

"He will be having a worse time than this," the prince said.

The big car swung around another shoulder and there, without warning, through the snow, the faint gleam of other light reflected back to them. How far? Two hundred yards? Three hundred? Whatever it was it was closing fast. Stuart, at the right rear door, loosened the .38 from his shoulder holster and dropped it into his right jacket pocket. The other hand was on a flashlight.

The big car, now in an apparent straightaway, surged ahead, pulling up on the smaller vehicle in an inexorable rush. Fifty yards, thirty, twenty—and the Renault swung sharp to the right and disappeared around a shoulder of cliff. The Lincoln swayed into the turn, skidded, caught and then they were on it. The big car's front wheels edged even with the Renault's rear, then pulled ahead halfway the length of the small car and then came a powerful swing to the right and the ripping crush of metal. Thrown forward by the impact, Stuart shoved himself back and grabbed the door, having just enough room behind the Renault to swing it clear.

Then he was out and the flashlight beam was on the other car where he could see the outline of a head and shoulders against the glare.

"Higgins!" he yelled. "Higgins! Stay where you are!"

The left door of the Renault was flung open and a figure tumbled out, sprawled to the ground, and then was on its feet running across the road—toward the abyss.

"Higgins!" Stuart yelled again and plunged in pursuit, half-conscious now that Lieutenant Haddad was out of the left-hand door and a dozen feet ahead of him, that much nearer the pursued. Stuart had the flashlight on, following the blurred bolting figure through the snow. Ahead of him he saw Haddad plunging in pursuit and then he saw that Haddad had a gun in his hand and was aiming at the fleeing back.

"Haddad!" he yelled. "No! Damn you, no!"

Then, back through the snow, there came a thin, high squall of pure terror—and Higgins vanished, disappeared, was, in less than a breath, gone.

Oh, the stupid, stupid sonofabitch! He's over the side, the stupid, insane, terrified sonofabitch. It was over, finished, but momentum carried Stuart forward.

Then at the lip of rock, he heard and, in the same instant saw, Higgins was straddling a thin pinnacle of rock, just over the edge of the chasm, his face staring up, white and wild-eyed, as gripped in madness as he had been in the cemetery in Wynnsboro. His hands were clutching and slipping on an outcrop above his head and he was wailing. And Haddad, poised in his own perilous imbalance, was striking at Higgins' clutching hands with the hard heel of his boot. Stuart saw it all at once and without having to think about it swung the heavy flashlight in a full-muscled arc. It caught Haddad in the throat and threw him back to the solid ground, choking.

Stuart went down to his knees, braced his legs into crevices in the rock, sprawled down on his chest, grabbed Higgins' wrists and, without real consciousness of his own peril or the furious strain on his wrists and shoulders, pulled Higgins up to solid ground and, without relaxing the convulsive tension of his grip, pulled him back away from the edge. Then he knocked him unconscious.

Haddad still lay in the wet snow, retching. Over him, flashlight in one hand, the emir stood competently holding a pistol aimed at the lieutenant's head.

"He was trying to kill him," Stuart said hoarsely. "He was trying to kick him off the cliff."

'I know," the emir said. "I saw. You took a terrible risk, Mr. Stuart."

"Why? Why? Is he insane?" Stuart asked, looking down at Haddad who was now drunkenly rising.

"I don't know. I intend to learn," the prince said. He shouted to the two uniformed policemen. They came from the car, one carrying two sets of handcuffs.

Driving down the mountain, Haddad was shoved into the front seat. The uniformed guard sat behind him with the submachine-gun muzzle conveniently close to the nape of his neck.

Higgins, groggy, totally cowed, hunched over the center of the rear seat between Stuart and the prince.

"I don't know what to do with him," Stuart said to the emir out of a vast and druglike exhaustion.

"Which one? If you mean the lieutenant, it will be attended to."

"No, he's yours. The other. If you've got one crazy officer, you could have more." Rage had gone out of him, and all he could feel now was the weary bitterness.

"I cannot yet tell you what affected Haddad," the emir said patiently. "But I doubt if it was insanity. I'll know in time. Meanwhile, I think you need rest."

"I cannot leave this man alone in your custody. I am sorry, and I am—my government will be—much in your debt. Neither do I know what affected your lieutenant." Stuart looked at Haddad's shoulders, now more stooped. "And I don't know if it was insanity, of course. It could have been ordinary jealousy."

"What do you mean, jealousy?" The prince's tone remained even but alertly inquiring.

Stuart brought himself, still reluctantly, to the distasteful necessity of tattling.

"Higgins' girl was also Haddad's mistress. They had some arrangement for sharing her."

"Oh?" The emir paused. "No," he said, when he spoke again. "I attempt to know my men. It is obvious that this time I failed to know all I should know. But I think no thought of a woman could have influenced him to act as foolishly as he did. No woman meant more to Haddad than convenience. No, it was something else."

"The question is, does that something else infect other of your men? If Henning—or Higgins—should die in a cell tonight, he would not be the first prisoner to be found a suicide."

"It occurs, of course, and I understand your concern. Would you prefer to watch over the prisoner yourself? It is not necessary, but it can be arranged—to relieve your unease."

"Thank you. I would." Stuart was both vastly relieved and drearily aware of exhaustion and the clammy, clinging wetness of his clothes and the rheumatic ache of abused muscle. *Christ,* he thought, *it would be wonderful to sleep for forty-eight hours —but, to lose him now, after we've shagged him a third of the way around the world. Impossible.* It was beyond five when the big Lincoln whispered over the cobbles and stopped at the Sûreté. Brief instruction from the prince sent the driver inside; he returned with three other armed guards who, without ceremony, hauled the prisoners out on the narrow curb. Stuart noted that Higgins was swaying drunkenly and might have fallen but for the men gripping his arms just below the shoulder.

They mounted the high stoop and entered the red-tiled hall which now, in its predawn desertion, returned hollow echo to voices and footsteps.

"Go with these men," the emir said, nodding at the guards holding Higgins. "They will make you as comfortable as possible for the rest of the night. I must warn you the accommodations do not resemble the St. Georges."

"And you?" Stuart asked.

"I have other business," the emir said. He motioned to the guards holding Haddad and started up the steep iron staircase.

22

"Come, Mr. Stuart, I believe we can answer your questions now." The voice took him by surprise where he sat on a hard wooden bench, just outside the dank and malodorous cell, fighting to keep awake. Throughout the hours he had envied Higgins who lay on the wooden slats of a mattressless, blanketless bunk behind the bars, snoring the dreamless sleep of the unjust.

At that, he had thought, *I can't blame him.* There are human conditions beyond honesty and good behavior which promote sleep. Among them are despair, exhaustion, and terror. *He sleeps fine, but I doubt like hell that he's going to enjoy waking up.*

He had not tried to question his prisoner. He was too tired for the effort in the first place and, in the second, it had been obvious that, for now, Higgins was too far gone to be anywhere near usefully responsive. *Sleep, you bastard,* he had thought, *you're going to despise the dawn.*

Tussling with his own exhaustion, the utter necessity of not yielding to it, he had not heard the director's approach. He looked around at the voice and was astonished to find the prince fresh shaven, freshly shirted and suited and shined, and showing no traces of the night's rigors.

"I'm sorry," Stuart said.

"If you will come with me," the emir said. "Lieutenant Haddad is prepared to explain himself."

"I'll be glad to hear," Stuart said tiredly, then nodded at the sleeping Higgins. "What about him?"

"There is nothing else to fear, as you will see. Take my personal assurance. He is safe. But because I know your concern, two of my most trusted men will watch while you are away—for only a little time."

Yes, Stuart thought with some lingering bitterness, *Haddad was also one of your most trusted.* He rose, stretched his aching frame and followed the prince, bitten by uneasy reluctance to let Higgins out of his sight.

They climbed a dark, stont stairwell out of the cellblocks, crossed the red-tile pavement, mounted the echoing iron stairway, and approached the tall oaken doorway. Stuart glanced at his watch, ten o'clock, five hours since they had reached the foot of the mountain with their game. A uniformed attendant saluted and swung open the door. The emir followed Stuart into the office.

Lieutenant Haddad lay sprawled in a wooden office chair, his hands cuffed to the stout arms, his head lolling on his chest. Then Stuart saw his bare feet. They were resting on the heels, spread wide, one ankle cuffed to a leg of the emir's desk, the other to the handle of a filing cabinet, and they had been flayed. The skin of the soles drooped in ribbons and the white of tendons showed through the smeared red flesh. Stuart felt his stomach turn over and, with effort, kept his face still. *I owe the bastard nothing,* he thought, *but all the same, God in heaven!"*

"He was reluctant," the prince said. "It was necessary to deal harshly with him."

"What did that?" Stuart asked, fighting to control his revulsion.

"It is done with the flat of bayonets. Unfortunately, they

sometimes cut," the emir said calmly. "It is effective." He nodded toward a guard standing beside the chair; wooden-faced,
the guard took a step forward and, with the edge of his hand,
slashed Haddad across the bridge of the nose. The lieutenant's
head came up and Stuart found himself looking directly into
eyes sick with measureless despair.

"You will now repeat to Mr. Stuart what you have explained
to me," the emir said without stress or emotion.

Haddad stiffened, struggled to pull himself upright against
his manacles, failed and let his head sink back to his chest. The
guard hit him again and once more the head came up. The
voice out of his chest was a whisper so low that Stuart scarcely
heard.

"I was responsible. Only I." The head fell again.

"Was it the girl?" Stuart asked, feeling pity, sick at the necessity of further torturing this tortured creature.

The head swayed woodenly from side to side and the whisper
came again.

"No. Not the woman. Nothing."

"Then why?" Stuart persisted.

"I was ordered. He was not to be caught alive. Ordered . . ." the whisper trailed away, and when the guard
slapped him again, the head merely rolled under the impact.

"He has fainted," the emir said. "No matter. I can tell you
the rest. Be assured that it is true. A man in his condition does
not lie."

"What's going to happen to him?" Stuart asked.

"That remains to the court. I think they will hang him—
publicly, as we do criminals, in the Place de Canone. I do not
tolerate traitors."

"What did he mean, he was ordered?" Stuart asked,
thinking at the same time the question was hardly necessary,
feeling somewhere in the back of his mind that he knew the answer, or some of it, perhaps not all, but enough to guess at why
Peter Higgins had murdered, out of a cemetery in Wynnsboro,
Carver Otis Barton.

"It is not necessary to risk boring you with details in which you will have no particular interest," the emir said. "It is enough to say that this man betrayed me. He was, as you know, chief of my narcotics division, head of the intelligence section against drug smuggling. It is true, as you know also, the nature of their work, if it is to be effective, sometimes necessitates an officer to seem to be the confidant of both sides. I say seem to be; in the end there should be no question of where his genuine loyalty must lie. Haddad was corrupted.

"This is of greater importance to me than to you and thus gratitude is now turned around. I might not have learned this but for the need of capturing the man who is now your prisoner."

"But why kill Higgins?" Stuart asked again, not really needing the answer, but needing to hear it uttered.

"Haddad was ordered by the people to whom he had betrayed his allegiance to make sure that your man was not taken alive. He dared not refuse and therefore he took unacceptable risks to carry out his orders—and the risks betrayed him—fortunately, for you and for me.

"The one vital thing you need to know, Mr. Stuart, is this: The decision to kill your man and the orders to carry out did not originate here in the Lebanon, or in Turkey."

"Where, then?"

"At the other end of the supply line. The orders came from America."

Well, he had heard it said aloud, but it had lost the element of surprise. Now Stuart felt in utter weariness that he had known it all along.

"That presents problems," he said.

"It does indeed," the emir said.

For what seemed to Stuart at least the fiftieth time, Higgins shook his head doggedly and muttered, "I'm not who you say I am."

"You're a fool, as well as stubborn," Stuart repeated patiently. "I told you, I saw you do it."

"Somebody else. Not me," Higgins mumbled. "You made a mistake."

The Air Force Kc-135 tanker, dispatched from Adana, Turkey, to Beirut, Lebanon, on the orders of the President of the United States who had this urgent necessity explained to him by the aged director of the Federal Bureau of Investigation in Washington, was reaching for the heights after refueling in Wiesbaden, Germany. Few caught murderers could get such exclusive and expensive transportation home to face their peers, but, after Stuart's report from the ambassador's office in Beirut, nobody in authority questioned its advisability in the present case. Wynnsboro lay seven hours westward. Whenever Higgins had slept, Jeff Stuart had clawed over and over again in his mind, searching for the key to unlock his prisoner's mulish refusal to admit who he was. In rare moments of self-indulgence he permitted himself to remember that he was flying in the direction of Amy Wynn.

"It wasn't a mistake," Stuart insisted. "I won't give you any crap about never forgetting a face. But this isn't crap. I'll never forget yours."

"Look," Higgins protested with another of his occasional feeble efforts at defiance. "You kidnapped me, shanghaied me. There's such a thing as extradition. A man has rights."

"Try your rights on the judge and jury," Stuart said in disgust. "You ought to be on your knees praying your thanks I didn't leave you in the hands of the Lebanese police. You should have seen your old friend and true buddy, Haddad."

"Why? What's he to me?"

"He was something to you, whether or not you knew it. They made hamburger out of his feet. Do you know why he tried to boot you off that mountain?"

"The broad, I guess. He was shacked up with her before I was."

"You flatter yourself, and, if you believe it, you're more of a fool than even I thought. Do you think—and you'll have to believe I saw what I saw—that the director of the Sûreté would mince his top cop only because he got an occasional hard on at your expense?"

Higgins looked out at the wingtip, abruptly fluttering in turbulence and down at cumulus engaged in its stately backward passage.

"She was a good lay," he said at length. "Why do I have to keep these damned things on?" He rubbed one wrist against the plastic seat arm. "They hurt."

"Not because I'm afraid you'll do anything—or could—to this baby-sitting carriage. You could, though, chicken out on me and hurt yourself—if you had the guts—which I doubt."

"I don't doubt it; I know I don't. What'll they do to me? Do you know?"

"Probably hang you."

"You've got the wrong man—you'll find out."

"I don't know how many times I have to tell you I saw you do it. Did you hate that man, the nigger, Barton?"

"No."

All right, Stuart thought, *he's leveling even if he doesn't know it. Now, there's the rest of it. I know what I've got is a thing that has killed, but the puzzling part is he's no killer. What shoved him? Rather, who?*

I will always wonder whether I belong where I am, he thought. *I wanted to chase this thing until I had it. Now I've got it at considerable expense and it is nothing, nothing that I wanted. I saw Barton killed. I saw this thing kill him. Barton would have despised himself for dying at this hand. I am glad I did not let him know. Now, I've got the thing and take it to a hangman, which is absolutely certain. I did not love Barton according to any church's law of brothers being brothers. He was something I half-glimpsed, half-understood, more than half not liked. But he was vital; and this thing here spilled all of it.*

"Haddad did not give a damn about the woman," he said. "He had nothing against you. He made his best shot at killing you because he was told to do exactly that and he was in the crap so deep he didn't dare not try it."

"More crap." It came out of dejection.

"Haddad doesn't believe that—or didn't. They hanged him this morning. Just before we left. I saw it."

"I don't believe it," Higgins said. "You've got the wrong man —I have to keep telling you."

"Wrong man, of course. That was why you tried to run off the top of a mountain in a blizzard."

"I was scared. How many times do I have to tell you I'm no hero? And how do you know which way to run? When some big sonofabitch you never heard of is ramming you through a snowstorm? You got the wrong man, I tell you again."

"All right," Stuart said. He got up and moved out of the metal shack built into the tanker and came back a few moments later, uneasily in a new onslaught of upper-air disturbance, balancing flat, green, seamed plastic garments which appeared nearly too cumbersome for his strength.

"We'll try these on you," he said. "Stand up."

"I can't," Higgins said. "These fucking cuffs. What you got there?"

Stuart dropped his load and fetched the key from his pocket and unlatched his passenger and told him to get to his feet.

"New style, pleated, Edwardian mod suit. Fits beautifully. Like it?" Stuart said.

"What the hell is this? Armor plate?" Higgins asked.

"Exactly," Stuart said. "In just about six hours now we are going to be landing in this airplane in a city called Wynnsboro, where you have been before. And you will be, from the ass up, covered with armor plate—only so that you land in one solid, stupid piece. Understand?"

"I don't get it," Higgins said, swaying under the weight of plastic-covered fiber glass and metal.

"You will when your friends gun you," Stuart said. "The orders to kick your ass off the mountain came from the United States. I suspect they originated in Wynnsboro. Where else?"

23

Somewhere above the middle of southern America, flattened and featureless except for the veined tracery of streams and superhighways 40,000 feet below, the Air Force KC-135 let its engines subtly diminish their patient grumble, and the airplane began to slide down the long hill of air. Jeff Stuart uncuffed his companion from a stanchion and nudged him awake. Higgins was still spasmodically sleeping off the hangover of terror he had acquired during those few seconds clinging with slippery and cruelly boot-crunched fingers to the thin lip of oblivion.

"Time to get into your zoot suit for the homecoming," he said, not unkindly. Stuart's grasp of slang was out of date at best, although his command of profanity when he needed it was adequate to any era.

Higgins looked at the plastic-pocketed armor with instant distaste, quickly flavored with apprehension as sleep fled enough to clear the way for awareness.

"I'm still the wrong man," he muttered.

"If you are, why are you paling up on me?" Stuart said. "You got forty minutes"—he looked at his watch—"to get zipped, buckled, buttoned, and tucked into that thing. I can't guarantee you'll need it, but I'd hate my own guts afterward if I'd guessed wrong and you did need it."

"Where we landing?" Higgins asked querulously. "You don't tell me nothing."

"More than you tell me, and that's a fact," Stuart said without heat. "But if you need to know, back to the scene of the crime—Wynnsboro. Where else?" Stuart regarded Higgins with quizzical interest. "Now you're even paler."

Higgins, weighted down in the shapeless mass of body armor, trying halfheartedly to hold himself erect against the burden—and failing—looked ludicrously forlorn. Stuart, occupation manhunter, took no pleasure in the spectacle of a creature hunted, caught, and helpless. Pity, it occurred to him, sometimes sprouts in barren soil. *At that moment across the street from the cemetery, had I been quick enough and he less quick, I would have left this thing dead beside Barton's corpse—and I am damned if it wouldn't have been kinder than what I do now. Now, he's for it. I'll see him hanged—and I'll never believe he was worth the rope.*

This body armor is no prank all the same, he thought. And he felt his own peculiar brand of apprehension. He had the thing he had gone eight thousand miles to get. He would deliver it where it had to be delivered to be tried by its peers. And he would make damned certain, within one man's competence, that it lived long enough for its peers and the hangman to do their work. The landing and debarkation ahead could be critical; someone had wanted to kill this Higgins badly enough to get a Lebanese cop named Haddad killed in his turn for trying to kick him off a Lebanese mountain. He had come terribly close to losing Higgins there and though he knew he could not give it name, he did not believe the threat had abated.

He knew he was, himself, still tired and bruised both physically and emotionally, and it was heartening to know that from now on there would be help. Nevertheless, he was tense as he felt the big plane flare out and heard the hard, hot blow of rubber striking concrete. The reverse thrusters bellowed, and he had to move swiftly to grab and steady his passenger as the sheer weight of armor pitched him forward. Then they were taxiing off the runway and the plane stopped and the engines whined down. Stuart stood up, hauled Higgins erect, and cuffed his right wrist to his own left. He shifted the .38 from its holster to his right-hand jacket pocket, kept his hand on the butt, and started forward toward the hatch. An airman came back from the front of the plane and was unbuttoning the hatch as they reached it. It opened on a blinding of floodlights and the brief, dancing suns of photographers' strobe lights.

There was no seeing through the barrage of light and Stuart was just barely aware of the dimpled steel of the ladder platform at the tips of his toes. Out behind the lights there was at first silence and then a confused uproar of human noise. Excitement, confusion, Stuart thought, not bloodthirst, for, though he did not doubt that the city of Wynnsboro dripped with lust, it was unlikely that those willing to voice it would have been permitted here at this moment.

But he knew that Higgins read into it the cry of the pack ready to rend him, for he felt the steel-clad weight of him pull back in the convulsive need to get something, anything—in this case Stuart's flesh—between him and what he could not face. Stuart himself, in that white glare, had never felt so pitilessly exposed. And he thought he knew that Higgins had real reason to fear—not from the noisy cries of photographers and reporters fighting for position—but from some far more deadly menace. He yanked at the umbilical cuff tying them together.

"God damn it, get out here!" he snarled. "I told you you'd get the movie star treatment." He felt Higgins yielding, shambling, unwilling, but coming. The fact was that Higgins was slowly, with terrible reluctance coming to cling to his captor, yielding the remnant of his destroyed will to the only force left to shield him from a ravening world. The process had begun on that high mountain road when Stuart had plunged out of the snow to pull him from under Lieutenant Haddad's crushing boot heel. If the prey can love the huntsman, Higgins had begun to love Stuart as the whipped and bawling child loves the mother who first whips him and then follows the blows with tendernesses. Not that Stuart was tender, but to Higgins there was nobody else, nothing else at all.

Stuart could now begin to make out a human mass around the foot of the ladder. And then somebody was yelling, hoarse and savage. "Shift those goddamned lights! Shift them, sonofabitch, shift them!" The glare quit, turned off, done with, and the voice bellowed again, "Shift them, I said! Shift them, not douse 'em! Jesus H. Christ!" And so the lights came on again, but this time the glare was not directly into their eyes.

Then Stuart heard a peremptory voice he knew. "Stuart. Bring him down. Hurry up!" Rembert's voice. He had known there would be help; he had not expected the silvermaned autocrat would bring his own aged and dignified cop's body to this scene. But then—a fleeting thought—why not? Hadn't he and the even more ancient director made their awesome reputations by being in at the kill? The big, news-making kills?

"Come on," he said to Higgins, tightening the pressure on the cuff, and Higgins came, awkward, slow in his fear and in his weight of armor, but coming. And Stuart saw two figures coming up the ladder to meet them. One, he knew, had to be Rembert, for where else on earth, grew such a mane of burnished silver? He did not recognize the other, in civilian clothes, until the four came together at the halfway point.

"All right, Stuart, good work." Rembert grunted. "We'll take him now."

"No!" The cry came out of Higgins somewhere between scream and moan, and now Higgins was not merely cringing behind Stuart. He collapsed against and into Stuart. This was not mere terror; this was the total failure of a human spirit drained of everything human but a final plea for compassion. "Stay with me!"

It was then, with some astonishment, that Stuart recognized the other man, saw the pistol in his hand, saw the expressionless face, the cold, impassive eyes, that passionless machine, Lieutenant John Kelley of the Wynnsboro Department of Police. It was not exactly a light suddenly dawned, for his mind had for months been hacking at a mystery which had no answer beyond his knowing that mystery existed. He still had no answer, but now he knew this much: Higgins had not totally fallen apart until he recognized Lieutenant Kelley.

All right, Stuart told himself, *Kelley is no stranger to this possession of mine and maybe that answers a question or part of a question, but it sure as hell leaves a lot of other and probably bigger questions without answers. Some help toward answering the big ones? I don't know. But I do know I don't want him locked up in Kelley's calaboose any more than I wanted him in the emir's pokey. There's too much I don't have any grip on, none at all. What I'm going to do about it, I don't know either. But I'm honestly glad Rembert's here. I can remember plenty of times I would rather have looked Medusa square in her snake coiffure than have looked at Rembert—but this is not one of them. If ever anybody needed the old silver fox, tonight is the night. Meanwhile, me lad, carry on.* He took a stronger strain on the cuff.

"What's the matter with the bastard?" Rembert demanded harshly. "You got him thinking you're his mother?"

"I don't know," Stuart said.

Higgins still clung against him. His breathing was a hoarse sob.

"I'll take him," Rembert said again.

"No, no!" It was ripped out of Higgins' throat.

"For God's sake—a baby-sitter!" Rembert's voice carried disgust. "All right, let him stay on the tit—but move him."

"Keep coming, just keep coming," Stuart said, taking another step down the ladder, wondering if he was getting through at all to a mind which, he suspected, was close to paralyzed. Higgins followed, stumbling, so close now the cuff chain fell slack. Rembert followed and Lieutenant Kelley went ahead and so they came to the last step and the ground and the strobe lights flashed into a renewed choreography of flame. There were more human noises and shufflings of protest among the newsmen, and for a moment Higgins stopped and the cuff chain tightened and brought Stuart up short.

"Straighten up and move!" Stuart snarled. "You're a VIP— for Christ's sake, straighten up and act like one."

There had been a narrow pathway ahead of them, but now it closed under the pressure of journalistic flesh and lens and Rembert was shouting, "Move those people back! Move them, God damn it!" The path opened again and Stuart saw that they were moving between rows of the gray shirts and blue trousers of the Wynnsboro uniformed force. And he saw immediately around Higgins, himself, and Rembert the closing in of a phalanx of men whose breed, he recognized, was of his own, that of the Bureau. *I should have known he wouldn't come alone,* he thought in relief.

He recognized, among the uniforms, the purse-lipped petulance of Wynnsboro's Commissioner Arthur Mayhew and had a second of amused reflection, not marked with much sympathy, on how Wynnsboro law must feel about this roughshod invasion by the federals. *There's damn little chance we're loved as brothers here,* he thought, *when we're bringing home their bacon— particularly when it happens to be a piece of bacon I suspect makes them want to throw up.*

The FBI wedge shouldered ahead to the rear doors of an armored police van. The doors, slightly to Stuart's surprise, were held on either side by men in Wynnsboro uniforms. He pushed Higgins ahead of him up on the one step and then the second and inside and pushed him down on one of the steel benches along the armored side. Rembert's florid face and silver gonfalon of authority came through the door.

"Look, Stuart, my car will be right behind you. We have other cars in front and in back of me, so just sit tight. OK?"

Just before the doors closed a third figure stepped up and into the van and sat on the bench facing Stuart and his prisoner and, once more, even through that extra epidermis of plastic and steel, he felt Higgins shudder and knew that he shrank. *Why the hell him?* Stuart thought in tired irritation. He found

himself staring at Kelley. Higgins, he had long since acknowledged, was no prize package in the best of conditions; almost
anything could turn him off, but why did it have to be Kelley
who put out his light entirely? The face on the other side of the
van was cold enough, the eyes steady and measuring, a kind of
slide-rule awareness. But menace? Threat? Certainly, in what
must have been a generally ignoble career, Higgins must have
been confronted more than once by a tough cop's professional
mask. Why Kelley?

All Stuart knew about Kelley really, he remembered, was
that he had got an ice pick through a lung while he and Amos
Wynn had stopped in the middle of a riot to haul Stuart himself to safety. And he had talked to him briefly in the hospital
only to thank him. And he knew that, among his fellows, Kelley
was accounted a tough cop, not a mean cop, not a brutal one,
but a machine who knew his job and did it well. Why Kelley?
An answer? Part of an answer? Nothing? It had to be more than
nothing.

"Surprised?" Kelley asked with a brief, thin smile.

"A little," Stuart acknowledged. "Surprised to see you on
your feet. Congratulations."

"Thanks. Penicillin, that other antibiotic junk. Besides I
heal quick. That isn't what I meant."

"Yes?"

"I meant surprised me taking this ride with you."

"Should I be?"

"I don't know. When you federals move in, you move pretty
hard. Take over, some people would say."

"The Bureau isn't always polite," Stuart admitted.

"Kind of an understatement, wouldn't you say?" Kelley said
with another shadow of something that could possibly have
been mirth. "If pride was one of my vices, I might feel hurt.
Take our commissioner; he's so hurt he's constipated."

"That why you're riding with the prisoner—instead of him?"

"Maybe, but I doubt it. He has dignity in addition to pride

and an uncooperative bowel. The combination, in a paddy wagon, might hospitalize him."

"But why you?"

"Even you federals seem to feel you ought to make some concession to local appearances. That's what I am—window dressing."

"Where are we going?"

"City lockup. More window dressing. After all if this pigeon you fetched did something wrong and did it here, that's where he belongs. Until he can get a change of venue, that is—or if he can."

"That's why they told me to fetch him here, naturally," Stuart said. "Not that I think he was happy to come."

"Probably not."

They rode in silence. Kelley sat watching the prisoner without expression, without malice. Higgins hunched under the weight of the body armor, head down, breathing hoarsely, his one free elbow crossed tight and low across his belly, his knees pressed together, in a spastic tension that Stuart, beside him, could sense. *It is,* he thought with some sympathy, *the age-old instinct of the threatened male to rally every force available to him to protect first, neither head nor heart, but the crotch where crouched the organs that alone most made life worth preserving. Even if he was seventy-five,* Stuart reflected, *if something came after him the first thing he'd cover up would be his balls.*

"How secure is your jail?" he asked Kelley. "It looked a little leaky to me, what I saw of it."

"You're afraid that fella's going to go over the wall?" Kelley asked.

"No. What I had in mind is what might come over the wall and nibble on him."

"Well, I'll tell you, you were right. It was, and mostly still is, a Model-T among jails. But when you federals moved in, once the word came you had the pigeon, they brought along architects and electricians and welders and steel plate and mirrors and closed-circuit TV and a lot of other gadgets and made us an outright gift of a piece of a jail that is strictly Rolls-Royce. Your boy wouldn't be safer in Fort Knox."

"Good to hear," Stuart said. "I went to some trouble and I would feel hurt if this"—he nodded toward his charge—"should by accident stub his toe or something."

"I suspect your bosses feel the same way," Kelley said tranquilly and returned to his calm appraisal of the huddled prisoner.

"Careful of his pecker, ain't he?" he said at length.

"If you were ever in a war, you might remember having some such general impulse from time to time," Stuart said.

"Oh, I know about that all right. But now you got him here, and some people think he might have shot somebody once. But you wouldn't think it to look at him, would you?"

"No, you wouldn't."

"Looks downright harmless, I'd say."

"He is," Stuart said. He was back to it: That Higgins was no stranger to animal fears he had long known. And Higgins was a killer, he knew, for he had seen him kill. And here was a calm, unthreatening cop and, in his presence, Higgins got deeper into the depths of his personal hell than anywhere else. Why? He did not think he was likely to learn anything by asking Kelley about it, but he also knew there was no reason why he shouldn't. There wasn't the slightest danger that he would put Kelley on his guard against anything because, he suspected, if Kelley had ever needed to be on his guard against anything whatever he would have taken care of the matter early.

"You know," he said slowly and clearly, "for some reason you scare the bejesus out of this man."

"I suspect most everything scares him," Kelley said calmly. "Especially cops. I'd say he's allergic to cops."

"It's more than that," Stuart said with equal calm. "It's not just that you're a cop. Higgins knows *you*. How, or why, or where, or when, I don't know. But he knows *you,* and the fact that he does scares the living shit out of him."

"You think so?" Kelley said without expression.

"I know so," Stuart said. "And I expect to find out why."

"Be my guest," Kelley said. "Meanwhile, I guess we've got where we are going."

Stuart felt the windowless van slow, then stop, then reverse and swing backward and stop again. The doors opened and Rembert stood at the opening, solidly flanked by FBI men with the disconsolate figure of Police Commissioner Mayhew trying to peer among them. It was one of the commissioner's several disappointments with the way fate had constructed him that he was hard put to see *over* any fellow human being more than eleven years old.

"OK, Stuart, bring him out," Rembert barked. Kelly still sat on his bench, watching with faintly amused sympathy, as Stuart got his overweighted charge to his feet and led him to the ground where they were immediately surrounded by Bureau agents.

The photographers' strobes had begun another wild firefly dance of incandescence, but this time Rembert's voice roared with real fury and his target was the Commissioner of Police.

"I told you no more, you stupid, fat-assed bastard! Now get your cops moving, for once, and get those photographers the hell out of here. At once!"

They faced a squat steel door in a stone wall. A uniformed Wynnsboro policeman unlocked and opened it and stood aside. It was the last local uniform they saw that night.

An FBI agent waited at a new, glossy steel panel which, unlocked, slid upward like a portcullis, revealing rows of steel toggle levers. There was a metallic clank and a steel door slid silently open. Stuart led his charge beyond into a fluorescent glare. Another door opened, not barred, but half-inch steel pierced by an eye-level window which Stuart knew, without being told, was bulletproof glass. Beyond was a cell with a bunk with steel mesh springs and no mattress, a washbowl, a toilet bowl without seat and, high up, the glint of a lens which Stuart knew would be television's sleepless peephole. The low mutter of machinery meant filtered air—and even that would be guarded.

"Uncuff him," Rembert said, "and then the other guys can get him out of his iron suit and put him away for beddie bye. You got him here—that's enough."

"There's going to be a guard on him?" Stuart asked, feeling the sudden onset of total weariness.

"Of course."

"Not Wynnsboro cops?" Stuart knew better, but it had been so long and he couldn't help asking and he couldn't let go of his unwelcome burden, yearn to as he might.

"Of course not," Rembert snapped. "A Wynnsboro cop couldn't get in here with a Sherman tank." Rembert was, not unnaturally, out of date in his military nomenclature.

"All right," Stuart sighed and rubbed the chafed left wrist which, it now seemed to him, had been forever a cord of life between him and Higgins.

He turned tiredly away and was at once galvanized back to life by an animal cry of fear, and he turned to see Higgins staring after him.

"You seem to have struck up a lifelong friendship," Rembert said. "Never mind, I've got a doctor who'll have him asleep in no time. You've got in your overtime and I guarantee he'll be fine. Come and tell me about it and then get some sleep, which I guess you need."

Stuart stood for a moment, saying nothing, looking back at the shrunken figure which was being efficiently divested of his armor. Something pulled at his heart, which he thought was ridiculous. And he knew that somewhere behind the exhaustion, deep enough but never so deep they could not be dug up, the questions still waited for him.

"Good night, Higgins," he said gently. "I'll see you."

He turned and walked out with Rembert, and as they went

beyond the steel door, which clanged shut behind them, and then the barred gate and into the open air, he turned to his chief.

"I am damned, sir, if I am going to tell you all about anything tonight. I am, as you suggested, going to get some sleep. But first I am going to make a telephone call."

24

Rembert, as Stuart knew, was autocratic, demanding and beset by an obsession about international Communism so dense and all-pervading that it clouded other areas of his head, but he was not inhuman. He began automatically to bridle at Stuart's revolutionary notion that he was going to sleep first and talk later. But, knowing Higgins to be well enclosed and as safely preserved as a Smithfield ham, he surrendered with grace and told a Bureau driver to take Stuart to his motel.

It was late, probably beyond midnight, but Amy answered the telephone promptly. It took him badly somewhere in the area of his tired nerve centers that her voice and words sounded both cool and uncommitted.

"So you brought it home," she said, not really asking. "I saw it on TV and I must say it didn't look as though you had got much for all that trouble. But I'm sure you feel better—fulfilled, they probably would have said at Skidmore."

"Amy, Amy . . . darling," he began to protest out of a dull disappointment, "don't you . . . oh, hell . . . do you . . ."

"You ought to get some rest, dear. I'm sure you need it . . . And I know I'm going to." And she hung up.

Good Christ, he thought stupidly, contemplating the dead instrument in his hand. *You waste the first third of a lifetime on various faceless blondes, redheads, brunettes, all with the same basic mechanical equipment, and then the good Lord lets you happen on the one who owns and operates all the same flesh and blood accessories but possesses in addition a brain, humor, warmth, laughter, and some bright and wonderful something that God himself couldn't define, and then you blow it for some reason you are too stupid to understand.*

He cradled the telephone and stood up and fumbled through the necessities of buttons and zippers and holster straps and let all of it fall where he stood. He remembered the remainder of a quart of Old Grandad must be somewhere in the top dresser drawer and, finding this to be a fact, tilted the bottle up and let his throat do its work. He looked with longing toward the bed, but even over the pungency of the bourbon, was aware of what travel and tension had combined to manufacture in his armpits.

And I'll probably sleep better, he told himself, trudging to the shower and turning the water on hard and hot. Finished there, he paused in front of the mirror just long enough to note that his five o'clock shadow was now well-past midnight and to decide not to do anything about it. *Moreover, you need a haircut again,* he told himself, *and it really doesn't seem like more than a couple of weeks.*

He spent perhaps two minutes in disconsolate cudgeling of his brain about Amy Wynn before the bourbon, the bath, and exhaustion felled him and he was gone. Somewhere, along the dark byways of oblivion, he became aware that he was dreaming that the naked body of Amy Wynn was in his arms, all its cool, silken length, its suppleness and entrancing protrusions, its eager giving or making an even trade or whatever the transaction was. He wallowed in his luxury of a nightmare, stubbornly refusing to surrender any moment of it, holding out against the treachery of waking up until he could hold out no longer. He surrendered at last bitterly and batted his eyes open and felt the sensation of life come back to fingers and arms and the entire flesh of man, and discovered that he wasn't dreaming.

It was a clear fact, but he didn't believe it since it was impossible. His gummed eyes acknowledged that the pale edge of dawn lay upon the day and he turned his head with dogged determination to confirm, by the testimony of the aching emptiness beside him, that the dream had merely, cruelly trailed him back into consciousness. The emptiness smiled at him out of gray eyes and generous lips and the remainder of the void rolled him, unresisting, onto his back and hitched up onto his supine frame a weight so proportioned and distributed and arranged to his satisfaction that he would not have traded it for everything in Fort Knox.

"Good morning," the emptiness said.

"How . . . how?" he said from somewhere out of the abyss of stupidity.

It sounded like a chuckle, but, with his eyes getting better accustomed to their work, it looked more like a self-satisfied smirk.

"What's the use of owning a motel if the owner can't have a master key?" she said.

"You own this?" Still stupid, and he felt that nothing was likely ever to better that condition, and he didn't care.

"Pa gave it to me at Christmas, along with some other odds and ends. He thinks it'll improve the inheritance tax situation. Pa hates the Internal Revenue Service. Passionately. That's enough. Go to sleep—it's only five o'clock."

"That's a hell of an order," he said and tightened the left arm on his burden while the right hand set out to exercise its squatters' right of exploring texture and shape and plane and curve from nape of neck, to shoulder blades, one and two, to the long, smooth declivity marking one rib cage from the other, to where it curved deeper at the waist and then began to rise to where, just before it slid down into the cleft of the body, now parting, he remembered a faint almost invisible fuzz of goldish down that, his fingertips believed, they could detect as fine as spider web. *Damn fool fingers,* he thought if he thought at all, *they can be conned into anything.* Then the hand, in loving impudence, queried further across the smooth round of rump muscle, tightening against him.

"Ah," he whispered, "such merchandise."

"Such a buyer," she said.

He rolled the weight back from him and kicked away the sheets and propped himself on an elbow and gave his eyes their turn. He bent forward and began to kiss her, starting just under the heavy fall of hair, across brow and cheek and now closed eyelid, where he could feel a flutter, and down to the hollow of the throat, where another stronger pulse presented itself, and down to breasts, first left, then right, and the willing rise of nipple. And then back to the wide smiling lips and opened mouth and the breath in both of them building in depth and strength toward the full urgency of heart and lung.

"No more talk," she said, moving to receive him, although he could not have said she moved at all. He drew her toward him and said, "No more," and drew her closer and heard the sigh and the whispered, "There!"

Well, it was no new thing in the world, they knew. It had been going on this way, or something like this, for eons and if it hadn't been in one form or another, neither of them would have been here now to believe sincerely, in these moments, that they had invented it and were entitled to a patent. Even in times of total, even-handed honesty—willing to grant whatever was due to a trillion past experimenters—they believed that they had improved upon all former practitioners at the minimum and probably better than that since this fusion was separate, unique, like no other and bound to be permanent if providence held within its gift any small supply of wisdom and justice.

And so now they lay quietly and savored it and each other and felt honestly smug and particularly favored, although, of course, they gave themselves the credit for it, which naturally they deserved.

And the telephone rang and she looked up at him in accusation and said, "Damn! Again. And this time, you answer it—or let it ring. And, let me add, I've known from the beginning that your business was insane." She started to sit up in indignation while he reached unwillingly for the instrument in its cradle. "You'd think a girl could be born with better sense," she added bitterly.

"Stuart," he said.

"Rembert here," the telephone said. "Get your ass out of bed. He wants to talk to you and won't talk to anybody else, the bastard."

Rembert, Stuart thought. *They're after me—and gaining. Why is it absolutely inevitable that every time my boss gets struck down by an emergency involving me I am required to come to attention with my pants off? They're gaining, sure enough.*

"Who? Higgins?" he said aloud.

"Who else?" Rembert said. "I'm having you picked up in ten minutes."

"Won't he keep five more than that?" Stuart said irritably. "I haven't shaved, and I haven't had any sleep to speak of."

"He won't care if you aren't shaved," Rembert said impatiently. "He isn't either. Hurry up."

He put down the instrument slowly and turned to look at Amy. She did not look pleased, although she was not yet sore enough for the luminous aura of shared and highly satisfactory completion to have evaporated entirely.

"I don't think you have to tell me," she said. "But why now?" She looked at her wrist. "Even yet it's only seven o'clock—five minutes to."

"He's asking for me," Stuart said.

"The thing you brought off the plane?"

"Yes, darling. The thing."

"You've got him. Why badger the creature anymore?" She shuddered. "The way he looked on TV . . . so . . . nothing. Trying to hide behind you, chained to you like some stupid animal. So stooped and scared and shapeless. What was all that junk you had him wrapped up in?"

"Body armor," Stuart said. "You didn't know this. Somebody tried to kill him in Lebanon—when we almost had him alive."

"Why?" She frowned her bewilderment. "What was there about Lebanon that would make anybody think it was worth the trouble to kill that . . . that thing? Who?"

"A Beirut police lieutenant, national police—they call it the Sûreté." He knew he didn't want to talk about this, or to recount his part in those moments at the edge of the cliff, although he could not have explained the reluctance on any firmer ground than that he might seem to be indulging in childish heroics. And he surely did not want to detail the methods which had been used to persuade Lieutenant Haddad to confess.

"I don't understand," she said, the frown deeper. "A policeman? Was anything done about it?"

"They hanged the cop," he said shortly.

"Sometimes you infuriate me," she said. "I don't understand any of this and you're not much help. If we get married, which I intend, I won't put up with this FBI mumbo jumbo, and you may as well know it now. Why would a cop, as you call yourself and all other cops—I may as well use the word, too, silly as it sounds—want to kill a runaway American?"

"He had orders, darling. Please, I'm not trying to be mysterious . . . It's just that . . . well . . ."

"Stop mumbling. Whose orders?"

"I don't know that. Not yet, anyhow. And if I did know now you're too bright to think I could tell you now, even you."

"Some prospect for a fiftieth anniversary, I must say. Besides, you might have shaved. I feel like I'd been ravished by a porcupine."

He smiled. "If I'da knowed you was comin' I'da baked a razor."

"If that's a Stuart-brand joke, I'm likely to change my mind about the whole thing."

He stood up and went to the bathroom and turned the shower on again—cold this time—and took his icy medicine more or less like a man and changed blades in the razor and hoed himself, meanwhile whistling without tune. He came back into the room and unself-consciously searched out fresh clothing and hitched himself into it while she, just as unself-consciously, sat on the bed with her knees up and her elbows propped on them, brooding.

"You know," he said, looking at her fondly, and speaking in tones of astonished revelation, "we appear to be awfully comfortable with each other. When was the last time you blushed?"

"At least we're not bored," she said with a quick small smile. "Jeff, you know I don't like any of this, don't you?" Her voice was puzzled and in some way pleading. "I couldn't tell you why because I don't really know, but I don't like it. It . . . it scares me in some dumb way. And it revolts me in another dumb way . . . this chasing half around the world just for revenge on the stupid pathetic thing you brought back."

"In another dumb way, I understand it, darling. That is I don't understand it, but I know it. The thing is, maybe, you just don't like cops."

"That's not it, Jeff. But I don't like vengeance . . ." She shuddered. "And I'm afraid, somewhere, somehow, of what all this might do to this place where I was born and where all my people have been born it seems like forever."

"It isn't vengeance, darling," he said gently. "You have to believe that. The law says murder is crime—so does the Bible for that matter—and Higgins did a murder. I saw him do it."

"All right, cop," she said, swinging the long, smooth brown legs over the edge of the bed and coming toward him. "I'll see what I can do about believing it." She came against him, tall and cool and silky, and raised her mouth for his. "Go do your duty while I try to think of a way to get out of here with a shred of reputation—fine fix for a motel owner. I love you."

They moved apart with reluctance, fingers still touching as he opened the door. There surged, in each, certainty and fullness of heart and thankfulness, compounded of both humility and pride. And neither knew that it had ended here, in this air-conditioned any man's shelter in a Southern city, and might never be mended.

The car was waiting under the portico in front of the motel office. Stuart glanced at his watch and saw it was seven thirty and knew it was likely Rembert would be building a head of steam. And he was. Rembert, frowning, was impatiently watching the sweep second hand of his own watch when Stuart came through the door of Commissioner Mayhew's office, which Rembert had cavalierly appropriated.

"You took your time," he said accusingly. "It wouldn't matter if you hadn't some way made the bastard think you're his maiden aunt. Before you go down there, we'll take a few minutes to tell you what we found out while you slept." It sounded like sloth condemned, and Stuart knew it was meant to.

Ten minutes later, beyond the new steel barricades and their system of space-age locks, Stuart stood in front of Higgins' cell for which a Bureau colleague, on this occasion, was serving as turnkey.

"The boss said to let me in," he told his companion.

"I don't know if that's too bright an idea," the other said with some reluctance, "but he's the boss."

"And to tell you to shove off."

"That's even dumber. But he's still the boss," the guard said and unlocked the door. Stuart walked into the winkless glare of guardian light in which Higgins already stood condemned to spend all the days, hours, and minutes still left to his allotment.

"How're you doing?" Stuart asked. Higgins stood up somewhat heavily and Stuart noticed, without surprise, that the fingers of his left hand seemed absently but constantly to caress his right wrist as though to assure themselves that the chain was gone.

"All right, I guess."

The voice snubbed Stuart short in astonishment. The voice was calm, unshaken, sad but shriven of both the shrill quaver of fear and sullen negation. He looked more closely; you could not say the face was serene but certainly it had abandoned that vibrating tension. What kind of alchemy of the spirit had been worked here and what Merlin had worked it?

"You look better," he said. "Feel better?"

"Not good, but I quit shaking," Higgins said.

"How come?"

"I don't know. But I got this far and ever since that mountain I wasn't sure I would. But I did."

It's a damned small favor to be thankful for, Stuart thought, and wondered what kind of anesthesia his own spirit would settle for under similar circumstances.

"You wanted to see me," Stuart said aloud.

"Yeah, I don't know anybody else. Not anybody else I'd want to see here anyhow. If you don't want, you don't have to." The voice was now soft and apologetic—but, more astounding, without any note of groveling.

"I've got time," Stuart said. "You need anything? Want me to get in touch with anybody for you?"

"No. Nothing. Nobody. I kind of hoped you could tell me what next. It seems like it'd be easier all around if I knew what to expect."

"OK," Stuart said. "Let's sit." He lowered himself to the steel slat springs of the mattressless bunk and, after a moment of hesitation, so did Higgins. "Cigarette?" Stuart asked, shaking out the pack of plastic-coffined Philip Morris filters. "They don't taste like much, but they seem to give your lungs as much chance as they deserve."

Jesus, he told himself, *if I ever saw anybody with less reason to worry about lung cancer!* He held a match and Higgins, holding the cigarette steady, sucked on it hungrily.

"Mr. Stuart, if you can tell me anything." Higgins hesitated and frowned as though hunting for what he hoped might be useful words to clothe chaos with precision. "What's going to happen to me?" Forced out of abject wretchedness, the words tumbled over one another. He had chosen as well as he could, and the choices could not be criticized, for, after all, that was the question, what would happen to him?

"Well," Stuart began and paused to sort things out. If something was going to start here, he didn't want to turn it off. On the other hand, he didn't want to badger the man either and he wondered, briefly, if he had brought with him into this barren steel place some of Amy Wynn's womanly pity. "Well, to begin with, are you still telling me I got the wrong man?"

"I don't know whether you have or not," Higgins said astonishingly. Then he stopped and looked around with an almost instantaneous resurgence of panicky suspicion. "Is this place bugged?"

"It was. Of course," Stuart said. "I asked the boss to turn it off and he said he would and I believe him." *Oh, hell*, he thought, *let's level with the poor clod.* "But you have to know that if you tell me anything important, I've got to tell somebody else. But if you do want to unload anything, maybe this'll help. Nothing you figure you want to tell me has any legal standing. You can't make a confession to me; nothing you can tell me would put a rope around your neck."

"Yeah," Higgins said, nodding his head sluggishly. "Yeah, I guess I see . . . sort of. But what does happen?"

"I don't know that I can tell you exactly," Stuart said. "You'll be arraigned: murder one. You've got a right to get a lawyer before that . . . either that or ask the court to get one for you. Then you can plead guilty, or not guilty, or not guilty because you claim you were crazy, put yourself at the mercy of the court or stand mute. That'll be up to you—and to what you think or what your lawyer thinks."

"Do I have to do what he says?"

"No."

"I don't have any money."

"I wouldn't worry too much about that. I'll be frank with you, Higgins; the kind of defense you need there isn't enough money to pay for. But there are lawyers around, big ones with big reputations, that would trip over themselves to be your mouthpiece for free."

"Why would they do that?"

"Different reasons. Try it this way for one: Some lawyers have a lot of ham in them and sometimes the bigger the lawyer the bigger the ham. Take one who's already made all the money the income tax will let him use, and there isn't too much left for him to be hungry about. Some get hungry for other things than money; for these there aren't enough newspapers or TV cameras in the country to satisfy what they're hungry for. Whoever your lawyer turns out to be, you'll be the excuse to get his name in the papers and his face on the tube."

"I guess I see that. Me being a half-assed celebrity gives him a chance to be the all-ass one, is that it?"

"That's it. There's something else you probably ought to know. You're a celebrity, right enough. What's more, you're a commodity. You say you're broke, but you don't have to be. Maybe what you need more than a lawyer is a literary agent. But a lawyer could do it because you've got a seller's market."

"What's that mean?"

"If you were outside this tin box right now and had the use of a telephone, I wouldn't even guess how much some magazine like *Look* or *Life,* or a newspaper or a network would pay for the exclusive use of you. But your lawyer will know, or if he doesn't, he'll know how to find out. He'll have you rolling in money."

And you poor misbegotten sonofabitch, Stuart was thinking, *who do you think will be getting all that money—or at least who'll be using it? Not you, my friend, not you. But counsel will get his fees, sure enough, while you get to take the high jump.*

For a moment, Higgins' face lit up and then, while reality

took its time seeping back into him, he looked merely curious.

"Big money?" he asked.

"The way I count big," Stuart said.

"It might help pay a lawyer," Higgins reflected.

"It might indeed. It might even leave enough after his bill to keep you in cigarettes—while you're here. But there's another thing about this whole question of your lawyer that I ought to mention. They're not all after the name in the paper, or a fast buck, or both. The real best of them really believe what they were taught in law school, which is to say that a man on trial is entitled by law—written or moral—to the best defense he can get. A man like that thinks, first, it's his sworn duty, and, second, since he may also be entitled to carry around his share of ham, he likes to win."

"Even if the guy is guilty?"

"You got some tricky ones, don't you?" Stuart said. He offered the cigarettes again and Higgins took one. "I happen to know you're guilty because I watched you finishing the job. But that's not the question for your lawyer: It's a question for your jury and nobody's going to tell a jury beforehand how guilty guilt is—or even whether it's guilt at all. The thing for your lawyer to think about is that you're entitled to the best he's got in him. That answer anything for you?"

"Yeah. Quite a lot, I guess. Thanks." Higgins was still rubbing his right wrist, but Stuart didn't think his mind was on it. "But to come right back to the beginning, Mr. Stuart, what do you think's going to happen?"

Stuart thought, *How did I get into this? What does he want of me or hope to get? Does he think I can hold his hand, tell him everything's going to be all right? How much help would that be when they blindfold him? On the other hand, how much do I think he can take of what I think is accurate? What is cruelty anyhow? Or pity? Or comfort? He needs a preacher, not a cop.*

"You know," he said carefully, "it's not just me anymore. You could tell me for twenty years I'd made a mistake about you, and we'd both know you were lying. But now it's more than me."

"How you mean that?" Out of earnest inquiry Higgins had been spurred to some quick, reflex tension.

"I work for an outfit with a lot of tools. You ought to know that by now," Stuart said. "You left a print of your right palm on the stock of that gun. You left your right thumb and forefinger on the key of that Chevelle when you pitched it. They're yours, all right."

"The hell," Higgins said. "I didn't know that."

"I'm not surprised. You were in a hurry when I saw you."

"But what's going to happen? What do you think?"

"Higgins, I don't know," Stuart said, feeling without resentment that this was getting to be more of a strain than really ought to be put on him. *It's not logical,* he thought, *it doesn't make any sense. Chase one, catch one, and the next thing, without reason or rhyme, you find yourself with a kind of responsibility for him.* "You're a white man. You killed a black one. This is the South. How do I know what a Southern jury will do?"

"But what do you think they'll do?" Higgins persisted.

"I think they'll hang you," Stuart said shortly. "You insist on it, all right, that's what I think."

Now, he thought; *now if he's going to fall apart again, he'll do it now. Brutal? Maybe—I don't know. The best way? I don't know that either.* He waited and he saw the face sag and go gray in the harsh light and waited and dreaded waiting for the animal wail of last night. But it didn't come and almost imperceptibly color crept back into the face and after it a kind of earnest, seeking composure. At last Higgins spoke.

"You said you saw me. All right, I'm not going to argue with you about that—not here anyhow. But I guess I ought to tell you this, Mr. Stuart. There was more to this business than you seeing me in that cemetery. Maybe it ain't going to change anything, but there was more, a lot more."

"I know that, Higgins. I've known it ever since Haddad

tromped on your fingers. Maybe even before," Stuart said gently.

"Yeah, that was funny," Higgins said with thoughtful solemnity. "I never thought Haddad would do me like that. We were pretty near buddies."

"He didn't have any choice. He had orders," Stuart said.

"Whose orders?" Higgins was momentarily alert again. "Why?"

"I don't know," Stuart said. "But they came from here. I think neither one of us needs to guess why. The point is, who?"

"Yeah, I guess that's the point all right." Higgins sighed and went silent. He sat without moving on the steel slats, shoulders slumped, eyes closed, chin down on his chest, breathing deeply. Stuart began to wonder if he had fallen asleep, whether he might still be retreating into oblivion because the burden of wakeful reality was too much to bear. *Not that I blame him,* Stuart thought, and wondered again as he wondered increasingly with each hour ticking out of Higgins' drastically reduced life expectancy, what conceivable reason could be offered out of either head or heart for his feeling anything at all for the human thing beside him? But it puzzled him that the graven image of the crazed thing in the cemetery was somehow fading and that, now, he had trouble recalling Barton dying under his hands.

"You awake?" he said at last.

"Yeah. Thinking," Higgins muttered and stayed as he was. *The Silver Fox isn't going to be very happy about this,* Stuart reflected, *when I get back upstairs and report that all I've got to tell him is that I've spent more than a hour pretending to be an amateur legal aid society. I don't know how much this man knows, but he has to know something. All I know is that, left to himself, he probably wouldn't kill a cockroach. So he wasn't left to himself and that's the point of all this, after all: Who didn't leave him to himself and why am I not finding out?*

"Mr. Stuart, are you a lawyer?" The question, coming without warning from the sagging figure beside him, was startling.

"Who? Me? I'm a cop," Stuart said.

"Not a lawyer?" It came in a tired sigh.

"I went through law school if that's what you mean," Stuart said. "I got a degree, but no, I wouldn't say I was a lawyer. Why?"

"I guess it sounds like a hell of a nerve." He stopped and swallowed painfully and finally rushed it out. "Would you be my lawyer?"

"What!" Stuart heard himself say out of utter incredulity. "Hell, man, I'm the chief witness against you."

25

People who had played poker with Amos Wynn or challenged him in commercial transactions over the decades knew, sometimes in grief, that when he felt like it his gnarled face might as well have been reinforced concrete for all the information it let loose. He was a close-held man. And a perceptive one. He knew that neither twitch nor tone had betrayed him when Jeff Stuart laid the drawing of Peter Higgins before his eyes on his own dinner table. And he was as aware as Stuart himself of the doubt and hesitation with which Amy denied recognizing the face. Like Stuart, he was curious about that, a tantalizing puzzle, more so for Amos than for Stuart because it was impossible that the drawing said to her what it said to him. He knew who the man was.

It had cost an effort of imposed will to contain the astonishment of seeing Higgins' face staring up at him from the drawing paper. Wynn had known his city so long and so intimately that he usually knew the who, what, or why of strangers in it. In this catalog Higgins was of little account, a hanger-on, an errand boy, an addicted loser, of minor interest as a probable minor crook, not worth much bother. He knew the face. But until the instant of seeing the picture it never would have occurred to him that this was the man whose trigger finger had sent a load of buckshot into Carver Otis Barton.

Having seen it, the rest was grade-school arithmetic, known sums to be added and subtracted and the answer promptly to be arrived at. Amos had seldom needed the answers printed in the back of the textbook. A momentary surge of rage smashed against his self-control—and broke itself there. He came out of it cold and ready to reason.

Amos would have been the last to hold that he had lived sixty-two years without error. But he also knew because the record upheld conviction that even his worst mistakes had been capable of amendment and the small ones had not mattered. But this was something else. This was out of reach. Amos distrusted anything he couldn't get his hands on to shape according to his will. He didn't believe in luck, even in poker. To his mind luck was less than twenty percent of facing six other men over a deck of cards. Bluff, for example, wasn't luck but a useful semiscientific tool. Bluff, to be used intelligently, needed a working knowledge of probabilities and more important a working knowledge of the other man's psychological mix. Luck did not deserve even the minor dignity of being reckoned the bitch goddess; it was only a bitch.

Now, uncomfortably, he found himself face to face with luck, and helpless to do anything about it. The only tool at hand was probability, and probability without knowledge to back it up was a frail instrument indeed. Probability here was a very different breed of cat from that which ran through a deck of cards.

A mistake stared up at him from the drawing. Such fragile

logic as could be applied here said, at first, that the mistake had a fair chance of going undetected. So long as Higgins remained an unidentified face—nameless, without a history, without a trace, without a knowable place in the world, a shock-haired, wild-eyed nobody capsuled in enigma—it was reasonable to hope the mistake could lay buried forever.

But nothing was going to guarantee that. It *might* work out and that was all. The possibility that the mistake might squeak through, however, by no means justified the mistake. Luck had tripped it up immediately when chance had placed Jeff Stuart in exactly the right place at exactly the right time to see the killer in action. But, he reminded himself coldly, if Stuart hadn't seen Higgins, somebody else might have and the result, depending on who did the seeing, might have been the same.

No problem might have existed if the matter had rested only with the Wynnsboro police since Arthur Mayhew could be trusted not to happen on unseemly ideas—or very many ideas of any variety for that matter. But Barton's killing was no per-functory back alley homicide, as perfunctorily forgotten. Wynn might not have anticipated the intensity of the national shock wave to be generated by Barton's violent end, but once the FBI was into it, he did not make the mistake of underestimating either the Bureau's resources or its determination. The jeop-ardy in which the mistake now lay had to be measured directly against the abilities and the persistence of the likes of Jeff Stu-art, with whom, he recognized, his daughter was falling in love.

He had considered whether his pilgrimage to Washington in the effort to lever the FBI off his city's back might have wors-ened the situation—and he decided that it had not. *It's about what they would expect of me,* he told himself; *nobody is likely to work up a sweat because a man known to be bullheaded goes around being bullheaded.*

So there, for weeks, the mistake lay dormant while Amos Wynn waited luck out and the FBI went prying and prodding around the world to cancel luck. For Amos there could be no twisting the fact and he didn't try to. And he didn't try to excuse himself; he had made a wrong judgment. He had banked a decision on the vulnerability of Giuseppe Gervase who could neither refuse nor doublecross the man who knew the truth of the bomb in the Ebenezer Baptist Church. He had neglected to take into account Gervase's blind greed. The knowledge goaded him. *You have always known,* he told himself, *that if something important has to be done you had better do it yourself.*

There may have been those in Wynnsboro at the time who had jumped to the horseback conclusion that Amos Wynn was somehow responsible for the death of Carver Otis Barton. If so, they did not know, had no evidence, and could have proved nothing if they had wanted to. But they would have been right, and right for the right reason: They knew that few deliberate acts of transcendant human importance came to pass in Wynnsboro without somehow being touched by his hand.

Wynn was not a bloodthirsty man and, though capable of hard brutality when he thought it was necessary, not a heartless one. Hatred for another human being was nowhere in him, for he was not himself small enough to waste energy on the futility of hatred and nobody else in sight was big enough to be worth hating. He was singularly free of passion except on two subjects: his daughter Amy and the city whose stewardship was his by heritage. In the end, he would be forced to reckon how terribly he had imperiled both.

He had decided the death of Carver Otis Barton coldly, without passion, without a flicker of anger. The man had come without invitation, unwanted. He had thrown the city into confusion deliberately, attacked its traditions and its self-respect, threatened to destroy its viable present and its hope of a viable future. Wynn did not need to prove to himself that Barton stood as a mortal peril to Wynnsboro and its people, white or black. The coming of the Teamsters and Barton's coming to support them and the useless tragedy of Lucy Clagget's death convicted the man. Wynn had warned him that the city could not and would not tolerate him, but Barton had elected to defy the warning. He could not be scared off, and he could not be bought off. He was immovable and incorruptible. In Wynn's calculation, the only answer left to Wynnsboro was Barton's death. He had ordered it with regret but without hesitation and without pity because he held it to be the final necessity. If a choice lay between the city and Barton, the city would be the survivor.

Once the killing was done, he had felt neither remorse nor guilt. Barton had known what he was getting into; he had made the choice of a brave and stubborn man and had lost, as he may have expected to lose. Wynn had respected the toughness of Barton's fiber; if he had not had that it probably would not have been necessary to kill him. The riot the night of the killing had shocked Wynn profoundly. He had thought he knew his people and could not have believed they were capable of such an outpouring of passionate violence over the death of one strange black man from out of a world they knew nothing of. He had pondered the phenomenon since but admitted to himself that it remained a mystery to him.

Nothing in him called upon Wynn to mourn Barton. But he felt some compassion for the dead man when, at length, he learned who had pulled the trigger; black or white, Barton had been too strong and too proud a man for the indignity of being cut down by the likes of Higgins.

Peter Higgins was the core of the mistake. And Wynn recognized that it was coming home to roost as soon as he learned that Higgins was a captive and would live to stand trial. Luck had now demonstrated the validity of any sane man's belief in its essential bitchhood. Wynn felt no particular apprehension for himself. He would not confess guilt and he would not accept retribution without a fight, for he had always believed that a man who reached adult conclusions and acted on them owed an obligation to take the consequences of those actions without whimpering—if he could not defeat those consequences beforehand. In their separate ways, Amos Wynn and Carver Otis Barton had been more alike than either knew.

But two considerations set upon him the terrible grip of hitherto unacknowledged fear. He had hostages: Amy and the city of Wynnsboro. His own destruction could bring them both down with him.

He watched the eleven o'clock television news with Amy, sitting in his darkened study with only the pale flicker of the screen to illuminate their faces. His own was impassive, but he knew, looking toward her as Stuart drew his stumbling captive down the ladder, that hers was a compound of eagerness and revulsion.

"What's going to happen now, pa?" she asked. The scene at the jail door, harshly lit by the floodlight glare, had blacked out. Its puppet actors had been replaced by the cheerful inanities of a late night talk show from New York. She got up and switched off the set. "After that? Ugh!"

"He'll be tried," Amos said quietly. "And, I imagine, hanged."

"It's all beastly . . . all of it!" she said in quick passion. "Pa, I'm scared. I don't know why I'm scared . . . but I am, deathly scared."

"Don't be, girl," he said. "It doesn't touch you."

"You're wrong. It touches all of us," she insisted.

He did not answer, and he stayed where he was when the telephone rang and she left to answer. He was still there when, later, he heard her leaving the house and heard the Porsche start. He believed he knew where she was going. *And there's that,* he thought, *another thing that could smash her. I never thought I would let my young get into a position where she needed pity,* he thought. *But I have. And it has to stop here. Yes, girl,* he said to himself, *I'm scared too.*

He got up heavily and went to the telephone and spoke briefly. "Be there," he finished and put the instrument back in its cradle. He went to the cellar doorway and down the stair to his gun room. He unlocked a glass-front walnut cabinet and selected a short-barreled Smith & Wesson .38 revolver. He loaded it with studious care.

He dropped the weapon into the right-front pocket of his tan gabardine slacks where it rested in reasonable comfort and without an ostentatious bulge. In recent years Amos had taken to having his pants tailored with generous pleats below the waistband as General Douglas MacArthur had done before him and for the same reason. Although most of him was still lean and big and bony, Amos had begun to grow a mature man's alderman. The pleats both accommodated the accretion in comfort and camouflaged it. His gut was one of the few affronts to Wynn's personal vanities.

He took the Cadillac. He knew the streets in Giuseppe Gervase's affluent neighborhood were paved smoothly enough to treat the big car kindly. Moreover the Cadillac, in spite of its costly length and opulent gleam, was less conspicuous than the jeep which bore his brand.

He parked in the shadows of Gervase's carport and went to the front door and entered without knocking. He knew he was expected, although not welcome. He knew that Marie Gervase was away with her mother in New Jersey. And he knew where to find Wynnsboro's least legitimate entrepreneur in his own house—close to where the money was. And so, entering, he crossed the dimly lighted, overupholstered living room, passed down a long hall and opened the door to Gervase's office.

Gervase was at his desk over which a hooded lamp burned, casting a circle of brilliance on the desktop but leaving the fleshy, carnivorous face of the man behind it in shadow. Wynn took an upright, oaken, ladder-back armchair, seated himself, and thoughtfully inspected his half-seen host. After a long moment he spoke.

"I don't see you too well. Turn on some lights." His voice was quiet, but there could be no debating its quality of command. Gervase got up in sullen silence, went to the wall, and switched on a ceiling fixture and returned to his desk. *Jumpy and sore and probably scared,* Wynn thought; *he should be.*

"That's better," he said. "You watched the eleven o'clock news?"

"No," Gervase muttered angrily. "I was out there. The sonofabitch."

"Why?" Wynn said conversationally. "To try to kill him again?"

Gervase started up, then sank back into his chair. "Kill him?" he said. "You got to be kidding."

"Cut it out," Wynn said. "I don't miss everything—too much, but not everything. I know what didn't work in Lebanon, and I don't think you went to the airport just because you like to rubberneck. You had people planted at the airport."

Gervase recognized that Wynn was stating a proposition rather than asking and decided nothing was to be gained here by lying and that, conversely, something might be gained out of truth since it was clear that whatever steps he might take he was faithfully serving Wynn's interest as well as his own.

"Never mind who. I had somebody—two. But shit! The way those federals had him tied up it'd take an atom bomb to get at him."

"Figuring to try again?"

"I don't know how," Gervase said gloomily. "It ain't the local cops that have got him."

"And you can't very well give him a squirt of roach powder through the air-conditioning, can you?" Wynn said sardonically. "You'd be knocking off half the FBI. You've got my sympathy."

"It ain't so funny," Gervase said. He remembered that he had a grievance in all of this, that he was entitled to righteous anger since he had got into his present predicament in Wynn's behalf, gaining nothing himself, not wanting any part of a murder that was bound to provoke an uncomfortable degree of attention and pursuit. Having practiced the art, Gervase had a good eye for calculating the risks of a killing against the obscurity or—conversely—fame of a potential victim. "Barton was your pigeon, sure as hell not mine. I did you a favor. I don't understand you, Am . . ."—he remembered in time—"I don't understand, after all the hell you raised because a no-account nigger got killed by accident in that church, then you turn around, like it was nothing, and want to knock off the biggest nigger in the country. Anybody'd know there'd be hell to pay." The hot eyes peered accusingly at Wynn past the flaring prow of nose.

"Don't call me Amos," Wynn said coldly. "I told you. Bombing the church was stupid and useless. Barton was something else. Getting him out of the way was necessary."

"God damn it, Wynn!" Gervase was not often forced to pity himself, and the rare necessity stirred resentment deep inside him. "You're in this as deep as I am. You're the big shot; you got to do something."

"We'll look that over," Wynn said quietly. "Meantime there're some things I want to know about I should have known before. I'm finding out I'm not entirely immune to stupidity either; it's an uncomfortable thought. I think I know why, sure, in fact; but I want the confirmation." The gun was heavy in his crotch, and he moved in the chair to shift the weight.

"Meaning what?" Gervase asked, and his eyes squinted in suspicion. He sensed a trap here someplace, ready to spring, and was already probing for a way to avoid it.

"Meaning why you sent that stumblebum to kill Barton," Wynn said.

"He was the only thing I had," Gervase said, cautious, on the defensive.

"You're lying," Wynn said without heat, merely stating a fact they both knew. "Don't waste my time on it. The money doesn't matter. I want the truth for a change."

"It's the truth, I sw . . ." Gervase said, wondering if it was possible for him to hate more than he hated this big, hard-eyed, wooden-faced, unmoving nemisis.

"Don't blaspheme yourself—you're dirty enough already," Wynn said. "You said it would be expensive, and I bought that because I knew, even better than you said you knew, that it would cause a stink and it had to be done competently. Tell me"—the voice had gone harsh—"what became of the professional you were bringing in from Mexico?"

Wynn had in effect signed Barton's death warrant with all the deliberation of the judge he held himself to be, and now he found it incongruous and unsettling to sit here recapitulating a bungled murder he had bought and paid for.

"He couldn't . . . I couldn't . . ." Gervase was reaching, without much hope, for a convincing lie.

"You're still lying. I want to know exactly how much of that hundred thousand dollars ever got to that sucker you planted out there in the cemetery with a gun. By the way, that tomb you picked belonged to the Montgomery family. They buried the last one twenty years ago, which was lucky for you. If the family had a live man left today, they'd have got you for that two months ago."

Here, Gervase thought under the choking pressure of helpless anger, *here I sit in front of him, pressured into talking about how a job got done just because he wanted it done. Who in all hell is he to sit there so goddamned sure that he's a better man than I am? Cleaner? Better? Who in the name of God is he to judge me?*

"Damn it, Wynn, he got it. Do you think I'd hold out—on a thing like that? Christ!"

"You'd hold out on your mother, Gervase," Wynn said, gazing at him with the curiosity he might expend on some loathsome insect. "And you did. How much?"

"I tell you the God's honest truth . . ."

"You wouldn't know it face to face. How much?" The demand carried the relentless insistence of a bulldozer. "How much, Gervase?"

"He got ten thousand here. But—" Gervase began.

"But what? And I don't believe the ten thousand either, Gervase. You wouldn't have paid him carfare if you could get out of it. You had something on him. You wouldn't have kept a slob like that around if you didn't. What was it, Gervase?"

"He had a conviction against him in Kentucky," Gervase admitted sullenly.

"What for?"

"Rape and assault. A school kid. He was nothin', Wynn, why should you care about him? And he got money, all along the way, I swear . . ."

"I didn't believe it the last time you swore either. I don't care about him, Gervase. Rape? Assault? A schoolgirl? A baby raper and you sent him out to do a man's work. It would be a pleasure to stomp you, Gervase. Your man didn't just kill Barton. He killed a little girl, too. Remember?"

Gervase remained silent and tried to meet Wynn's contemptuous stare and couldn't and looked away, feeling the sting of salt in the corners of his eyes, wanting desperately to scrub away what he knew were tears of rage but not daring to betray himself, wondering how or whether he was ever going to get this remorseless monster off his back. As bad as any part of it was the humiliation. He was the one men feared; how was it possible this one could make him grovel? He needed to get strong again and, guarding the movement in stealth, felt down alongside his hip in the crevice of his leather padded swivel chair for the steel hardness of the reassurance that was always there, ready for need. *The big bastard could hound me to it,* he thought, and felt a little better. *It could come to that.*

"I'll ask you about something that's had me puzzled some," Wynn said curiously. "Puzzled because it's out of character. How was it you gave this Higgins as much as a dime—and let him get away alive?"

"I don't get you," Gervase said.

"You tried to get him killed when they caught him," Wynn said patiently. "Why didn't you get him killed before he ever left town? Or anywhere along the way? Why did you wait until they had him? It puzzled me. It's out of character. Killing Barton was something else—you bungled that trying to do it cheap, we both know that. But killing Higgins afterward wouldn't have cost you anything; it wouldn't even have mattered if you'd bungled that, too. Why was it, Gervase?"

"Why should I want him killed? I had nothin' against him," Gervase muttered. But he was remembering how simple it might have been.

"You don't have to tell me, Gervase," Wynn said. "I'll tell you why. You kept him alive because you figured somehow, someday, some way or other you could use him to get me." Wynn, without taking his eyes off his victim where they had stayed now without wavering for half an hour, shifted again in the hard chair and, as though idly, thrust his hands into the deep pockets behind the pleats of his trousers and reared back, as though tired of holding an upright position and tilted the chair until its front legs were off the floor and the tall bowed back rested in easy balance against the wall. Gervase watched the movement in covert suspicion, and Wynn knew that he was watching.

I wonder, the big man was asking himself, *how much or how long it will take to goad him into moving. Sooner or later he will, either when he gets some guts into him or gets so terrified he does it out of reflex action. It would simplify things all around if he tried it. But I wonder, I wonder. I've never killed a man, not in cold blood, not because I intentionally drove him to it, forced him to commit suicide. Killed, yes, but not this way. Do I want to do it? Or have I got any choice?*

"Isn't that right?" he said. "Isn't that the way it was, Gervase? You kept him alive to get me. Either to get me off your back. Or make me pay. Isn't that right, Gervase?"

"Have it your own way," Gervase snarled. "What do you want?"

"Why, the same thing you want, Gervase. To have this cleaned up and forgotten. But you know it isn't going to be easy, of course you know that. They've got your sucker, and they've got him where you can't touch him. So how long, Gervase, do you think it's going to be before he starts talking? How long do you think?"

"If he talks he gets to you, too," Gervase snarled. He had quit thinking and now hate saved him, at last, from the humiliation of squirming under that relentless stare. He felt the steel under his hand in the recess of the upholstery and his hand tightened on it, and all he could see were the gray eyes, taunting and contemptuous. Only the eyes—and the quiet maddening voice. Everything else was a blinding swirl of rage.

"Not if you weren't here, Gervase, not if you weren't here." The soft voice pounded in his ears like a shout.

Gervase jerked up the gun from its hiding place in the chair, and even as he did so felt himself hammered back by a blow high in the chest, a blow so hard and white-hot that he knew his chair was crashing backward and over. He heard and felt the hard crack of his head against the floor.

26

Somewhere between quietly and ecstatically content and obscurely troubled—if that compound were chemically possible—Amy turned the Porsche into the gravel drive and parked in the carport against the coming sun which could brutally mistreat its crimson paint. She looked at her watch; it was coming up on eight o'clock, and the sun was not only coming but already in full malignant arrival.

Marty will be up and so will pa, she thought. She wondered a little whether her reception was likely to prove as unusual as the circumstances, but she approached the house without embarrassment and with no thought of subterfuge. No Wynn, so far as she knew, ever had been susceptible to either; the Wynns plotted their courses without regard to the generality of mankind and without waiting for the sanction of other Wynns. By and large they expected to get the second since the only orthodoxy one Wynn required of another was an unshakeable awareness that he or she was a Wynn and nothing less. Wynn pride unquestioningly assumed a right to stand tall and stride free.

She had showered and restored her face before leaving Stuart's room, and the plain gold-colored linen dress she had put on around one A. M. hadn't been on her long enough during the night to be anything but freshly unrumpled now. And she was hungry, so she walked directly from the front entrance to the kitchen.

Her gesture was unusual for a morning greeting but because her mood toward humanity called for demonstrative affection in general she paused in the kitchen long enough to give Martine Pullen a quick one-armed hug. "Morning," she said and turned toward the door to the terrace.

Martine, when she felt like it, had a flashing, delighted smile, and she gave it now. It struck an answering chord of pleasure in Amy, as it had frequently since Marty's return to the house a month after her father's funeral, to recognize a change in their relationship. Before the night of the girl's tormented outburst, Amy now knew, Marty had been to her, one, a servant, and, two, a precocious and obliging child to whom it would be a self-indulgent pleasure to proffer the charity of a college education. Lately, among other revelations, she had come to understand that Martine studied not only high school English and math but also the works of such as Malcolm X, Eldridge Cleaver, Le Roi Jones, James Baldwin, and Martin Luther King and was knowledgeably aware of profound tumult well beyond the orderly horizons of the Wynnsboro public schools. She recognized that the youngster was groping her way into an expanding world which must be both terrifying and profoundly exhilarating to her, and she did not begrudge the girl her right to seek her place in it.

The change was subtle: Marty was still, one, a servant, and, two, a bright child whose education would place its fiscally insignificant claim upon the Wynn bank accounts. But the change was there; Amy now looked upon Marty with the respect she would accord to maturity in her own race. Her education was no longer charity but rather an obligation to the fulfillment of man which anyone in his right mind, who could also pay for it, would be honored to honor. The two women— for Marty was nearly a woman and in some ways a full adult who knew already the cruel bruises of maturity—now shared friendship as well as affection; that was the difference.

"You hungry?" Marty asked. "You pa's already eating. A lot of food goes into him—for one man."

"Starved," Amy said. "How about papaya and two poached eggs and buttered toast and bacon and a quart of coffee? And grits since I'm a Southern belle—or belly, whichever you prefer."

"Coming up," Marty said and smiled that sudden sunburst again. Amy went out the door.

Amos Wynn, facing a yellow mound of scrambled eggs which was dwindling not at all and turning gelid despite the reputation for gluttony just bestowed upon him by Martine, knew she was coming. He had heard the Porsche drive into the carport and had heard voices from the kitchen. He knew where she had been in the night and supposed that she knew he knew, but he did not expect her to avoid him. As a Wynn, she would not; as a Wynn, he would not have it any other way.

She had been heavy on his mind even as he had returned to the sprawling mansion in the blackness shortly before dawn had begun to wrench away the night. He now believed it inevitable that she was bound to get badly hurt, one way or another. The question now was how much, if at all, it would be possible for him to mitigate the wound, to contain it within limits tolerable to her spirit and her resolution. He did not doubt the capacity of her fiber to withstand pressure, but passionately he wished that she might not be hurt at all.

There had been a curious and deadly inevitability about the way the night had gone, he recognized now. He did not know with absolute certainty whether he had gone out in the night determined to kill Giuseppe Gervase, although he had known then and still knew in the bright freshness of the morning that it would have been the only way to guarantee safety for Amy, for Wynnsboro, and—peripherally and less vitally—for himself. The trouble there was, he knew, that safety for them and safety for himself were inseparable.

He did know that he had not completed the job, at least not immediately, but he thought it at least likely that the way he had left Gervase the job had more than a chance to complete itself. As the two guns went off simultaneously, he had had a curious sense of how closely Gervase's bullet had passed over his right shoulder and how near to his neck and he had heard it smash into the wood paneling against which his chair was tilted. And he had seen Gervase and his chair flop backward.

He had tilted the chair forward and risen deliberately to his feet and crossed the room and circled the desk to look down on the fallen man. He had at first thought he was already dead, but then he had seen air bubbling in the froth of blood spreading on the man's flamboyant, short-sleeved sports shirt. And so he had knelt and felt for the pulse and found it erratic but still strong.

He had not in that moment nor did he now feel any pressure of guilt. It was true that he had deliberately goaded Gervase into firing and that, seeing in the man's eyes that he was surely going to do it, had still waited for the mad wince of action to fire at the same time. It had been a duel, a fair contest with evenly matched men firing blind, aiming to kill, not to maim.

Finishing him off was something else. Looking down at the helpless mound of obese flesh, he recognized the necessity for the *coup de grâce*, but knew at the same moment it was impossible. A duel was one thing. To now finish killing a thing incapable of defense would be murder and he knew, without having to reflect on it, that it was impossible for him to do, no matter what the cost.

He had left the house walking erect, had backed the Cadillac out of the carport, had driven away to an intersection where he knew he would find one of the stainless steel telephone booths he had lately caused the council to install here and there in Wynnsboro. He had called St. Francis Hospital emergency rather than police headquarters, feeling instinctively that if Gervase was to have any chance at all it would be improved by his being retrieved first by an ambulance and a trained intern or resident rather than by a pair of ham-handed policemen in a squad car.

Thereafter he had driven twenty miles to the lake and got a canoe out of the boathouse and paddled to where he knew the mud bottom lay at least a hundred feet beneath the keel and dropped the weapon overboard. He knew there was small chance, if any, that the bullet in Gervase's chest would ever be identified since the weapon had come down to him through two grandfathers and his father and its origins had long been lost in frontier antiquity. Then he had driven home. *I am not a professional,* he told himself, *and I do not know whether he will live.*

He had not yet got around to examining the difference between commissioning the extermination of Carver Otis Barton from ambush and his automatic refusal to insure the safety of his own vital interests by a simple act of completing the killing of a creature he had nearly killed already. But he would in time.

Amy came to the other side of the table, looking fresh and lovely, in riotous and joyful full bloom. She took the chair facing him and said, "Beautiful day, pal"

"So're you," he grunted and knew to his surprise that she had brought him up far enough from painful reveries to smile at her. "It's an old prerogative of Wynn women; they're lookers." The gray eyes in the gnarled brown face were steady on her and fond, but she sensed rather than saw a thoughtful sadness in them. *I've hurt him,* she thought in regret; *I'm sorry it couldn't be helped.*

"I don't suppose you need to guess where I was," she said calmly and smiled back at him, feeling the warm swell of her love for and gratitude to the outsize, indomitable crag that was her father.

"No, I don't," he said. "You look pleased with yourself. It shows."

"I am. Are you upset?"

"I dunno," he said. He laced the handle of his fork through hard fingers, and when he cracked his knuckles absently the metal bent double. "If you mean am I going to yell and holler and go for a horsewhip, no, I'm not. I've had you around too long and know you too well to jump the tracks because you all of a sudden spent the night with a man. But I won't pretend I enjoy the idea. Jealousy maybe. A man has a daughter and by a shortage of luck—or because the Lord planned it that way—he's got only the one and he knows, if he has brains enough to count on his fingers, that sooner or later he's not only going to lose her but he damned well ought to. But no law says he has to enjoy it. If I'm upset, that's the way I'm upset."

"Thanks," she said. "I'm going to marry him."

"I would have thought that," he said, smiling again. "It was never a family trait to let go of something, once they decided they wanted it. It's a property-minded family."

She grinned at him. "In this case, I feel more like the property than the owner. Or it's even-steven, which would be even better."

"I suppose you know I would never try to pick your man for you, but that never did mean I wouldn't be interested," he said. "He's your choice, not mine—and to get down to cases it's your business and not mine. But, more or less incidentally—well, no, to be truthful, not incidental at all because I made it my business enough to butt in and ask—I know a little about him. He's something more than a big foot policeman. Did you know he has a law degree?"

"No," Amy said. "I didn't ask and it wasn't what I was interested in."

"Probably not," Amos admitted. Bringing up a daughter and cognizant of its dangers, he had told himself before this, forced a man to be realistic about the motivation which set a man and a woman on a collision course toward each other—and it wasn't a law degree or any other kind of degree. On the other hand, he thought, the old man ought to be practical enough to think about such things.

"There's another thing you may not have thought about," he said. "It could turn out to be an embarrassment—for you—for him—for both. It has for other people. Does he know how much you'll be worth?"

Amy looked at him inquiringly, then smiled. "How could he? I don't know myself."

"I should think he ought to know by this time that I'm not dead broke," Amos mused. "You ever consider that—or talk about it together?"

Amy's expression was mildly Machiavellian. "Nope. He bought me dinner once, and *he* didn't seem to be flat broke either. How much will I be worth?"

"Around thirty million dollars—give or take a few. To tell the truth, I don't know myself."

"Whooo-eee!" Amy said. "That's money. What am I supposed to do with that?"

"I should've had you briefed long ago," Amos said, suddenly aware again of how soon and how vitally her ability to cope with the Wynn heritage could become all important. "A man gets in the habit of thinking he goes on forever, which is damn foolishness. You'll find it's more work than fun, but you'll have help: lawyers, trustees, executors, accountants up to the hips and over. But in the end the decisions come down to one place, the responsibility. The Wynns have been responsible here for a long time, and responsibility doesn't run out just because people named Wynn do. Your man will have to be told what he's getting into."

"You're not afraid he'll pick it up and run off with it?"

"No. It's not that portable in the first place. In the second place, you're a woman grown; you've seen enough men, of one kind and another. Admitting I'm prejudiced in your favor, I think it's a safe bet, now that you've finally got your mind made up, that you didn't pick a sprinter."

"Thanks again," Amy said. "I don't think so either, although I can't say I'm crazy about the job he does now. You've been snooping—you admitted it—why didn't he go into law practice?"

"I don't know, girl. I didn't snoop that much. What bothers you about his work?"

"I'm not sure. And I can't define it," she said, frowning. "I think he feels some kind of holy commitment to it—but to me it's not a holy job. A . . . hunter. And you saw what he brought back here last night—from half around the world. Oh, I don't know, pa. . . ." Her voice trailed off unhappily.

"It had to be done. He stuck to what he had to do until he did it. I can't help admiring that—even if I don't admire the FBI worth a damn." His fingers, still grasping the fork handle, turned it over and whitened and the metal bent the other way. "When I was a kid, they called that kind of stubbornness a virtue, and I guess it is."

"Well," Amy said, with a sudden air of decision. "I'll try to keep him busy with your thirty million bucks. Whooo-eee again."

Daughter, Amos said to himself, *I'm praying for you. Not for the thirty million . . . for you.*

About the time Amos Wynn and his daughter arose from the table on the terrace, Jeff Stuart was trudging up the stairway from the new leakproof, air-conditioned, jealously guarded, solid stainless steel cell in Wynnsboro's cellar jail. He still wore a bemused expression as he entered Commissioner Mayhew's commandeered office. Rembert, who had been on the telephone to the director in Washington most of the morning, looked up irritably.

"You've been at it long enough," he said. "I hope it was worth it."

"You didn't listen?" Stuart asked.

"No, I didn't listen. Didn't I tell you I'd turn the thing off?"

"Yes. You did," Stuart admitted. "But you didn't say you'd keep it off."

"Well, I did. What do you think I am—dishonest?" Rembert's frown was deepening dangerously.

"No. But curious."

"Well, what'd he say? What'd you get?"

"Nothing much," Stuart said cautiously. "He made a condition."

Rembert snorted. "He's in a hell of a condition to make conditions. What's his proposition?"

"He wants me to defend him."

"What!" Rembert finished the word with his tongue against the roof of his mouth and the mouth open. He left things that way for the time it took to rally his forces and add, "Good suffering Jesus, man, you're what's going to convict him!"

"That's about what I said," Stuart said mildly, still looking baffled.

Rembert was staring at him incredulously. "And I thought I was kidding when I called you a baby-sitter," he said. "What went on anyhow?"

"Mind if I sit down?" Stuart said. "This'll take a while." He pulled a chair back from in front of the desk, sat, reached for a cigarette, lighted it, and dragged smoke deep into his lungs and let it out in a long gray sigh.

"Well?" Rembert said impatiently.

"I'm just trying to get it organized," Stuart protested. "Well, what he mainly wanted to know was what was going to happen to him. I didn't know whether I ought to or not, but I finally decided there wasn't much point lying to him. I told him I thought they'd hang him."

"How'd he take that?"

"Surprisingly well. He's found something somewhere inside himself that's calmed him down. Damned if I know how; he'd been acting like a bowl of waterlogged jello ever since we grabbed him off that mountain."

"Strange," Rembert said, musing. "Strange. They'll do it sometimes—when you least expect it. What else?"

"He wanted to know what procedure he can expect. I told him how it'll probably go, arraignment, murder one, his plea, no chance of bail, naturally. And I told him he had the right to a lawyer, of course—either one he picks or the court picks for him."

"What'd he say to that?"

"Said he didn't have any money."

"Hell, man. He won't need money."

"That's what I told him. He could have any of them, Bailey, Foreman, Belli, Williams. He could have half the American Bar and never spend a dime. They'd use him, sell him, or take him on just for the kick of doing the law in the eye—or all three."

"That make him feel better?"

"Not noticeably," Stuart said, shaking his head in puzzlement. "He said he didn't know any of those people."

"He sounds crazy," Rembert said, sitting up abruptly. "You think he is?"

"No-o-o-o," Stuart said. "But he certainly is different." He shook his head again.

Rembert joined him so that, for a long moment, they resembled a pair of puppets in the hands of a puppeteer suffering from locomotor ataxy. "What brought him around to you, for God's sake?"

"I don't have any idea. But now I think he'd got around to something like that even before I got there. I don't know, but he led me right to it, sure enough. Startled me."

"I wouldn't be surprised," Rembert said dryly. "But doesn't he know you're the state's eyewitness, the only one the state's got?"

"He ought to. I've told him enough times I saw him do it."

"And even if you were his mouthpiece, the state would have to subpoena you as a hostile witness and put you on the stand and make you say you saw what you saw. You couldn't duck it. There'd be no taking the Fifth on a thing like that, bud. And no claiming a privilege. It would be something you happened to have your peepers on—long before he ever became your client. He's got to be crazy."

"Yes," Stuart said wearily. "I told him."

"He still wants you? Hell, you're his hangman."

"He still wants me."

"What'd he offer you? Anything besides his love and devotion?"

"There's that," Stuart said thoughtfully. "It isn't what he offered me. It's what he said I wouldn't get if I didn't."

"Straighten that out for me," Rembert demanded, frowning again.

"Well," Stuart said, getting at it with care. "He said there was more to this, a whole lot more than just what I saw."

"You believe that?"

"Ever since I laid a hand on him I've believed it more every hour. You've seen him. I've seen him even more. He's a rabbit, a mouse. He killed Barton all right; I've got to believe that because I saw it with my own eyes. I've either got to believe it or somebody has to convince me I had the DT's that day."

"You're sure you really did see him?" Rembert demanded, sudden doubt in his eyes.

"Of course I saw him. Him, Higgins, nobody else. But now I can't believe it. He did it, but he couldn't have done it— and I know that doesn't make sense. But he did do it and that means somebody made him do it, some godawful pressure. I'd sooner believe Little Red Riding Hood was a wolf killer than believe that worm went out all by himself on his own hook and deliberately plugged Barton. He wouldn't even do it for money —although, of course, he must have got some. Somebody financed his vacation because it's a cinch he didn't. But who? Why?"

"He must know both who and why."

"That comes with me being his lawyer."

"Which you can't do."

"Of course I can't do it. But I'd give my shirt to know who or what pushed him into it. We chased him hard enough, and we had to because he *is* the killer. And we've got him and we can hang him. But that isn't going to solve Barton's murder any more than I'm likely to get to be director of the FBI. All we've got is the finger that pulled the trigger and it doesn't mean damn all. Let's remember who Barton was, what he meant in this country, what he meant to the President, what he meant in terms of how much further apart his murder drove the blacks and the whites in this country. We can't let that go with just stringing up a punk like Higgins."

Rembert didn't seem to be listening. His eyes had narrowed in speculation. With the regularity of a metronome the fingers of his right hand were tapping on the desktop and he seemed to be far away.

"I could fire you from the Bureau," he said suddenly. "Hire you back afterward, of course—no loss of seniority—I'm sure the director would let me fix that."

"What are you talking about?" Stuart said.

"Turning you loose to be his lawyer. You say he'd spill to you if you're his mouthpiece. So if you were, we'd know what he knows. Why not?"

"Wait a minute, now," Stuart said. "Just wait a minute. This *is* nutty. First place, I'd make him a hell of a poor lawyer, even if I wasn't the main prosecution witness. I've never practiced; all I ever did was get admitted in Minnesota. I've never defended anybody, not even a shoplifter."

"Isn't the point," Rembert said. "You just said it yourself;

what's important is to find out what he knows, what was behind him, what really got Barton killed."

Stuart's eyes were narrowing and angry. "You know damned well I can't do that," he said coldly.

"Why not?"

"Because I told him he's entitled to the best defense he can get. And he is. Legally, morally, any way you want to put it. Whatever he knows is his and it isn't the FBI's unless he decides to give it to the FBI. What he might tell me as his lawyer wouldn't belong to the FBI either; it would still belong to him and nobody else. I wouldn't know it as a Bureau agent; I'd only know it as his lawyer—and, Mr. Rembert, *that* is privileged."

"You'd still want to know who the real killer is. Or wouldn't you?" Rembert demanded.

"Of course." Stuart was shaking his head in bafflement again. "But, believe me, in the impossible case I ever should turn out to be that man's lawyer, he'd get exactly what he's entitled to and that is the best damned defense I'd be capable of giving him. Not one thing less. Believe me!"

"You're not seeing it all, son," Rembert said softly. "Not yet. Think about it. Think about it. The best conceivable defense Higgins can possibly get this side of the hangman is for us to know who pushed him and why they pushed him and what they pushed him with. Think about it. If you could prove he was helpless to do anything but what he did, there's that one thin chance you could get him off with life. Otherwise, he hangs."

Stuart reached for another cigarette, lighted it, inhaled, let the smoke drift out, and stared at the ceiling. He kept on staring and did not speak, and Rembert watched him in unwonted anxiety.

"You may be right," Stuart said at last. "You can guarantee there wouldn't be any Bureau pressure on me?"

"I can guarantee the Bureau. But nobody can guarantee the prosecutor. You know he'll put you on the stand."

"Yes, I know. That couldn't be ducked—and I wouldn't try. I did see him."

"Hell of a mess," Rembert said. "A mess any way you look at it. But I want the guy behind him, you want him, the director wants him, the President wants him, the country wants him. Tell me this, you've been on this for weeks, months. What do you know about Higgins?"

"Nothing really, except basically he's a worm. He was a sort of handyman for a local hood. Guy that runs whorehouses and slot machines and roadhouses and restaurants and, so they do say around here, runs dope from the border north to Chicago, Detroit, and New York too, I guess. All around unsavory type. Name's Gervase."

Rembert sat up.

"What was that name?"

"Gervase. Why?"

"How do you spell it?"

"*G-E-R-V* for Victor *A-S* for Sam *E* for Edward, pronounced like it had an acute accent on the last *E*. Why?"

"Look in there, front page," Rembert said, picking up the Wynnsboro *Times* and shoving it across the desk toward Stuart. "There's a man named Gervase in St. Francis Hospital. On the critical list. Somebody shot him last night."

27

Rembert's fingers were busy on the desktop again and he was frowning, but the halo of silver hair, Stuart noticed, was in marcelled good order as always.

"Now what?" Stuart said.

"I guess the way to put this on the road is to fire you first," Rembert said. "You can write out your resignation, stating why . . . no, skip the explanation. It would look peculiar when the prosecution put you on the stand."

"It's going to look peculiar anyhow," Stuart said. "I didn't just see him. I chased him eight thousand miles, and when we got back, half the people in the country must have seen us on the tube."

"It won't be the weirdest thing that ever happened in court," Rembert said. "Besides, you're not in court yet. I can see complications coming."

"Are the complications you're thinking about any different than the ones I am?" Stuart asked, ungrammatically.

"For one, you're not famous," Rembert said dryly. "You're no Foreman or Williams. You're not even a Belli. You're a lawyer—but only just. The only thing you have going for you in a claim to defend Higgins is that he wants you. The judge, whoever he turns out to be, won't have to listen to you—or Higgins either."

"I know that, of course."

"If he decides the whole schmeer is too ridiculous . . . too downright . . . bizarre is the only word . . . he'll laugh you out of court and appoint whoever he wants as Higgins' counsel —and you have to admit he'd be absolutely justified."

"I know," Stuart said tiredly. "Nobody says I want to defend the slob."

"Higgins does." Rembert got up and began to pace up and down the room. He stopped and lifted a slat of the blind and peered out into dazzling sunlight and dropped the slat and returned to the desk. "Lousy place," he said.

"It has its compensations," Stuart said, thinking of Amy Wynn, feeling a quick, unbidden swell of joy.

"What's that?" Rembert asked sharply.

"Nothing. And that's wrong. I do in a goofy way want to defend him. He isn't much, but I seem to find myself feeling sorry for the misbegotten jerk. He was helpless—he still is."

"That's one of the poorest excuses for murder I ever heard." Rembert snorted. His big face took on his cross-examiner's look. "Just how much did he tell you? In detail?"

"You didn't listen in? Again?"

"No! Damn it."

"If I'm his lawyer, what he told me is privileged," Stuart said. "I know you don't have my resignation yet, but you will two minutes from now." He reached into an inside breast pocket and took out a ballpoint pen. "Got any paper?" he asked.

Rembert tore a sheet from a ruled yellow pad before him and handed it across the desk. "Here," he said, "if you insist on going formal."

Stuart wrote the date and time and scribbled quickly, *I hereby resign as an agent of the Federal Bureau of Investigation. Effective immediately.* He signed it and slid it to Rembert. "If I'm going to go at all," he said, "I guess the only way to go is formal. All right, he talked a lot. A lot of it was pointless or anyhow didn't have anything to do with this."

"Maybe I ought to be the judge of that." Rembert frowned.

"Maybe you hadn't," Stuart said. "I'm his mouthpiece—for now anyhow, so I'll be the judge. I'll tell you what I think won't hurt him."

Rembert stared at him, unwinking, his eyes quickly going wintry. "Just remember, Stuart," he said coldly, "you're dealing with murder. You're a law officer."

"Not anymore," Stuart said calmly. "I'm an officer of the court—and that's different. And I'm defense counsel—which is even more different. And I'm still trying to find out the real reason Barton got killed here—which may be altogether different."

Rembert studied him without favor. "All right, do it your way," he said at last. "But don't try to get fancy."

"I'm not," Stuart said. "Some of the things he told me aren't relevant. Other things may be marginally relevant, but maybe we can get along without those and I don't want to talk about them because if I did I might be getting him into more trouble than he is already. Needlessly. He is my client."

"He's already got all the trouble there is," Rembert said impatiently.

It was true enough, Stuart thought. A rape conviction and a sentence still unpassed in Kentucky could scarcely be compared with first-degree murder in any rational scale of values, but still who knew what was going to count for how much when a jury got down to weighing the sins of Peter Higgins. The man he had killed was black, but the girl he had raped was white. That made a difference and Stuart was not minded to put that fact in the scale unless he had to.

"Did he admit he killed Barton?" Rembert demanded impatiently.

"Of course he killed him. I saw him do it. Remember?"

"No, damn it! Did he admit it to you?"

"I'm not going to say that," Stuart said doggedly. "He was in the cemetery. He was in that tomb. He had a gun. He ran away. All that I saw."

"All right, all right," Rembert said. "It comes to the same thing."

"Not necessarily," Stuart said cautiously. "What if he admits everything I saw but still swears he didn't kill Barton?"

"Of all the damned fool . . ." Rembert exploded. "That's impossible!"

"Maybe . . ."

"I warned you not to get cute."

"I'm not trying to get cute. But you'll admit I'm in a peculiar position."

"Peculiar is no word for it. What else?"

"There's a cop in this town. Lieutenant of detectives. Name's John Kelley. You know him?"

"Yes. Seems like a good man. What about him?"

"Higgins says he drove his getaway car."

"What?" Rembert's eyes narrowed.

"That's what he says."

"Do you believe that? It's insane."

"I told him if he lied to me and I found out he lied—and I would—no more lawyer. I don't know whether I believe it or not."

"Well, I don't. A cop? Kelley would have to be out of his mind." Rembert paused and pulled at his lower lip. "Give me a cigarette," he said.

Stuart looked startled. "I thought you hated the things."

"I do. Give me one."

Stuart shook out a cigarette and struck a match for the assistant director who pulled one deep drag into his lungs, coughed, and, with a look of disgust, threw the smoldering tobacco across the room.

"Filthy things," he said. "Either that or absolutely sure Higgins would never be caught."

"The only way he could be sure of that would be to be sure he'd be dead instead of caught," Stuart said.

"Exactly. He almost was."

Stuart shook his head. "As far as I've been able to find out, Kelley's the class of the class of this police department. Tough and honest, that's his reputation."

"You can be one without the other," Rembert said sententiously. "There's no knowing what kind of skeletons Kelley might have in the closet."

"I'm going to believe Higgins," Stuart said.

"Why? It's insane."

"Not because he's my client, but because of other things."

"What other things?"

"Higgins was a jellyfish when I hauled him off that plane. Scared silly; I didn't know a man could get that scared. . . . But when we ran into Kelley on the ladder . . ." Stuart shook his head again.

"What?" Rembert demanded.

"All of a sudden he was scared twice as bad."

"It doesn't prove anything necessarily," Rembert protested. "Working for a crook like Gervase it's logical Kelley might have joggled him before and he remembered. A man in his position, any cop would scare him. A cop he knew could scare him even worse."

"Maybe," Stuart said doubtfully. "But if Kelley *did* drive that car it could fit with something I think . . . or I guess hunch is a better word . . . more and more all the time."

"What's that?" Rembert asked suspiciously. "Don't get the idea you *are* a Percy Foreman—or even a Belli."

"I'm not. The last thing I'm likely to get in this idiot business is delusions of grandeur."

"What then?"

Stuart drew a deep breath and let it out in a long sigh. "Higgins pulled the trigger, all right. I believe that. But I think what killed Carver Otis Barton was the whole damned town. I don't think there's a soul in the city limits that can plead innocent."

"Now you're insane." Rembert snorted. "Your list of defendants include your girlfriend?

"What about my girlfriend?" The demand was instinctive, but then, Stuart realized, he had to consider Amy Wynn in the light of what he had just said. He had condemned the city, and that made Amy part and parcel of his accusation. She had to be. If Wynnsboro was responsible for the death of Carver Otis Barton, so was Amy Wynn. You couldn't generalize murder and then excuse one person because fate or whatever had decreed her innocent of all things except love for you. You couldn't have it both ways.

"I know you've been seeing Amos Wynn's daughter," Rembert said. "I know I told you to, but I don't think it's all business either."

"No," Stuart admitted, "it isn't. I'm going to marry her."

"Not if you're going to try to send the whole town to the pen, you're not. Orange blossoms and murder trials don't mix."

Stuart would have been hard put to define all that lay behind the feeling of black depression that crept over him like flowing lava.

"I'm not trying to say everybody in town got together and decided that Barton had to die," he said slowly. "But they weren't against it either. Barton represented everything this town has rejected for generations. He was anathema here—even to most of the blacks—they've got Uncle Tom bred into them. I know; there must be five hundred or a thousand people in the city who should have recognized Higgins' picture—but do you think one soul would admit it? Not one, black or white. They all played dumb. And they stayed that way until finally, for whatever reasons they had, one black man and Miss Wynn admitted they recognized him."

"Do you always call her Miss Wynn?"

Stuart knew he blushed. "No, of course not."

"What was her reason for coming across?"

"We were in a place where she'd seen him do something—and that made her remember."

"Saw him do what?"

"Get ham-handed with a hostess."

"You think she really didn't remember him until then?"

"I don't know," Stuart admitted. "I'm trying to be honest with myself. I guess what I believe is that subconsciously she might not have wanted to remember."

"Hmmm," Rembert said. "Strange. All of a sudden she tells you. I wonder."

Stuart knew he was blushing again: At bottom, he believed now, Amy might have kept what she knew to herself had they not become so drawn to each other and had not the beginning of love softened her reserve. Amy he knew, love or no love, was Wynnsboro to her core. The two were not incompatible except in the strange and terrible circumstance that Barton was dead here and dead by premeditated violence. What was it Amos Wynn had said? Executed. That, he knew, was what had happened: Wynnsboro had executed him for crimes against its essential nature.

"How come the black man came across?" Rembert demanded. "What reason did he have?"

"He got around to it eventually. He had to, and I admire him for it," Stuart said.

"Why did he have to?"

"He had two daughters. They both got killed. You could say both were accidents. Only the accidents happened to them because they believed in what Barton was here for."

"I see," Rembert said. "So you're blaming the town, but the only real evidence you've got is that nobody went out of his way to help you identify Higgins."

"No, there's more," Stuart said. "Not that I could make a murder case out of it."

"What more?"

"I think there must have been a more or less general knowledge around town that if Barton came back, and if he tried to push the Teamster organizing operation, something was going to happen to stop him."

"Can you prove that?"

"I don't know. I can try. There's a man named Gabriel Jardine."

"Who's he?"

"Runs the textile mill here. Managing director."

"What have you got on him?"

"Hearsay. He got half-squiffed and talked in front of a black bartender at the country club."

"You'd have hell's own time trying to do anything with that in court."

"I know it. I wouldn't even try. And even if I could prove it, it wouldn't necessarily be guilty knowledge. All I'm trying to say to you is that the whole town rejected Barton and what he stood for. He wasn't welcome here. When he came here, he signed his own death warrant. And nobody on earth could make me believe that Higgins nominated himself for the job of executioner. And, of course, I know who did nominate him. He told me."

Rembert sat up abruptly. "Gervase?" he demanded.

"Yes, Gervase. Higgins' boss. Higgins' own executioner . . . only it didn't come off. And how am I to prove that . . . with Gervase up there in St. Francis dying—maybe dead already."

"He wasn't two hours ago," Rembert said. "You're going to see him, naturally."

"If the Lord lets me. I saw him once. If it isn't any better the next time, I might as well not bother. But I know a little something more about him this time. Hearsay again. Higgins."

"Now what have you got?" Rembert said. "I will swear the minute I get your resignation in hand and you become a living lawyer you also at the same time get to be a terrible pain in the ass."

"I'm not trying to be. I'm trying to think. If you read the reports . . ."

"I read them." Rembert was beginning to show the signs of impatience which, on him, were not unattractive since red went well with silver.

"A church got bombed here, you recall. Before Barton ever showed. They had a Teamster organizing session and the place was fused and a man got killed."

"What about it?"

"Higgins says Gervase set up the bombing."

"Gervase sounds more delightful all the time."

"There's more, and if even half of it is true and you could prove it, there'd be enough to hang him higher than a kite. Hearsay again, or just about. Higgins. He told me that four times in the three years Gervase had him on the string he had to drive a pickup truck out to a lake ten miles from town with Gervase's goons along and packages in the back. They dumped the packages in the lake. Higgins doesn't think the packages were animal crackers."

"We can drag the lake," Rembert said thoughtfully. "Who were they?"

"Higgins swears he doesn't know—except he thinks he might know who one was because he never saw him after that."

"Who?"

"Colored numbers operator. Named Davis."

"It isn't going to help us much to know about Gervase's sins if he kicks off first. What makes Higgins think he knows about the church? Give me another cigarette."

"You blew the last one."

"Never mind if I did." Rembert took the offered cigarette, dragged on it, and discarded it while Stuart watched with curiosity.

"You'll get cancer," he said. "Gervase had a colored kid hanging around. Named Dowdy, a dumb bad kid, even more dumb than bad, I gather. Related to that saloon keeper I tried to talk to the night of the riot, the one that got killed in the riot.

"The night of the church bombing, Higgins says, Gervase chased the kid out of town . . . for good. Higgins says he took Gervase's pickup truck—the same one he used on those trips to the lake—the hearse, so to speak—and gave the kid a lift to the railroad junction east of town where he could hook a freight and disappear. Higgins says the kid was so scared and mad—full throttle on both—he told him how Gervase made him do the bomb job. Higgins said the kid swore he'd get Gervase someday."

"Yes?" Rembert drummed on the desk again and stared at the ceiling in speculation. "So maybe that's who plugged Gervase. What a place!"

"Maybe, maybe not. Probably the fewest thing Gervase ever had was friends who wished him good health. I favor another explanation for Mr. Gervase's present affliction."

"Foreman, again," Rembert said cynically. "What are you pulling out of your hat this time?"

"The pieces fit. The trouble is not enough pieces. Take Gervase—he's a hood and a red-neck and there's reason to at least suspect he's a killer—the kind that doesn't do it himself but knows how to get it done. He makes his living in a variety of ways, almost none of which are honest. The trouble is he goes

out of character when you try to figure him as the guy who put
out a contract on Barton. Not that he didn't do it, because I believe he did. But why would he do it? Barton was no threat to
Gervase; the worlds they operated in hardly even touched except in the remotest way. The only things Gervase was likely to
hold against Barton was that he was black and he was from out
of town. That isn't enough to explain just up and going to the
trouble of getting him killed. Gervase, by reputation, is anything but stupid. I can believe he might get somebody killed almost just for the fun of it—so long as he knew there wasn't
much chance of a backfire—or no chance at all. Barton was
something different. Gervase had to be bright enough to know
that making a dead man out of Barton would cause a terrible
stink, as it did, since we made most of it. So why would he take
that chance?"

"Ask Gervase."

"Just pray we get the chance," Stuart said. "Just pray he
wakes up—and talks."

"You say he's not a gabby type. Why would he?"

"I admit there's not much chance of it, but if we can pile
enough on him, he might try to make a trade. There's another
thing that puzzles me, and that's why he let Higgins live as long
as he has."

"And, as you say, almost didn't."

"Yeah. Higgins told me that after Kelley picked him up and
dumped him with some money and orders and a hot car to
drive, he got passed along. That stop in Matamoros was the
only thing that wasn't on the schedule, him and that baby
whore. After he got to Mexico City, everything was on the rails
again and greased all the way: Havana, Madrid, Marseilles,
Beirut. All along the road he was taken in hand by somebody
who knew about him and had orders about him and skedaddled
him on to the next stop. Why?"

"You're getting at something. What?"

"Higgins was no Barton. A dead Higgins wouldn't embarrass
anybody. Why didn't Gervase have him knocked off right away?

Higgins was the only witness Gervase would have to worry about. Why wait until he was caught and then have a Lebanese cop try to kick him off a mountain?"

"You tell me."

"Because a live Higgins must have meant an asset to Gervase. Alive he could be used for something. Dead he was useless."

"But alive—dangerous."

"So whatever he was worth alive had to be something with a high potential, something worth a risk."

"I admit it makes a kind of harebrained sense—the way you put it together. But . . . harebrained is the right word."

"I don't think so. Not if my hunch is right. I believe this town was Barton's essential killer. If it was—or some part of this town was—keeping Higgins alive gave Gervase a real nut-crushing grip on Wynnsboro."

"Theory."

"If you want. But there's another thing: Gervase's a hundred-carat skinflint. So why keep an expensive live Higgins when a dead Higgins could be had for peanuts or less? Not that he didn't diddle Higgins anyhow. He'd promised him fifty thousand bucks to go into the cemetery with the gun. Higgins never got anything but a handout here and there along the road—just enough to keep him running."

Rembert sat up and looked alert. "So he did admit to you he did the job?"

"I didn't say that. I said he got an offer for going into the cemetery and Gervase more or less welshed on it. I'm still his lawyer. So then take the rest of it."

"What rest? You're being ingenious, I admit, but you're not proving damn all."

"I know it." Stuart, dark eyes brooding in his scarred face, dug his blunt fingers into his already and customarily disheveled hair. "If I'm going to believe hearsay, and I sure can't just ignore it simply because it's hearsay . . ."

"All right don't ignore it. Spin it out until you run out of things to spin out."

"All right. So we've got Gervase. Somebody has gone to the trouble of plugging him and he'll probably die before we can do anything about him. We sure can't while he's unconscious. But somebody took the trouble. Dowdy? That's possible, but the most the Dowdy kid had against him was that Gervase gave him a raw deal and scared the bejesus out of him.

"But if Gervase arranged the Barton murder, which I believe, whoever got him to arrange it would have a persuasive reason for plugging him. The only thing I don't understand about that is why, after plugging him once, they didn't finish the job. That's a conundrum."

"Don't talk fancy."

"Sorry. Then if you admit that Gervase is, at best, an unsavory sonofabitch, what is a cop like Kelley—Gervase's natural enemy—doing apparently in cahoots enough to give Gervase's choreboy a lift out of town?"

"I think you'd better talk to Kelley."

"I intend to. I also intend to have a word with the blabbermouth drunk. Jardine."

"You say he runs the textile mill. Who owns it?"

"The company name is Wynn Textiles, Inc. That's the name practically everything in town goes by—including the town itself."

28

Aside from the fact that he had fallen in love here and had been more than richly rewarded for doing so, Jeff Stuart could find nothing about this summer in the city of Wynnsboro to award him either pleasure or satisfaction. He had lost Carver Otis Barton here and accounted the loss a personal defeat as well as a more general offense against the good and the growth of civilization in a nation which he revered.

Now, he wondered, in just what spirit should you approach a man to whom, probably, you owed your life when your present purpose was to accuse him of complicity in an assassination? It was another scorching day and the old courthouse sweltered in musty dankness. Lieutenant John Kelley's office door stood open on the dim corridor, and a tired wind blew through it from open windows, carrying only a discouraged movement of air and no relief. Kelley, thin and saturnine, standing in front of a gray-steel filing cabinet, wearing a tieless short-sleeved shirt and apparently not sweating as Stuart knew he was, turned at his footstep and appraised him out of coolly expressionless light-blue eyes.

"I've been expecting you," he said. "Have a seat." He moved behind his scarred wooden desk and seated himself in an equally battered swivel chair which squeaked as he leaned back, and continued his inspection of his caller. His holstered pistol,

Stuart noticed, lay on the desktop within easy reach. He had a feeling that Kelley never allowed himself to get very far removed from the tools of his authority.

"Why?" Stuart asked.

"Inevitable." Kelley shrugged and permitted a thin smile to show for a moment. "You spent two hours with the prisoner this morning and more than that this afternoon. Either you were talking—or he was—or you both were. I wouldn't guess you were just holding hands."

"You keep track of things around here."

"It pays to around a jail—particularly when uninvited guests show up and take over the joint," Kelley said without evident resentment.

"If you'd caught Higgins, that wouldn't be necessary. Now I guess it is," Stuart said.

"You could be saying that if we had caught Higgins, it wouldn't be necessary to take over because he might be dead," Kelley said evenly. "That's possible, of course, although we don't as a matter of policy mistreat prisoners."

"I'm not suggesting that you do. But we all know that fugitives on the run sometimes get damaged in the process. How's your wound?"

Kelley shrugged. "Healed. A little stiff, that's all."

"It took guts to stop and pick me up," Stuart said. "I want you to know I understand how much guts it took."

"We don't like guests getting beat up," Kelley said. "Which doesn't change the fact that it was a damn fool place for you to be."

"White guests?"

"I didn't specify a color. I said guests."

"You could call Barton a guest," Stuart said.

"You could—and you couldn't. Nobody invited him that I know of. Anyhow Barton ran into something that he probably knew he stirred up himself. He wasn't just touristing around— the way you seemed to be."

"I wasn't exactly touristing. And nobody invited me either.

But I agree it was a damn fool place to be as it turned out. For getting me out I thank you and I'm sorry you got hurt."

"Don't thank me. If I'd been alone I might have let them have you. But Mr. Wynn wouldn't and that's why we stopped."

"Wynn is quite a man," Stuart said.

"You can say it again—and you'll only be about a quarter the way there . . . But that's not why you dropped in, I think."

"No," Stuart said, wondering at the man's self-possession. *He knows where this is bound to go,* he thought, *he has to know, and he isn't going to turn one hair.* "As you suggested, Higgins had some talking to do."

"I wouldn't be surprised. He has a lot to try to weasel out of —and he's not going to weasel very far keeping his trap shut. Nor, I would guess, by opening it."

"He mentioned you," Stuart said.

"Yes?"

"He said you met him on the other side of the cemetery. Over there on that empty stretch of Magnolia. After that, he said, you drove him to where the car was stashed—the Chevelle he dumped in the junkyard in Atlanta."

Stuart wasn't really expecting a reaction. Everything he knew about this cold, efficient policeman denied that he could be taken by surprise, and he was not.

"Now why would I do a thing like that?" Kelley said calmly. The faded blue eyes were unwinking, almost casual in their quiet inspection of his guest.

"I don't know. I wonder. For some reason I don't really see you playing Good Samaritan to a scared jellyfish like Higgins. Even less, I guess, in cahoots with a bum like Gervase."

"So he got Gervase into it too? That doesn't surprise me quite so much."

"Why not?"

"The way I understood it around town, Gervase more or less owned Higgins. Maybe he didn't like being owned. It could be, now he's in the soup, he's trying to get anybody else he can into it with him. Gervase would be a natural for it. Could be . . ."

"Incidentally, got any idea yet who shot Gervase? Or why?"

"We're looking," Kelley said. "If he comes to, we might get some better idea."

"It wouldn't have been you?" Stuart asked abruptly, knowing perfectly well that even if this wild shot in the dark happened to be square on target Kelley wasn't going to betray anything.

"No. It wouldn't have. Except he's a bastard, I've got no bones to pick with Gervase."

"There's a hook-up somewhere," Stuart said doggedly. "You and Higgins and Gervase don't fit together worth a damn. But I believe you did help Higgins take it on the run."

"Prove it," Kelley said.

"Maybe I can't," Stuart admitted. "I'll see what I can do. You know you'll get put on the stand, don't you?"

"That's all right. If Higgins' defense puts me on the stand, they'll have to put him on to say I did it. The prosecution will make confetti out of him. His word, my word, which one would you take?"

"In this case, his."

"You sound like his lawyer," Kelley said, looking at him quizzically, showing more expression than he had at any moment in the interview.

"It's a possibility," Stuart said. "Not his lawyer, just a dumb cop trying to find out why Barton got killed. As I say, the cast of characters doesn't fit—unless—"

"Unless?" Kelley lifted an eyebrow slightly.

"I don't exactly know. I'll neighbor around and see if I get struck by lightning. Thanks for your time." He got up to go, deciding against offering his hand.

"Be seeing you," Kelley said.

Back at the motel, crossing the lobby, Stuart received and noted the mynah's raucous indecent proposal, walked to the cage and returned the bird's impudently perky stare.

"I don't think you're a consenting adult," he said. "Up yours." At the desk, the clerk handed him his key and a message slip which, he saw, was a request to return a call to a number in Baton Rouge. There was no name, but, after a puzzled second, he supposed it must be Blaisdell and wondered what might be on the Teamster's mind.

In his room he shrugged wearily out of his sweaty jacket, looked contemplatively at the telephone, turned up the air-conditioning and decided that he needed a shower more urgently than Blaisdell needed to talk. He took the first shock of it as hot as he could endure, soaping himself luxuriously, including his scalp which itched, and finished with the needle spray from both shower heads so icy cold that he came out of the stall squalling in protest.

Toweled down, he fixed a tumbler of bourbon and branch, took it to the bedside stand, and sat on the edge of the bed and picked up the telephone. *If I can talk to Rembert bare-assed,* he reflected, *I guess I'm not violating the social graces any more talking to a Teamster the same way. At the moment I abhor the very thought of any kind of clothing: it was the saddest day in all evolution when man first met a haberdasher and got talked into covering his raw pelt.*

He recognized the melodious baritone immediately, named himself, and asked, "What's on your mind?"

"Got to thinking about you," Blaisdell said. "Now that you've got your pigeon."

"We've got him, but he isn't much of a pigeon. More of a canary."

Blaisdell chuckled. "Singing, huh?"

"But out of tune," Stuart said. "Can I help you with anything?"

"I don't know," Blaisdell said slowly. "As I say, I was thinking about you—and the canary, of course. You remember we considered whether your getting your hands on him might not make that town a little less uncommon."

"I don't know," Stuart said, uneasily foreseeing the direction in which Blaisdell would go, wondering whether it might be good or bad or neither in terms of what he himself was after. "We haven't had him long enough to know."

"But you're getting something. As long as he sings."

"A little," Stuart admitted. He knew he was not prepared to go into detail with an outsider. He still stood aside from whatever the Teamsters proposed to do in Wynnsboro; that was their affair and Wynnsboro's affair. Now he found himself in a strange dual role, but the Bureau's secretive habit of mind was still heavy on him. And, in any case, he would not with Blaisdell explore the nuances of his conviction that all the things and people he had touched—Higgins, Gervase, Kelley—were merely instruments arranged in a bizarre concatenation to carry out the purposes of some more overpowering will. There was no other feasible way to explain their outlandish partnership.

"Enough to make the place a little edgy?"

"I don't think so to tell the truth. It's possible, but nobody but me knows what he's had to say. All the town knows is we got him and brought him back. There's curiosity, naturally."

"I don't suppose it fits in with your ground rules to give me an idea of what tune he's singing."

"No." Stuart's reply was abrupt.

"I wouldn't have thought so," Blaisdell said without resentment. "You have to operate your way; we have to operate our way. We'll be moving back in there directly. Never really moved out as a matter of fact. I just thought I'd let you know."

"That's kind of you, but you know I told you, what you do or don't do in Wynnsboro is not the Bureau's business—unless you do something or something happens to make it our business. If you want my horseback guess, you might be rushing things. That is, if you figured that catching Higgins would help you. I doubt if the powers that be here are any fonder of the Teamsters today than they were yesterday. Or distracted enough not to notice you."

Blaisdell chuckled again, warmly.

369

"We both know who the power-that-be is around there," he
said. "I may be seeing you. Good luck with your canary."

29

He had telephoned her because he wanted her
badly and she had come to him eagerly. She opened the door to
his room without knocking and walked straight into his arms
and waited until after she had kissed him to say, "Hello, darling cop."

He held her back and looked at her and said, "You're the
loveliest thing I ever saw or felt. Thank you."

"For what?"

"For coming here, of course."

"What else would I do? Since you wouldn't go to the lake
with me?"

"I'm sorry. I want to. But we're somewhere around the last
quarter of this game. I can't get very far away from anything."

"I knew there must be a good reason why I don't like the
cop business. Besides all the other reasons I don't—or suspect
I don't. Your captive is locked up. I don't see why you have to
sit here like a mother hen."

"There's something else, darling."

"I imagine there always will be. What is it this time?"

"A man was shot last night . . ." he said slowly. He won-

dered how much, if anything, he should tell this girl he loved
without any reservation whatever and without limit. And at the
same time he thought how absurd it was to think anything of the
sort since he was automatically making reservations and setting
limits by wondering how much he could tell her.

"I know, our homegrown Sicilian *tong*. What happened? Did
he finally serve somebody a bad steak? Oh, I'm sorry—I didn't
intend to joke. He really was shot. But what does that have to
do with you . . . I mean, us?"

"Nothing with us, I think," he said cautiously. "Just I have
to be around . . . in case he doesn't die."

"I don't understand," she said, puzzled. "What has
he . . . ?"

"Maybe nothing," he said, deciding to evade again, just why
he couldn't have said. "Higgins . . . the one I brought back
. . . worked for him. I have to know all I can find out about
Higgins."

"Cops . . ." she said in only half-simulated despair.

It was not until they lay together on the bed, her naked body
in his arms, that he realized that his urgent need of her was not,
this time, sexual. By that time it was too late for anything but
shamed embarrassment on his part and something between
shame and confusion for her. It was difficult to credit how this
night's unwanted constraint could have done otherwise after
their few awakening times together had been so instinctively,
simply and unaffectedly open and joyous and mutual and entirely without shame or reserve. Now a strange, unbidden reserve lay heavy upon them.

"I'm sorry," he whispered in something that sounded very
much like a groan when, with her close and beloved in his
arms, he realized that he was flaccid and worse, was going to
stay that way.

"What's the matter, darling?" she said with worried anxiety.
"Have I done something? Said something?"

"No, damn it. No," he said with the angry roughness of his
embarrassment.

She laughed shakily. "Well, don't swear at me."

"I'm not cussing at you," he said. "At myself."

"It's all right, darling," she said soothingly, but he heard the confusion in her voice. "But it must be me. I must have done something. Are you sure?" She got up on one elbow and bent to kiss him, and for no reason he could understand he had to force himself not to shrink from the touch of her lips. *What the hell is wrong with me,* he asked himself in puzzled anger. *Some stud!*

"No, it isn't all right," he said. "But I don't know why. I'm no good for anything, darling, and I don't know why. I know I love you, but the fact is I'm impotent."

She laughed that rather quaking laugh again, and he knew it was teetering on the edge of tears. "It certainly set in suddenly, if you are. Did you get struck by lightning . . . or something?"

I know what I got struck by, he realized in a flash of guilty insight. *I've done her the lousy injustice of equating her with this lousy town, and it's bothering me. Jesus Christ, Barton is dead. Let him rest. Quit gnawing on it and make it stop gnawing on you. You're probably full of crap anyhow. Somebody killed him, sure enough, because he's dead, but who nominated you judge and jury and gave you the right to condemn the place and everybody in it? Including your girl, your beloved girl, your magic, warm, beautiful, gay, funny, loving and loved girl? But this place, this Wynnsboro is a murderer—I know, I feel it, I hate it.*

He turned to her in fierce resolution, willing his body to want her, and she responded eagerly. She pressed herself against him and her thighs were opening to him and her hips moved in anticipation and invitation.

"Now, darling," she whispered even as he, in a sick shame, understood that nothing was going to happen. He cursed and rolled away from her, acutely conscious as he did of the fleeting touch of her aroused nipples and their departure from his flesh.

"Oh, Jeff, what is it?" she whispered. She was hurt and shamed and afraid of something she could not understand.

Something had happened to them, and it was both incredible and impossible. As swiftly and overwhelmingly as the joyous wonder had come, it was now inexplicably gone. "Oh, Jeff." She wanted to wail or hammer at his hard body in outraged humiliation; she didn't know which.

"I'm a damned idiot," he said angrily. "Also I'm cheating you. Maybe that's the matter."

"Don't," she said urgently. "You're not cheating me, and I love you."

"I don't mean cheating you with this—or maybe I do. Maybe the reason for this is that I was cheating you in something else."

"I don't understand." She propped herself up on both elbows and looked down at him out of troubled eyes. "If I thought you were capable of cheating, I wouldn't be nutty about you."

"I am, though," he said. "I hold out on you. Here I tell myself there's nothing held back between us, that everything is up and up between you and me, and even when I tell myself that I know I'm lying to me. It's Barton and Higgins and Gervase and Wynnsboro and the whole mess. I could tell you that I don't level with you because in the Bureau you're supposed to keep your mouth shut and you do it so long it would be a habit even with your mother. It's true in a way, but not true enough, not between you and me."

"I know you're not supposed to talk about some things. It's all right. I understand."

"That would be all right—if that was exactly true. Only this time it isn't true, not exactly. Anyway I'm not in the Bureau anymore."

"You are not in what anymore?" She was startled, disbelieving, and it showed.

"I'm out of the Bureau. I resigned."

"Oh, I'm glad. But in the middle of this thing? I don't get it, darling. I don't know what you're talking about."

"I quit so I could defend Higgins. He asked me to be his counsel. I accepted."

She shook her head in bewilderment.

"It's not possible! How can you say or think the things you've said and thought all the time and then . . . how could you say you saw him kill that man and that that made it personal—and chase him halfway around the world and catch him and haul him back here like a Roman emperor behind your chariot—all trussed and chained and ready to hang—and turn completely around and say you're going to get him freed? Jeff, I don't believe I heard what I thought I heard."

"You heard all right. Except I didn't say I was going to get him freed. He'll probably hang all right. But I'm going to do what I can to prevent it."

"In heaven's name! Why?"

"Because I don't think he's guilty."

"Not guilty! You said you saw him do it!"

"I know. I did. He did. He pulled the trigger all right. But he was innocent of intent. He didn't want to do it. He was made to do it. And that, illogical as it may sound, somehow seems to be the matter between us right now."

"That's crazy," she said.

"No. I can't make love to you because I accused this city, in my heart, of the murder. And you're part of the city. Now do you see?"

"Oh, darling. No I don't see. But I see you have to find who pushed that wretched creature. You have to know. To save us."

"I know who pushed him. Gervase."

She stared at him, her gray eyes so enormous that they seemed all of her face. "Doesn't that settle everything?"

"Not until I find out what pushed Gervase."

"Darling, give this up. It's destroying you. It's killing me."

The telephone rang.

"I knew it." She sat up and reached for the instrument and handed it toward him. She began to laugh, but the laughter turned into sobs even as he said, "Hello, Stuart."

"It's Gervase. He came out of it," Rembert said. He had himself in hand, but Stuart could feel the electric intensity of his excitement. He felt his own rising. Maybe now there'd be an end to this, and, for her sake as well as his own, he made a conscious effort not to remember the tear-stained face he had left back at the motel she owned and where, just now, he had felt a deservedly unwelcome and unsavory visitor.

"What kind of shape is he in?" he asked, trying at the same time to sort and assemble the few tools which might pry something useful out of a man who had every reason not to tell anything and a wary animal's instinct against doing so.

"How do I know? I'm not his doctor. All I know he's not dead yet."

"Can we see him now?"

"We can't. You can. They didn't want anybody, and they absolutely balked at both of us. I picked you because you know the whole schmeer."

Stuart could guess what the choice had cost Rembert, the veteran hunter denied his place at the kill.

"I don't know if you made the right choice," Stuart said with slightly dishonest politeness. "I could be too tangled up in it."

"You'd better be the right choice," Rembert said coldly. "You've only got ten minutes, and there'll be a doctor sitting on your shoulder, so it may be less than that. It was all I could do to keep them from having a Wynnsboro cop roosting on the same shoulder."

"Lieutenant Kelley, for instance," Stuart said—and shuddered.

A polite but patently disapproving head nurse met them on the fourth floor.

"You will have to wait for the doctor," she said and nodded at a bench.

"Where is he?" Rembert demanded.

"Busy," she said curtly and went back behind her desk. Stuart was conscious that she was keeping a suspicious eye on them, and he knew, from small familiar signs, that Rembert beside him was fuming. *How sick is Gervase?* he wondered. *Sick enough, perhaps, to be afraid of death and possibly willing to unburden before he went to his reward? I doubt that. Mad enough at whoever shot him to want to get it off his chest? And who did shoot him? And why? Did it have anything to do with Barton? It seems likely. Ten minutes! What can you do with ten minutes on a man like Gervase, a man with so much to conceal and a lifetime of practice in concealing it?* The thought that he stood so near to the possibility of answering the unanswered question—and the likelihood of failure—was so intense that he felt physically sick.

"Mr. Rembert, Mr. Stuart?" The words broke into Stuart's preoccupation, and he looked up to see a man in a white jacket, short, poised, eyes hidden behind the glint of spectacles. "I'm Doctor Graham."

They stood up and offered their hands and the physician met them with a quick, firm grasp.

"I'm sorry to have to impose ground rules, and I am afraid you will find them strict," the doctor said. "The patient is a very sick man, and I preferred not to permit any interview."

"It is necessary," Rembert said.

"So I was told," the doctor said dryly. "The call came from the Attorney General. I felt obliged to accede—within limits."

"How sick is he?" Stuart asked.

"Very."

"Is he going to live?" Rembert demanded.

"I don't know. That's why I agreed. If I had known he would survive, I would not have permitted it. You understand, Mr. Stuart, I will be with you. I will not interfere unless I believe you are upsetting him—dangerously. If I stop you—you'll stop. Is that understood?"

"Damn it, doctor, the man is a killer—several times over," Rembert growled.

"At the moment, he is a patient," the doctor said. "Understood?"

"Understood," Rembert said, the unwillingness heavy in his tone. *How,* Stuart was wondering, *how are you going to get anywhere being gentle with a man like Gervase?*

"Come on then," the doctor said and turned away. They followed.

Tensed, Stuart was still aware that Rembert had halted outside the door and was standing, resentfully unwilling, beside a uniformed policeman in the dimly lighted corridor. He had known, of course, that a patient of Gervase's unsavory eminence and his present condition would be guarded, but this was carrying police procedure too ironically far. A guard under Lieutenant Kelley's command!

A dim night-light was burning over the bed, and Dr. Graham silently motioned Stuart to a straight chair at the head of the bed. Stuart sat and was conscious of the doctor's presence at his shoulder.

Gervase's eyes were closed. Stuart was struck at the sight of the whole face on the pillow. It was deeply sunken all around on either side of the huge prow of nose and that seemed pinched, even in the half-light. The closed eyes seemed to have retreated, and the thin, sneering mouth now sagged open. Except that a shallow breath now moved in and out it reminded him of the mouths of dead men he had seen before. *This one has had it,* he thought, *whatever the doctor thinks. Gervase has had it.*

The doctor circled the bed and leaned over and spoke, "Mr. Gervase, are you awake?" Stuart saw that the doctor had taken up Gervase's wrist and his fingers rested lightly on the pulse. Gervase's eyes slowly opened, and he looked up into the doctor's face and said, "Yeah," in a thin, harsh whisper.

"This man must talk to you—for just a few minutes," Graham said. "Don't excite yourself. Just take it easy."

Gervase's head rolled toward Stuart and Stuart, leaning close, saw that they were vague and wandering. Then, in amazement, he saw them come alight with life and rage, a look at once sneering and defiant, lighted with anger.

"The fed!" he whispered. "Who the hell let you in here?"

"I won't be long, Gervase," Stuart said, forcing his voice to calm and quiet—thinking at the same time how little mercy this pitiable and contemptible animal deserved. "There are a few things that have to be asked."

"Who asked you to ask anything? Get the hell out of here."

Stuart was conscious of the doctor's wary movement toward him. *This is going to hell in a hand basket,* he thought in despair and spoke quickly, but still quietly, "Who shot you?"

"None of your goddamn business," Gervase croaked. "It's my business. I'll take care of it."

"Maybe you can't," Stuart said quietly. "Maybe you'll have to leave it to us."

"Fuck you," Gervase said, the weak voice slightly stronger. "I ain't croaking."

Stuart looked up and saw the doctor's eyes on him, carrying urgent warning. The doctor's fingers held steady on Gervase's wrist.

"Gervase, you know we have Pete Higgins."

"That piss ant! Keep him." Gervase's head rolled away toward the doctor, and his voice sank back to a weary whisper. "Get him out of here."

"Only a few minutes more, Mr. Gervase. Take it easy."

"Take it easy, my ass."

"Higgins says you made him kill the black man," Stuart whispered. *God, how far can I go? How soon are they going to lower the boom on me?*

The question seemed to rouse Gervase's fury again. "Who gives a shit what he says? Get out. Leave me alone. I'm sick."

The doctor moved again. How the hell deal with this? Stuart knew he wasn't going to last long. He supposed—correctly—that it was only the doctor's own nonprofessional fascination that had permitted him to stay this long and even that wouldn't let it last much longer. Stuart decided to lay it all on the line in one shot; when he spoke, his voice, still a whisper, was a brutal demand.

"Gervase, listen to me! There isn't much time for you to answer. Who shot you? Why did he shoot you? Who made you make Higgins kill Barton? Why? Why did Kelley help Higgins get away? Why did you try to get Higgins killed in Lebanon? How many other men have you killed, Gervase? I know of four." He was aware that the doctor had dropped Gervase's wrist and was moving around the bed swiftly. "Get it off your chest, Gervase." His voice rose to brutal demand. "You're dying, Gervase."

The doctor's grip was hard on his shoulder, dragging him up from the chair. The doctor's voice was as hard as his own, "Come on! Now!"

The heat had gone out of Gervase's eyes, and the voice had sunk back to a tired, bitter apathy, "Fuck you, cop."

They were out of the room and the doctor's voice was low and angry. "God damn it, I told you to go easy. That was cruel. It was unnecessary. You broke your word!"

"You don't know how necessary it was," Stuart said wearily and turned to Rembert. "Let's go," he said.

It was four o'clock in the morning and Stuart and Rembert still sat in the stale, tobacco-laden air of Commissioner Mayhew's office, tiredly inventorying what they knew to be true but had no possibility of proving. *He looks old now, really old and beat,* Stuart thought, looking across the desk at his silver-crowned superior. He felt old himself, immeasurably old—and defeated.

"If he lives," Rembert said for perhaps the tenth time, "we can get him charged as an accessory in the Barton killing."

"On Higgins' word?" Stuart said, for the same tenth time. "What else is there?"

"Higgins' belief that he killed a colored numbers guy named Davis. Higgins' story that he made the Dowdy kid bomb a church. We can dig, but even if we dig deep, we're not going to answer the real question. Who shot him? Why? Who shoved him into the Barton thing? Anyhow he isn't going to live."

"Who made you a doctor?" Rembert said with asperity. "Graham said he didn't know."

"I don't know. All I say is he isn't going to live."

Who knows what governs truth or its revelation? Who knows? Who knows? The telephone rang at four ten and, with a puzzled look, Rembert lifted it from the desk and answered and, suddenly alert, handed it to Stuart. "For you."

"Yes?" Stuart said into the instrument.

"He wants you. You'd better hurry," the voice said. After a baffled moment he recognized the voice and said, "All right, Doctor Graham. We're on the way."

He was too worn, too tired, too long defeated to get excited as the FBI driver hurtled them toward St. Francis with the reckless urgency which Rembert had commanded. *There is something inevitable, something ordained about this,* he thought.

Dr. Graham was talking to a priest in the lobby when they went through the door. Stuart half-heard the priest saying, "Yes, he was a Catholic—of a sort" as the doctor took his arm and propelled him toward the elevator. "Come on, Mr. Stuart. It's touch and go."

Stuart bent over the bed again and was shocked at how far the face had drawn tighter into its final retreat from life.

"He's here, Mr. Gervase," the doctor said, bending low, once more automatically reaching for the pulse.

The eyes flickered, came open dully, looked at Stuart and closed again. The voice was halting, barely audible.

"Cop?"

"Yes, Gervase," Stuart said.

Gervase seemed to arch himself and the eyes opened again and lighted with burning intensity.

"Listen cop. Wynn shot me. Amos Wynn. He made me get the nigger killed. Now you know it. Fuck you." The eyes closed again.

"Gervase?" Stuart said, "Gervase?" He felt a terrible urgency to hold this spirit a little longer.

Gervase stirred slightly but kept his eyes closed. "You want more, ask Wynn. Fuck you."

Long afterward, when there was time to wonder, Stuart won-

dered half-guiltily whether his visit earlier in the night had
been the shock that pushed Gervase over the edge. Once, troubled by the thought, he asked Dr. Graham. The doctor said he
didn't know, that nobody could be certain.

30

"All right. Thanks," Blaisdell said and cradled the
telephone on the scarred and stained desktop of his tiny office
inside the barren warehouse Teamsters hall in Baton Rouge.
He sighed and reached into the desk drawer for one of his cigars in its aluminum torpedo tube.

"That's that," he said. "I don't know that it's going to make
a lot of difference, probably none."

"What's what?" Andrus Thompson, another cigar held aslant
between his teeth to keep the smoke away from his good right
eye, tipped his chair forward from its tilt against the wall, the
front legs cracking loudly as they came down on the floor.
"Who was that?"

"Fella in Wynnsboro. I had it fixed for him to call when it
happened—if it happened."

"I ain't no mind reader," Thompson said irritably. "When
what happened—if?"

"If that fella that got shot up there kicked off. He did."

"Gervase?"

"Yeah, Gervase. Boss man for that fella they say shot Barton.

And I guess he did, all right. I wish they'd kept him alive a while longer."

"Why? How'd you figure to use him?"

"I never knew that we could, but we might have. They've got Higgins for killing Barton. But Higgins is no-account trash. He's white all right, but he's such a nothin' that nobody's going to care a real damn whether they hang him or not. Now, Gervase was something else, a crook but a big white crook. A well-known nigger-hater. If they'd kept Gervase alive long enough to prove he made Higgins do the killing—if he did—we'd have things a lot different.

"The blacks up there, no more than the whites, ain't going to get much of a boot out of hanging Higgins. But if Gervase was behind it—if he was—the blacks would be so goddamn mad it would make things a lot easier for us."

"Yeah." Thompson was frowning, and, looking up, Blaisdell recognized again something he sensed more and more often in his black lieutenant, the tension of rage barely held in leash. The effort of containing it, on these occasions when memory or some new frustration thrust it upon him, unconsciously tightened Thompson's face into a mask of hate and made the cords in his neck stand rigid against the dark flesh. "You think Gervase sent Higgins to plant the thing that gave me this?" He touched the patch over his left eye socket.

"Andrus, you know I wouldn't know. It could be—if Gervase was in the habit of having Higgins do his dirty work."

"Well, I don't," Thompson said in a tight voice. "I don't know that Gervase wasn't the one that got the church bombed. I wouldn't be surprised if he was—in fact, I'm so willing to believe it that I practically do already. So I ain't mourning if he's dead; I only half-regret I didn't get the chance to do it myself. But no white man could've got in to plant that bomb, which don't mean anything except that Higgins didn't do it. Gervase could've had a nigger do it."

Blaisdell looked at him with concern and sympathy. "I know it ain't going to do any good to ask you to stop fretting about your eye, Andrus," he said. "But I wish you could; it eats on you, and that's a fact. Try looking at it this way: It's a war and people get hurt in wars."

Thompson sneered. "When they get a chance, they hurt back," he said. "I sold this, all right." He touched the patch again. "But I haven't got paid yet."

"It ain't going to bring your eye back, but there's some payment in getting that town organized," Blaisdell said. "I want to see your work pay off."

"There's still Wynn," Thompson said in the same tight voice. "I've been giving thought to that man."

"There's still Wynn," Blaisdell agreed. "But I think we can lick him."

"Maybe, maybe not." Thompson paused, staring at the floor, and his face was knotting up again. "That ain't quite the way I've been thinking about him."

"How do you mean?"

"Little things that don't prove anything by themselves and maybe not even if you take them all together. Like this: you remember the drunks blabbering in the bar—talk about how Barton wasn't going to get a chance to get away with a march?"

"Of course. Sure. What about them?" Blaisdell was leaning forward in abruptly aroused interest.

"They were both Wynn's men. Wynn executives. Wynn directors. Where do Wynn executives get their orders? Where do you guess they get just about all the ideas they've got?"

Blaisdell's eyes narrowed in concentration. "So that's where you're getting to, Andrus," he said softly. "I've considered it. It's possible. But there's no proof—and no way to get any."

Thompson's eye glittered. "Sometimes a thing proves itself— if it makes sense—and hardly anything else does. There's another thing: Who shot the guy that they just told you is dead?"

"Gervase was the kind of man that almost anybody that ever had anything to do with him wouldn't mind going to his funeral. It could have been a hundred people—all with a good reason."

"Sure, sure," Thompson said impatiently. "So why didn't they do it long ago? Why just now? With Barton dead? With Gervase's man in the jug waiting trial and you already know he's singing anyhow some to the FBI? Who stands to make the profit if the Teamsters drop dead in that town? I tell you, some things prove themselves."

"Not in a court, Andrus," Blaisdell said. "And that's where it counts. How you reckon a court in Wynnsboro would handle Amos Wynn?"

"This ain't necessarily a matter of courts," Thompson said.

"Some things maybe. Not this. It could make sense, but it doesn't make proof. You can devil yourself thinking it, but you can get hurt saying it out loud."

"I've been hurt already," Thompson blurted out of the anguish of his rage. Once again, gently prodding, he fingered the emptiness under the eyepatch. He made a short, hard noise of laughter. "You think it would be appropriate for me to switch this black rag for a white one?"

31

Now that he tensed himself to support the burden of irrevocable knowledge, Jeff Stuart recognized its quality of inevitability. He had been fumbling toward this sure and certain target from the beginning and some hidden part of his being had known it, while the conscious part of his mind had not—or had at least stubbornly rejected it. But it had been there, all right, and that explained a lot, the most important being the stealthy growth of his sense of guilt toward the woman he loved. He had moved steadily, irresistibly to trap her and to snare her in this trap was to crush her. And to destroy himself.

What were the choices now? He could still quit and thus perhaps save her; Rembert was furious at him because, in the first blinding shock, his instinct had been to refuse to tell what he had heard at Gervase's deathbed. He had used the transparent plea that revelation would thrust against the interests of Higgins as his client; he did not believe that and neither, obviously, did Rembert.

But would his surrender now really save Amy in the end? Would it? Might not her perceptive instinct surely tell her what his own had tried to tell him and he had, until now, refused to acknowledge? Wasn't she already more than halfway there? If not, why her instinctual revulsion against his pursuit of the killer? Why her haunting sense of unease that the manhunt threatened some greater, darker danger? And his quitting now would be inexplicable to her after the months of pursuit. His quitting would have to be explained to her and if he refused to explain it—or evaded—her own intelligent curiosity, honed the sharper by their profound involvement with each other would likely lead her all the more quickly to the unholy truth. Damn Amos Wynn's proud soul to hell!

If he didn't quit, what would happen? He would have to tell Rembert, and, once told, there would be no possibility of turning back in a probably vain hope of protecting Amy. He would have to go into court and testify to Gervase's dying declaration —and put Dr. Graham in the witness chair to confirm it. He would owe it to his client to tell the name of Carver Otis Barton's real destroyer. He would inevitably bring down all that seven generations of Wynns had built out of fierce protective pride and tradition. He would destroy Amos Wynn, and he would smash Amos Wynn's daughter. And he would, of course, lose her.

Either way for himself, Jefferson Stuart, there was no salvation. He was the certain loser. It had struck him, in despairing temptation, that by quitting he might hold her love. He had dismissed it; Amy deserved a better man than that. If he quit— and kept her—he would have to live out a life with her knowing that he had quit and carrying the load of concealing the truth from her all their days. And, he knew, if he quit, he would have Amos Wynn's contempt to endure. That was impossible—and he dismissed it.

The question now was how she was to learn the truth. She had to learn it and any way she did was bound to be a murderous blow. Let her find her way to it in lonely agony? Or let her be struck by it in swift cruelty in the hope that the shock, once taken, could then be survived? He did not know, and he knew that now he and Amos Wynn had between them a powerful community of interest. It was unlikely that either—or both together—could now find any miracle of real use to Amy. It was a thin hope. No hope at all, in fact. But he knew he had to face Wynn. Damn his proud soul.

Where was a minor question, but he did not want to confront the older man in the Wynn home. For one thing, Amy might well be there. More obscurely, he now felt that her house, the place lighted by her being, was forever off limits to him. In his soul the tie between them was already cut: it had been cut by the cruelly haphazard edge of chance and it was an irony that had forced him to use the blade.

He telephoned Wynn at home, fearful as he heard it ring that Amy might answer. He was spared that. The girl, Martine, answered and said that Mister Wynn was at home and she would tell him. Who was calling please? Stuart gave his name and waited and soon Wynn's even-toned dryly quizzical voice came on.

"I need to talk to you, Mr. Wynn," Stuart said.

"All right," Wynn said. "Come on out."

"Somewhere else if you don't mind."

"Private, eh?" Wynn said evenly. "Where are you?"

"At the motel, sir."

"All right, I'll come there. Half an hour all right? What's on your mind?"

"I think you'll agree it would be better in person," Stuart said cautiously.

"Some things are," Wynn said.

Stuart never saw Amy's father without being struck by his size and strength and air of solid, self-confident composure. It was so even now, even under the dead weight of knowledge. *I ought to hate him,* he thought, *and I suppose I do. But he's Amy's father, and in some dim way I half-understand him. But understanding him doesn't change anything. He took terrible chances and he lost; none of it is forgivable, but the worst is that when he made his gamble he inevitably took her along.*

Amos Wynn looked around the comfortable room and decided on the biggest chair in it.

"If I had suspected when I built this place that I would ever be in it I'd have had some decent furniture put in," he said. "Now, what's on your mind? I don't imagine you got me here for nothing."

All right, Stuart thought, *there isn't any other way to get at this.*

"Mr. Wynn," he said, "I know who ordered Barton's murder."

"Execution," Wynn said calmly. "Who?"

"You, sir."

"So you got to that, did you?" Wynn said, his calm unbroken, measuring Stuart in quiet appraisal. "Tell me where and how you came on this essentially insane idea. I don't imagine you're joking."

"No. I was with Gervase just before he died."

"I don't know how much you know about Gervase," Wynn said. "He was not a reliable man."

"Does it matter?" Stuart said, making an effort to hold his own nerves in the same iron control with which Wynn held his. "So long as he told the truth? That time? And both of us know that he did."

"You seem convinced. It does not follow that I am—or anybody else will be."

"It took me long enough to get there. But I see now there wasn't anywhere else to get to. Gervase was dying when he named you. As his killer. And as Barton's. A priest had already confessed him."

"A small man running for cover, laying off his bets. If Gervase had a soul, which is open to question, he would naturally want to buy it a free ride."

"There were other things."

"Such as?"

"John Kelley drove Higgins' getaway car."

"Does he admit that?"

"No, not exactly. He doesn't deny it either—in so many words."

"Good man, Kelley," Wynn said impassively.

"I suppose that was what made me take so long getting to you," Stuart said. "It was an incongruous operation—unbelievable except that it was true. I couldn't somehow see Kelley involved with people like Gervase and Higgins. And if I couldn't see Kelley in that kind of a partnership, I couldn't see you. But I should have known it had to be true—you as much as told me yourself the first time I talked to you when you said Barton was executed—not murdered."

"That doesn't follow either," Wynn said, unmoved.

"It does when you take the effort to reflect that nothing important happens in this town until Amos Wynn decides on it."

Wynn's big quiet body stirred slightly in his chair, but Stuart was aware that if the man was in any discomfort it could only be physical. His gray eyes, now fixed speculatively on Stuart, were as unwavering as ever.

"Tell me, son." Stuart flinched inwardly at the diminutive,

for, even now, he felt the cruelty of the thought of how close he had come to becoming this man's son indeed—not flesh of his flesh but one flesh with his daughter. "What do you propose to do with this preposterous allegation?"

"Whatever I have to do," Stuart said shortly. "Take it to the witness stand. I came here to find Barton's murderer. I've found him. I can't let you get away with it."

"Around here, they'll laugh you out of court."

"I can demand a change of venue and get it for exactly that reason. My man can't get a fair trial in a town that you own lock, stock, and barrel."

"Your man?" Wynn's heavy, grizzled brows went up a fraction of an inch.

"Higgins," Stuart said. "I'm his lawyer."

"Oh?" Wynn stared at him speculatively. "Funny. After you chased him around the globe. Incongruous, you could say. The judge may not allow it."

"If he doesn't, I'll coach whoever does represent him."

"Young man, I haven't lived this long without being in fights —and winning more than I lost. I know all the holds and if necessary the dirty tricks. And, as you know, in this state—anywhere in it, I enjoy certain built-in advantages. A change of venue wouldn't make much difference that I can see. Young man, you're in a fight that you don't have hell's chance of winning."

"I'm not sure of that. Any way you look at it, that family name you're so imperious about is going to get dirtied."

"That's possible, of course. And I will regret that—not particularly because of me, but because of the name itself and because of my daughter. But I doubt, young man, if you really understand the momentum of history. The Wynns have been here well over two hundred years. The name has had mud slung at it before—more than once. The stuff dries up and falls off in time; the Wynns go on. I think you want more than that; you want a conviction. Can you get that on the unsupported word of a dead man? Who, by common knowledge, was vermin. I think not."

"You forget something," Stuart said. "The Wynns have run out. The name dies with you. You leave the dirt to your daughter, who won't be able to wait for the dirt to dry up and blow away. You'll leave her a lot of money, no doubt. The rest that you leave her she'll hate having. You've got that wrong about me wanting a conviction. It is the last damned thing on earth I would have wanted. I sure as hell didn't want to get to you, and I never dreamed that I would. You stood so tall. The power in this town, no question, but a hell of a lot more than that: its character, its pride, its integrity, the whole works. And so I follow this filthy trail back to its beginning and what do I find? You. A murderer by the crummiest kind of proxy. Want a conviction? Wynn, you damned near broke my heart."

Stuart had been speaking quietly and evenly, but then rage and grief broke through the control he had laid upon himself. He was aware that he was shouting at the huge, quiet figure across the room.

"Damn you, Wynn! Damn your soul! Couldn't you see what you were doing to her? How could you have had the arrogant guts to let her in for this? What kind of monster are you?"

Amos Wynn took the outburst impassively, leaving a space of silence after Stuart subsided. At last he spoke.

"I know you and Amy have been sleeping together," he said without expression. "And I suppose that's why you're particularly upset now that you think you've got me in a bind and suppose you have to do something about it."

"We were going to be married," Stuart said, strangely relieved to know that this, too, was now out in the open. He desperately wanted to feel no obligation to this man.

"And now you doubt if you ever will be," Wynn said.

"I know damned well we won't," Stuart said hotly. "You took care of that when you took care of Barton—had him taken care of since you apparently didn't have the guts to do it yourself. Damn it, man, she's your daughter! I cannot for the life of me understand how you had the guts to take the chance."

"The Wynns," Amos said calmly, "have always taken chances when they had to. You don't build anything playing it safe. Play it careful and tough and close to the vest, but don't play it queasy."

"You had too much in the pot this time," Stuart said bitterly. "Amy's life."

"And you feel that you have—or had—some right to claim some custodial capacity for that life—probably because you fell into bed with each other. Amy's a woman grown. I gave up trying to run her life for her before she was sixteen. I respected her capacity to run her own. She'll stand up under whatever you try to do to her old man. The Wynn women are strong women."

"You put them to a hell of a test," Stuart said.

"I'll have to ask you to believe that I regretted—and regret— the necessity." Wynn kept his eyes steady on Stuart. "This city is not just a town. It is a body of people, of custom, of tradition, of beliefs, of ways of living and working, of governing and being governed, of accepting responsibilities and of having the capacity and the guts to make sure that they are fulfilled. The peculiarities of Wynnsboro, if you want to call them peculiarities, have been tested. They work, they meet our necessities. The destruction of these things could not be tolerated."

"Are you admitting you had Barton killed?"

"Don't be ridiculous," Wynn said, raising one grizzled eyebrow slightly.

"No, I guess you wouldn't," Stuart said. "And I don't suppose it will make much impression to tell you that instead of preserving something you thought worth hanging onto, you succeeded in destroying all of it, along with your daughter and yourself. Maybe you won't be convicted; I admit you're a power around here. But only around here. Maybe nobody here will believe you're guilty—or if they know damn well you're guilty they'll write it off as just another nigger killing and good riddance. But there's a lot of country outside this kingdom of yours, and, believe me, Wynn, they'll believe you guilty, all right, and they'll bring the whole shebang down on your head—and Amy's head."

"That, too, is possible," Wynn said. "It doesn't change the fact that a man has to stand where he stands. I am not obtuse. Old values are being ripped up by the roots. I am aware that even here they can be destroyed—but not while I can prevent it."

I don't know whether to pity him or hate him, Stuart told himself. And then, in sudden insight, he realized it was neither. This man was granite; he would not seek pity and he would not accept it if offered. Or hate him? You could hate him only because his gamble had inevitably involved his daughter—and he had lost. You could try to hate him for Barton's death, but it wouldn't quite work, repugnant as the deed had been. You had to recognize that he was utterly sincere in his belief that Barton's death was, in fact, an execution and not a murder. His beliefs were wrong, but to him they were gospel and immutable. He had been true to what he was, to what seven generations of Wynn ancestors had made him. By his lights he had played fair. He had warned Barton. Barton had defied him. And he had killed—without passion. Was it insanity, a special madness bred into his fiber? Perhaps. It had been sin—but was he the sinner? No, you couldn't hate him and certainly you could not pity him. You could only pity Amy and yourself. You could not even pity Barton, only Barton's wife and son. What, then, had you left? Only grief and bewilderment.

"There is one thing left," Stuart said. "I'll let you decide it. Who is going to tell Amy? You? Or me?"

"That you're trying to get me?" Wynn gave the question calm, inward-looking study. "That you propose to muddy the name of Wynn? That you're quitting her because of who her father is?"

"You know better than that," Stuart said. "I'm not quitting her and you know it. You've put us where she has to quit me. I

love her and I would save her if it were possible. It isn't. Even
if I could force myself to let you off the hook, she'd know the
truth—by that alone if nothing else. Your daughter is not a stupid woman, Wynn."

"I'm aware of that, and you're probably right. But you're after
me and you want me to tell her that. You've got a fallacy there.
In the first place, I don't think you're going to get me."

"Whether I get you isn't the issue. The issue is Amy."

"I have that in mind, son. And I'm trying to take its measure.
If I did tell her, it would be an admission that I give a damn
whether you're trying to get me. I am not about to put that
load on her. I am not going to shake her faith in me. The fact
that you are after me would not do that. Even if she was convinced that I killed Barton, she would understand why I believed it necessary. But she has always known that I carry my
own loads; me telling her would be offloading some of it onto
her and I won't do that. She is going to be hurt badly enough
anyhow. I don't think more than she can bear because she's a
sturdy woman. But just knowing *you* are after me is going to be
a crusher. You see, son, I know Amy did not fall for you lightly;
she doesn't do anything important lightly. It's going to be asking a lot of her to see you and me squared off against each
other. She's going to have to choose between us." For the first
time, Wynn frowned in thought. "I don't know which way
she'll go," he said at length. "Whichever . . . I'll accept."

"I know which way she'll go," Stuart said bleakly. "There's
no question. I know. I wish to God I could spare her—that we
could. And I know we can't."

"I believe you. And I can see that nothing I could say to you
or offer you—for her sake or even for your own sake—is going
to turn you off. I admit I admire that about you; you'll go
ahead hell-bent because you think you have to.

"And that's likely to smash up whatever there is between
Amy and you. Frankly, I don't care if you get smashed. You're
playing in a man's game and you know the stakes. I do care if
she gets smashed, but the only way I could stop you would be to

kill you. Frankly, I've considered it, but I'm not going to do it. That would smash her even worse.

"No, son, I see your problem. But don't count on me to solve it for you. You understand I can't do anything to dignify what you're going to try to do to me—least of all, dignify it to Amy."

"I understand," Stuart said.

The hotel chair creaked under the strain as Amos Wynn got up to leave.

Orville Dickinson was a federal district judge, which would have pleased the late Carver Otis Barton until he found out that Judge Dickinson owed his appointment to the persuasive intercession of Senator Moses Kirkwood who, in turn, owed his instructions to exert himself in Judge Dickinson's behalf to Amos Wynn. The judge, aware of the sources of his dignity, felt a powerful sense of loyalty to Wynn and only slightly less so to the Senator.

Leaving Stuart, Wynn was preoccupied with the threat to Amy's happiness and filled with a dread far deeper than he had acknowledged to Stuart or would have admitted to any living soul. It was true that he did not fear for himself, for it was literally true that Amos Wynn was one of that rare company of men who do not know the meaning of fear—for themselves. He now admitted to himself that he had made a serious error by commissioning the execution of Barton to Gervase. He had seriously considered doing the job himself but had rejected the idea as less practical than turning it over to one of Gervase's efficient gunmen. The mistake had rested in his failure to take Gervase's greed into account—and Gervase had botched the job by sending the cheapest and least efficient of men, Higgins.

It was too late, of course, to dwell on that monumental stupidity, and meanwhile there was other urgent business thrust upon him in Wynnsboro's behalf. Thus he went straight from Stuart's motel to Judge Dickinson's austere chambers in the federal building.

The judge was a white-haired man in his middle seventies,

who wore upon a thin, ascetic face a perpetual air of benevolent calm and austere judgment. It was true in a sense except that his judgment was a quality which came to him in times of need in a pure strain direct from Amos Wynn. His chambers were another haven where an outsize chair had been installed long ago to accommodate the dimensions of Amos Wynn.

Wynn took his reserved seat while the jurist eyed his caller with curiosity, wondering what it would be this time. Wynn seldom went calling for purely social reasons.

"Judge, we have a problem that I think is tailor-made for your attention," Wynn said without preliminary.

"All right, Amos—if it's legal," the judge said, with a thin attempt at levity.

"It's legal enough. Did you know the Teamsters Union is still trying to pry out a beachhead here?"

"Not particularly. They fall outside my province."

"Not anymore, Orville. My information is they're going to try another organization march here."

"They won't get far with that, will they, Amos?"

Wynn shook his big head in negation.

"A year ago, no. Nor six months ago. Maybe not now either, but I don't want to take the chance. I used to know what went on in the niggers' heads, but I'm no longer as sure as I once was. They went over the fence when that man Barton got himself killed here—and I have the uneasy feeling that they're edgier than they used to be. Against their own best interest—but there it is. I want that march stopped before it gets started."

"An injunction?"

"Exactly."

"How do you propose I support an injunction, Amos? It needs to look reasonable—and in the public interest."

"It will. You're averting a clear threat to public order. The riot last spring gives you all the support you need. The riot after the killing."

The judge sat up in quick attention.

"That reminds me of another problem, Amos," he said. "It is causing me a certain amount of concern. I'd like to have your ideas of it—if you have one. You know I value your counsel."

"What is it, Orville?"

"Damnedest thing. Unprecedented in my experience."

"All right, spill it."

"That FBI man, Stuart the name is—ex-FBI man, I should say, came in to see me with some weird information. He says Higgins, the man he ran down and fetched back here as Barton's murderer, now wants him, Stuart, to defend him as counsel. Isn't that the damnedest thing?"

"Stuart hasn't been admitted to the bar in this state, has he? So far as you know?"

"No. And he's never practiced either. But he was admitted in some Midwestern state, I forget which one for the moment. Insane, isn't it?"

"Well," Wynn sat for a time, thinking. "I suppose the defendant's wishes carry some weight. Do you have to agree?"

"No. But I don't know whether I should. What do you think?"

"I think you should agree, Orville. The Northern press and radio will be all over us when the trial opens. They'd raise hell if you refused to let the guy have counsel of his choice. I'd let it go if I were you, Orville."

"I suppose you're right. But it certainly is unprecedented. By the way, who should I name in that injunction?"

"Fellow named Blaisdell. Teamster business agent from Baton Rouge. And a colored organizer named Thompson. If I think of anybody else, I'll let you know."

32

Leaving the federal building in the late afternoon, Amos Wynn, conscious of change, looked up speculatively at a brassy overcast roiling in from the west. The air was hot and heavy and unaccountably depressing. *Something coming in,* he thought, *but I am not the meteorologist and don't intend to be.* He drove to his home and housed the Cadillac under the carport roof and went into the house and down to the basement gun room and picked up the telephone.

"Zeke," he said when he got an answer. "The plane ready?"

"It's always ready, Mister Wynn. Where you want to go?"

"Baton Rouge and back tonight. But you tell me. It could wait. I see there's a little weather out there."

"Nothing it won't take," the pilot said. "Maybe some turbulence."

"All right. Half an hour," Wynn said and dropped the instrument back into its cradle.

I wonder, he thought, and went to one of the glass-fronted teakwood cases mounted on the wall. *Those people are not your friends,* he reminded himself, *not even slightly.* He took a ring of keys from his pocket and opened the case and took out a snub-barreled Sharps derringer, a sleeve gun. *This would do it,* he thought, and broke the weapon and looked into the bores against the light. Clean, which of course he knew they would be. From a chest against the wall he took a box of .41 ammunition and pressed two brass cartridges into the breech.

He started toward the stair, paused in midstride, turned, broke the gun again and took out the cartridges and put the weapon back on its pegs. *No,* he told himself, *this ain't that kind of a trip.*

But, if not, what kind of trip was it? Preventive medicine you could call it, but very late in the case. Judge Dickinson, by this time, had surely dictated the injunction to his secretary and it would be rolling out of her typewriter with, pushing it up around the platen rubber, all the dictatorial force of law. Was it just? Unjust? It really didn't matter because justice was not the issue here. The crux of the matter was that once it had cleared the keys of her typewriter and had Orville's dignified signature it would, indeed, carry all the force of law—until tested in some higher tribunal and perhaps even after being so tested.

He would not need to wait for a copy of it. It would have been impossible for Amos Wynn to conceive of his word being doubted anywhere in his state and probably in any other state as well. His was not an idle tongue, and he knew Blaisdell would not question it—any more than he would question Blaisdell's word. If he said an injunction existed and violation of it would be likely to provoke serious trouble, Blaisdell would believe that it did, indeed, exist.

He did not, with his own eyes and ears, know Blaisdell, but he knew of him. He knew that he was tough and gentle and sensible and had both integrity and the capacity for violence, which he would prefer not to use, would if he had to but would probably not waste on profitless gambles.

The question now was whether Blaisdell could be convinced that Wynnsboro held no profit for him. But there was always that unguessable margin. To some men, sensible or not, an ultimatum was intolerable. These could not find anywhere within themselves the capacity to yield. Barton had been one of that kind; it had cost his life and the lives of the Clagget girls. And,

Amos recognized, he wore the same brand. What then of Blaisdell?

Zeke Appel had been right about the weather. The Bellanca
bucked its way up to 7,500 feet, often dropping sickly, then re-
covering and thrusting on into the rough and angry sky. At alti-
tude Appel found the going so heavy that he turned off the
auto pilot, dropped a third of his flaps, and slowed the plane to
just above stalling speed.

"Sorry," he said. "It's going to be a slow flight, but I got to
take some of the pressure off her."

"Doesn't matter," Wynn said, "just get there." He ignored
Appel's skillful struggle as entirely as he would have ignored a
flight smooth as velvet. He knew the errand he was now engaged upon probably stood not much more than a fifty percent
chance of success. But he did know that if Blaisdell defied
Judge Dickinson's order and came to Wynnsboro the injunction would still work. The Teamsters would be stopped, at
least temporarily, until the injunction fought its way up
through the courts and either, in the end, failed or survived.
That could take years, at least many months, certainly until
after Higgins' trial had ended and—with it—whatever Jeff Stuart and the FBI would do to the name and legacy of the Wynns.

But it would certainly be better—for the town, for Amy's
eventual peace of mind, and, incidentally, for his own continuing
command of the Wynn heritage—which meant Wynnsboro—if
Blaisdell could be convinced of his defeat beforehand and
could be persuaded not to test the force of the injunction in
Wynnsboro streets.

There was more of an element of gambling here, more of not
well-justified optimism, than Wynn liked to bet on. He did not
trust luck, but also, as a realist, he recognized that he was no
longer as free as he was accustomed to be to manipulate the
odds on the risks he would take. This one seemed at least reasonable—and, in any case, he stood a chance to win the contest
whether or not Blaisdell would consent to stay out of Wynns-

boro at least until the higher courts had reviewed Judge Dickinson's order.

But he knew there were some things he could no longer preserve. He could no longer save the Wynn name, in this generation, from the stain of murder. Stuart would see to that, for Stuart was a man incapable of quitting. But, as he had told Stuart and it was exactly true, the Wynn name had been stained before and the Wynns had survived. But it was also true, and painfully so, as Stuart had told him, that the long male line of the Wynns died with him. And the burden of the stain would be shifted to Amy. He had told Stuart that he had considered killing him and, truly, he had. But the proposition was impossible, and he had rejected it. He knew Amy loved the man and he would not destroy what she loved even though he knew that the two would inevitably be lost to each other, indeed, though Amy probably did not yet know it, were lost already.

And so now he would go to confront Blaisdell on his own ground. He had considered the possibility of physical danger and, if it existed, the need to meet it head on. And he had rejected that, unloaded the weapon he had selected, and returned it in peace to its pegs in the teakwood cabinet. Certainly he was not now going among friends, but it was unlikely that Blaisdell would see any potential profit in offering him physical violence. Blaisdell, whatever might be said of him, was a sensible man, a realist in a rough business, none rougher.

"I'll be letting down now," Appel said. "On the ground in ten minutes. You need me with you?"

"No," Wynn said. "I won't be gone long, couple hours at most. Call ahead and order a car for me." The Bellanca fought its way down the hostile slope of disordered air, flared out jerkily, and touched down at the Ryan Airport north of the city.

It was a quarter after six when the Bellanca taxied up to the terminal, wheeled around and parked, and the propellors stopped turning. An Avis Mustang, freshly washed and vacuumed, was waiting for him, the key in the hand of the girl attendant at the booth inside the door. Wynn eyed the car with cool distaste.

"Haven't you got something I can get into?" he asked. "That car wasn't tailored for me."

The girl smiled apologetically, looking up and down the six feet four longitude of him and the breadth of latitude to match, and said, "No, it's not. Or you are not. Surely you don't match. But it's the only one left."

"All right. It'll do," he said and turned to the pilot. "You do the paper work, Zeke. I'll be back." He looked around the building, recognized a telephone booth and went to look up the Teamster hall address and to locate it on the city map in the front of the book. He went out and folded himself laboriously into the car and drove south, skirting the eastern edge of the city, on U.S. 61.

He recognized the place by the narrow black and white street name where a graveled road intersected the four-lane interstate and by a glimpse of the weathered, paintless warehouse set back in its copse of pine. He swung across the median and pulled up in front of the warehouse. He maneuvered himself out of the light car and approached a door sheeted in galvanized iron and was mildly interested by the black lick marks of flame up the front and an unmended hole in the wall where one of the two bombs of the year before had gone off. *They've got more troubles than Wynnsboro,* he thought, and wondered whether there might be some advantage in knowing that.

He tried the sheet iron door and found it unlocked. Inside the hall was cavernous, stifling in its heated gloom—and empty. A dim light burned beyond a glass enclosure at the side of the hall and he went there and tried a door and found that, too, unlocked. Inside, in the dusk, he could see empty desks and filing cabinets and hooded typewriters. A voice called, "Who's that?"

He followed toward the light and the sound of the voice and found himself filling the narrow doorway to a tiny office. Behind a desk heavy with disordered paper, he saw a black man peering up at him curiously from one eye. The man was slender, very dark, and, at sight of him, the face drew itself into a careful hostility.

"My name is Amos Wynn," he said.

"I know what your name is," the black man said. "What you want?"

"To see Blaisdell," Wynn said.

"He ain't here," the black man said.

Andrus Thompson had seen Wynn before, both in pictures and at a distance, and such was the size and the composed bulk of him that he had no question of his caller's identity.

"Who are you?" Wynn asked.

Instinctively, without his being conscious of the gesture, Thompson's hand went up to caress the patch where his left eye should have been. He was unprepared for the surge of rage that swept through him. *The sonofabitch cost me this,* he thought, *and the sonofabitch doesn't even know who he did it to. And wouldn't care.* Thompson loved no white man, not even Blaisdell, though he respected him. But this giant, this monument of such sublime indifference that he could kill and maim without even bothering to identify his victims.

"Thompson," he heard himself say. "First name's Andrus."

"Oh," Wynn said. "I recognize the name. You got that in the church in Wynnsboro last April. I ought to have known."

"That's where I got it," Thompson said in a tight voice. "What you want with Blaisdell?"

Wynn eyed him in cool detachment. "To talk to him. When'll he be back or where can I find him now?"

"You can't, not now. He's in Washington. You can talk to me. When Blaisdell ain't here, I'm Blaisdell."

"I doubt it," Wynn said calmly.

"It's a mistake to doubt it," Thompson said, the one eye steady on Wynn's gray pair. "If I couldn't talk for Blaisdell I wouldn't have been in that church last April. The one that made you remember who I am. What you want with Blaisdell?"

"You could give him a message," Wynn said, deciding.

"What message?"

"To get in touch with me. Come up to see me, if that's convenient. If not I can get down here again—or to Washington if he won't be back tomorrow or the day after. This is Tuesday, I'll want to see him before Friday."

"What about?" The sheer mass of Amos Wynn was impressive to any man and the more so because it was always encased in granite self-possession. The fact that he was impressed did not, however, diminish Thompson's hatred. It was more than the whiteness of Wynn's skin alone; it was the contempt, the disregard for his own black skin that was implied by Wynn's calm assumption that he was here engaged with something less than he was, had always been less, was condemned to be less by immutable law.

I wonder if the white sonofabitch came here carrying a gun, Thompson wondered. It was possible. He didn't know. Blaisdell's .38 Colt, always loaded, he knew was less than a foot from his right hand.

"You can go a little further," Wynn said quietly. "He's got that march—or whatever he wants to call it—staged for Friday. Tell him to call it off."

"He won't," Thompson said. "We won't."

"It would be a waste," Wynn said. "More people could get hurt. There've been too many hurt already. The march has been enjoined. There'll be two hundred police there to see that it stays enjoined."

"You're right about the too many hurt," Thompson said. He touched the eyepatch again and let his hand drop nearer the upper drawer in Blaisdell's desk. "A little queer you'd be thinking about that now."

"Yes?" Wynn's tone was politely questioning.

Thompson had begun to let the fury boil unchecked within him. This was the enemy, always had been the enemy. The author of humiliation, casual injustice that was not even recognized as such because the author was blinded to it, casual brutality, casual indifference, casual assumption that he, Andrus Thompson, was something marked with a fatal flaw that made him inferior. In a strange, mad way he was enjoying the rage, the hurricane of emotion. He reached into the drawer and took out the gun and held it so that Wynn could see it.

"Put it away, Thompson," Wynn said quietly.

"No," Thompson grated. "I'm going to kill you, Wynn. Here. Now."

"Why?" Wynn said. "Put it away."

"For this, if nothing else." He touched the patch with his left forefinger. "But there's more," Thompson said. "There's more —but this is enough," he said as he fired.

In that instant Amos Wynn understood by the tension of his one-eyed face and the hot madness in his one eye that Andrus Thompson was going to fire, and he braced his chest to receive the blow, thinking at the same time with a kind of bemused contempt that the poor sonofabitch has made a mistake: *I am not responsible for his eye.*

33

In the end, telling Amy Wynn was half as complicated and a hundred times as devastating as the worst Jeff Stuart had anticipated in all the brutal hours before he did tell her. If, meanwhile, he was having trouble with head and heart and stomach muscle, his agonies differed from hers only to the

degree that he knew what was roweling him and she did not—
quite. If helpless ignorance is an illness—which it often is—her
situation was probably the worse of the two.

He had called her, and, understanding his urgent need of
her, she had gone to him gladly. She had not known why he
needed her—as he did not—but knowing that the body can
sometimes furnish solace when other resources cannot, she had
offered that. Then followed that shaming business, for both of
them, in bed together. And his running off, in almost palpable
relief, at the summons of the telephone. And she had let herself
get weepy which, in its own way, was another humiliation.

Ever since she had been holding a lonely conference with
herself, bruised by the twinges of self-doubt, ridden by
bafflement, demanding answers of heart and instinct and not
getting very many. *Come on, Amy,* she told herself, *you're a big
girl now and ordinarily you're not too stupid. You've got a lot
invested here, too much to let it go without doing anything
about it. Whatever it is, you know it's serious, not simply some
momentary lover's whim whose causes can't even be remembered a day—or an hour—later.*

She considered the possibility that it had been a bad investment in the first place. She reminded herself that she wouldn't
be the first woman who ever made a dumb mistake about a
man. What had fetched her in the first place? Certainly it
wasn't what he did for a living. She knew she shared a prejudice
common to mankind against the things implied by the word policeman: officiousness, interference, casual brutality, a halter on
freedom, vengeance, authorized cruelty immune to redress, the
implication that all other men are evil. But then, of course, it
had been obvious that he was none of these—except in his relentless determination to run down Barton's killer. But then,
having caught him, he was now of all incomprehensible things
turned about full-face to become his victim's protector! Maybe
the key to the surrender of her own heart was there somewhere.
He was anything but what his credentials said he ought to be.
No, she could not say she had made a fool's investment. What

had really fetched her were the things her heart said were true: thoughtful kindness, quiet generosity, warmth, a fundamental humility, the capacity for pity, a vulnerable heart, and, with all that, a quiet fortitude to see the course he ought to follow and then follow it. *No man can fake these qualities,* she thought. *The phoniness would show through; it had to.*

And then, of course, that capacity for the honest lusts of the flesh. For a little while she wondered if that could have been the thing that had gone wrong. Had she tumbled too readily into bed with him, too easily acknowledged her own body's appetites? Should she have put up barriers, teased, made him pant, artfully retreated behind a spurious virginity? Had he marked her for an easy lay and, having found that to be true, withdrawn himself from a commitment made too quickly? *That,* she told herself, *is schoolgirl nonsense—or, worse, a whore's nonsense. We knew who we were and what we wanted and how badly we wanted it and for how long.*

Well then, what was it? For it was certainly something monstrous. She knew she could not understand how he had somehow translated his manhunt into a feeling that he had betrayed her. But that was what he had said, and she had to believe he meant it, incoherent as he had been about it and incomprehensible as the idea was to her.

But was it entirely? She had all along had inside herself that gnawing unease that he represented some deeper peril. Not in himself, but in what he represented. Not to herself, but to what she represented. She knew and was sometimes irritated by knowing that he did not tell her everything about his work, and she told herself that was foolish as well as selfish and had an element of jealousy about it. She knew he had a right and probably a sworn duty as well to keep some things behind a wall she was forbidden to enter, but the plain fact was, she acknowledged, that in loving him she wanted to own every part of him. She believed she had no secrets from him; conversely, how could he keep things hidden from her? Illogical? Of course. But true, all the same.

And, she told herself fiercely, she had a right to know. If what he represented implied some danger to her, to both of them, to the things she represented, sworn duty or no sworn duty, she had a right to know.

She waited out the morning, toyed at a lunch for which her normally lusty appetite was missing, and brooded away half the afternoon. She understood, subconsciously, that she was waiting for the telephone to ring and told herself that was idiocy. The radio told her that the man named Gervase was dead and she recalled that he had spoken of Gervase in the humiliating night and supposed that Gervase's death could be what was preoccupying him now. He had his work; let him alone to do it and, in God's good time, with prayer, the barrier, whatever it was, could be torn down.

Restlessly, she took the Porsche and drove out to the cottage at the lake, thinking vaguely that a swim, an exhausting workout of the body, might relieve the endlessly circling exhaustion of the mind and troubled heart. She dozed restlessly after a mile and a half in the water and awoke in the dark with nothing changed.

It was after midnight when she made up her mind. Whatever had come between them, she told herself, was too big to tolerate longer. And she could not find the answer in a troubled man's impotence, nor in obscure, evasive explanations that were no explanations at all. Whatever it was had to be named in plain English, and she would not wait. It had to be confronted so that it could be defeated. And, whatever it was, she knew she would not let it make her weep again.

She had the key in her hand when she walked along the second floor balcony and came to the door of Jeff Stuart's room. A light glowed behind the draperies and so she knocked softly, but there was no answer. She started to put the key in the lock but changed her mind and tried the knob. The door was not locked and she walked in. The bedside light was burning, driving its glow straight down against his eyes, but he was asleep, on top of the coverlet, naked. The scarred face was frowning and the room smelled of whiskey. He looked vulnerable, defenseless, wounded even in sleep.

She moved quietly across the room, picked up a half-full tumbler smelling of stale booze and crossed to the bathroom to empty it and, passing the dresser, noticed a whiskey bottle two-thirds gone.

So, she thought, *my drunken friend. Too boozed up to call. I'll show you.*

In his imagination, against his will, there had been pictures of what he had to say to her and how she might receive it. He had lived through hours of that, through the deepening afternoon and into the night. She would be shocked. There would be a hurricane of grief. There would be horror. She would not be able to believe; it would be too much to comprehend anything except that he had betrayed her, betrayed her love, gone out in madness to tear her to bits to bring all her life and pride and faith and dignity down in destruction.

She would collapse, since this was too great a burden to ask any spirit to endure. He should have known better since she was Amos Wynn's daughter and the granddaughter of all his ancestors.

His own sense of guilt and betrayal bled him without mercy. He was not to be spared that, then or later. And, of course, it spelled the end for them. His fear of what he had to do to her probably was worse than the sense of his own loss and grief, although he had no yardstick to measure the precise depth of either abyss.

Three times he tried to reach her at home, but Martine reported that she was away and she did not know when Amy would return or where she had gone. The last time he called it was after midnight. By then he was wondering whether Amos had changed his mind and decided to tell her. He didn't know whether he hoped so or not. But if Amos had not told her he could not imagine where she might have gone. Uncertainty over where she might be, and why, added its illogical extra quotient of worry. For what he had thought would be until time ended for him, he had believed he hated Amos, but as the hours passed he realized, in some surprise, that what he now felt for Amy's father was sorrow and pity.

Sometime in the dinnerless night, devil-driven, he had begun to drink. He had drunk until he recognized that he was drunk and then drunk more. What was unendurable had to be driven back out of sight until in some unbelievable future it could be endured. He did not know when sheer exhaustion of nerve and heart and body laid him low in sodden, hurtful sleep.

It was the same dream, come to him in mercy when he needed it most. He could feel the weight and willingness of her body. The tumbled heavy hair was in his face and even in darkness he saw the shimmering highlights in the chestnut mass of it. The welcome and welcoming flesh was against his own. He could smell her, that particular compound of costly fragrance and cleanness and an indefinable something more that not only said woman, but said *his* woman. Their bodies were truly coupled, and he felt the throb of his flesh within hers and the slow, exultant pulsation of her answer, and they were moving, more swiftly than he wanted, toward climax.

He came out of the dream knowing that he stank inside and outside and felt the full, dispiriting clangor of the whiskey in his skull. And it was no dream.

And so all the rest of it came back in a black wave of horror. He rolled away from and out of her and groaned and said, "Oh, God, Amy, I didn't know. I was asleep." The dream, turned to black nightmare, was left unfinished.

"Don't blame yourself for that," she said. "I was raping you."

He stared at her out of despair and in darkness and then he told her. There were no well chosen words, no pace, no tone, no prescription for this. It came out haltingly, clumsily, and she heard him out in silence.

But if Amy Wynn had been told, on professional authority, that it was possible for the human heart to go physically cold in a healthy chest, she would not have believed it. Now she did. It was ice.

She got up and turned on the bedside light again and spoke in a voice so expressionless and rigidly controlled that he scarcely knew it for hers. "I think this is not anything to talk about in the dark."

She turned to look down at the beloved, half-ugly face, expecting to want to touch it with soothing fingers in pity and sympathy for its hurt. But she saw that it was a stranger's face, a face she had never known or could remember seeing. The place in her chest was still ice.

"Is this what I felt all along?" she asked wonderingly. "Vengeance?"

"No. I didn't know. I didn't even guess until that man Gervase told me when he was dying this morning. Maybe I should have guessed. But how could I? He's yours. It was impossible."

"But you got to that. And you think pa had the nigger killed." The gray eyes were huge and steady on his face. There were no tears. But the pain was there, guarded, forbidden now, coldly controlled but nakedly visible.

"I know he did."

"I don't think you can surprise me. I felt something coming. I knew something was. I just didn't know what . . ."

"Amy . . ." He stopped again.

"Maybe I have to believe you. The thing I can't believe is the way you say it was done. That isn't pa. If he had asked me, I would have done it for him myself. It's something somebody like you has no way of even beginning to understand."

He wanted to protest that he did understand. He wanted to take her in his arms and forbid the wound to hurt. He wanted to shield her and, God help him, he wanted to shield Amos Wynn.

"Now what will you do?" she asked calmly.

He forced himself to look directly into the steady gray eyes.

"What has to be done."

"I guess that's inevitable. Does pa know this?"

"Yes. He came here when I asked him. We talked about it. I told him. He wasn't surprised, I think."

"No, he wouldn't be. Of course, he saw it coming better than I did. I felt it, but he knew it."

"I had hoped he would explain it to you. I thought, coming from him, it might hurt less. I didn't want to do it. I thought he could reach something I can't . . . make you understand why he believed it was necessary."

"Don't worry about that. I understand, all right. And I know he wouldn't tell me. He would force you to do it yourself. He wouldn't take the chance of letting me suspect he might be afraid of you. Pride, I suppose."

"Yes. Pride. And evil."

Where had it gone, Amy thought, looking down at him. Where had the beloved face gone? Why couldn't she see it now? And she had been so sure, so utterly damned sure. This stranger. Her father. Her choice? There wasn't any choice. There was only the pain.

"He has begun to fight you, you know," she said. "So have I. I understand you, all right, but we won't let you win."

"I hope I lose," he said honestly. "But I can't turn back from it."

"I know that," she said. "You won't walk away from it."

Neither of them knew that the fight was ended already in Baton Rouge—and that both had lost.

She sat up on the edge of the bed beside him, looking down at him, thinking, *God, if I could cry, if I could only cry.* She reached across him and took the big-fingered hairy hand and laid it against her left breast.

"Feel that," she said. "That is where the heart was."

She got up and walked across the room and with deliberation picked up her clothes and began to dress.